THE

LIGHT

AT THE

END

L. M. AFFROSSMAN

ISBN: 978-1-914399-58-9

Printed and bound in Great Britain by Clays Ltd, Elcograf S.P.A.

Cover Design main image by Mercat Design. All Rights Reserved

SPARSILE BOOKS LTD

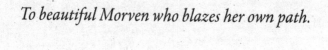

To beautiful Morven who blazes her own path.

The soul can never be cut into pieces by any weapon, nor can he be burned by fire, nor moistened by water, nor withered by the wind.

Bhagavad-gita
Chapters 1–6

ONE

DARK

—So, what do we have here?
—Male, approximately forty. Suspected fracture C5 to C6.
—Sir, can you hear me?
—Initial GCS, eye response, 2.
—Sir, can you tell me your name?
—Head block. Triple immobilization of C-spine.
—All right, my darling. We're just going to take a look.
—Starting fluids.
—Get the X-ray machine in. Tee up scan. Alert theatre.
— Bloods off including crossmatch.
—What's that, my darling? Are you trying to say something?
—Look at his eyes. He's screaming.
—Rate 160. Morphine, 15mg stat.

LIGHT

—BP 90 over 35. Pulse 120.

—Verbal response, 2. Motor response, 1.

—Can you call X-ray again, please?

—PO2 89 , BP falling. Pulse 164.

—He's in shock.

—Adrenaline?

LIFTING. SUNBURSTS. SUPERNOVAS. THE INCREDIBLE
BRIGHTNESS OF BEING.

—Where's the X-ray?

—Shit. Fracture dislocation C5, 6. Need to get him to theatre.

—Sandbrook's on his way.

—Where's the Somnipradine?

—The brother hasn't signed the permission.

—Get it from him. *Now!*

DARK

No sound. No light. No smell. No touch. Gone. Vanished. Disappeared. What's this? Something stirring in the black?

'Hello. I'm Mr Sandbrook, your surgeon. Do you remember
me?'

Ripples across dark water. Shadowless. Down too deep.
Shipwrecks disintegrating inside barnacled ribcages of whales.

Submerged city. Broken columns. Shoals of tiny luminescent fish streaming through crumbling arches. Following me. The lapis eyes of a woman behind a floating picture frame. She wants to tell me something. *Wait!* Swims away past the statue of a man in flawless Carrara marble, buried to his shoulders on the ocean floor.

Ting…Ting…Ting… A full second between beats.

'Blink if you understand me?'

Ting…Ting…Ting…

Cogs and clock towers. Old Father Time, hinged from the waist, striking the hours with a bronze hammer.

'Good. I want to tell you a little bit about what's happened to you. Blink again if you understand. Excellent. Well done. I'm afraid to say it's not good news.'

Weightless. I have no body. I am. I am not. I am. I am not—

§

I am.

§

The fluttering of my eyes attracts my attention and suddenly I'm awake. I know three things at once. One: I am in hospital—chill disinfectant smells, mechanical sounds pinging and groaning. Two: I have a raging thirst making my throat feel like the inside of an active volcano. Three: this is all I remember.

There are machines all around me and one in particular that beeps at one-second intervals.

Ting…Ting…Ting…

Movement catches my eye. The door is swinging open and a man in a slightly rumpled suit appears carrying a phone in one hand and a disposable cup in the other. The man is familiar but it's the cup that I'm really interested in.

'Thir—sty.'

'Darius?'

Sebastian—I know him. Baby brother. Little Seb. All grown up now—almost drops his coffee when I speak. He was looking at his phone. How very Seb. He comes over and stares into my eyes in an oddly clinical way. 'You're awake?'

Brilliant deduction, Poirot. 'Wat—er.'

'Here.' Wetness against my lips. *A sponge?* Taken away. 'Thirsty.' Seb starts twisting a lock of hair behind his ear. Old habit only resurrected when he doesn't want to answer. 'I'm sorry. I'm not allowed.' He offers me a tentative smile. 'You seem better today. More lucid.' *More lucid? Have I been awake before?*

'How's the memory?' On the point of answering, 'What memory?', something sea-shifts inside me. A tidal rush of images—headlights blunting themselves on lampless country darkness. A vague light feeling of movement, almost balletic. No response from the brakes. Steering wheel about as useful as a child's toy, and a solitary scream piercing the dark. Suddenly I know something. Something vitally important then it all rushes away before I understand what it is I know.

Seb is watching me. 'Did you remember something?'

'I—' A door opens inside my head. There's a question I haven't asked, and I can't believe I'm only asking it now. 'Mum?' Does she know where I am? Has anyone called the hospice? God, she must be out of her mind with worry. The strangest look crosses Seb's face, almost of exasperation. 'Don't you remember me telling you?'

'Telling me what?' He shakes his head and briefly closes his eyes. 'I'm sorry. She died two weeks ago. Heart attack. Nothing they could do.'

That's not right. The last thing I remember is visiting her. She was sitting in a chair next to the window, knees covered with a crocheted blanket. Everything about her was sharp, her chin, her nose, her eyes. She smiled a rainbow of emotions at me and came straight to the point. *I was thinking of your father. Do you think it's true that we'll meet again in the next life?* A lie would be kindest, but she'd see through that clearer than the sparkle in a jeweller's eye. *I don't think there is an afterlife. So sorry, no. I don't think you'll see Dad again.* She sat back in her seat and smoothed the blanket. *Good. I thought I might have to spend eternity picking up his socks.*

'Darius, did you understand what I told you?'

'Yes.'

'That Mum is dead?'

'Yes.' We fall silent. Things are disintegrating. Hard to make sense. 'Seb?'

'Yes?'

'Does Mum know I'm here?'

'Oh Darius.'

Leaves in a whirlwind, thoughts speed off.

§

I'm awake again. Seb is sitting by the bed but on the other side now. He needs a shave. How much time has passed? Everything's so hazy. My thoughts…they run away…won't let me follow after them…

He brightens when he catches me blinking. 'Welcome back.'

'I slept.'

'Technically you went into shock. Your eyes rolled back and all the machines went crazy. Everyone was running about. Then you slept.'

'Mum?' Seb's face clenches.

'I know, Seb. She's gone.' He grins with relief then tries to hide it.

'How are you feeling?'

Good question. How am I feeling? The truth is, I don't know. Fact: My mother is dead. I understand this and I have no reason to believe Seb is lying, but I feel nothing. No pain. No grief. It's as if the information is about someone else, something I heard through glass or read in a newspaper over breakfast. *Yes, I agree, very tragic. Are you going to eat all that bacon?*

'Darius?'

I'm spared the embarrassment of answering by the door swinging open. A man—grey hair and matching beard, eyes a startling contrasting brown—enters followed by a much younger man who peers through spectacles the size of satellite dishes. The older man looks at me with a kind of business-like interest which reassures me. There's something old school and no-nonsense about him.

Half expect him to yell something like, 'What the hell are you doing lazing about in bed, Colvin? Don't you know there's a war on?' Part of me wants to oblige and leap to my feet. If only I wasn't so dog-tired. I can't even lift my head from the pillow and I'm less alert than I was a minute ago. Objects are surrounded by a fiercely burning corona of light while the objects themselves are in shadow.

He takes out a small torch from his pocket and shines it into my eyes. His breath smells of cloves. After a moment, he says, 'Good.' He doesn't explain what is good. 'I'm Mr Sandbrook, your surgeon. Do you remember me?'

'Yes.' I don't.

'Can you tell me your name?'

'Darius...Colvin.'

'Excellent. Do you know where you are?'

'Hospital.'

'You're at The Grange. A private facility. You'll get top-class treatment here.' He examines my notes. 'You didn't faint when they tilted you into a sitting position today. Very good. Excellent. Your blood pressure is stabilizing.' The younger man makes a show of taking notes and Sandbrook glances at him as though surprised to see him there. 'This is Mr Berrycloth, who is in training,' he says, although he appears to be reminding himself. He turns back to me. 'You understand what has happened to you?'

'He's more lucid than yesterday,' Seb interjects. Sandbrook freezes for a second as if sensing a fly landing on the back of his neck. *Oh Seb!* I feel the embarrassed pang most patients feel when relatives inadvisably express opinions to medical professionals. Perhaps I should apologise but Sandbrook repeats the question. 'You understand what has happened to you?'

Black waves of fatigue rise behind my eyes. Can't think straight. Seems easiest to say, 'Yes.' I answer *yes* to a few more questions I barely hear, then Sandbrook turns his focus to Berrycloth. 'Mr Colvin doesn't remember meeting me before his accident. But he is an excellent art dealer. I bought a little van Dongen from him last year. Didn't let me have it cheaply either. Now, can you give me your summary of the patient, Mr Berrycloth?'

Berrycloth shuffles forwards. He gazes down at me through the satellite dish spectacles then stutters out, 'The patient is a thirty-seven-year-old male with no significant prior medical history. He was admitted following a car accident. Head injury and whiplash. Fractures fifth and sixth cervical, some displacement. Bilateral loss of power and sensation from the neck down...'

Is he mad? I try to object but panic leaves me breathless. All I can do is stare intensely at Sandbrook, making thin wheezing sounds that barely ripple the air. *Interrupt him. Tell him he's wrong. Tell him he's some jumped-up little med school undergrad who doesn't know what he's talking about. My limbs won't move because I'm so tired. Because I'm lying still to let you examine me. Because—*

Berrycloth is doing something at my feet. 'Mr Colvin, do you feel that?'

Feel what? 'No.' At my thigh. 'No.' My hands...my elbow. No. No. No! Fear and fatigue are attempting to sedate my brain. Mustn't sleep. Move! Move something. Anything. Wiggle a toe. Twitch a finger. Prove them wrong. Close my eyes with the effort. Gasp out, 'There... moving toe ... Look!'

Berrycloth stops talking. Sandbrook adjusts his glasses and bends down to examine my foot. 'Which toe?'

'Big one...left.'

'Can you move it for me now?' Sweat beads my forehead. 'Again. Can you try again?' A river of exhaustion is trying to sweep me away. I cling to a branch of consciousness, squeeze my eyes tight shut and make a supreme effort. *There.* The seconds pass.

Ting...Ting...Ting...

Sandbrook straightens. ''Fraid we're not seeing anything. In cases such as these, we have to be guarded. Each case is different and we cannot accurately predict how much or when function, if any, will return.' His hand moves up and down. Is he patting my thigh? I feel nothing. 'We'd hope for maybe ten per cent. I am sorry but we have to be honest.' He smiles almost coyly at me, an adult playing along with a child. *I hear sleigh bells too.*

He continues talking about what lies in my future—of feeling in hands, feet, limbs—but the ten in ten per cent starts to expand inside me until the *one* is a spear sticking straight through my brain. The *zero* is a screaming mouth. My mouth, screaming all the way down to my lost bones. Sandbrook is calling for Diazepam 5mg stat and everything is in motion. Everything but me. I'm the ghost in the machine, the eye of the storm, the vanishing point.

How do you define a loss of ninety per cent? I'm not connected to my body. A floating head. Everything below dead weight. I'll never walk again. No legs. No arms. Jesus, I'll never fuck again. Never touch. Where are my hands? Get me out of here! Are you listening? Something terrible is about to happen!

TWO

LEXIE:

I don't see the dead. At least not like they portray it in dramas. War correspondents, firemen, soldiers reeling from some Michael Jackson video corpse hovering in the room with half its face shot away. Truth be told, I don't see them at all. But I do hear them. The sickening crunch if ribs give way under compressions. The AED's tinny inhuman voice, *Shock at five...stand clear...* Wail of relatives in the background. *Get them out of here.* That particular thud an unconscious body makes as it jerks on a table. Weird vocalisations, grunts and moans everyone agrees isn't fear. And right at the end, as I'm wiping the sweat from my eyes and pretending that it's business as usual, avoiding the nurses' eyes, so I don't have to admit the stinking rotten unfairness of it all that makes me want to rage against the dying of the light—after all that, comes the tuneless herald of oblivion, one long dead note: flatline.

I still hear it as I lie in bed watching dawn bleach out the night, wondering when the bottle of wine I drank or the second Zopi I took will kick in. Maybe my eyes start to grow heavy around six. Then the alarm goes off at six thirty, and it's back to work as usual.

For some reason the department of Neurology at Jimmy's is located on the top floor. Someone—Liv? Most likely Liv—once pointed out that the hospital has the layout of a human body.

'Think about it. Neurology's exactly where the brain would be. Cardiology is at the centre. And all the colectomies take place in the basement. The architect clearly had a sense of humour.'

'Like when he painted the walls the colour of faecal incontinence?'

'Obvs. He wanted us to remember what a shithole the place is.'

Pointless to look at my watch again so, of course, I do. Ten past. Shit. Shouldn't have taken that second Zopiclone. The price of a few hours' blankness means sleeping through the alarm only to wake stiff and wrung out and still hearing the voices of the dead. Okay, Lexie, get it together.

The faecal smell hits me as soon as I enter the ward. It's hidden under a layer of chlorine and artificial fragrances but it's there all the same, along with stomach acids and the metal scent of blood. *Same old. Same old.* Breathe in deeply and hope to dull the olfactory neurons before the gag reflex kicks in.

Typing my password—F-U-C-K-U-2—when a voice says timidly, 'You can't be behind there.'

When I don't turn around, the voice clears its throat and squeaks, 'Staff only.'

'I am staff.'

'Can I see your ID?'

'No.' The computer tells me my password is wrong and I thump it with the heel of my hand. Wait a minute, maybe it's S-C-R-E-W-U-2. As I'm typing it in, the voice insists, 'You have to leave, or I'll be forced to call Doctor Song.' Straighten up and face her. Probably her first day. Got that shiny, freshly painted look. 'I am Doctor Song.'

Newbie's eyes travel from my short, choppy blonde hair with its meridian line of dark roots to the slight forward jut of my jaw, all the way down the bony sexless frame hidden beneath leathers and terminating in heavy biker's boots, then the pause—wait for it—back to the face, and the double take at my eyes and their epicanthic folds. I narrow them into imperious slivers.

She swallows several times. 'I'm sorry. I didn't—'

'It's fine. Where's Grendel's mother?'

'Who's mother?'

'Sister Bosko.'

'Oh! She's talking to pharmacy. She wants to speak with you.'

'I need to get changed first.'

'She told me to tell you she's been keeping a log.'

'Really? I always wondered what she did while I was working.' Newbie gasps.

'What will I tell her?'

'Tell her to keep writing that log while the doctor saves lives?'

§

Start rounds with a thumping head and a mouth drier than the canals of Mars. Coffee? No chance now with Grendel's mother sniffing about. Send the student nurse down to the Macdonald's stand? Worth a shot. First day. Doesn't know any better. Have to pick my moment.

So, what's on today's menu? Two new epileptics admitted, one with a CT scan with some ominous dark patches on her frontal lobes. An elderly man with confusion. A teenager with persistent headaches after a motorcycle accident.

'How bad are the headaches?'

'Bad.'

'Can you be more precise?'

'I feel worse than you look, Doc.'

'Good one.'

As I'm examining Mr Cooper—a retired music teacher who can only speak in musical notes after stroke damage to Wernicke's area of the brain—an alarm goes off in Colonel Halpern's bay. 'Excuse me. I'll be right back.'

'Doh ray me la fah fah fah?' Mr Cooper suggests anxiously.

First thing I see are the crumpled sheets then Colonel Halpern's more crumpled body beneath them. There are lights flashing on the Vital Signs monitor and a series of discordant notes beeping blue murder. 'Colonel?' I've got my stethoscope on his chest when he murmurs, 'Sorry to disappoint but I'm not dead.'

'Pity. We could use the bed.'

He opens one eye. 'What's wrong with me this time?'

'Monitor says you're not breathing.' A swift kick and the alarm falls silent. The concerned face of one of the crash team appears around the curtain. 'False alarm.'

'Again?'

'You know the colonel, ward's worst hypochondriac.' Lift his chart and give it a quick scan. Not good. Chandra upped the pain meds last session. 'How's the pain?'

He shifts uncomfortably. 'Manageable.'

Just what we want to hear. Trouble is, the colonel comes from a school where unbearable pain is described on a scale of *not-so-bad* to *manageable*. Suspect his dying words are going to be, *Mustn't grumble.* 'I'll up your midazolam. How's the double vision?'

'Hard to tell. All you medical chaps and chapesses look alike. Know you of course. You've got those Chinese eyes.'

'Korean.'

'That's right. From your mother.'

'My father. My mother is Irish.'

'Ah yes. You told me that. Where you get your blonde hair from.' I get it from a bottle. An attempt to show solidarity with my Celtic roots. It worked. Everyone said I'd made myself the spit of great Uncle Liam.

'Okay. Let's see if the midazolam does the trick. You need to rest now.'

'I DO NOT NEED TO REST!' Colour drains out of the colonel's face and he sinks against the pillows. In a gruff voice he says, 'Sorry. Got eternal rest beckoning every time I close my eyes. Off, off into that good night as they say. Need to be lucid for the time that remains. Things to do. Ends to tie up.'

'We'll see what we can do.' Looks like he's dozing off and I'm about to tiptoe away when he suddenly asks, 'Do you dream, Dr Song?'

Heart skips a beat. 'Of course. Everyone does.'

'Funny things dreams.'

'Are they?'

'Yes. In the blink on an eye you forget who you are. You forget your nearest and dearest, forget your spouse, forget your children.' He doesn't notice that my face has gone strangely rigid and continues, 'Been with my Elsie fifty years this Easter. Last night I dreamt I was married to a complete stranger. Never seen the woman before. Yet I accepted it without question. We had a son too.' He adds this last a little wistfully. Children not a blessing of his long marriage. 'Lovely little soul. Blond curls. Cheeky chappie grin.' His fingers twist the bedcovers fretfully. 'Silliest thing is, now I'm awake I miss him. What do you think it means?'

'I don't know.' I wish I could get him off the topic, but he's clearly working up to something. He fiddles with the bedsheets and avoids my eye. 'Some say the people who come to you in dreams are buried memories, that they might be people you've met before in other lives.' He hesitates, embarrassed. 'But that's just nonsense, eh? Pure poppycock.'

Wishful thinking? Drugs and endorphins? 'Don't ask me. I'm just a lowly body mechanic. No-one teaches you at medical school how the soul works.' He doesn't answer. Flagging now, eyes fluttering, but just as I thought he was losing the battle with sleep, he opens them wide and asks, 'Have the trial chappies got back to you?'

'Not yet. But I'm hopeful of hearing soon.'

'Need to get the old noggin working again.' He lifts a hand weakly and taps his temple. 'Get the troops under command, eh? Before that other chap has the boots off me.'

'What do you mean?'

'What's his name? Something like Chalmers. Indian chappie.'

'Dr Chandra?'

'That's the one. Angel of Death.'

'Dr Chandra is one of the sweetest doctors in the hospital.'

'Always asking me if I want to be resuscitated. Do I want to sign one of those DNA thingies?'

'You mean a DNR?'

'That's what I said.'

'I'm sure Dr Chandra is just thinking about your welfare. Resuscitation can be a nasty business.'

'Taking his side, are you?'

'It's not like that—'

'Stick together your kind.' My hands freeze on the tubular bar of the bed-end. 'Our kind?'

'Yes.' Angry spots of red appear at the centres of the colonel's pallid cheeks. 'You lot. Doctors!'

Doctors? Of course, doctors. I give his hand a squeeze. The fingers feel like thin icicles. A little more pressure and they would snap off in my palm. The Angel of Death might not have come in the guise of Dr Chandra, but his eclipsing shadow can't be far away. Try to impart some warmth into the lifeless fingers. 'No-one's going to force you to sign a DNR against your will. I promise.'

As I turn away the colonel says something I don't make out. Ignore it? Already falling behind. Probably won't even remember asking in a few minutes. I go back. 'What was that?' His voice is very weak. 'Is it selfish?'

'I don't—'

'Saying no to Dr Chandra, I mean. Wanting to go on the trial so I can hang on for a bit longer. Not being ready to step through the veil.' No. Not this. I'm not ready. Nothing to steady me. Not even a fucking coffee. The whites of his eyes are thick and discoloured, panes of old glass sinking towards the bottom. 'Is it selfish…to want a little more life?'

Squeeze his hand a little tighter. 'No. It isn't. It isn't selfish at all.' Without saying goodbye, I turn and walk rapidly away.

Outside the colonel's room the faecal smell is stronger, but it isn't the reason I want to throw up. Need something to take the edge off. What a cliché, the doctor who can't get through the day without drugs. I haven't got my breath back before Grendel's mother appears. Climbed out of her snake pit specially to come find me. 'Mr Caldwell wants to see you.'

'Did he say why?' She doesn't dignify this with an answer, but her brows rise Macdonald's-arch-style. Stupid question. Consultants don't explain themselves. Even God finds their ways mysterious. 'I'll go up at the end of my shift.'

'You're to go now.'

Uh oh.

THREE

DARIUS:

A plopping wetness drip-dropping on my cheeks. Is it raining? Slowly, as though hoisting something heavy into the air, I raise my eyelids.

'Darius!' Seb's tear-stained face hangs over me like the moon.

'Wh—what's going on?' A moment ago I was floating across a Jackson Pollock canvas of white swirling blackness; now I'm back watching Seb wiping his eyes furtively with the cuff of his jacket. 'Do you know where you are?'

'In hospital. Yes. My neck—'

'It's—'

'I know, Seb. It's broken. Nothing below the shoulders. I remember everything now.'

'Not everything.' He delivers this statement like a punch, and I see now what I hadn't noticed before: the dark impasto smudges beneath the eyes, damp dark hair sticking to his face on one side, standing up in feathers and combs on the other. A man near breaking point. *Christ, what have I done to you?* Impotent rage strains against chest muscles that don't respond. 'Seb, it's okay. It's okay.' I would swap kingdoms just to be able to reach out and squeeze his hand right now. 'It's all right. I know. Mum's gone.' As I say the words my heart lights up with pain so exquisite it takes my breath away. Yet still I can't grieve. 'I know, Seb. I understand now.'

A flash of relief then a shake of the head. A hand smears down the side of his face. 'Yes. But do you remember dying last night?'

I blink stupidly, an exaggerated cartoonish blink that should reveal pulsating question marks floating on the surfaces of my pupils. 'Died?'

Seb nods. 'Everything's been going so well these last weeks.'

'Yes.'

'But last night—You really don't remember?'

'Being dead? No. You'd think I would.'

'What do you remember?'

'Not much. Sandbrook was talking then there was this blitz-krieg of pain pounding inside my skull. And something else. More than just the pain. Fear. I was scared shitless.'

'Yes. You rolled your eyes and said, *Something terrible is going to happen.*'

'Yes. Yes, I recall that now.'

'An impending sense of doom. It's part of it.'

'Part of what?'

'Dysreflexia.'

'Dysre—whatia?'

'Dysreflexia. Apparently your body's automatic nervous system went into overdrive because you had an untreated urinary infection. It's par for the course in your condition, I'm afraid. He did mention it to you.'

'Yes.'

Sandbrook: soft voice, clove-scented breath. 'It's a dangerous condition. If you flush from the neck up and have the mother of all headaches we need to know.'

'I'm used to headaches. I've suffered from migraines most of my life.'

'Not like this one. I promise you, it's quite unique. You'll feel as though your doom is upon you.'

'I died?'

Seb stares down at his shoes. 'You went red. Your whole head. It was as if you'd been shot through with pigment. We're talking full on *Crimson Lake* here. You were burning up. Then you passed out. I found out later your blood pressure had skyrocketed.'

'But you say I died?'

'All the alarm bells went off and half the staff came rushing in. They gave you nifedipine which should have worked, but you stopped breathing and your heart gave out.' As if in terrified response, my heart starts beating frantically against my ribs. I breathe deeply in and out to calm it. Seb is still staring at his shoes. 'One of the junior doctors wanted to start CPR, but there was a problem. They were afraid it would destabilise your neck. I don't know the details. I think I cried out or said something because just then a nurse noticed me and she hustled me out of the room.' He pushes a hand through his hair and holds it briefly at the back of his neck. 'I was outside the whole time not knowing what was happening. But Sandbrook came out later and told me you were stable. Apparently they saved your life with some experimental drug they're trialling. They asked me to sign the permissions when they brought you here. I can't remember its name.'

'Somnipradine?'

Seb looked startled. 'You know about it?'

'I think—I think I was awake.'

Seb's eyes saucer. 'You can't have been. You flatlined.'

'I know, but I remember.' A kind of waking that no-one seemed to notice. A floating quality about it. Seeing and feeling things that couldn't be real yet somehow were. 'The hands of the wall clock were going backwards.' Seb shifts his weight uncomfortably and glances at the door. He wants me to stop. But I can't stop. 'Sandbrook has a bald patch at the back of his head.'

'How would you—? I mean you can't. Unless—' He looks round wildly. 'That monitor. Perhaps you caught a reflection. Or wait.' He snaps his fingers. 'You met him before. He bought a painting, remember? You've transposed a memory.'

'Seb, I was there.' In amongst all the chaos—the alarms going off and Sandbrook ordering a second bolus of Somnipradine—my vision drifted to the bed where I saw the body of a man. Bare-ly recognizable, a withered, shrunken thing, a dry husk with all the essence squeezed out. Looking at it was like looking at sand blowing over some shrivelled entombed face.' The expression on Seb's face is telling me to shut up, but I can't help myself. 'Time was moving differently.'

'Time?'

'Yes. Suddenly Sandbrook was in a different part of the room though he hadn't moved from my line of sight. I asked as loudly as I could, *What is going on?* But no-one answered.'

'You had no pulse.'

'I know. One of the junior doctors was saying, *It's not working.* I heard him, Seb. I saw myself dying.'

'Then what?'

'I noticed that the ceiling was being eaten away by the night sky. It was so strange, growing in depth and intensity, a deep in-digo colour shot through with violet and pierced by tiny winking pinpoints of light. At the same time I was conscious of strange contradictions, of travelling yet standing still, of being nearby yet already at a great distance, of leaving everything behind yet feeling no sorrow, no sadness. To be honest, the nearer those alien con-stellations appeared the more I was filled with an immense sense of peace. Even when I heard Sandbrook say, *A third bolus.* And Berrycloth arguing, *Sir, his heart can't take it.*'

'They went ahead. They gave it to you.'

'All I knew was there was a violent tug yanking me backwards. I looked down and I could see that I was anchored to the body on the bed by an umbilicus of pulsing energy. It was impossible to see except for the shimmering reaction of the light about it, and it terminated in my chest.'

'They found your pulse after the third injection, but it was erratic.'

'I found myself floating above the corridor outside. I saw you hunched in a seat gnawing at the knuckle of your hand.' Seb im-mediately drops his hand.

'Did you speak to me?'

'No. I was confused. Part of me wanted to leave. But seeing you, I wasn't so sure. I wanted to comfort you, but the sky was calling. Then there was another tug and it felt like my heart was being ripped out. Darkness fell across one half of me, and I saw the stars on my left side winking out. Suddenly I was scared. I mean really scared. I pulled and tore at the umbilicus but it felt like elephant hide. I couldn't budge it. Then there was a bang, and I was falling the way you do in nightmares, and everything went black.'

Seb falls back in his chair. He hasn't blinked once. 'Well…' he says. 'Well—'

'You think I was dreaming?'

'Don't you think you were dreaming?'

'I wasn't dreaming. I was—' I have no idea what I was.

Seb rubs the back of his neck. 'You died while they were pumping seven colours of shit through your veins. No wonder you're going all Damien Hirst on me.' We laugh a little, both embarrassed but for different reasons.

'Seb?'

'Yes?'

'Why was I out there?'

'Out where?'

'On that country road. In the middle of the night. Why was I driving so fast?'

'No-one knows.'

'I'm so sorry. I'm so very sorry. For what I've done to you.' Wretched drips of salt escape from the corner of my eyes.

'Hey, it's okay.' Seb looks more alarmed than when listening to my ravings about the afterlife. A scratching sensation as a paper napkin dabs my skin. 'It was an accident. And you haven't done anything to me.'

'I don't know what's going to happen.'

'Simples. You'll come live with me.' Dear old Seb. He means it. He really does. It hasn't sunk in that I'm all ghost and no machine. 'You can't look after me.'

'Sure I can.'

'Every pet you've ever owned has died of neglect or starvation.'

'That's not my fault. Who knew gerbils needed fed every day?'
'It would never work. I can't let you do it.'
'Seriously bro, how are you going to stop me?'

§

As Seb leaves, I try to wave, forgetting nothing will happen. How long before my brain accepts this new normal? Seb hasn't taken it in either. Doesn't have a clue what it means, what's ahead of him. Christ, he's all I've got. And what has he got stuck with in the bargain? A talking lump of dead flesh. Less fun than a gerbil.

Not like there's someone to share the burden. Thirty-nine years old and what to show for it? No wife. No kids. When was the last time I saw Susan? Susan? Suzanne. God, can't even keep her name straight. Why did she leave? Lack of commitment. Yes. Mine, not hers. Always on a plane. Paris, Venice, Madrid. Always chasing the next big breakthrough. That dizzy feeling when you know the painting you're looking at is the real deal. What did she say? I could fall in love with any woman as long as she was staring out of a Renaissance portrait. Married to the job. Darius Colvin, art dealer and modern-day eunuch. O God, why was I driving so fast? What was I even doing on a country lane in the middle of the night?

It's so dark in here. Did Seb turn down the lights? 'Hello? Is anyone there?' Weird prickling at the nape of neck. Cold feeling in the pit of stomach. Something's wrong. It's the meds. It's just the meds. Close my eyes tight and when I open them, an orderly is standing in the doorway. Thank God. She's holding a tray with tea and toast and smiling at me.

'Can you help me? I think something is wrong.'

Her smile disappears and she says, *hungry feeling you're hope I. morning Good.* Then she retreats backwards and closes the door. Hot air blows over my face. *Wind blowing. Face hot. Cracked. Like mudflats. All dried up. Wind hot, hotter. Touches skin, like sucking. Pulls head down. Eyes slit-wise. Blue-tongued lizards baking on rock. No lizards now. Not for days. Panting. Got to breathe breathe. Too fast and Wind takes all. This valley is new. Hard, steep sides. Floor soft, sandy then sharp. Rocks everywhere. Everything strange. Not real. This place. It wasn't in the Black.*

'You don't look like brothers at all.'

'No.' A new nurse—middle-aged, well padded—is standing at the side of the bed. 'You're dark like your dad.' We seem to be in the middle of a conversation. 'Your brother's been so worried about you. Sat by your bed for days.'

'Mmmm.' How long has she been here? She really didn't notice anything? The pressure cuff is peeled from my arm. 'BP is 130 over 80. That's very good. Mr Sandbrook will be pleased.' She pats my shoulder with a show of nursely sensitivity—she's done her homework, knows where I have feeling. 'You're very lucky, you know. We only started the Somnipradine trials a few weeks ago.' Lucky? Yes, lucky to be brought back to one-quarter life while three-quarters of me died weeks ago. Lucky to lie here and think about how I've ruined my life. Damn Sandbrook. Damn his trials. Why didn't you let me go?

I close my eyes and pretend to drift off until she takes the hint and leaves. But, after she's gone, I lie staring at the ceiling trying to make sense of what just happened. I know three things. One, I have suffered severe trauma and so it's likely dreams may be more vivid as my body tries to make sense of what the hell I've done to it. Two, I am on strong medication which explains a certain tendency towards hallucination. Three, I believe neither of those things. Because I was there, in that high-sided valley with the hot dry wind blowing in my face, standing on feet that didn't belong to me.

FOUR

LEXIE:

Caldwell is well over six feet tall, bald and carries the body mass of a much smaller man. His bones are so thinly papered in crinkled flesh that it's rumoured patients worry more about his health than they do their own. He's talking on the phone and doesn't look up when I enter so I loiter for a few seconds, pretending an interest in the floor, then throw myself gracelessly into a chair and fold my arms across my chest. Defensive? You betcha.

Caldwell is nodding. 'I see…and there was no question of… No? No. Good.'

He puts the phone down, gets to his feet and crosses the office in a couple of strides to the window. He stands there, hands clasped behind his back, staring silently down at the asphalt desert of the carpark before suddenly asking, 'What do you imagine the costs are to keep a hospital like this running?'

Is he expecting a figure? 'I don't know.'

'Take a guess.'

'Millions?' I can see the ammonite shape of his skull bones through his naked scalp.

'Millions,' he agrees. 'And do you know how important it is to our reputation that international drugs companies choose Jimmy's to run their clinical trials?' I'm not expected to answer so I don't.

'Many times the salary of a junior doctor who thinks she knows better than the rest of us.' Caldwell pauses and glances over his shoulder while my guts twist themselves into a series of interlocking pretzels. What does he want: acts of contrition, fall at his feet, burst into tears, blubber apologies? Clench my jaw and stare back feeling like a cat staring at the headlights of an oncoming artic, an angry, stupid, suicidal cat too full of ancient ancestral pride to have the sense to leap out of harm's way. Eventually Caldwell turns back to the window. 'Did you understand you were not officially part of the research program?'

'I applied for a place earlier in the year.'

'Were you or were you not officially part of the program?'

'No.'

'No.' Caldwell rolls the word ruminatively around his gums. 'And did it occur to you that forging an acceptance for a patient who had been refused a place on the trial might have invalidated the whole process?'

'Yes.'

'And if he had died while being incorrectly administered Somnipradine—'

'He wouldn't have.'

'*If* he had died his widow would have been within her rights to sue?'

'Yes.'

'And knowing these two things do you still consider that you made the right choice?'

The question hangs in the air between us like a noose. *Answer him.* Try to lift the muscles of my face in a placatory smile, but the effort causes my left foot to start tapping madly and a bolus of something bitter makes me swallow down the apology like an uncoated pill. Caldwell makes an impatient noise. 'Do you consider you made the right choice, Dr Song?'

'Yes.'

'I see.' There's long silence, and I'm beginning to hope that perhaps the interview is over, when he says, 'I've seen it before of course, the young buck who thinks he can teach us old boys a thing or two. I say 'he' because I usually see this behaviour in men. Or more rarely—' He pauses with the affected delicacy of the cleverly camouflaged predator. 'In women trying to be men.'

'I wasn't…' I have no idea what I wasn't and the sentence trails off.

Caldwell is back in his seat, hands clasped on his chest, elbows sticking out at an unnatural angle like folded wings. Find myself thinking wildly, *Praying mantises don't paralyse or poison their prey. They hold them in place and devour their brains while they squirm their way to death.*

'Let me ask you another question, Dr Song. What do you think the primary remit of a hospital doctor is here at Jimmy's?' *A trick? A trap? What does he want me to say?* I can hear the noise of rush hour traffic outside, its colicky rumble interrupted from time to time by the thin operatic wail of sirens. *The primary remit of a hospital doctor?* Resignedly I say, 'To save lives.'

'No, Dr Song.'

'No?'

'No. You are surely familiar with the word. Certainly saving lives is an aspect of our function but it is secondary—perhaps not even that—to the great responsibility we share. Can you think what that might be?' Dumb shake of my head. 'Then let me make it plain. Fighting death is a fool's game. You've been a doctor long enough to know that people come in here to be patched up, handed pills, sliced, diced, zapped with radiation then sent on their way and told they're cured. In the meantime any doctor worth their salt knows there is no cure for the malady of being alive, that every one of the trillions of cells that make up a human body is on a suicide mission, preprogrammed to burn, brightly but briefly, before winking out and returning to the black infinity of death. The best we can achieve is to scoop a few grains of sand from the bottom of a rapidly running-out hourglass.

'And to achieve even this doubtful triumph we require almost as many pounds sterling as there are cells in our dying organisms. So, Dr Song, our primary duty is not, as you would whimsically have it, to save lives, but to prevent ruining our reputation, tying up personnel in court and risking NHS MILLIONS!' He raps an accompaniment to these last syllables with his knuckles on the desk.

Dig my fingers into my ribs until the pain makes my eyes water. 'I don't regret my actions. A man's life was at stake.'

'A very old, very frail man. A man who, according to his records, had exceeded his expiry date by at least a decade.'

'But he had a chance. The data on Somnipradine shows it outperforming every neurostimulant in the field.'

'And if you had perchance temporarily blunted the Reaper's sickle, what then?' *Don't answer. Just making things worse.* Caldwell taps his forefingers together. 'No suggestions? Allow me to illuminate you. The press would have got hold of it. No—' He stops my protest with a raised palm. 'They would. They always do. Tomorrow morning we would be reading lurid headlines over our cornflakes: *NEW DRUG CHEATS DEATH. IMMORTALITY ONLY A COUPLE OF PILLS AWAY.* And when our overlords in the pharmaceutical world got wind of it, they'd pull the plug faster than you could say DNR. The trial would collapse and all the other trials would follow suit.' Caldwell rubs his hands together. 'Well done, Dr Song, by the end of the day you would have saved one antediluvian patient at the expense of curing millions in the future. While, clearly, you believe you have an exemption from the maxim, *first do no harm*, I cannot make my mind up if you are to be congratulated on your evil genius or ridiculed for a lack of insight, so breathtakingly myopic, they should name an entire branch of ophthalmology after you.'

Outside the door a phone starts ringing. Someone picks it up and speaks in a low voice. Caldwell is staring at my trembling leg. Force myself to hold it still until the effort makes my teeth ache. *Please let him be finished.* He isn't finished.

'There are rumours about you, Dr Song.'

'Oh?'

'Rumours that suggest you have become afraid of death.' The room freezes. I hear myself say in a voice that doesn't sound like my voice. 'That's not true. It just—I mean who would say that?' I sound hysterical. Got to keep it together.

'Several of your colleagues have expressed concerns.'

'Look, if this is about Grendel—Nursing Officer Bosko—'

'Sister Bosko is a highly respected member of staff whose opinion I take very seriously. But no, this isn't about the good Sister. A number of your close colleagues have expressed doubts.' He rustles some papers on his desk and reads aloud, 'Overly aggressive resuscitation procedures. Extending the duration of CPR beyond reasonable expectation. Willful disregard of DNR protocols. Shall I go on? No? Something of a slippery slope, eh? Once you start to feel that your decisions are more valid than those around you, it can only be a tiny step to forge a patient's eligibility and place him at the cutting edge of medicine.'

Thrust out my bottom lip, the way I used to in childhood fights, and say in a flat, dull voice, 'I was right. You know I was right.' There is a long silence in which Caldwell sniffs once and I swallow several times. The longer this goes on the dustier my mouth feels. I can see a jug of iced water on Caldwell's desk. Would it be inappropriate to ask for a drink? What do I have to lose?

Before I can ask, Caldwell shifts in his seat and his mandibles part. 'We seem to have reached something of a stalemate, Dr Song. I suppose this is the moment when I tell you that, despite your maverick ways, you're too good a doctor, dammit, for us to lose. Well I'm not going to tell you that because you are a perfectly ordinary ten-a-penny junior doctor, and we have no room for medics who want to throw the entire system into disarray by tearing up the rule book and playing God. Every doctor in this hospital is part of a team, Dr Song. Even me. We know it and we work for the greater good, like cells working together to produce a healthy body. There is a name for a cell that goes rogue. We call it cancer and we CUT IT OUT.'

He lifts a pair of half-moon spectacles and places them on the end of his nose then opens his laptop. Clearly the matter is at a conclusion. Some instinct propels me to my feet. 'You'll have my resignation today if that's what you want.' He looks up slowly. This is it. I've called his bluff and aimed the barrel of my gun square between his eyes. Everything freezes. The only movement is a mild blepharospasm making my eye twitch Clint Eastwood style. I swallow and he blinks in slow motion. Playing along? Or did I imagine that? 'Very good, Doctor Song. Collect your things and go now. You can email me the letter.'

'But—'

He looks at me enquiringly, an executioner enquiring whether the block is at a comfortable height. Outside a siren howls into life and goes shrieking off into the distance like an angel of death.

§

Walk down back to the ward in a state of split consciousness. One part of me is replaying the words *you're fired* over and over on a continuous loop, while the other part slinks home, tail between its legs. A moment of panic when I can't get the ward door open. Has my security pass been cancelled already? No, just a wrong number. Chest feels tight. Don't think. Just get it over with. Collect my things. Say my goodbyes.

Newbie stares at me with round appalled eyes as I pass the nurse's station. Jesus, does everyone know? Grendel's mother is nowhere to be seen. Good. DNR doesn't cover what I'd like to do to her. I hope the colonel will forgive me.

'Is his wife here?' That's Chandra's voice coming out of the colonel's room. Must have called him in to cover my shift. A nurse answers, 'She's on her way.'

'I'll call it now. Time of—'

No, no, no, no, no. The door swings wide and smashes against the wall. NHS too cheap to replace broken doorstops. Everyone looks around at me, but my eyes are on the colonel's bed. One of the nurses is reaching for the sheets. 'Wait!' They look to Chandra who gives a tense nod.

'When?'

'Just after you left.'

'Adrenaline?'

'Yes.'

'Vasopressin?'

'Of course. There was no response, Lexie. We shocked him more than eight times.' Chandra goes on talking about compressions and intractable VF and flatlines, but I'm not listening. My eyes are fixed on the colonel. His body looks limp and broken, a lost old teddy bear with his stuffing torn out. *Come on, you stupid stubborn old man. Open your eyes and say, "Sorry to disappoint. But I'm not dead."*

In a few minutes the nurses will return clad in gloves and aprons, bearing the mortuary trolley. They'll remove the IV and take out the cannula tube piercing his vein. They'll drain his bladder and pack gauze into his orifices. They'll clean him—even his dentures—and dress his wounds. They will tie his big toes together and remove his wedding ring and hold it securely at the nurses' station until his widow claims it. They'll put him in a clean hospital gown, and finally swaddle him in a sheet, tucking in his feet, then pull it up over his face until the last vestiges of his humanity are neatly erased.

There's a bleep from the monitor and several small peaks appear. Chandra and I watch them knowing them for what they are: ghosts, little fizzling embers beneath a fire that has burned itself out.

'Come on.' Chandra is at the door. Behind him, the last of the peaks collapses, a shooting star falling below the flatline horizon. It's over.

Chandra's eyes brim with sympathy. 'He had a good life, Lexie. Longer than most.'

'Fuck you. He still had things to do.'

FIVE

DARIUS:

Awake. A shining moment of relief followed by horror at finding my living brain encased in a flaccid scarecrow body. Five weeks and every awakening the same. Life sentence. No parole. Not even the strange dream of that high-sided valley to break up the monotony. Hot air blasting my face and the wormy feel of sand between my toes. Still with me when I close my eyes. Like a powerful memory. Everything hard and solid and real. I was there. One hundred per cent. Offer my conclusion to the indifferent face of the blood pressure monitor. *More real than you.*

Sudden harsh featureless light makes me blink wildly. An orderly has switched on the fluorescent bulbs. 'Time to go.' I was expecting the young red-haired physio eager to wheel me off to what they laughingly call the 'gym'—hands bandaged to handlebars because you can't grip, or strapped into frames so you can feel gravity as God intended, and all the broken, useless people hanging there praying that our bowels won't open and empty themselves in front of everyone.

Wait for him to offer an explanation which he obligingly doesn't. He slides me across the transfer board from bed to wheelchair, like it's an open bedpan and he's forgotten his rubber gloves. Fine. We match silence for silence until a creeping sense that decisions are being taken without my consent makes me blurt, 'Where are you taking me?'

The physio jabs his finger at an elevator button. 'Down to the MRI suite.'

'An MRI? Has something changed?'

'Couldn't say.'

'Who requested it?

'Doctor.'

'Dr Sandbrook?'

'No. The new one.'

'I have a new doctor?'

'Guess so. Chinese woman. Used to work at St James's General.'

'What's she like?'

'You don't want to know.'

Now I desperately, urgently, frantically need to know. 'Tell me.'

'Rumour is she got kicked out.'

'For what?'

'Couldn't say.'

'But isn't The Grange meant to be—' I dredge up something Seb told me '—a haven of excellence?'

'Couldn't say. But I heard her father pulled strings and got her the job here.'

The lift arrives and he wheels me in backwards. I can't see which button he presses, but a moment later the doors slide apart and a rush of cool antiseptic air hits me in the face. I'm wheeled down a silent corridor with doors on either side. The smell of antiseptic grows stronger. A set of double doors displays a radiation symbol. Beneath it a notice reads:

RESTRICTED ENTRY.
AUTHORISED PERSONS ONLY!

The doors open. Inside, there's a narrow bed protruding from the belly of a machine that looks like it belongs in a monstrous laundromat. A woman with choppy blonde hair, clearly dyed, and imperious eyes like slivers of volcanic glass, approaches. 'Good. You're ready. You remember what I told you about the procedure?' Remember? How can I remember? I've never seen her before. She frowns. 'I'm Doctor Song. I started here at The Grange last week.'

I give an *of course* grunt which fools her not in the slightest, but she says, 'I'm going to give you the contrast agent now. It's very safe, and we're here to take care of you.' She's holding a syringe. She fits it to the canula in the back of my hand and pushes the plunger. I feel nothing. Her expression is business-like. 'Any questions?' Only a number bigger than infinity. Should I say? Will I be marked down as unstable? She looks at me very closely as if she senses something is wrong, but before she can interrogate me further, a young nurse appears at her side. 'We're ready, Doctor Song.'

'All right then.' She gives me an encouraging smile. 'Let's see if we can find an explanation for what's happening to you.'

'Wait! I don't understand. What do you mean?' I can't seem to make myself heard. Mouth filled with sticks and debris. Sounds muffled and stuck together.

'This won't take long.'

Another transfer board and I slip onto a sliding surface that glides me into a doughnut-shaped hole into a tube so narrow the curving walls are only inches from my face. Makes me think of submarines trapped on the ocean floor. Sailors lying dead within them. My ears ring in the silence. 'Everything okay?' Doctor Song's voice comes through the earphones.

'Yes.' I sound timid and strange.

'You'll hear a lot of odd noises. It's just the magnetic field. Nothing to worry about. Okay?'

'Yes.'

'If you're worried about anything, just say.'

'Thank you.' A faint whirring sound, bicycle wheels running along tarmac. Close my eyes and begin counting down from one hundred. *Ninety-nine, ninety-eight, ninety-seven...* At ninety-four the sound grows much louder, an atonal cacophony of weird notes and dissonant pitches, an insane orchestra playing with jackhammers and jets.

'Still okay?'

'Yes.'

'Darius, are you okay?'

'Yes. Yes, I'm okay'

'C…you…ear…m…'

'I can't hear you.'

'.you…hear…can't…I'

'What?'

'c…y…eeeeeeeeeeeeeeeeeeeeeeeeeee'

'Hullo? Hullo?' In the earphones nothing but static. *A glitch in the comms. A momentary distraction. She'll be back in a second.* 'Hullo? Can you hear me? Hullo?' Trapped. Locked in a coffin. A head floating in a tank. A genie imprisoned inside a bottle. 'Is anyone there?' Shouting brings on a fit of coughing. Lungs filling. Can't empty them. The machine is screaming. Walls collapsing. A scorching wind blows in my face.

FIRST LIFE

Beginnings

The memories of Dreams-the-People

SIX

Wind blowing. Face hot. Cracked. Like mudflats. All dried up. Wind hot, hotter. Touches skin, like sucking. Pulls head down. Eyes slit-wise. Blue-tongued lizards baking on rock. No lizards now. Not for days. Panting. Got to breathe breathe. Too fast and Wind takes all.

The valley is not like in the Before. Hard, steep sides. Floor soft, sandy then sharp. Rocks everywhere. Everything strange. Not real. This place. It wasn't in the Black.

§

Stop. Stop! This isn't happening. In the MRI suite. Winter outside. Winter, MRI, Doctor Song; magnetic field. Say it again. Fast. One hundred times. Mouth feels dry. Tongue sticking to the roof of mouth. Feet sinking into sand…

§

Salt taste on lips. On tongue. A pelt of hot no-air presses my skin. Water to mouth. Last few drops. Keep going. No time to stop. No time for drawing memories. Insects. A cloud buzzing around my head. Yesterday hands flapping. Kept them away. Today weak. Let them bite.

Pause. Sniff air. Only dry, harsh empty emptiness. No memories here. The sky is a hard flat rock. Hands and knees. Digging stick. Plunge. Scrape. Scratch. Then bowl. Plunge. Scoop. Toss. I am hopeful. The bowl has earth memory. Soft wet clay. Clinging. Moist. Tree memory in the digging stick. Look for roots. Find the water. This sand. This bed. Where is the river?

'Where is the river?' Crooked-Mouth asks. Her voice is a lapwing calling at night. First-Father scratches his head. 'The river is here,' he says. 'We came to the river. The river is here.'

'The river is here,' First-Mother agrees. She lifts her digging stick. Second-Mother and Third-Mother go with her. Second-Mother is carrying New-One on her back. 'We will find the river.' I watch them go. I watch them so I will remember. I do not tell them that I looked at the Black and the river was not there.

§

Thirsty. No, not my thoughts. Not my memory. What's happening to me? Doctor Song? Can anyone hear me?

§

Dust. Rocks. Sand trickles between my fingers. Dry. Dead. Hands bleeding. Pain of me. Tongue thick, fills my mouth. Flesh thin, cracking. Like faces of First Father, First-Mother. Only death here. The wind blows sand. I am not hopeful anymore.

'They are all gone,' says First-Mother. 'All that swam here. Silver-Tail and Four-Spines and Long-Eels and Specked-Eel and Not-Leaves and Upside-down and Swims-Along-Bottom. All gone. The river is not here.'

There is nothing to drink. Crooked-Mouth breathe breathes too quick. 'Stop,' says First-Father, but Crooked-Mouth doesn't stop. Her tongue lolls out, like dog. First-Father says, 'Stop!' But all day she is crying and breathe breathing. Her eyes swallow the Moon. One eye is the Moon sailing across the night sky while other is reflection on dark water. Crooked-Mouth has become dead.

§

I'm weeping. Weeping for a girl who died hundreds of thousands of years ago. A girl I never knew is tearing out my heart.

§

Crooked-Mouth lies down in the earth. Her mouth eats the Black. Third-Mother weeps, beats on her breast. There are no flowers. No gifts for Crooked-Mouth when she eats the Black. Everyone is weeping. Killed-the-Leopard punches a tree. Dead leaves fall to the ground. Third-Mother takes a bead from her necklace. I know this bead. It came from the river. Smooth like skin. Shiny like a clever eye. She puts it in Crooked-Mouth's grave.

Carries-Short-Spear is angry. He points at me. 'Why do you not weep? Crooked-Mouth has become dead.' The others stop weeping. They are angry with me also. Carries-Short-Spear chases me away. I think he will throw his spear at me, but he pushes it under my bad leg. Makes me fall. I taste the ground. It tastes dusty dead. When I try to get up, Carries-Short-Spear pushes me down. First-Mother watches. She does not look sorry. Carries-Short-Spear turns away in disgust. He goes back and leaves me to watch. They are closing the earth over Crooked-Mouth. Everyone is weeping. I am not weeping. I will see Crooked-Mouth in the Black.

§

There are bones nearby. Clean picked. The colour of old teeth. Ribcage half sunk in the sand. Like fingers clasping. One tusk long, straight. One broken, gone. Not in the now. An old fight. I go near and nearer. Fear in me. There is drumming heart. There is roaring inside ears. But I go close. Good foot first. Bad foot drag follows. The bones are whispering. Reach out, fingers touching. There is memory here.

I use a bone to make Crooked-Mouth's mark. They are singing. I would like to sing. But they do not ask me. They have their backs to me. They are singing for Crooked-Mouth because Crooked-Mouth has no voice now. She is eating the black.

I have ashes. When the trees burn down, I creep crawl back. They are hot but I can touch. Clever fingers find an egg. Bald crow, broken, empty now. I use it to hide the ashes.

There is no water to mix the ash. I spit. Nothing comes. Spit again. Small trickle. Enough. Under my rib I prick with the bone. Teeth bite down hard. Tears are leaking. But I go on. The singing for Crooked-Mouth has stopped. They will say she eats the Black. They will not say her name now. I think of Crooked-Mouth and am not hopeful.

Under my ribs, I prick a bird. Crooked-Mouth's voice was a lapwing at night. I make it very small because Crooked-Mouth was small. She gave me a honeycomb once. She touched my marks. Crooked-Mouth was small, but her heart was big.

They do not sing now. They lie down and disappear from themselves. They will be back when the sun returns. I lie down.

But I don't disappear. My eyes are open. Inside the Black my eyes stay wide, watching.

I think she will not come. I must not wish the Black. The Black must come of Itself. I do not wish for Aurochs, but he comes. When the fire dies. When the forest is no more. He comes. No feet. Floating. There is a fierce glare in his eyes. The truth of it is not in words. It is in knowing his knowing. He shows me the river. The river is not there. First-Father is taking us to the river. But the river is not there.

Now Crooked-Mouth is in the Black. She smiles and her teeth are like scattered pebbles. They gleam white in the darkness. 'Crooked-Mouth,' I say. 'I am happy to see you. Is there plenty to drink in the Black?' I am so glad tears want to come down my face. Crooked-Mouth is sad now. She has something to tell me. I must make memories on my body of First-Father and First-Mother and of Second-Mother and Third-Mother. I must make memories of Carries-Short-Spear and Kills-the-Leopard and New-One. And when I have made the memories I will be done. I will take their memories and I will go far.

'Where will I go?' I ask.

Crooked-Mouth does not know.

'Who will remember me? If I go, who will say my name?'

Crooked-Mouth does not know.

'I don't want to go.'

But Crooked-Mouth is not there. Aurochs is in the black. There is a fierce glare in his eyes. I cannot move. His blood boils within me. Snorting breath choking me. Terrible hooves trampling me—

I sit up. I am no longer in the Black even though it is still dark. Crooked-Mouth has told me to go. Aurochs has told me to go. I will not go. Where will I go? I am very thirsty.

There is a scream. I am running. Foot drags. The sun has climbed up. They are back. But New-One has become dead. Second-Mother goes down on hands and knees and beats the earth with her head. She beats until blood comes but no-one stops her. Carries-Short-Spear is angry. He points his spear at me. I think

41

he will hurt me, but First-Father shakes his head. He sits down. He is weak. He needs to drink.

New-One is in his grave. Kills-the-Leopard gives him a hawk feather to take into the Black. They sing but it is not loud like before. Kills-the-Leopard and Carries-Short-Spear go looking for water. We sit under a big rock in the shade. The air is hot, hotter than yesterday. Everywhere the light dazzles, eyes cannot see.

I think of water. Cool. Beautiful. Moving like snake swimming down throat. First-Mother tries to sing but her voice is all cracked. She is silent. Third-Mother is panting. Her eyes are sunk in. When First-Mother touches her, she sits up. She cries, 'Crooked-Mouth is here.' We look to where Third-Mother points. We cannot see Crooked-Mouth. We are afraid. 'I do not see Crooked-Mouth,' First-Mother says. 'Where is she?' But Third-Mother is not speaking. She has become dead.

First-Mother wants Third-Mother to lie down in the earth. But no-one digs. No-one sings. No-one gives gifts. I make a mark for Third-Mother under the mark for Crooked-Mouth. I make a circle because Third-Mother's belly was always round.

§

'Doctor Song?'
'Yes?'
'We're here to take Darius Colvin back to the ward. Are you ready?'
'Yes. Go ahead. Okay, Darius. You did really well. Feeling a bit sleepy? Let's get you back.'

§

The sun has nearly gone into the Black when Carries-Short-Spear returns. His head droops. He has lost his spear. 'Where is Kills-the-Leopard?' First-Father asks. Carries-Short-Spear's face is like the moon when a cloud passes over. He sits down and cradles his head in his arms. 'We went a long way. There is no water. We went far. Then further. No-one can go further and come back.' First-Father says nothing. Carries-Short-Spear sits down. He scrapes the sand with his heels. 'Kills-the-Leopard fell down. He has become dead.' He is looking at me.

I make a mark for Kills-the-Leopard. I draw a leopard leaping. I mean it to be fierce but my hands are weak, shaking. It does not come out the way I want. I worry that it will not be a good memory and Kills-the-Leopard will be alone in the Black. No-one speaks. First-Father holds First-Mother's hand. They do not talk of New-One or Third-Mother or Crooked-Mouth or Kills-the-Leopard because they are eating the Black now. Carries-Short-Spear is holding Second-Mother's hand.

When they have all disappeared, I look into the Black. It is a long time, but Gazelle comes. She has a gentle look in her eyes. She tells me I must put the memories under my skin and then I must go. I ask her where will I go? She does not know.

The next day we lie in the shade. My body burns like the sun. I am covered in dust. I start to make the marks for First-Father, First-Mother. A rock for First-Father because he is as old as the rocks and his face is cracked like one. For First-Mother I draw a row of small people because she is mother to us all. Carries-Short-Spear is watching me. 'Why are you doing that?' he asks. 'Why are you making their marks. They are not eating the Black.' This is surprising. I did not think Carries-Short-Spear cares about my marks.

A fly crawls across his face. He does not flick it away. 'You are making their marks. But First-Father and First-Mother are not eating the Black.' I do not answer.

'We went far,' he says. 'Kills-the-Leopard and I went far. Then further. No-one can go further and come back.' I am making a mark for Second-Mother. I make a curve like her mouth which was always smiling. He says in voice not like his voice, 'Have you done one for me?' I open my hand. There is a short spear below my fingers. It points up as though flying.

Carries-Short-Spear looks at it long then longer. He says, 'I am a hunter. When I chase kudu and antelope and gazelle, I see with their eyes. I run on their feet. They are my brothers and I feel their blood boil when death comes closer. When Kills-the-Leopard is there, I feel him too. He is my brother. 'But you—' He does not speak for long. Then longer. He looks down at Second-Mother. She is sleeping. When he looks back at me his eyes burn in his

43

head. 'I hear you. You think we have all disappeared. But I hear you talking to the Black.'

I curl my fingers around Carries-Short-Spear's mark. I put it behind my back. He says, 'You know where there is water.'

'How could I know? I am covered in dust. My lips are cracked like yours.'

He says, 'You talked to the Black. You know.'

'How could I know? You and Kills-the-Leopard travelled far. Then further. No-one could have gone further.'

Carries-Short-Spear begins to cough. I know this coughing. Long before Crooked-Mouth lay down in the earth, Gazelle called to me in the Black. There was a spear driven into her side. She showed me what it is to become dead. I looked through her eyes and saw the world grow dark. She coughed, like Carries-the-Spear is coughing and blood comes from her mouth. There is blood on Carries-the Spear's mouth now. I feel his mark burning deep in my palm.

It is two more days and they have all become dead. I am too weak to lay them in the earth. They will not eat the Black. They will become rot then bones. Like Aurochs and Antelope and Elephant. They will become disappeared.

When the Black comes, I wait. But no-one calls to me. I am sitting by alone. My lips are cracked, my belly shrivelled. Everything smells dusty gone. Time to go.

I am at the river that is not there. Look for rock, the one that is like lion crouching low. Hands press into sand. Dig. Scratch. Scrape. Find them. Horns plugged with grass. Close to ear. Shake. Listen. Close to mouth. Do not lose a drop. Then over lips, down throat. Like rain bursting on to parched earth. Like river cutting through black stones. Pure, clear and filled with life, life, LIFE!

Long before Crooked-Mouth lies down in the earth, Aurochs comes to me in the Black. He is skinny thirsting. His ribs show. His head droops. When he talks to me, his tongue lolls out swollen, dry. He gives me his horns. I fill them when the river is here. I hide them under the rock that is like lion crouching low.

Leave First-Father and First-Mother. Leave Carries-Short-Spear and Second-Mother. Leave the river that is not here. Leave the safe places. Leave Crooked-Mouth. Sorrow for Crooked-Mouth. No saving. Carries-Short-Spear would hunt me, kill me. I am not a hunter. Crooked-Mouth cannot leave. Sorrow for First-Father. Tell him of the Black and Aurochs skinny thirsting. But he says only, 'Here is the river. The river is here.'

Carries-Short-Spear and Kills-the-Leopard went far. Then further. No-one could go further. I have Aurochs' horn. I have my marks. I am Dreams-the-People and I will go into the Beyond.

§

The voice comes from far away but I hear it clearly. 'So, how are you feeling now?'

'Seb, I've remembered the strangest things.'

SEVEN

DARIUS:

'Darius?'

What am I looking at? The unfamiliar doctor with the choppy blonde hair 'Yes?'

'You called me Seb.'

'Sorry. I was sleeping.' She looks are me strangely. 'You think you were sleeping?' Stare at her helplessly. What other explanation is there? She taps a pen against a clipboard. 'Do you know where you are?'

'Hospital. My room.'

'And where were you before?' Walking across a dying landscape a hundred and fifty thousand years ago. 'The MRI suite?'

'Are you asking me if you were in the MRI suite?'

'No. I was there. You were there.'

'What day is it?'

'I have no earthly idea. What do days matter when you spend your time looking at the ceiling?'

She concedes the point. 'Can you tell me what we were discussing before you called me by your brother's name?'

My lips feel dry. It's a trick question. Has to be. 'I was asleep. The sedation hadn't worn off.' There is a silence. I watch a frown form on her forehead then professional tact smooth it away.

'Darius,' she says gently. 'You had the MRI last week.'

LEXIE:

Out in the corridor, a voice calls after me, 'Doctor Song?' Turn to find a tall blond man approaching. He holds out a hand. 'Sebastian Colvin. Darius's brother. Call me Seb, please.' Take his hand a little stiffly. Beautiful men have never been kind to me.

'You don't look like your brother. He's so dark.'

He laughs. 'The good angel and the bad. You just have to work out which is which.' There's an awkward moment while neither of us speaks. He wants something.

'Can I help you?'

He gives a guilty-child smile and rubs the back of his neck. 'I—Look, I'll just come right out and say it. I'm worried about my brother.'

'Of course.'

'No, you see. I think—at least I have reason to think—' He stop starts like this for a while until I make the universal *Doctor-with-better-things-to-be-doing* gesture then his cheeks redden and he says in a rush, 'I'm worried about his mind.'

'His mind?'

'He's been saying strange things.'

'Such as?'

He hesitates. 'You know he recalls nothing of the accident?'

'Yes.'

'But he—' He hesitates again. Change to my *You-can-tell-me-I'm-a-doctor* face, until he continues. 'He claims that he's been experiencing someone else's memories.' Everything inside my head goes very still.

'Go on.'

'It's not like him. Last time I was up he was going on about caves and the land drying up and pricking his skin with dyes.' He breaks off and I start talking reassuringly about PTSD and trauma and the effect of heavy painkillers, but he interrupts. 'It's more than that. No-one knows him better than I do, and he sincerely believes he was there, A hundred-and-fifty-thousand years ago experiencing the birth of art or imagination or something.'

'And he only started making these claims after the accident? No history of mental illness before?'

'None. Even after the accident. He didn't mention anything like it until after his bout of dysreflexia.'

'These memories from prehistory?'

'At first he talked about being dead. A kind of out-of-body experience, I think you'd call it. Then he began to get all worked up about some lost tribe of neanderthals.'

A hundred-and-fifty-thousand years ago gives them as much likelihood of being human, but I don't correct him. 'And if you challenge him?'

'He argues, quite coherently. In fact, he's so persuasive there are times I've wondered if I'm the mad one. Other times, he just changes the subject. It's as if we've been having a different conversation all along.' He's staring at me, and I know what's coming next.

'What do you think? Is it brain damage?'

Adopt the *doctor-as-politician* stance: in other words, I answer without answering. I use phrases such as, *too early to tell* and *treatments being considerably more advanced than they were ten years ago* until he's thanking me for my help and going off no wiser than he was when he started.

§

Liv answers on the third ring. 'What's wrong, baby sister? You haven't been fired already? Dad's going to be pissed.'

'Fuck off, Liv. I need your help.'

'Ouch. That must really hurt.' That's the trouble with phoning Liv. We stop being two professionals in our thirties and revert to being kids rolling about the floor fighting over the tv remote.

'I need you to speak to Dad.' There's a low whistle at the end of the phone.

'Jeez, Lexie. Why don't you speak to him?'

'You know why.'

'The man put his reputation on the line to get you that job.'

'He got me a job in a glorified care home. It's one up from mopping the floors.' I expect her to argue. Instead, she says, 'Mark called. You didn't tell me you two broke up.'

'Old story. Girl wants to fuck boy. Boy wants to marry girl. It was always going to end badly.'

'You mean you were fine until he started needing you.'

'Oh of course, I forget you're a psychologist. What's wrong with me, Dr Song? Do tell. Is it daddy issues?'

'Definitely. And probably mummy ones too. Do you want to know what your real issue is?'

'Why not? Just don't expect me to pay you at the end of the session.'

'You think you're a man.'

Now that makes me laugh. 'Kind of fashionable these days, isn't it?'

'You don't want to be a man, Lexie. You just want to act like one, the worst kind of man you can imagine. I've seen this kind of behaviour before, generally in women with philandering fathers or ones who've felt betrayed by men.'

'How about I'm the brains and you can stay the beauty?' It's untrue. Liv is sharper than a laser scalpel, but I can't let her have everything.

There's a heavy sigh on the end of the line. She used to make that sound when she was about to lose at arm wrestling. 'What is it you need?'

'It's about Somnipradine. They're trialling it at The Grange.' I wait for her to say, *My God, they're trialling Somnipradine there.* There's a silence until I say, 'You knew, didn't you?'

'Dad and I thought you'd be pleased.'

'Well, thanks for the intervention.'

'Swallow the bitter pill, Lexie, and let someone help you for once. Actually, for twice, as you're about to ask me for something.'

'I've got a patient showing an anomalous reaction.'

'Anomalous how?'

'It's hard to explain. But there's something big going on. I can feel it.'

'Well *feeling things* is at the heart of all great scientific methodology.'

'Are you going to help me or not?'

'What do you expect me to do?'

'Ask Dad if he's heard anything. He's got contacts. I need to know if there have been any findings that suggest Somnipradine is linked to enhanced memory.'

'That's all?' Liv sounds sceptical. Damn, she knows me too well. But what can I say, *what if Somnipradine is linked to memory capable of going beyond this life?* That sounds crazy even when I think it.

'That's all, Liv. I promise.'

Another sigh. 'All right. I'll see what I can do.'

§

It's the end of a shitty day before a ping on my phone alerts me that Liv has left a message. I feel wrung out. We lost two patients—an elderly woman who was suffering from a colonic carcinoma and a young woman who suffered complications from advanced MND. Somnipradine didn't save either of them.

Liv's message is typically terse. *Look in your email.* I should wait until I get home. It's the sensible thing to do. So, of course, I lock myself in a cubicle in the ladies and start scrolling. At first, I can't find it. Damn you, Liv. Is this your idea of a joke? But no. There it is in the spam folder between a plea to '*Tell us how we did*' from a store I can't remember ever buying from and a chance to earn millions while working from the comfort of my own home. The article is recent and details some preliminary findings from an American study. It's drily written, full of statistical data and underscored by words such as, *inconclusive* or *until further research is possible*, but there are links to other articles that contain anecdotal material.

In Pennsylvania, a young boy with no discernible heartbeat received Somnipradine after arriving at an ER. His physical recovery followed a rapid trajectory and he passed a number of cognitive tests without difficulty before being released. However, upon returning to the family home, he began to manifest strange behaviours. He refused to enter his bedroom, repeatedly telling his mother, "We don't live here." He would describe his 'real home' as having a distinctive wallpaper "with cranes and pagodas". He also mentioned that the room would shake when trains went past the window. His mother confirmed that they had lived in a cheap apartment in Tioga, "practically on the rail line", and that there had also been chinoiserie wallpaper in the small second bedroom. However, the family had moved out of the apartment when the boy was six months old and the mother could not recall ever having talked about it in his presence.

In New York a woman in her thirties was admitted to an ER in Lower Manhattan after a suicide attempt. She was unresponsive and was administered two boluses of Somnipradine, which stabilised her life signs and led to a full recovery. Although she scored highly on the mini mental state exam, her therapist noted several strange behaviours during their interviews. The woman became agitated after a porter of Latino descent came to fetch her for a routine exam. She insisted that he had taken her daughter though it was known that both her children were male. She claimed that her daughter had been 'sold' while she had been away working in the fields.

When questioned she would give consistent responses, saying that her daughter's name was Liling and that her own was Nuo. (The patient was of Italian Jewish descent and her husband was unaware of any east Asian connections.) She was unable to give a family name and kept repeating that her daughter had been taken by the 'flat noses' while she was in the fields. Repeated attempts at reassurance met with resistance. It was noted that she was repeatedly wringing her hands, and when questioned, she answered. "These are not my hands. These hands are too soft." A mirror was fetched and in response to her own face, she said, "Who is this woman?" During the 'episodes' (none of which lasted more than fifteen minutes) the woman appeared lucid and sounded coherent.

Over a matter of months, she was convinced that she did not have a daughter and the episodes ceased. She was considered cognitively stable and released, although the husband raised concerns that she may have learned to hide her false memories. He also claimed that, despite behaving normally, she sometimes appeared distracted, as though secretly listening to some invisible source.

A six month follow up was not possible as the patient had made a second, and unfortunately successful, suicide attempt. Although there is gathering evidence for a link between Somnipradine and increased brain activity, primarily in the amygdala and hippocampal areas, no direct conclusions can be drawn at this time...

§

A ping on the phone is from Liv. *What time are you coming home?* What time is it? The numbers on the phone don't make sense. After midnight? I can't have been sitting here for six hours. The pain in my lower limbs begs to differ. I suspect if I don't get up soon, I'll have to limp through the next week bent over with a dowager's hump. Come on, Lexie, go home, get some sleep. The research will be here in the morning. My eye catches an article entitled, Positron Emission Tomography (PET) in post Somnipradine patients. I click the link.

EIGHT

DARIUS:

Dr Song listens to me, head cocked to one side. 'And the pain is located in your scrotum?'

'Yes.'

'May I take a look?'

'Yes.' Why do I want the ground to swallow me up? Every indignity known to man has been visited upon me in the last weeks. Who needs the bowels of hell when your own bowels have lost contact with command central?

'There?' She glances up. I didn't realise she had started. I felt nothing. We play this game for a while, her sticking something sharp into my manhood, me trying to tell myself the world isn't a cold dead empty thing below my neck. I try not to think about my penis, a shrivelled slug not responding to her hand.

'Darius?' The concern in her voice brings me back. Oh, the horror. There are tears in my eyes and, even worse, she has spotted them. 'Is something wrong?'

'I'm fine.' She holds my gaze a fraction too long then gets to her feet and walks over to the sink. Over the sizzle of the water, she says, 'I can't see anything. It could simply be phantom sensation. But there's always a risk of urinary infection. We'll do a test and I'll see about antibiotics.'

'Thank you.'

'How long ago did the pain start?'

'I'm not sure.' She flips the tap off with an elbow. 'Days? Weeks?'

'I—' She's looking at me closely. What can I say: *I first noticed the pain after I met you?*

§

Once Dr Song has gone, Duvet—my name for the well-padded nurse with the comforting air—enters. With the help of an orderly, she manoeuvres me into my wheelchair and checks my head support before whisking me off to the winter garden for a change of scene. The winter garden is a euphemistic term for a chilly room with whitewashed walls and French windows looking over three long terraced lawns. She leaves me there so I can 'enjoy the view'.

There's a glamour of frost on the bare branches of the trees and the grass is sticking up in stiff white needles. Funny, I never liked the cold but now the sight of it makes me ache to the centre of my soul. To be outside, breath puffing out in white plumes, footprints stencilling wet green trails across the lawn.

Impulse makes me nudge the head controls of the wheelchair and I roll forwards, dilapidated dalek-style, until the sight of my reflection in the glass pulls me up. I don't recognise the emaciated broken man looking back at me, eyes lost in shadows above the hollow cheeks. He makes me want to hurl myself out of the wheelchair. To punch and kick until pain overwhelms me. But my will has no dominion and I sit, inert as paint on canvas, while my mind forms fists that hammer against my skull. *We take it all for granted. Then, in an instant, it's gone. Everything. Forever.*

The distinct sound of footsteps coming down the corridor breaks into my thoughts, and a moment later Duvet enters followed by an elderly man in a pristine three-piece suit. His back is so stooped his body forms a question mark over the crook handle of his umbrella. A spatter of freckles is visible on top of his scalp. 'Douglas?'

'My dear boy.' Douglas Carnegie shuffles into the room and hands his umbrella to Duvet with such casual authority that she takes it meekly and leaves without another word. He studies me intently before sighing and shaking his head. 'A terrible business. Poor Amanda.' He pulls his chair a little closer. 'I'm sorry not to have been up sooner. That brother of yours said you didn't want visitors.' *Did I tell him to say that?* He was probably right. I didn't want to see anyone. 'I'm glad you're here now.'

'Quite, quite.' Carnegie looks away, embarrassed. 'It's good to see you up and about.' He freezes. 'Well not up and about exactly, but I mean—'

'It's fine.'

'Well now, we all miss you, of course. Dottie sends her love.'

'Is she still burning the coffee?'

'No. She's become a fourth wave feminist apparently. We have to burn our own coffee now.'

'She might have to make an exception for me.'

'Good. Humour. Nobody does that these days. Too much damn self-pity. Humour got us through two world wars, you know.' He pats my leg awkwardly. I wish I felt something. 'It'll get you through too.'

'I hope so.' To fill a silence I ask, 'How's Seb doing?' At the same time Carnegie says, 'Need to talk to you about that brother of yours.'

'Sorry, what?'

'Your brother.'

'Got himself in hot water, has he?'

'Oh, he isn't bad. He just isn't you.' He lifts a portfolio. My old one. Recognise the familiar smoky scent of leather anywhere. It wrenches my heart a little. Douglas is unravelling a canvas. 'Take a look at this.' He holds it out to me then colours and clears his throat noisily. 'Sorry. Thoughtless of me.'

'It's all right.'

He places it on my lap and lets me study it. Psyche in the wilderness. Canvas support. Plain ground. Just a hint of the under-drawing. Psyche crouches petrified at the centre of an arid land-scape, butterfly wings crumpled and useless against her spine. She's beautifully rendered but it's the background that draws me in. The cracked baked earth. The primordial sweep of the cliffs. No protection. No escape. A valley walled in on either side.

'Well?' Douglas says.

'Have I seen this before?'

'Not to my knowledge. It only came in last week and it's not catalogue listed anywhere as far as I can tell.'

'Seb thinks it's an original?'

'Came to me yesterday raving on about coming across an un-known Giulio Romano.'

'His evidence?'

'He was going on about the sensuous distortion of the figure. Reminded him of Raphael to begin with. The expressive sfumato—you see it most clearly in the curvature of her neck—caught his eye. That and the exaggerated way the artist uses colour instead of shadow.'

'Did he say anything about the wisps of cloth covering Psyche's thighs?'

'Not a word. What are you thinking?'

'Prussian blue.'

'You're sure?'

'No, of course not. You'll need to get a pigment analysis done. But see those greenish notes? Don't look right. The artist wants us to think it's a Renaissance colour, most likely ultramarine. But if I'm right—'

'Of course you're right. It can't possibly be a Romano. Eighteenth century or later.'

'Well, it's a first-class copy. The forger knew what he was doing.'

'Don't cover for him. The boy's a fool and you know it. I'd have got rid of him ages ago if he didn't look so much like your mother. Lovely lady. Did I ever tell you I carried a torch for her when I was young?' He has, many times. Carnegie is nodding to himself. 'Yes. Yes. She was beautiful. All the boys wanted to be with her. I used to watch them buzzing around and wished I could tell her how I felt. Ah well, she's gone now and Sebastian is all that's left of her charm.' He sits for a moment, an old man lost in the past then, catching himself, brightens. 'But you, my boy, have her brains. You're as sharp as ever.'

'Thinking is pretty much all I have left.'

'Quite so. Quite so. But in our line of work, it's all about what goes on behind the eyes. Insight. Imagination. A touch of Lady Luck if you will.'

My balls feel as though they're on fire. Try to think of cool water gently pouring over them. 'I'm sorry, what?'

'I was asking if you wanted to come back.'

'Back?'

'Not to the office, of course. I thought about it, and it just isn't possible. All those stairs. How on earth did women manage them in corsets and crinolines? No, work from home, my boy. All the creature comforts at your fingertips…Not literally, of course. Not *your* fingertips… dreadful business. I meant—what I meant—'

'I understand.'

'Look the nub of the matter is, the firm needs you. I need you. There's a job needing done and you're the man for it. What do you say?'

A chance? A chance to go home, to rebuild my life. Can I really do it? Pick myself out of the ruins and carry on? Pretend I never had a body. Start over again. 'Look Douglas, don't think I'm ungrateful—'

An awkward pat to my shoulder. 'Say no more. I quite understand. This isn't like getting over a busted leg. You need time to heal, to get back on your feet… not literally of course, in a metaphorical sense…Well then.' He stands up. 'I must be off. Things to do. Need to find out if Dottie finds photocopying empowering.'

'Thank you. For coming to see me…and everything. It's a very generous offer. I just need time to think. Maybe if it wasn't so hot in here. My brains feel a little fried.'

He gives me a strange look. 'You do that, my boy. I'll visit soon.'

After he's gone, I sit for a while trying to process our conversation. But it's hard to think. The pain is growing worse. It must be an infection. Surely Doctor Song should have the results by now. I need that antibiotic. What if the dysreflexia comes back. Murderous heat is spreading through me, and sweat is beginning to drip into my eyes. 'Hello? Is anyone there?' Where's Duvet when I need her? Have to get back to my room. Cooler there. I could make it to the elevator, but how would I summon it? Frustration is a hard stone grinding inside my chest. Perhaps it's cooler at the window. Hit the wheelchair control with my chin. Nothing. Again. No response. Not now. Not when I need it. 'Hullo?' Where is everyone? The sounds have all gone—people out in the corridor, the ping of the elevator arriving, doors swishing open and shut—vanished. I'm in dead space. Something isn't right.

'Can anyone hear me?'

'No,' says a voice in my ear, clear as a bell.

SECOND LIFE

The Eunuch's Tale

The memories of Refined Ink

NINE

'No.'

'No?'

The knifer looks at me with oily impenetrable eyes, then picks a tooth with an immaculate fingernail. 'Not for nothing, no.'

'I can pay you back later.'

'Six silver taels or you're wasting my time.'

'Look, I'm good for it. My family's—' Pull myself up short. What was I going to use to persuade him, *my family's reputation*—no currency in that now. The knifer looks bored. He's a businessman and clearly I am not a promising customer. 'Please,' I say. The oily eyes show a flicker of compassion or possibly just irritation. 'How old are you?'

'Twenty years…next spring.'

'The Emperor likes them younger. Ten years or less. Ensures purity.'

'But adult men are not forbidden from joining the service.'

'Adult men can pay.'

Nothing left but to thank him in tones dripping with sarcasm then take my leave.

Walk for a while through the shopping district where it's easiest to lose oneself in crowds. Low-grade silks, precious stones, blood oranges, the colours collide and blur, and it's only then that I realise I am viewing everything through the floating prism of my tears.

It's foolish to go near home, but my feet are tugged along by my heartstrings and my will can exert no mastery. My father's house is respectable but unimposing: a fitting residence for a scholar and honoured member of the Pavilion of Literary Profundity. Viewing it, like a thief, hidden in the shadows of a neighbour's garden wall, I see now that it is also a fitting mausoleum. The windows are boarded up, and a scroll attached to the door bears the Emperor's seal. I can't read it from here but I am certain it speaks of His Majesty's justice. After all, is it not said that the ruler alone may strike like lightning and his wisdom is beyond question? In finding my father guilty of a great crime against the state, he is to be admired for his diligence and all-seeing eye.

My neighbour's dog is barking. Time to move along. The crowds are thinning and the shops are beginning to close. Owners are taking down lanterns and rolling up awnings. Everywhere, the aromas of food: sesame, garlic, roasted chestnuts, pomegranates, the musky smell of bear meat, the gamey scent of wild mushrooms. I haven't eaten for two days. Shock and fear has kept my appetite in check but now my senses are overwhelmed and I need to eat more than I need to draw breath.

Without meaning to, I head towards the vegetable market. Scraps can be found there once the stalls have cleared. Perhaps I can boil myself a soup from spoiled leaves. But the closer I get the slower my steps become. After all the market has a dual purpose, and one of them is far from vegetal. When I am almost at the end of Luomashi Street—a stone's throw from my destination—I freeze.

The strangeness of my behaviour attracts an urchin. 'Three wén to see the heads.' My stunned silence has him mistaking me for a tourist. 'It's a good price. Five of them and I can tell you their stories. A whole family. Father, mother, son and two daughters.' He gives a salacious grin. 'In their *prime*. They sliced the old geezer up with the death by eight cuts. He never cried out but thanked the Emperor and called on his ancestors to forgive him. It was beheadings for the others, and they didn't go meekly I can tell you. Squealing like stuck pigs, especially the little ones. Quite the show. The executioner damn near cut off his own thumb trying to get them to hold still.' He demonstrates with a chopping motion then sucks his thumb for effect. I can't speak. I can't move. The urchin clearly wonders if I am capable of understanding decent language as he continues with exaggerated slowness and sweeping gestures of his hands. 'All right, two wén. You won't be disappointed. Magpies have had their eyes out.'

I am running, the urchin's pain-filled howl in my ears. My blow landed on his nose. Unfair, he's only a child trying to earn his supper. And what am I? The disgraced son of a scholar executed for treason. I should have died alongside my mother, holding my little sister's hands and telling them to be brave. Propping myself against the blood red city wall, I eject a graceful arc of bile.

§

'Mr Colvin, would you like to go back to your room?'
'I'm fine here, thanks.'
'I'm just outside if you need me.'
'Thankyou...No, wait. I need to explain...'

§

REFINED INK:

I'm back, a week before my fate changes forever. I have the strangest feeling of having travelled a long distance although I know I've never been further than the *Chaobai* river. While I'm pondering this, Father calls me into his study. 'Ah, there you are. I need your help.' He waves a hand at his copy of the Analects of Confucius. 'I am trying to resolve the meaning of the word *jen* which I have noticed in a sentence which also discusses *li*.' When I stare blankly, he sighs and explains, 'The appearance of the word for *perfect virtue* so close to that of *profitableness* is worrying. I must be certain there are no additional nuances that might have been missed before making the entry into the *Great Work*. You see?'

'Yes, Father.' I would rather offer my three preciouses up to the castrator's knife than spend another day poring over books in Father's cramped study. As soon as he becomes distracted by a dense passage in *The Classic of Filial Piety*, I slip out and am on Chengxian Street and beyond the Harmony and Peace Palace before he can ask me to fetch some dusty tome of textual analysis. I wonder how long he will sit there, hand outstretched, before he notices I'm gone.

The day is warm, the locust trees particularly sweet smelling. I'm tempted to savour them, but there are more pressing matters. Old Lasting Happiness welcomes me to her establishment with the warm embrace of a mother. Had my mother ever worn cheap silk and kissed me with breath reeking of sour wine and poppies. 'So, are you here to play or to chat with beautiful girls?'

'Play first.'

'Ah,' she said, wagging a finger at me. 'First you play. Then you *play*.'

I join the other men at the table who greet me with cordial grunts and nods. Fragrant Spring and little Plum Blossom seem especially pleased to see the handsome son of a scholar. After all, they've been serving pig farmers all day, who stink of shit and grunt and scratch themselves as much as their charges.

As we play, ewers of rice wine magically appear at my side, held by Plum Blossom who devotes herself entirely to making sure my cup is never empty. The candlelight grows unsteady. Plum Blossom's hair trinkets become the Empress's jewels. Her powdered face belongs to an ivory goddess in a temple shrine. She's never looked so beautiful. Everyone seems beautiful tonight. Old Lasting Happiness' leathery skin takes on an erotic glow, and even the pig farmers are not bad chaps. It's not their fault that their Fates were cruel.

All sense of time is lost. If it's possible, I lose even more interest in the ambiguity of Confucius' Analects or of the importance of Father's magnum opus. I lose all my money and even my jacket. But I don't realise any of this until I'm manhandled out of the flower house—still loudly professing my love for Plum Blossom—and thrown into the street. I kiss the ground, with my tongue, deeply as a lover.

Stumbling home, the drummers in the towers match their beat to the throbbing in my head. A blackbird sings out notes of death as I pass by and a cat with jade eyes follows me all the way to the Tonghui bridge. I don't have to be sober to tell the omens aren't good. Best hurry back to father and hope I haven't been missed.

A hundred paces from my home a stranger leaps from the shadows and hits me on the chest. I would have cried out but a hand covers my mouth. 'Please, young master, not a word.' Something familiar in the voice makes me straighten up and the hand falls away. My old nurse is standing before me wringing her hands and looking as though the world is ending. Her anxiety touches me deeply. 'It's not so bad. I have another jacket. Father will never notice.' Tears begin streaming down her cheeks. 'Young master, he's gone. All of them have gone. You mustn't go back.'

The pleasure from the wine has subsided into an acidic sloshing inside my stomach and my temples are beginning to tighten. Nothing she's saying makes sense. 'I need to get inside.'

'You can't go. They've been arrested.'

'Arrested?' The word feels odd on my tongue. I can't keep hold of it.

'The Imperial Guard came and took them all away.'

'But—' The world is swimming. 'On what charge?' She glances over her shoulder then stands on tiptoe and whispers in my ear. 'Treason.' The remnants of my inebriation instantly dissolve and I am excruciatingly, miserably sober.

'You're lying. No-one is more loyal than my father.'

'Why would I lie? Treason is the charge. It's the Emperor's justice and the Emperor is never wrong.' But treason? The word burns my lips. No-one can come back from that. Although she has already said, I ask, 'Mother and my sisters?' She nods. 'They came for you too.' The road feels unsteady. The wall reaches out and catches me.

'They will hunt me down.'

'No, young master. They won't.'

'Why not?'

'Because they already have you.' I stare at her—now all too in focus—face. Has grief driven out her wits? An owl hoots and she glances fearfully up. 'Best we move along.'

We walk back to the Tonghui bridge, keeping to the shadows, while she explains. 'When the Imperial Guard turned up at the door, your mother ran to the kitchen and ordered the kitchen boy, Excellent Fortune, to put on your spare jacket. When the family were called to assemble, Excellent Fortune went with your mother, whose glare warned the others to say not a word.'

Shame lights a fire in my entrails. 'If he doesn't admit the subterfuge, they will execute him.'

'They will kill him anyway.' She pats my hand. 'It is his fate. As it was mine to be returning from the market and able to pass myself off as a neighbour's servant. They didn't give me away. Not even the littlest.' With that her tears begin to flow again. We stop a moment to allow her to compose herself and I look back at the darkness that had swallowed my home.

'I can never go back.'

'No.'

'What am I to do? I have no other family. Father's brothers all died in the plague last year.'

'I am going to my sister's house. Perhaps she will take you in too.'

The house turns out to be a hovel made of mud. It looks as though it would wash away with the first heavy rains, but old nurse assures me that it has stood there for generations. A withered apple of a woman, whose kindly eyes are those of my nurse, answers the door. I think she would allow me to stay even if we sat one atop another. Her husband, by contrast, is a brutish man who makes his living as a tanner. I smell him a full five minutes before he arrives.

'No,' he says, arms folded across his chest. 'His presence is inauspicious.'

'Inauspicious? Is that how they talk in the tannery now?' He turns red with shame then purple with rage. The silk dyers would have envied his mastery of colour. 'He's UNLUCKY!'

'Of course he's unlucky. His whole family are about to die.'

'Bad luck is catching.'

'So are fleas and you've brought enough of those home.'

He folds his arms across his chest. 'I have spoken.'

So that's that. I'm out on my ear. Weeping, my nurse gives me the few coins she has on her. Then I am standing on the threshold with the night swirling at my back. 'What am I to do?' Reaching for my hand, she turns it over and studies the palm. After a few minutes I can't help saying, 'Well?'

She frowns. 'It's difficult.' After another minute she says, 'Interesting.'

'Shut the fucking door!' yells the tanner and we both jump.

'Tell me.'

'It's strange. The journey line is strong but it's tangled around the fate line.'

'What does it mean?'

'You will travel but in a strange way. And you will find love but not for long.' With that the tanner yells again and she shut the door. All I can do is walk away, arms around myself to keep warm. I miss my jacket. I miss my family more. What journey can I possibly take when I only have a few coins and no prospects? A sharp west wind blows over me and I realise that she didn't say anything about my lifeline.

TEN

'*Darius?*'

'Yes.'

'*Is everything okay?*'

'Perfectly.'

'*Do you know who I am?*'

'Doctor Song.'

'*Do you know why you're here?*'

'They brought me here after my accident.'

'*Darius, where is here?*'

'The marketplace. Where they killed my family.'

§

REFINED INK:

On the third day after their arrest, my family is executed in the vegetable market in accordance with the justice of the Emperor. I don't go. Shame more than fear holds me back. I can't bear to see the terror in my little sisters' eyes or the helpless resignation on the face of Excellent Fortune, who the touts are betting will be first to die. I spend the day and my last wén on sour-tasting wine in Old

Lasting Happiness' flower house, plunging myself into a temporary oblivion while my family face an eternal one.

Afterwards, with nothing better to do, I wander the streets, up and down, not caring how wet and cold it is. No-one recognises me. I hardly look like the son of a respected scholar anymore. But eventually, driven by hunger and desperation, I sneak back towards my old home.

It looks like a gutted animal, shutters ripped off, door smashed, the entrails of our family life spilling out across the ground. A new family is already taking possession. They're busy throwing debris through the broken shutters and don't notice the strange sad ghost, with red-rimmed eyes, watching from across the street.

Slowly—so slowly I don't even realise I'm doing it at first—I wipe my nose on my sleeve and walk over. The leg of a battered old stool my father would never let my mother throw out—*My dear, no scholar requires testaments to his dignity beyond that of his wisdom*—is half covered in shredded embroideries that were intended for my sisters' dowries. I bend down to pick up a scrap from one of my father's valuable books. 'Oy, what do you think you're doing?' The angry voice belongs to a red-faced man who's waving a fist from an upper window. 'You just wait there. I want a word.' I sprint off and don't stop until a curtain of tears comes down to blind me.

In an alley smelling of piss and worse, I turn the scrap over. It's a passage from *The Classic of Filial Piety*. My father has high-lighted a line in which Confucius argues that carrying out blood vengeance is the fulfilment of a son's duty. Stare at it for a long time, the words lodging deep within the broken fragments of my heart. I don't dare say it aloud, or even allow the thought to form inside my head, but I recognise my destiny and accept my fate. I will do it. I will kill the Emperor.

§

Of course to accept one's fate is simple. Fulfilling it is another matter altogether. How can I, a penniless young man in soiled clothing, gain access to the Forbidden City let alone the Emperor's

Divine Presence? I think for many hours, coming up with plans then rejecting them, knowing in my heart there is only one way. But can I do it? Not even the meekest lamb goes willingly to the butcher. Over and over I returned to the story of Princess Miao Shan, whose filial piety was so great, she willingly sacrificed her arms and eyes to save her wicked father. Could I do less for a father who was as gentle as the falling snow?

They say noble sacrifice is golden, yet it bought me nothing from the knifer. He wanted to crack his teeth on cold metal and no argument of mine could persuade him otherwise. What to do? Emptiness growls in my belly. How can the feel of nothing hurt so much? Can't go without food much longer. My head swims and I'm shivering though the day is not cold. The ghosts of my little sisters weep in my ears. Another try. If ever there was a mission doomed to failure…but what choice have I? What choice?

It is not the knifer who answers the door but his servant. 'No beggars,' he says and tries to shut it in my face. 'I need to see your master.' That thin, broken voice, is it really mine? Pull myself erect and summon the memory of my family's dignity. 'He is expecting me.'

'He's out.'

This I know. I watched him leave from behind a willow's frondy veil then counted to one thousand to be sure he wasn't coming back. 'I have an appointment.' Servant looks doubtful but I hold his gaze, my superior rank evident in my stance. His eyes travel down my dishevelled clothing. It's possible that I have sold my last to raise the fee. 'You'd better be telling the truth,' he grumbles and reluctantly lets me inside. I fear he will lead me to a room to wait, but he takes me straight to the *Ch'ang tzu*, a hut set a little apart from the main buildings. 'Wait here.' He is barely able to keep the grin from his face.

It's cold in the hut. They say it reduces blood loss. On the table are the knifer's tools, a cleaver, a curved blade, evil-looking pincers—all wickedly sharp. Looking is a bad idea. My preciouses jolt back like an animal scenting the abattoir. But my feet are creeping forward, and all the time I'm whispering comforting words as if trying to distract a frightened child. There, there. Nothing to be afraid of. It doesn't hurt a bit.

A bowl on the table is decorated with dragons. Some sort of liquid inside. Do I drink it or apply it? Rumours abound about a numbing medicine. A direct application then. My hands are surprisingly steady as I undo my clothing. How much to put on? There are no brushes or spoons so pouring seems to be the only option. It slops over my scrotum and penis but at least the job seems thorough.

Count the seconds waiting for it to take effect. I am aware of a faint tingling which quickly builds to a roaring heat. The affected skin turns fiery red. Grip the edge of the table trying to ride it out but it crashes over me, blood-filled waves of pain. The redness rises up and up until it fills my eyeballs with bright liquid fire. I would say anything...do anything. Even my tears burn. Clasp my scrotum with one hand, the handle of the curved knife in the other. And cut and cut and cut...

§

I am sitting on a mountain peak with my balls hanging over the edge. Both balls and penis are attached to huge weights and the pressure is tremendous. I can't remember why I'm here. Sometimes there is darkness and beautiful deep red lilies bloom out of the black. Like drops of blood in water. They bring tears to my eyes and when I wipe them away a dragon is sitting on a mountaintop far in the distance. He opens his mouth and his tongue, miles long, comes rolling out across space and licks me between my legs. Is someone screaming?

§

The light is insistent. It tickles my lashes and unsticks the strands of gluey sleep that hold my lids shut. Dragon's breath in my face. Meaty, filled with death. 'Ah,' says the knifer. 'You're awake.'

'Thirsty.' My voice is a bullfrog's croak. The knifer is examining my lower body. 'A mess,' he says disdainfully. 'What were you doing? Turning yourself into pork mince? He holds a bloodied lump of meat above me pinched between thumb and forefinger.

'Half hanging off when I found you. If I hadn't come home when I did, they'd be selling you to the butcher by the pound.'

'Thir—sty.' The knifer is still tutting. 'I've seen crows do a prettier job on a carcass.' How can I make him understand. Try to reach for him and a searing pain makes me scream. 'Don't move.' The knifer's voice is impatient. 'Despite your ham-fisted butchery, I managed to insert a spigot into the wound. Without it, you'd have closed tighter than a virgin's thighs and died screaming by the end of the week.' I file this information away so that I can feel its true horror when there are less pressing issues at hand.

'Thirsty.'

'Well, you can forget about that.' His dragon's breath is in my face again. 'Wound has to heal. It's barely scabbed over and you can't be pissing it open again.' His head turns. 'Boys.' Two thickset apprentices appear, bull necks, hands like hams. 'You know what to do.' I have no idea what they are about to do but some instinct made me croak, 'No, please.' My whimpering is ignored, and with a wrench that sends flames up my spine, they drag me to my feet. 'Gently now,' the knifer chides. I feel a glimmer of warmth towards him until he adds, 'I won't have the delicacy of my stitches undone. That's craftsmanship that is. Now walk!'

Back and forth. Back and forth. My legs buckle and I moan piteously but I am set on this path and cannot escape. A red mist descends. The dragon on the mountaintop hisses and sizzles. His demons have me by the armpits while a voice commands, *Keep going! Keep going!*

I am on my back. How long have I been here? Nothing makes sense. My world is a forest of new pains. Night follows day follows night follows day. No water has passed my lips for three days, and in that time I have learned that thirst is quite unlike hunger. Hunger waxes and wanes. It is possible to forget hunger, if only briefly, but thirst rages through your body in a relentless ghostly torrent. The knifer raises my head. 'Drink this.' Expecting water I lap it up but it tastes strange, bitter. Catches the back of my throat, making me cough. 'What—what is this?'

'It's good for you. A mixture of hyacinth, crocus and strong liqueur. Promotes healing. Drink it down and then you can have some water.' I obey and the knifer pats my shoulder. 'Good lad.' I think I would cry if there was enough moisture left in my body for tears.

I am ready for my greatest challenge. After a period of blackness which could not be called sleep, the knifer and his apprentices reappear. One helps me to my feet, which I am proud to say I manage without collapsing, while the other holds out an undecorated bowl. I look from it to the knifer. 'I can't.'

'Yes, you can. We've taken the spigot out.' A glance at the older apprentice. 'Nice work. Go ahead. You can do it.' The pressure inside my bladder is unbearable but fear is paralyzing me. The knifer sighs. 'Fetch me the jug.' The smaller apprentice runs out of the room then returns with a large jug and matching basin. The knifer places the basin on the ground then lifts the jug above his head. Is he going to throw the contents at me? He tips the jug and a thin stream of water pours out and splashes into the bowl. 'No.' Turn my head and close my eyes, but that sound...that sound. Before I know it a second splash joins the first and I feel the most immense relief I have ever felt in my life. It is almost orgasmic. Of course a cramp follows that makes me double over but the knifer assures me that this will pass with time. The main thing is I've urinated. 'And if I hadn't?'

'Don't think about it,' he says.

ELEVEN

REFINED INK:

A hundred days pass and I learn many things about my new body, chief amongst them is how to walk. The centre of my body has been dragged towards my neutered groin and so I tip forwards, feet slightly splayed, steps small and careful. The knifer nods approvingly when he sees me. 'He's ready.' The Chief Eunuch is informed and we wait to be summoned to the Forbidden City. While we wait, I am presented with my lost preciouses carefully preserved in a leather container. My name is written on a label attached by a thread. It is an emotional moment. The apprentices look awestruck and even the knifer swallows hard before saying, 'Guard them well. You'll be reunited in the next life.'

The next day word comes from the Forbidden City. The knifer reads the message, his brows rising. 'The Chief Eunuch is coming for you.'

'Is that usual?'

The knifer looks at me as if he might have cut off the wrong bit during the castration. 'No. That is in no fucking way usual.'

§

The Chief Eunuch is a large bald man with soft rippling skin. I stand very erect before him in my new blue robes, although it hurts to do so. He makes a circuit around me. 'So this is the one?' The knifer makes a face at me so I bow several times and say, 'Yes. I am he.'

'Indeed.' He clasps the most prominent of his chins between two fingers and studies me closely as though I might be hiding part of me from sight which, considering my preciouses are clutched in my shaking hands, is something I could hardly be accused of. 'Well,' he says at last. 'We will see what we will see.' With a gesture as graceful as a dancer, he turns and I understand I am to follow him. No-one says anything and I do not look back, but somehow over the last hundred days I have grown attached to the knifer and, in leaving him, I feel a wrench as though I am losing a father for the second time.

We pass through the Meridian Gate, over the River of Golden Water and towards the Hall of Supreme Harmony, though we do not go in but veer east. 'These are the eunuch quarters,' he explains. 'That will be your bed over there. You may place your preciouses on the shelf behind.' I look about. Narrow beds in rows. No wall hangings or rugs. Less palatial than I had imagined. He sees my

71

face and his lips make a moue. 'Such a long look. These quarters are for junior eunuchs only. Over time a smart individual may see himself rise through the ranks. And the rewards can be—' he covers his mouth, titters delicately '—not inconsiderable. Of course it is easier for those who are gelded young. You may have heard of the extraordinary trajectory of my rise.' His hand rests on my arm. The fingernails are immaculate. 'In less than ten years I found myself with the ear of the Emperor. An organ, I'm sure you'll agree, far more worthy than the one I sacrificed.' Before I can appear suitably impressed, there is a cry. 'Father!' A young eunuch—Mongolian by the look of him, twelve, thirteen years of age—hurries into the living quarters and bows.

'Well? I suppose you have good reason for interrupting.'

'Please. The Emperor requests that the new eunuch be brought into his divine presence at once.'

'The Emperor requests it?' The atmosphere in the room drops several degrees.

'Yes, Father. At once.'

'Get out.' The young Eunuch does not understand. He stays where he is, wondering if he has misheard. 'Didn't you hear me? GET OUT!' The Chief Eunuch punctuates the imperative with a swift kick, which is explanation enough for the young eunuch who flees in terror.

Only when the door flaps shut does the Chief Eunuch turn to me. 'Is this your doing?'

'No, I swear.'

'Do you take me for a fool?'

Fall to my knees. His feet are surprisingly large. If he kicks me I will certainly lose an eye. 'I would not dare.'

'Is it bribery? Connections? Have you been casting spells?' As he accuses, his voice slides higher—dying cats, zither strings snapping. I want to cover my ears. I keep my head low.

'Please. I admit my fault and beg your correction.' There is silence. I sneak a peek. His chins are wobbling while volcanic eruptions under the skin are sending red flares across his cheeks and down his neck. His eyes narrow, almost disappearing into pouchy folds of flesh. 'Follow me,' he hisses.

We set off, passing through a door inlaid with brass and then one with silver and finally through one inlaid with gold. I have never seen such grandeur and I tremble a little with awe, but also with fatigue because I have grown unused to walking more than a few steps. My awe turns to puzzlement for the hall is empty. The dragon throne, before which I had thought to prostrate myself, is unoccupied. As if reading my words, the Chief Eunuch explains, 'The Emperor's extreme wisdom and modesty prevent him from using the Palace of Heavenly Purity for trivial matters.' He aims the word 'trivial' at me as though spitting on a beggar. 'His Divine Majesty has thus moved his residence to the smaller Hall of Mental Cultivation.' After this he is silent until we reach our destination.

The door here is plainer but defended by two fierce-looking guards. At the sight of the Chief Eunuch, they stand back and usher us through. I am impressed and would say so except that clearly my opinions matter not an aborted rat's foetus to the Chief Eunuch. Lower my head, follow meekly.

'Majesty.' The Chief Eunuch falls to his knees and I follow suit.

'Please.' The voice is softer than I expected. The Chief Eunuch gets to his feet, but when I attempt to follow, a sharp pinch reminds me I am less than a dirt-eating worm.

'This is the one?' His Majesty is inquiring. 'The one who cut himself?'

'Your Majesty is discerning as always.'

'I wish to see his face.'

'Get up.' The Chief Eunuch pinches me again. I rise and come face-to-face with the occupant of the Dragon Throne, Son-of-Heaven, Great Emperor Harmonious Justice himself. It is said that Heaven's chosen are not like other mortals, and now I can attest to this with my own eyes because the Emperor is the strangest man I have ever seen. He is wearing a jade-coloured coat of extraordinary cut, bright blue stockings and a curling wig, which stands proud above his head and reaches down past his shoulders.

One of the first lessons a eunuch must learn is to keep his thoughts to himself. It is a lesson at which I now spectacularly fail. The Emperor's eyes glitter. 'Are you an admirer of European dress?' I have no words despite the sharpest pinch yet by the Chief Eunuch. The Emperor smiles indulgently. 'The style is common in the English court at present. Such a strange people. I find it allows me to understand them better when I take on their garb. To walk in another man's shoes so to speak.' He studies my face again, clearly wondering if I am a mute, and I am bracing myself for the Chief Eunuch to pincer my flesh again, when he suddenly says, 'Leave us.' The strangest thing is, he's talking to the Chief Eunuch.

'Majesty. If I might be so bold, the boy is a mere novice. He has received no training. Dare I suggest that he requires my presence as a guide and mentor lest he commit an offence that—'

'You may not.' The Chief Eunuch's eyes blink wide as though the Emperor's words have been blows to his cheeks. For the smallest fragment of time he makes no response then bows with exaggerated grace. 'His Majesty's wisdom knows no bounds. I shall be outside should my humble presence be required.' And that is that. Suddenly I am alone with the murderer of my entire family.

Will another moment like this arise? I'm not prepared. I thought it would take years. Now the deed could be done in seconds. The Emperor is taking off his wig. He places it on a stand and shakes out his natural hair. 'Rather itches,' he explains. 'I believe the English shave their heads.'

Perhaps there is something heavy enough to smash his skull in or at least to render him unconscious while I finish the job. A jade lion? A Ming vase? 'Ah, you have a taste for art,' he says spotting my roving eye.

'The Emperor has many beautiful things.'

'It speaks.' He laughs but not in a cruel way. His hand pats my shoulder. The most powerful man in the entire world pats *my* shoulder. 'I am something of a collector. But I am also, by a certain way of thinking, part of the collection.'

'I don't understand, Majesty.'

'Don't you? Neither do I. Not completely at least. I believe it has something to do with earthly immortality. Mortal men have such short memories.'

'Your Majesty will never be forgotten.'

'Do you think so? You are a sweet boy for saying it. I like your direct way of speaking. Where did you say you were from again?' I trot out my story: a life of noble impoverishment in the provinces; the terrible accident that took my father from us; a young man's determination to regain the family honour, only to be robbed on his way to the capital and forced to take matters into his own bloodied hands. By the end of it the Emperor has tears in his eyes and I am openly weeping. 'My poor dear boy.' Suddenly my hands are clasped in the Emperor's own. 'To have suffered so much hardship.' A slight frown. 'All those years toiling in the fields?'

'Yes, Majesty.'

'Yet your hands—'

'My hands, Majesty?'

'They're so soft.' After the slightest hesitation I say, 'The knifer bathed them in rosewater every day to prepare me.'

'Really? How remarkable. I shall have him send some to the Empress. Her horny toes would benefit.' He laughs, and I am so pleased with my quick thinking that I am laughing along with him before I remember the horror of what I am doing.' The doors opening behind me save me from the shame of my betrayal. A young man is ushered in. 'Ah,' says the Emperor, eyes lighting up. 'They're ready then.'

'Yes, Majesty.' The young man gives a low bow. He is carry-ing several rolled-up sheets of paper and he holds them out. 'If it pleases His Majesty to see them.'

'It pleases me very much. Bring them over.' He indicates a large rosewood desk. 'Spread them on there. Good. Good.' Then turning to me. 'Prepare yourself. We are about to see a marvel of the Occident.' But I am already marvelling. I have never seen a foreigner before. He is dressed in the simple blue surcoat of a lower court official, and he wears it with grace. Has the world gone mad? Foreigners dressed like courtiers and Emperors dressed as

Englishmen. It feels like a dream, and I wish the Chief Eunuch was here to pinch me. The Emperor notices my hesitation. 'Come see, dear boy. The detail is quite extraordinary.'

With a sudden awareness of the strangeness of my new gait, I creep forward and stand next to this stranger with skin the colour of a winter snow moon. Could he be ill, I wonder. The papers have been unrolled and we are looking down at several sketches of the Emperor. He is dressed in his current attire but portrayed in several poses. One, a portrait of head and shoulders catches my eye—the Confucian in me is discomfited by the thought of a body severed through the chest—but I say nothing. The Emperor is delighted. 'I am particularly taken with the one where I am spearing a tiger. I did, you know. In my youth. My companions ran off and left me to face the beast alone.' In his youth I can believe. I find it less credible that he performed the act while dressed like the King of England. The foreigner, however, seems suitably impressed. 'Your Majesty is a wonder.' His vocabulary is excellent but the strangeness of his accent makes it hard to tell if there is a trace of irony in his tone. I search his face. His eyes are like two thin discs of luminous jade but their expression is inscrutable.

Another interruption. The Chief Eunuch is back. He falls to his knees and presses his head to the floor. 'Majesty, forgive my thoughtless intrusion.' The Emperor is displeased. He straightens his back and clasps his hands. 'Speak!'

'The Russian Ambassador is here. He urgently requests a meeting with Your Majesty.' There is a silence. I hope the Emperor is considering kicking the Chief Eunuch in his non-existent balls for his impudence, but he lets out a sigh. 'Never a moment to call my own.'

'Majesty?'

'Have him wait for me at the Palace of Heavenly Purity. I shall change my clothes. The ambassador, as I recall, is not blessed with an excess of imagination.'

The Chief Eunuch sweeps out in one direction and the Emperor in the other. Suddenly the foreigner and I are alone, forgotten. He starts to roll up the portraits.

'Wait!'

He pauses. 'Yes?'

I don't know. I only know that I don't want him to go. 'You—you didn't tell me your name.' A frown. Why should he have? We are the Emperor's toys. When his attention leaves us, we wind down. 'They call me Second Son.'

'But that is not the name your father gave you.' He is looking at me curiously. I have never been looked at this way by a man. An invisible pricking writes strange characters on the back of my neck. 'You have another name.' Why am I persisting? He runs his fingertips along the edge of one of the portraits. 'Lodovico Salvestro Zabarelli.'

'You are an Englishman?' He laughs. 'Italian. My family are Venetian…from Venice,' he adds when he sees my blank stare. A city in the north of my country. A very beautiful city.'

'I would like to see it.' What am I saying? I will spend whatever is left of my miserable life in the confines of the Forbidden City. To cover my confusion I ask quickly, 'Are you of noble birth?' The jade eyes crinkle in a smile.

'Our names are inscribed in the Golden Book but much of the family's wealth is gone. What is left will go to my brother.' He turns an elegant finger on himself. 'As the younger I was always destined for the church.'

'A Christian?' My blood runs cold. The Emperor has forbidden such practices amongst the Manchu. Even discussing them would put our lives at risk. But I am curious. 'How is it you are at the Emperor's side?'

'We are of the Jesuit brotherhood. I think the Emperor tolerates us because we have contented ourselves with learning your ways, and we do not marry so there can be no complications in our relationships.'

I cannot hide my surprise. 'You are also eunuchs?'

He stares at me. 'In a way, yes. You could say that. But we do not geld ourselves.'

'Yet you are trusted?'

'We take a vow.' I am still trying to process the ridiculousness of this response when he suddenly says, 'You haven't told me your name.'

'My—' Shyness overcomes me. For the last hundred days I have been *boy* or *new eunuch* or *scum-sucking-worm's-belly*, when the Chief Eunuch is around, until I have half-forgotten I was ever called anything else. I try it out now, a little shocked at its unfamiliarity. 'Refined Ink.'

'That is a beautiful name.'

Tears spring to my eyes. 'My father gave it to me. It is all I have left of him.' Lodovico puts down his papers and hurries to my side, puts an arm about my shoulders. 'He must have been a very scholarly man.'

'A farmer.' I have betrayed my family again. The Chief Eunuch is wrong. My station is less elevated than a scum-sucking-worm's-belly. I am not even worthy to kiss such a creature's non-existent feet.

After a moment Lodovico lets go of my shoulders and gathers his sketches together. 'I must return to the studio. Master Castiglione is waiting for me. He will be annoyed that the Emperor has not given his opinion.'

'Will I see you again?'

The translucent jade eyes search mine. 'I would like that.'

TWELVE

REFINED INK:

To have found love with Lodovico both puzzles and thrills me. Wasn't it true that I have always loved the sensual touch of women? Was something lacking I failed to recognise? Or is it because I hover in this strange space between the sexes, seen neither as man nor woman? It doesn't matter. I won't be reunited with my preciouses until the afterlife, and all I know now is that love is the celestial body that lights my days.

But the Forbidden City is not run on the whims of a young eunuch who has fallen in love. Every day is filled with work, work, work. The Chief Eunuch assigns me the dirtiest and nastiest jobs he can think of, chief amongst them oiling his sweating feet which protrude from beneath his robe like a couple of gnarled tree roots. 'That's it,' he purrs. 'Caress them like you used to caress your cock.'

Spending time with Lodovico is nearly impossible. We meet sometimes while crossing the chequered pathways between palaces falling into step with one another, and those moments are precious jewels gathered in my heart—his fingers grazing mine as though by accident, a shared look; once he pushes a folded scrap of paper into my hand, and when I open it there is a sketch of two lovers locked in passionate embrace. That night I carefully slit my robe and slip the sketch inside next to my heart.

Every day I awake to find that the world is set to music. It plays through me making me vibrate in harmonious fashion in time to the earth's rhythms. Song is everywhere. In the rustle of leaves, in Lodovico's breathing. I even sing when I carry out the slops, ignoring the Chief Eunuch's narrowed eyes following me suspiciously.

Spring bursts blossom-fresh on the air and Lodovico pulls me behind a crimson pillar and kisses me. Not once in all the times I spent with Fragrant Spring and little Plum Blossom in the flower house have I been kissed like this. It makes my soul shudder. I think I could die now and be perfectly happy. I have forgotten my reason for entering the Forbidden City. I have forgotten my mission. Even the ghosts of my little sisters have grown so faint beneath the singing world I hardly notice them. I am filled with contentment, like Old Lasting Happiness's cat stretching itself in the sun. Then the Emperor sends for me again.

§

When I arrive at the Hall of Mental Cultivation, the Emperor is waiting, dressed as a classical poet from the Han period. He is in a thoughtful mood. 'I wish you to read to me.'

'Majesty?' He indicates a book with a marked page and settles back on a divan, eyes closed. In the corner a beautiful young musician prepares to accompany me on the pipa. My eyes bounce wildly round the room. Is there a door I can escape through? There is not. The pipa player catches my eye then strums a note very deliberately. My cue to begin. In a shaking voice, I read the first lines.

Trees decay. Leaves fall.

The cold air everywhere

laces my frozen face …

I know this poem. My father used to read it to me and the melancholy evocation of autumn would send thrills through me. *Read it again, papa. Read it again.* Suddenly I feel old. Only the very young pursue sadness willingly.

'You're not reading.'

'Majesty?' I come to a stuttering stop.

The Emperor's eyes are no longer closed but fixed on me. 'You are reciting,' he says.

'I know this poem, Majesty. It is one of my favourites.'

The Emperor sits up and studies me, one hand beneath his chin. 'Such a strange boy. Straight from ploughing the fields yet with the sensual lips of a poet.' I daren't speak another word. The pipa player is looking at me and I think, *she knows.* They all know. There is a jade lion on a pedestal next to the Emperor's head. Would I have time to grab it and dash his brains in before he could call for the guards? Too late. He's on his feet. 'Come. I wish to show you something.'

I follow him through several antechambers until we come to a door which he unlocks with a golden key taken from his belt. 'This room is rather special,' he says, offering me a shy smile. 'Only exceptional people are allowed inside.' The tip of a long fingernail tilts my chin. 'Are you exceptional, strange one?'

'I would not dare to dream it, majesty.'

'Such modesty You are like a maid on her wedding night.' He steps inside and beckons. Every drop of my blood drains out through the soles of my feet. I swallow. 'Majesty?'

'Come now.' His voice is a silk thread tangling itself around me. It drags me unwillingly towards it.

What did I expect? A torture chamber? A flower house dedicated to undreamt of sexual depravities? It's nothing of the sort. A long thin chamber made longer and thinner by a lining of shelves along one side. There is natural light from a narrow window set high on one wall, and everywhere there are extraordinary works of art. Crystal chandeliers drip from the ceiling. Glass paintings reveal unfamiliar landscapes and figures. In one, a man—a foreigner like Lodovico—lies in a peculiar narrow bed, staring blankly up at the ceiling. It's very convincingly rendered, but something about him makes me inexplicably sad, and I turn away to examine a silver figurine caught in a moment of exquisite agony. Closer inspection shows his tiny arms chained above him and a beautifully wrought silver eagle pecking out some internal organ, possibly his liver. I wonder how he offended his Emperor. Further down there are paintings of fabulous cities set alongside turquoise fringes of water. But the end of the room is where breath stops inside me.

A twilight scene. Strange wild landscape of rock and sky caught on the very edge of the light before the long shadows of night descend. The sky is the colour of sadness. How else to explain that insistent, haunting blue? But it is the single figure occupying the scene who commands the onlooker's attention. A woman, shrouded in the folds of a black cloak, stars of night-blooming jessamine constellating her hair. A Madonna as Lodovico has described? A foreign goddess? No, there is too much human about her. She has turned her head to look out of the canvas and her eyes are poignantly, desperately asking a question of the observer even as her painted lips stay mute. Unconsciously move my head closer to hear what she is saying.

'You have an eye for Euroiserie.' The Emperor is amused. 'The chiaroscuro is magnificently worked.' I wish he would stop talking. Though he's right about the shadows. Once, I dismissed their use in painting as 'dirty marks', making Lodovico laugh until the curls in his beard shook. Offended, I insisted, 'A painting should be filled with divine light, not sullied with darkness. There are no shadows in Heaven.' He stopped laughing and pointed towards the gathering twilight. I looked up, and as I did so, he whispered in my ear, 'How bright is a star without the blackness of the night sky enfolding it?'

The Emperor is still at my side clearly waiting for my response. 'Who is she?'

'Who *was* she? The painting is more than two hundred years old. She was painted by a fellow countryman of our Jesuit friends. The reason I have such a soft spot for them. Tell me, do you find her beautiful?' Do I? Her eyes are the same turquoise colour of the water in the other paintings. The Chief Eunuch would answer, *Of course, majesty. She is without compare.* But something about her draws a kind of truth from me that I can't hide. 'I find her strange.'

'An excellent answer. I find her strange too. And I am used to Europeans. But she is also rather compelling. I think she has a secret, don't you?'

'Majesty?'

He sighs, but not unpleasantly. 'I'm overwhelming you, sweet boy. Let us speak in generalities. What do you think of my collection of occidenterie?'

'Magnificent, Majesty. But—' I pause. Have I overreached? His fingernail traces my lips and the curve of my chin.

'But? Speak freely. Your mind is pure. It cannot offend me.'

'I only wondered why Your Majesty hides all these treasures from sight.' His expression stiffens and he turns to the side examining a marble figurine of a woman with snakes for hair. I feel a tightening in the ghost of my scrotum. Should I throw myself on the floor and plead for mercy or grab his neck hoping I can squeeze hard enough before the guards drag me away? Without turning around, he explains, 'When I became Emperor, I issued an imperial decree emancipating the slaves. It seemed wrong to me that a man should give his labour without recompense.'

'Your Majesty has a noble heart.'

'You are kind to say it. I assure you the Europeans think I am quite mad. After all, they have been enslaving the people they call Tartars for centuries although now I believe their taste has turned towards Africa. I am quite guarded when talking to their ambassadors lest they report that the Emperor of China is insane.' His eyes slide towards me. 'Think of that. The ruler of the greatest civilization on earth dismissed as insane by hairy barbarians.' Where is he going with this? I wish we weren't alone. He rearranges the figurine, turning it this way and that to find the perfect spot. 'We are the most advanced civilization the world has ever known. Everything we do outranks the dirty little cities on the other side of the world. It is what makes my ministers suspicious of foreigners.' He runs a finger across the figurine's serpent mane. 'Of foreign *things*.' A glance at me to see if I understand and I see a terrible pleading behind his eyes, a visceral need to be understood.

'Your Majesty is wise to hide beauty from eyes that cannot appreciate it.'

'How right you are. In the east I am the emperor who keeps Euroiserie. In the west I am the ruler who frees slaves. Sides of my character best kept for a select few.' He looks hard at me.

'His Majesty's secrets will always be safe with me.' He looks so pleased I feel confused. Have I somehow misjudged the man?

'Well now, perhaps your expression will resemble our twilight beauty with her delicious mystery. Come, we must return before we are missed.' His arm entwines my shoulder, and we leave the room like old friends. I feel the turquoise eyes following me.

THIRTEEN

'Darius, I want to run some tests. Is that okay?'
'Of course.'

'Can you count back in sevens from one hundred, ninety-three, eighty-six and so on.'

'Ninety-three, eighty-six, seventy-nine...'

'Very good. Your brother came to see you yesterday. Can you tell me what you talked about?'

'He's worried the Turnbull he put into auction won't reach the reserve price.'

'Will he be in trouble?'

[silence]

'Darius, will your brother be in trouble?'

'The Emperor won't like it.'

§

REFINED INK:

It's the middle of night. My eyes are wide open, uncomprehending. Where am I? The ceiling soars. Moonlight illuminates wisps of ghostly incense hanging in the air. Beyond the window, a nightjar pipes out thin notes. Something on my lap—an uncomfortable weight. It is the Emperor's head. His eyes are also open. But they are empty of everything, even incomprehension. My skull hits the bedhead and the nightmare shatters around me in eggshell fragments. All that is left is a sickly yellow yolk of truth—the Emperor is dead!

A million thoughts fly through my head, none of them making any sense. I am in the Emperor's bed. The Emperor is dead. I have missed all my opportunities to act heroically. I have failed my little sisters. I have failed my ancestors. I am the unluckiest man in the world—save perhaps for the Emperor. Who is DEAD! I don't know what to do. I need to get out. I can't get out. The door is too heavily guarded. There's nowhere to hide. Unless—

§

The golden key feels heavy in my pocket. Sound of my padding feet walking rapidly across tiled floors. It's too dark. The ante-rooms have changed shape. The blackness throws solid objects in my path. Shadows lurch. What if I can't find my way again? My thoughts are unravelling. I can't pull them together. A door slams into my face. Paw its surface like a blind man. It's locked. I can't go further. I'm here.

Inside, the collection glows eerily in a sliver of moonlight. The window is higher and narrower than I had supposed. Perhaps I can stand on something to reach it. As I think this, one of the shadows moves. Almost at once it stops but I have learned shadows are more than dirty marks. They draw your attention to what they're hiding. I am not alone. Is it a thief? A murderer? Can I convince him to let me go? 'I mean you no harm. I won't even look at your face.'

§

'Darius?'
'Darius?'
'Darius?'

§

A figure steps out from behind the shelves, is bathed in moonlight. 'Lodovico?' He is the most beautiful sight in the universe. I don't even think to ask what he's doing here. He comes towards me with the saddest expression on his face. 'Refined Ink, I thought I would never see you again.' He knows what I've done. How can he know? But then he adds, 'I am leaving for Venice in the morning.' Did I hear right? It's too much. I begin to weep—or perhaps I am already weeping—Lodovico has me in his arms. He smells of faraway exotic shores, incense and oil paint, familiarity and strangeness. He strokes my hair. 'What has happened?'

'The Emperor is dead.'

Lodovico stiffens and holds me at arm's length. 'Are you certain?'

'Yes.'

'But how?'

'He—died in my arms.'

'Oh, my poor love.'

'No!' His sympathy is too much. Push him away. 'You don't understand. It was my duty to kill him.'

Lodovico's round eyes grow rounder. 'You are an assassin?'

'He murdered my family.'

'The Emperor?' Lodovico cannot follow these ravings and my knees have grown weak. We collapse onto the floor below the window. In silence we sit there, shoulder to shoulder, knee to knee. When my voice returns to me, I say, 'I'm sorry I am not the man you thought me.' Lodovico does not look at me.

'Neither am I.'

'You are not a murderer.'

'No, but there are many other things I am not. A Jesuit for one. Though the Emperor's artist, Master Castiglione, is ignorant of that.'

'What else?' I ask weakly.

'I am not an honest man. You might call me a thief though I haven't stolen anything yet.' For a moment nothing makes sense. Then everything makes a horrible, stomach-churning logic. I do not even have to ask which item he is here to steal. 'What are you going to do with her?' Lodovico pushes his hands into his hair, the hair that curls—not like the Emperor's wig—but long and rolling like the waves of a gentle tide. 'I am going to restore my family fortune. She belongs to us. The painting was stolen from my grand-mother by an agent of Pope Clement.'

'Is he your Emperor?'

'In a way.'

I am suddenly more afraid for Lodovico than I am for myself. 'You will never get out of China. The minute its loss is discovered, search parties will be looking for you everywhere.' Lodovico's eyes are pools of shadow. I wish I could see his expression. A squeeze to my shoulder.

'I have thought of that. Christianity may be banned but there are still families who practice in secret. They will smuggle me out.' Can this be happening? My life is a magpie shot through the heart, spiralling down, down into blackness. Fingertips against my face. 'Trust me. It's a good plan.'

'It's lunacy. It will never work.'

'From a man who killed the Emperor with his thighs.' The absurdity of our situation makes us shake with silent laughter.

'A thief who isn't a thief.'

'A murderer who hasn't killed anyone.' That sobers me.

'There were opportunities. But each time—I don't understand. Something stopped me.' I hang my head in shame.

'Have you heard of a prince called Hamlet?'

'No.'

'I will tell you about him when we reach Venice.' Venice? Lodovico places his hands over mine. 'Come with me.'

It's unthinkable. Might as well ask me to grow wings and fly. I can't think of anything to say but to repeat the mantras I have learned since coming here. 'I serve the Emperor.'

'There isn't an Emperor to serve.' My hand is in his and he drags me to my feet. 'Come on.'

'Where?'

'We have to get you out of here.' There is a knotted rope dangling from the window. While Lodovico quickly removes the painting, I climb slowly, painfully—my wound troubling me as much as my thoughts. A ladder stands against the other side which I force myself to descend so gradually that Lodovico practically stands on my head as he comes down it. Moonlight turns the pathways grey. Nothing moves. Not even ghosts.

'I thought there would be guards here.'

'Guards outside would arouse suspicion. The collection's best protection has been simply not to exist.' Will I exist in your world, Lodovico, I wonder. But Lodovico is busy hiding the ladder and the rope then we are hurrying along the outer wall of the Palace of Mental Cultivation.

'Please stop. Where are we going?'

The moonlight catches Lodovico's eyes and they shine like a cat's. 'To the artist's quarters.'

'Master Castiglione—what will he say?'

'He won't say anything. He's away on business. And by the time they come looking for you, we will be gone.' I feel dizzy. We are dangling over a precipice on a thread of insanity.

Master Castiglione's quarters are sparsely furnished but sketches, silks, paints and inks crowd the tables and spill across the floor.

It reminds me of my father's study and a lump comes to my throat, preventing speech. I want to sleep, but ropes of fire are burning along my nerves and, when Lodovico indicates the bed, I perch on the edge and grip the edge until my knuckles turn white. The simplicity of the plan worries me. Are we supposed to walk through the gates with the Emperor's most treasured possession slung over Lodovico's shoulder? What happens when the guards search our belongings?

I look anxiously towards him hoping for some sign of reassurance, but he seems in no hurry, stretching out the canvas and muddling about in the palettes and pigments. His slim hands flutter over them in perfect rhythm, a pair of mandarin ducks working in harmony. I sit silently, watching, hypnotised by the curve of his neck, thinking of myself lifting his hair, lips on his—'Wait! NO! What are you DOING?'

An ugly gash of paint blots the canvas. Turquoise eyes vanish beneath a blindfold of zinc white. Lodovico is holding up his brush, seminal dregs of paint dripping from its tip. I am sick to my stomach.

'Shh.' A finger against his lips.

'Shh? SHH! Have you lost your FUCKING MIND? You've destroyed it.'

'It will wash off.'

'IT WILL—what?'

'It's a water-based pigment. I can remove it.'

'You can?'

'Of course. Did you think I was going to waltz through the gates with a stolen painting under my arm?' Lodovico laughs. He makes it sound so easy that the huge gaping flaws in his plan retreat like shadows at midday. Then rush back in again when I notice the inky blackness beneath the door is suffused with pearl. The Chief Eunuch will wake the Emperor for his first audience at daybreak. To calm myself, I ask, 'What will you paint?'

'Something simple. A crane or two. After all emptiness is a fundamental principle of Chinese painting. The more I leave out the more serious the work will seem, and lucky for us, this pigment dries quicker than a whore's tears. If I work fast, we can leave within the hour.'

I stand up, panic-stricken. 'I have to go back.'

Lodovico drops his brush. 'Are you crazy? You can't go out there. This is the safest place for you. I can provide an alibi if it comes to it, and—'

'I forgot. There's something I have to do.'

'Now?'

'Yes, now.' Lodovico is staring at me. He's wondering if I am betraying him. If only there was time to explain. Plant a kiss on his lips, and briefly the gates of Paradise open before slamming firmly shut again when I pull back. 'Meet me under the lian li tree near the Hall of Imperial Peace.' I try to sound positive. 'But first finish the painting. Two cranes symbolise longevity. One and a half cranes may suggest a poor outlook. He doesn't move, a bird welded to a frozen lake, but as I make to leave, he grabs my arm. 'If you're not there—' Grip him tightly and press my face against his shoulder. His robe feels like a curtain hung before Heaven. All that separates me from all I desire.

'I'll be there. I promise.'

§

Shadows blotch the eunuch's quarters mixing with night fumes rising from slack, gaping mouths. Rotten pork, fermented rice and a dash of urine from the less continent of my brethren whose knifers lacked the delicate touch. Slowly. Slowly. Not a sound. The sharp edge of a bedstead collides with my foot and pain rains down a blizzard of stars behind my eyes. Gulp down my cry and listen. A pig's grunting as someone turns over, the rumble of a snore. That's all. Limp forward, upper teeth buried in my lower lip. Toe is screaming seven colours of agony but fortunately my bed is only a few paces ahead. I'm almost there. Just enough light seeps from the door behind me to see the shelf. It is conspicuously, gut-wrenchingly empty. If nothingness has a shape, the shelf is groaning under it. Even so I take another few steps unable to believe the evidence of my eyes. *Where is it?*

'Lost something?' a voice hisses.

FOURTEEN

REFINED INK:

Each time I wake up, my face is bloodier and there are more teeth on the floor. The Chief Eunuch is sitting on a carved chair, feet resting on a stool. He seems bored.

'What did you do?'

'Nothing.'

The blow is to my ribs this time. It would have felled me if I wasn't already on the floor. When the pain clears from my eyes and I can draw breath again, the Chief Eunuch is waiting patiently for my answer. 'It's pointless to lie, worm. We know everything.' Then why bother asking? But it isn't information he wants, it's confession.

'What did you do?'

I don't even get a chance to answer before the mountain of flesh, with fists the size of my head, kicks me again. When I wake up this time, I have the impression I haven't been out that long. The Chief Eunuch is looking angrily at Flesh Mountain. 'I've told you before. Do not interrupt me.' He senses I am awake and turns in my direction. 'Well?'

I can't take another blow. By the smell of things, I have already lost dignity in both directions. 'I—Please, I didn't mean to.'

'Ah, now we are getting somewhere.' The Chief Eunuch leans forward. 'What didn't you mean to?'

'To...to kill him?' For the first time I see confusion on the Chief Eunuch's face. 'You killed him?'

'Yes. But I swear I didn't mean to.'

'And what was the cause of this crime? Jealousy? A lover's tiff?'

'No, nothing like that.'

'And the murder weapon?'

'There wasn't one.'

'You killed him with your bare hands?'

'With my thighs.'

'Your thighs!'

'It was an accident. I didn't know.'

'You didn't know you killed Lodovico Salvestro Zabarelli?' The world goes dark.

'Lodovico is dead?'

'You killed him.'

'No.' The Chief Eunuch glances at Flesh Mountain. 'Kick him again.'

When I have stopped screaming, he asks in a weary voice. 'Did you or did you not claim to have killed Lodovico Salvestro Zabarelli?'

'No.'

'Then who do you claim to have killed?' Life flashes before me but it's too late to lie. 'The...the...the...'

'The?'

'Emperor.'

All the sound is sucked out of the room. The Chief Eunuch's features pull into a tight knot. I feel like screaming but there's no air in my lungs. Nothing happens until time suddenly jolts forwards and a tall skinny eunuch is standing by the Chief Eunuch's chair. 'Find out,' are the only words I hear. He bows and leaves. 'While we are waiting,' the Chief Eunuch says, 'let us return to Master Castiglione's apprentice.'

'I barely know him.' Flesh Mountain rests his weight on my hand. 'I—HEAVEN'S MERCY—I speak to him sometimes, that's all.'

'He is your lover.' A glance and the pain in my hand eases. 'You helped him steal *The Twilight Madonna*.'

'It belonged to his family.'

'It belongs to the Emperor. Now you are going to tell us where he is hiding.' For the first time I look up with unfeigned amazement. Lodovico is gone? Did he run as soon as I left? Did he think I was betraying him? Or did the Chief Eunuch delay the search for the enjoyment of torturing me. 'You seem confused, worm. Let me jog your memory.' He holds out his hand and Flesh Mountain hands him a tubular-shaped container. Tears spring to my eyes. My preciouses. 'Rather a *small* thing to risk your life over,' the Chief Eunuch sneers. Flesh Mountain titters. There is a charcoal brazier near the Chief Eunuch's seat. I know what he is going to do before he does it and squeeze my eyes shut, but Flesh Mountain digs his fingers into my lids and pulls them up. The Chief Eunuch is holding my preciouses above the brazier. Already there is a smell, nauseating yet faintly delicious. I would vomit if there was anything left in me. 'Roasting worm meat. Perhaps we'll feed it to you. Unless—' I look at him hopefully. 'Unless you tell us where lover boy is.'

'I don't know. Please. I'm telling the truth. I don't know.' My preciouses sink closer to the flames. Maybe I will faint. Can you faint if you can't close your eyes? The door opens and the skinny eunuch returns. He whispers something in the Chief Eunuch's ear. He nods. 'Seems you were telling the truth about the Emperor at least.'

The Chief Eunuch returns to his seat and taps my preciouses thoughtfully. 'Sit him up.' Flesh Mountain lifts my boneless body on to a chair where I slump, mangled limbs dripping over the edge. What will be my punishment? Perhaps they will roast me slowly over the brazier until my flesh drops off. It seems too merciful.

'By some dog's fart configuration of fate, it appears you have done the world a favour.' The likelihood that he is talking to me seems so remote that I do not respond until Flesh Mountain drags my head back. With as much dignity as I can muster, I raise myself up and look the Chief Eunuch in the eye.

'I'm glad he died peacefully.'

We stare at each other for a moment then the Chief Eunuch and Flesh Mountain share a glance before collapsing into rutting pig squeals of laughter. 'Did you hear that? He's glad the Emperor died peacefully.' Every bone in my body feels crushed and both my ears are ringing painfully, but oddly the laughter hurts more than anything. I'm trying to form my broken mouth into a look of contempt when the Chief Eunuch dabs his eyes. 'Priceless, worm. You really are a pearl inside a stinking oyster. You didn't need the knifer. You were emasculated all along.' I try to respond but only manage to gurgle and spit.

'Let me get this straight, the Emperor orders your father sliced up, like a dish of minced pork then rolls the heads of your mother and sisters after him, and you still wish him a peaceful death. What could he have done to make you angry, worm? Murder your pet Pekingese?' He sees my face. 'Oh yes, I know who you are. I knew right from the start, Willow Refined Ink. As a matter of fact your father was a friend of mine. I thought about him as I passed the death warrant along to the executioner.'

'Then you knew he was not a traitor.' The words taste like blood in my mouth.

The Chief Eunuch stops laughing. 'Do you know what treason your father was guilty of?'

I don't want to know. I can't stand to think about it, but that won't stop the Chief Eunuch. He leans forwards so close I smell rot on his breath.

'Let me enlighten you. The act so heinous your entire family had to be wiped from the face of the earth was a word.' No. That can't be right. He's lying. Except he isn't. 'Your father was creating a dictionary, wasn't he?' I don't move a muscle, but something affirms the question because he continues, 'Your father wrote a dedication to the Emperor. In some that might have been sycophancy, but I knew your father well enough to believe he was genuine. You don't see the problem? It's simple enough. In his eagerness to praise the Emperor, your father wrote out the characters for His Majesty's name in full, not a single stroke left out—an act the smallest child knows is forbidden, but in a scholar what else could it be but sedition?' I shake my head. The ringing in my ears grows louder. Not that. He couldn't have. Not because of that.

The Chief Eunuch waits until I have finished snivelling. 'Have you heard it said of our illustrious departed Emperor that he freed the slaves?'

I look up, puzzled. 'Yes.'

'That he wiped out corruption in the administration?'

'Yes.'

'That he removed judicial immunity for palace officials?' I hadn't known but nod.

'His Majesty is a good man. That is the official line at least.' Where is he going with this? I nod warily. The Chief Eunuch sighs. 'Then perhaps you also know the impossibility of running an empire when you can't so much as bribe a laundry maid not to starch your undergarments.' I have no idea how to answer. 'The trouble with good men, worm, is that they don't understand how things work. They think goodness is a kind of light they can shine on corruption then darkness will simply evaporate. But darkness is there for a purpose. It balances the world. Yang must have Yin. Shadows emphasise the light.' He catches my surprised expression. 'Yes, I have learned from Master Castiglione. The Emperor considered himself a beam of light, true and unwavering. Such beams destroy darkness wherever they see it.' His eyes burn into mine. 'Down to the smallest, most innocent particles.'

With a delicacy surprising in a man his size, he gets to his feet. 'I am a shadow, worm. I work silently. Much of what I do goes unnoticed, but I am always there. For years I have been waiting for my time to strike, planning down to the smallest detail how to depose an emperor on my own terms, how to restore balance to the world. I have given my life to this. I have suffered many indignities and hardships to reach my goal. To become the man who single-handedly liberated China from the crushing tyranny of supreme self-righteousness. Then a cockless abortion, who doesn't know how to wipe his own arse, crawls out of his flea-infested hole and FUCKING RUINS IT FOR ME!'

'Kill me.'

'What's that, worm?' The sound comes bubbling through my bloodied lips.

'Kill me.'

'Oh dear, no. Death is far too good for you. It will console me to know that you are alive and suffering for what I sincerely hope is a long and unhappy life.' He claps his hands and Flesh Mountain's twin enters the room. He gives a bow, then regards me in a slavering wolf sort of way. 'Our friend here is going to aid in your torture until we are quite certain you don't know where the Twilight Madonna is. Then you will be sent to a province so remote I doubt you could find it on a map, where you will serve in a temple located on a mountain so high it doesn't have a name. What do you think, worm? A fitting punishment for a thief and a murderer?'

With great difficulty I lift my swollen jaw and hold his gaze. 'As long as Lodovico is free, I am happy with my fate.'

'Free?' The Chief Eunuch is amused. 'Do you think a milk-faced Italian is going to get far carrying artwork, stolen from the imperial treasury, under his arm? Nonetheless, worm, I like your youthful optimism so I'm going to send you a gift to brighten your days as a monk.' He glances at the Flesh Mountain twins. 'These two can be my witnesses. Each year, on the Night of Sevens, I will send you a basket. It may or may not contain anything. But one year, I promise, it will hold the head of Lodovico Salvestro Zabarelli.'

He wouldn't. He couldn't. He's bluffing. Smiling, he takes a step back and the Flesh Mountain twins close in.

FIFTEEN

Refined Ink:

It's cold. It's always cold up here. When I first arrived, Abbott Boundless Endurance was still alive—although it was sometimes hard to tell because he was brittle as a twig in winter and given to sitting motionless for hours. Several times the brothers began laying fruit at his feet and lighting candles only for him to open an eye and ask what was for dinner. The Abbott said I would get used to the cold. It was the only lie he ever told me.

The handbell ringing next to my ear sets off a volcanic shudder through my body, sending me clutching for the edges of my sleeping mat, as if this one solid object can prevent me from plunging off the vertiginous ledge we call home. I do this every morning. It makes the brothers laugh. 'Come on, sleepyhead,' Brother Ten Thousand Blessings says. 'Time for meditation.' He helps me get up. My limbs are very stiff these days. It's easy to grow old on a mountaintop.

I follow him across the Heavenly Bridge, a narrow structure that connects our sleeping quarters to the temple across a deep chasm where I once dropped a pebble over the side and counted. It disappeared and I didn't hear it hit the bottom. But I am falling behind. It's hard to catch my breath these days and the twisting of my back and limbs—which healed poorly despite the Abbott's best efforts—slow me down.

Dizziness makes me clutch my stick. The bridge sways. The stars whirl. If I fall now, will I plummet straight down, like the pebble? I am so light these days perhaps I would float, feather-fashion, gently into the next world. Below, the clouds form a thick soup boiling away the rest of humanity. Sometimes it would be easy to forget that there is a world below. But not today. Today, after meditation and prayers, my annual gift from Beijing will make its way up the mountain. The new abbot is kind enough to remind me of the date, but I didn't need a reminder. Even though we don't count the days, I know. I always know.

After breakfast the head man of the village appears. Even one extra body makes our tiny living quarters cramped so he won't stay long. He greets me with respect, swaddled in goatskins against the cold and clearly impressed by the lightness of my monk's garb. It doesn't occur to him I am freezing my ghostly balls off. He hands me the basket, bows and leaves me to open it in what privacy I can find. There isn't any, but my brothers are kind enough to busy themselves with other tasks. I am glad of this because, for the first time, the basket is heavy, and this is the moment I've been dreading. I squeeze myself into a corner and sit down to open my gift. Most years the basket is filled with hay. Often accompanied by messages such as, *We're closing in, worm.* or *Not long now.* Once, bizarrely, the note read, *Happy Holidays.* The basket is never heavy.

Time passes in contemplation of my gift. So many years have gone by. Will I recognise him? Will he look scared or peaceful—or maybe even pleased to see me? I hope you had a long, happy life before they found you. I hope you made it back to Venice and returned the portrait to your grandmother, and I hope you thought of me a little whenever you looked at it. I draw in a deep breath then slowly lift the lid.

There's a box inside, rough heavy planks nailed together. My heart hammers loud enough to cause an avalanche and there is pain in my right arm. But I need to do this. I need to. Even blackened with death and corruption I need to see him. I have no tools, but I manage to work the nails loose enough to allow me to prise open the lid. Inside is another box. Lacquer this time. A painting of two cranes on top. I'm more afraid than ever, but I force my trembling hands to open it. I'm coming, my love. I'm coming. Another box. Sick at heart, I see that the Chief Eunuch is playing with me. He has sent me some elaborate message this time, perhaps to celebrate my twenty-eighth year on the mountain.

Finding it hard to breathe, I open a further three boxes until I reach the last one, a small rectangular container which slides open easily at my touch. They are there inside, nestled on a scrap of silk: my preciouses, a little charred, not to mention wrinkled and wizened as old walnuts, but my chance to be made whole again, to walk the earth in a new life as a man. There is a note which I can hardly read through my tears. It is from the new Chief Eunuch informing me of the death of the previous one and thanking me for the favour I did the world. He is sorry my deed cannot be formally recognised but offers to free me from my vows and to allow me to travel wheresoever I choose.

Can it be happening? My chance to find Lodovico again. He wouldn't want to see me. Not after all these years, not after the Chief Eunuch tortured my bones out of shape. But to see him. Just for a moment. To hear his voice even from a distance. Tucking the smallest box into my robes, I struggle to my feet. I want to find the Abbott and to thank him for his kindness over the years, but there isn't time. My days are few now. I know that. I must leave immediately. I see Brother Ten Thousand Blessings eyeing me curiously and I wish I could tell him that ringing the handbell in my ear each morning was funny but now he needs to find a new joke. Instead, I offer him a brief toothless smile and head off.

It's twenty-eight years since I was brought up the mountain, broken in body and spirit and barely aware of where I was. I hope I can find my way back down. There's a tightness in my chest that sends tingles all the way down to the fingertips of my right hand. It's starting to snow. I must take care not to fall. *Wait for me. I'm coming.* Already the temple is at my back. The snow is growing heavier. It's like the snow that has settled over Lodovico's features over time. Those round jade eyes growing more translucent and further away every year. Snowflakes are getting in my eyes. So many faces lost in it. The Emperor. My old nurse. What did my father look like? I can't even remember the Chief Eunuch. All that is left of him is the lopsided ripple of his sneer. Only one face is clear. Of a woman with night-blooming jessamine in her hair and twilight at her back. Why her? Why someone I don't even know? I will ask Lodovico about it when I find him.

My arm is quite numb now. If I keep my stick in my left hand, it will make the going a little easier. Above my head, a vortex of dying butterflies is spiralling down to earth. How far away is Venice? On another day, I might be frightened. But fear is leaving me along with feeling. I've lived my life. It's time to go. *I'm coming, Lodovico. Watch me step out into a blizzard of stars.*

SIXTEEN

DARIUS:

Light. So much light. Dividing. Opening. A thousand-petal lotus floating on a lake of silence.

'Do you know who I am?'

'Lodovico. I knew you'd come.'

'I don't understand what you're saying?'

A woman is staring down at me. No, Lodovico is staring down at me. No, a woman. My heart is turning over with love and pain. 'Where is Lodovico?'

'You said something.'

'I thought—Is Lodovico here? Is he coming?'

She's frowning. 'You spoke…I thought you spoke…It sounded like you were speaking a foreign language.'

Words inside my head. Sounds…shapes. I had them a moment ago. Water sinking into sand.

'Doctor Song?'

'Darius? Are you back?'

'I—' Rove my eyes around the room. Blood pressure monitor, swivel tray, coverlet pulled tight over body inert as a mummified corpse. 'I'm back.'

'Where have you been?' Think of asking what she means or making a joke to deflect the question, but an immense weariness has settled over my heart. I am sadder than I've ever been. Sadder than when I woke up after the accident. And my grief is for a man I never knew, who probably never even existed.

'Darius, can you tell me where you've been?' *Where have you been?* Not *How have you been* or *What were you dreaming?* Flick my eyes towards her. Does she understand? I'm afraid to speak. Lodovico's eyes—no, Doctor Song's eyes—are kind. 'I know something is going on. Tell me.'

'Something strange is happening to me.'

'Your brother told me that you're remembering things that are troubling you.' Of course, Seb told her. He never could keep a secret.

'Strange things. They're not—' I'm going to sound like a madman. 'They're not my memories.'

'Can you tell me what you mean by that?'

'It's not my life I'm remembering.'

'You're saying your memories come from someone else?'

'Yes. Not exactly. They are my memories but I'm not me.'

'I don't understand.' *You* don't understand. Walk a mile inside my head. 'It's hard to put into words.'

'Try.'

What have I got to lose? I already sound insane. 'I've had memories from a time so far back even forming thoughts felt new. And, most recently, I remember living as a eunuch in Qing dynasty China.' She tries to hide it, but she's startled. Not what she was expecting. Too specific? Something wary enters her face. 'How can you be certain they're not dreams?

'I can't explain. They're just not. They're consistent. When I'm there, they feel as though they run on real time, with none of the gaps and jumps you'd expect. No flaws in the logic. No being chased around the kitchen table by wolves or sitting my exams in my underwear.' She smiles when I say this and tilts her head very slightly. It gives me a pang. Lodovico used to make that same gesture. To cover myself, I ask quickly, 'How long have I been 'gone'?'

'Seven. No, eight days.'

Blood pounds in my ears. 'That's not possible.' Her silence tells me it is. 'You're saying it was obvious this time? People noticed?'

'No. No-one knows.'

'Except you?'

'Except me.'

'But how?' She lifts a chair and straddles it backwards, leaning her elbows on the padded back. Clearly this is no routine visit.

'You've heard of micro-expressions?'

'Tiny unconscious gestures that give away a person's thoughts.'

'Exactly. We all have them but in tetraplegics they are exaggerated. Presumably to compensate for the lack of ability to gesture with hands and arms.'

'And I've been doing this?'

'It's a natural response. Earlier, when I asked where you had been, you considered not answering. Your eyebrows drew together and you looked off to the side. Then you checked to see if I was watching.'

'Was it that obvious?'

'Only if you know what to look for. That's my point. When you're 'gone' you carry on holding lucid conversations in the here-and-now, but the micro-expressions disappear.'

It's too much to take in. I still feel the chill of mountain air against my skin and Lodovico is watching me behind my eyelids. 'Do you know what's happening to me?'

'I don't want to jump to conclusions. It's possible you're experiencing what we call hypnopompic hallucinations, intense and disturbing dreams just before waking. Or, we could be looking at a kind of rationalization by the brain. Humans are storytellers after all. Your brain might simply be spinning narratives as a way of learning to accept your new situation.'

'I don't follow.'

'Think about it. In your prehistoric past life you can walk again but your leg drags. Next you manifest as a eunuch in a Chinese-themed incarnation which represents the urinary tract infections and loss of physical sensation.'

Is she right? These past weeks, I've been marinading in a vat of drugs a sixties rock band would baulk at. *Dreams-the-people* equals my broken spine. *Refined Ink* is my withered manhood. It makes perfect sense. I'm grieving. I'm rationalizing. *Crooked-Mouth*? *Lodovico*? *The Madonna with the turquoise eyes*. What do they represent? A loss so profound it runs straight through me in a bottomless night-filled chasm. It opens up and I feel myself falling. Crooked-Mouth is waiting of me there in the Black. 'No!'

'No?' Doctor Song is in a different position in the room. Time jumped again. She's standing by the window and has turned to look over her shoulder in response to my cry. Should I mention the gap in my consciousness? I open my mouth not knowing what I'm about to say and find myself saying, 'Do you know what I do for a living?' She blinks. Clearly this is coming out of nowhere, but she answers, 'You're an art dealer.'

'That's right. I've spent my entire working life authenticating works of art. There's a lot of science behind it, of course. But really it boils down to an art, a feel for what is genuine and what's fake. It can't be put into words. It's an intuition for what's true.' She isn't saying anything. Her eyes have wandered to the door. Thinking about what I'm saying? Or planning her escape? My voice rises in a surreal zigzag. 'Look I know how insane this all sounds. But what I mean is…what I'm trying to say—' What the hell am I trying to say? What can I possibly say to convince her that I'm not disappearing so far down the rabbit hole Alice couldn't find me with a GPS. She turns her head to look at me and I hold her eyes, Lodovico's eyes. 'I know real when I see it.'

§

At around seven-thirty, Seb bounds in without knocking. He splits the air with a Cheshire grin and pulls out a wad of notes before flourishing them in my face. 'Ahoy, matey, the good ship, Sebastian, brings spoils to lay at your feet.' The notes confetti flutter on to the bed. 'Hard cash. A little passé but nothing sounds so much like success as the rustling of crinkly paper, don't you think?'

'Where did that come from?'

'A little fairy with four hooves and a bias towards going *neigh*.'

'I thought you'd given up all that.'

'Don't be so serious, brother.'

'You promised.' The smile disappears from Seb's face. He sways a little and flops down in a chair, while a struggle ensues between his head and his neck muscles. Clearly he didn't come straight from the track. At last he lifts his head and looks at me out of the eyes of an abandoned puppy—a puppy abandoned in a cocktail bar during happy hour. 'I'm sorry, Darius. Things have been so stressful. I just needed a win, that's all.' Of course he did. What a total shit I am. Seb has been here for me every day, and I'm acting like some sanctimonious arse.

Needing to find a way to make amends, I offer up my own guilty secret. 'I think she believes me.'

'Who?'

'Doctor Song.'

Seb frowns. 'Doctor Song thinks you're remembering past lives?'

'She thinks it may be related to all the trauma I've been through.' Seb can't hide his relief.

'Well that makes sense. For a while I thought you were going the way of Uncle Ralph.'

'The time he thought he was the hound of the Baskervilles?'

'Barking mad, poor soul.' Old joke. Heard a million times. Makes me smile then makes my heart ache. I think Seb will want to ask more questions but he seems preoccupied.

'I hear the Old Man offered you your job back.'

'It's just an act of charity. I can probably be written off for tax purposes.'

'That's not true. He loves you. Never tires of telling me that you're the one with the gift.'

'Look on the bright side, the gods just tipped the scales massively in your favour.'

'Don't say that. You'll be back. I don't think he can do without you.'

'No-one's indispensable, Seb.'

'Think how he backed down when you wouldn't authenticate that Giorgione sketch in his friend's private collection. He'd have lost the plot with anyone else.'

'He knew it was the truth. Art critics use Giorgione like a waste-paper basket. Any painting or drawing around the turn of the sixteenth century they can't attribute to Titian or Sebastiano, they announce must be Giorgione regardless of subject or style. I just refuse to play along.'

'And that's why you'll be back.'

'You know, it's strange.'

'What is?'

'Hard to put into words.' Words a sane person might use. 'I suppose I always thought…in as much as I ever gave it any thought that, if I'd had a past life, I would have been an artist.'

'Caveman and eunuch not top of your list then?'

'It's ridiculous, I know. I'm lying here broken into a million bits and I'm disappointed that I still can't draw.'

Seb gives me the kind of look that you give small children who didn't win a prize at a party. 'There's another way of looking at it.'

'Really?'

'Think about it. You said what's-his-name—Dreamy People.'

'Dreams-the-People.'

'Yes, him. He was right at the beginning of abstract thought. Tattoos were his art. His body was his canvas.'

I hadn't thought of this. 'Go on.'

'And the eunuch—'

'Refined Ink, yes?'

'He was in love with an artist. Art stayed with him even in his final moments.'

I'm touched that Seb has listened so closely. 'I think I saw him.'

'Who?'

'Lodovico, the artist.' Seb gives me a startled look.

'You had another episode?'

'No. I think it's Doctor Song.'

'You think—what you're trying to say—what you think is—No. I have no idea what you think.'

'I think Doctor Song was once Lodovico. And before that she may even have been Crooked-Mouth.' Seb's mouth is hanging open. This is not a good sign. He tries to say something several times then changes his mind, finally settling upon, 'Did she say something that made you think this?'

'No. It was in the way she was looking at me.'

'Looking at you?'

'It's hard to explain. Do you think there's something special to a human soul? Something that makes it different from billions of other individuals on the planet. Some unique marker carried between lives?' Seb is rubbing the back of his neck and making furtive glances at the door. He used to do the same thing when we were children telling ghost stories late at night under the blankets. At last he says, 'Have you told her?'

'I didn't want to freak her out.'

'You saved that treat for me.' I've gone too far. Said aloud, it sounds even weirder than when the thoughts are inside my head.

Seb is looking at me as though I've mentioned I might be growing wings so I can fly. As if I haven't put him under enough strain.

'I'm sorry. You're right. I'm confusing dreams with reality. It's just—' A hot upsurge of emotion takes me by surprise, laminating my eyes with burning tears. 'There's not much to hang on to in here.'

Seb pats my shoulder awkwardly. 'Don't say that. You'll find a way through this. You always do.'

§

'He's a loon.'

'Seriously?'

Liv raises a manicured eyebrow. 'You asked for my professional opinion.'

'I'm still waiting.'

'You don't want to hear it, baby sister.'

'Don't call me that.'

'Sorry, Doctor baby sister.'

'Will you be serious?'

'Fine. You have a patient who's just been through a life-changing trauma, who's been oxygen deprived more than once and is now showing signs of psychosis. Order a Psych evaluation and support follow-up. End of story.'

She's right. I know she's right. 'You're wrong. There's more to it.'

Liv rolls her eyes. They look like delicate bird's eggs. 'There isn't more to it. You're just getting too involved.'

'Is that your professional opinion, *Doctor* Song?'

'Sure is. This guy is safe. He's going to lie there and look wounded and he's never going to ask you to marry him. It's exactly like that obsession you had for what's-his-name...Colonel Saunders.'

'Colonel Halpern.'

'Same difference.'

'Do you even know your own patients by their names?'

'Waste of neurons. I call them all, *Hmmmm.*'

'You do understand psychology is a caring profession?'

'Do you understand you're forming an attachment to this bloke because forming any kind of lasting relationship with a normal man is impossible for you?'

'Do you know—' My phone ringing interrupts. Unknown number. Probably a scam about to do me out of my life savings. Better than listening to Liv. 'Hello?'

'Olivia?' The voice on the end is all smiles.

'No, Dad, it's Lexie.'

'Oh.' I know this *oh*. It's the 'o' in disappointment and loser and no-hoper. He surprises me by adding, 'Good. I wanted to speak to you.' Checking up on me already. Why Daddy, I didn't know you cared. 'I'll come straight to the point. This obsession with Somnipradine has to stop.' I throw Liv an evil stare which she accepts with a look of puzzlement. Then again, she can't hear the other side of the conversation. 'Look, I don't know what Liv—'

'Your sister has nothing to do with it. I have other sources.' Sometimes I think of my father as a giant octopus, tentacles extending in all directions. My Irish half is probably being racist. My Korean half doesn't care. 'You sent me the articles in the first place.' I sound defensive. There is a sigh on the other end of the line. 'I thought you had an interest in the subject, that you had an academic paper in mind. Instead, I find out you've been talking about past life memories and other ridiculous things.' How does he know that? Who have I talked to? Liv? Sebastian? All the rest has been online research and chatroom discussions. My God. Is he monitoring my internet activity? I try to sound as calm as possible. 'My theories are borne out by the articles.'

'Sketchy, anecdotal data at best.'

'It won't be if I can show—'

He interrupts. 'You are allowing your unaddressed phobia of death to colour your judgement.' He hears my gasp. 'Yes, I know all about your neurosis.'

Throw Liv a look that's positively psychotic. He's shouting now. 'This isn't good enough. I won't have it. I won't have my daughter putting her name to theories that throw the whole trial into disrepute.'

Something in my brain goes ping. 'Dad, is someone leaning on you?'

'Don't be ridiculous. I simply won't have the family name caught up in lunatic conspiracy theories.' He goes on but I don't really listen to the rest of the conversation. When I put the phone down, Liv has the grace to look abashed.

'Sorry. He wormed it out of me. You know how he is.'

'Forget about it. It could happen to any spineless blabbermouth with no understanding of human psychology.'

'Forgiveness is good for the soul. You should try it sometime. Hey, where are you going?'

'I need to do more research. I just got the confirmation I need that I'm on to something.'

SEVENTEEN

Lexie:

Prisoner A8312NJ is smaller than I imagined. She's wearing a slightly dirty pale blue tracksuit and her hair hangs in greasy strands behind her ears. My approach makes her lift her gaze from the floor so that I see her face is thin, hollowed out, eyes almost lost in valleys of purple shadow. A fading yellow bruise stains her left cheek. She's more pathetic than threatening. Not my idea of a child-killer.

'Brigit Carlisle?' I hold out my hand. 'I'm Doctor Song.' She takes in my blunt cut blonde hair and biker boots and doesn't move. Should have worn a suit and hung a stethoscope around my neck. Flash a professional smile. 'Thank you for agreeing to see me.' No response. Hesitate a moment then, pushing aside thoughts about the stained seat and what made those stains, sit down.

Now that I'm here, I don't know where to begin. The room is large and noisy with families making excited seagull noises around their incarcerated loved ones and children squabbling over packets of crayons and cheap photocopied colouring sheets. On three sides warders hold up the walls, ostentatiously bored. They make me feel claustrophobic yet exposed, as though I'm the one who's imprisoned. Bad place for an attack of déjà vu.

'Did you bring me anything?'

'Sorry?'

'From the shop. You can get things.' I glance over at a kiosk in the corner of the room selling crisps and biscuits and coloured boxes of vapes. 'I'm sorry. I didn't—' A bony shoulder lifted, a tight smile. 'Don't matter.'

'I'll get you something after we've talked. Whatever you want.' She nods vaguely, goes back to looking at the floor. Emotions don't break the surface of her face. What's she on? Risperidone? Citalopram? The big fat lie that Big Pharma psycho drugs leave you unaltered. A clock on the wall shows that it's five past three. I've only got an hour and no idea when they count it from, the start of the visit or when I entered the building? No more time-wasting.

I adopt my doctor-means-business voice. 'I want to ask about the fire. Is that okay?' She doesn't answer. 'You were upstairs making beds when it occurred?' A nod. 'And by the time the fire brigade reached you, you were in respiratory distress.'

'You know more than me then.'

'Do you know your heart stopped twice in the ambulance?'

'I've heard.'

'And that the crash team worked on you for forty minutes to bring you back.' She glances around the room at the shabby paintwork and the worn stained chairs. 'Wasted their bleedin' time then, didn't they?'

'Brigit, are you aware that they gave you a drug called, Somnipradine?'

'Gave me a lot of drugs.'

'Did they tell you that they had given it to you?'

'Might have done. Dunno.' The hands of the clock are clasped at quarter past three. Need to speed things up.

'Prior to the fire you had a history of drug abuse?'

'Never said I didn't.'

'But you claim that you were clean for eight months before the fire occurred.'

'I was clean.'

'The investigation found that the fire was started by an untended candle near some drapery.'

She looks at me warily. 'Yes.'

'So you weren't trying to kill yourself or harm anyone?'

'My kids were in that house. What do you think?'

'I think something changed after you left the hospital.'

'Dunno.'

'You had never been violent before?'

'No.'

'Yet you came home and—' I can't say it. 'You—'

'Killed my son.' The words are toneless but there's a flicker behind her eyes. Is she challenging me?

'Did something happen when you saw your son again?' Her shoulders tighten. It's almost as if she pricks up her ears. Need to keep pressing. 'Had you ever had violent thoughts towards him before? You were diagnosed with postnatal depression?'

'They said that later. Wasn't true. I was never depressed.'

'What was your relationship like with your son before...before the fire?'

'Don't know what to tell you. He was my youngest. Nothing special. Not cuddly like his sisters. He was an angry baby. Always screaming. Sometimes though, he'd go quiet and stare at me like he hated me. Like we were mortal enemies or something. He was just a funny kid, that's all.'

'But you didn't hate him?'

She looks up sharply. 'Not then. No.' Her fingers are picking at a scab. 'In the hospital. I started remembering things.'

'Can you tell me about that?' I pull out a notebook, wishing they'd let me record our conversation. My phone was taken at the desk. Give her an expectant look but she presses her lips together, looks away. 'Brigit, I know you're afraid to talk about this. But I'm here to listen. No judgement. I promise.' She doesn't answer. *Come on. Don't clam up on me now*. 'Those memories didn't belong to you, did they?' Liv wouldn't approve. Leading the patient. A big psychoanalysis no-no. But I can't go back empty-handed. Not now. 'Brigit? Did the memories belong to someone else?'

Her head turns slowly. 'I remember a bright place. It was filled with rooms, huge rooms bigger than a church. You could hear people's footsteps echo when they walked across the floors.'

'Did you recognise it?'

She gives me a look. Her notes say she grew up in a council flat in Brixton. 'Never seen anything like it. Not even in pictures.' She scrunches her face at me. 'I remember that smooth white stuff everywhere—alabaster, that's what you call it. And there was gold. Masses of gold. And two great winged bulls at the entrance. I remember playing under them when I was a child.' *Winged bulls?* I've seen them at the British Museum. Where are they from? Egypt? Babylon? I wish I'd paid more attention.

'Can you tell me more?'

'He called it the palace without rival.'

'Who did?'

'The King.'

'Who was this king?'

'He was my brother.'

'Your older brother?' Her records say she's an only child. Suddenly she's looking straight into my eyes. In a split second this defeated slumped-over woman has become dangerous. 'I was the eldest living son. My father passed over me in favour of my younger brother.'

'Why?'

A shrug. 'A king may do as he pleases.' This isn't Brigit talking. Everything about her has changed: her body language, her speech patterns, even the dilation of her pupils seems different. Is she play-acting? She didn't strike me as having the breadth.

'Can you tell me your name?'

She changes position, then changes it again. She can't get comfortable. 'I was named after the sun god, the great god of justice, He who feels the world's iniquity as a searing wound.' She lifts an eyebrow. 'No-one could deny that Father had a sense of humour.'

'What was your brother's name?'

'I will never speak it.'

'You resented your brother?'

'My father tried to salve the wound by making me king of a great city, but that only made things worse.'

'Why?'

'They ignored me.'

'Who did?'

'The rulers of Nippur, Uruk and Ur. Even the rulers in the Sea Land. Whenever there was a matter to be resolved or a plea for aid, they went to my brother. Never to me.'

'Did you hate your brother?'

'He was King of the World. I was his subject.' Nice sidestep.

'Was he a good king?'

'A good king?' She pauses to take out a vape. It's the metallic blue of a comic book rocket. She drags on it then blows out cinnamon clouds in my face. 'He killed lions by piercing their mouths with a single arrow. He destroyed the sanctuaries of Elam when they rose against him and robbed the tombs of their kings preventing their ghosts from sleeping. He sowed the land with salt and *salahu* so nothing would grow.'

Sounds like a real teddy bear. 'Did his actions make you angry?'

'The people were angry.' Another sidestep. 'His ways made them restless.'

'Brigit. What happened when you left the hospital?' She looks right at me. There's nothing glassy or unfocussed in her expression but somehow I know she can't see me.

'He sent me a summons to go to the palace.'

'Your brother sent for you. Did you go?'

'He was King of the World. I was his subject. When we arrived, we were taken into the garden where he had the heads of the Elamite kings hanging from tree branches while their wives—stripped naked as serving girls—were forced to dance beneath. One of his enormous eunuchs was standing by with a whip at the ready if they faltered. He laughed when he saw me fighting to hide my emotion, and said, *O brother. Our father was right. You are too tender-hearted to be King of the World. Come, I want you to see my new hound.*'

'Everything all right?' A warder is at our side. Has she noticed something? Her sudden appearance flusters me, but Brigit answers, 'Yeah, miss. Everything's fine. Just having a chinwag with the doctor.' The warder gives a bored nod, leaves.

'Brigit?' Scan her face anxiously, afraid the moment has been lost. 'Did your brother show you the hound?' Strange look crosses her face. It makes me think of someone laughing with pain. 'He led me there, arm around my shoulders. He led the courtiers. He led the visiting ambassadors and the envoys from Egypt. All of us, brightly coloured hens with our wings clipped, following him to the kennels. He was laughing before we got there.

'His Master of Hound greeted us, falling on his stomach and proclaiming his unworthiness, but I had seen his face—green-tinged chalk, a man whose work sickens him—and I was afraid. I wanted to leave but my brother squeezed my arm, saying, *As the seed of my father's loins, I will hear your opinion first.*'

She breaks off and says nothing, despite my urgent prompting. 'Brigit? Brigit, can you hear me? What did he show you?' One of the warders is watching me. She says something to a second one and they both look over. The hands of the clock are at ten-to. 'Brigit, please. I'm trying to understand. Tell me what you remember.'

A deep inhalation as though coming up for air. 'I saw his hound.'

'Yes?'

'It was Tammaritu, King of Hamanu. My brother defeated him at the battle of Susa. I remember him as a fine warrior, someone who deserved to die with honour, but now was on his hands and knees, a dog chain through his jaw.' She looks at me pleadingly. 'This was the moment I knew my brother had to die.'

A bell shrills out a sharp *trrrrring* and a voice announces, *Five minutes.* Brigit slumps against the back of the chair. 'Brigit, did you kill your brother?'

She stares at me strangely. 'I haven't got a brother.'

'Not now. Before.'

'Oh that.' Suddenly she's disinterested. 'You said you'd get me something from the kiosk.'

'I will. When we're finished. But I want to know if you remember anything else.' A shrug. 'Dunno.' Is she toying with me? There's no time for softly-softly. 'What happened when you got back from the hospital?' She stares daggers, doesn't answer. 'When you came home. Do you remember what happened?'

'I saw him.'

'Who did you see?'

'The King of the World.'

'How could you do that?'

'He was in his cot staring up at me.'

'You mean your son?'

'It was him.'

'But he was just a little boy. Barely two years old. How could you know it was your brother?' She makes a restless gesture and her eyes slide away.

'Dunno. I guess, if you meet up with someone you haven't seen in a long time, they'll have changed a lot. Got fatter. Got thinner. Changed their hair colour. Got older. But you still know it's them. You can't disguise yourself from people who know you, now can you?'

Of course she's right. Recognition is a complex interaction between perception, memory and semantic knowledge. Sensory cues, expression, scent, even handwriting can give a person away. Can the same possibly be true between lives? Nerve endings fire off needles of excitement down my arms. My mouth is dry. Barely aware that all around chairs are being scraped back, coats are being pulled on, I press on, 'You thought your little boy was your brother from a previous life?'

'It was him all right. The way he looked at me. He knew about the fire.'

'The fire in your home? Before you were taken to hospital?'

'No. The first fire. In the Long Ago.'

'What happened in the fire?'

'We rose against him, but he came from the north. With his great army, he laid siege to my city until the dismembered bodies of the people were spread out as funerary offerings and my children were near death, their mothers driven mad with grief, then he came with his men in the dead of night and laid torch to my palace.'

'He tried to burn you out?'

'He blocked the doors and set guards around the walls. I could not escape. My home became my funeral pyre.'

She exhales a gauzy plume of smoke and I see it. Just for a heartbeat, the face of a king. 'This is where you died.'

'Yes.'

I can't help myself. I have to ask. 'What is it like? What did you see?'

She taps the vape against the heel of her hand. 'Death is slow-footed in a fire. I burned and burned. Trapped inside my roasting flesh, my heart, my bones turning to ash. All around the light was the black and orange of a dying sun. I remember in particular the moment when my sight burned away and when I could no longer hear the screams of my children because my ears were gone.'

'Do you remember the moment of dying?'

'I remember darkness. I was in the underworld for a long time, a place with no desires or feelings. I was there only as a mountain is there, as a river is there.'

'What changed?'

'I was here.'

'Here? In this life you mean?'

'I was just here. I did not ask why. I simply was.'

'With no memory of your former existence?'

'I did not know I had been a king. I did not think of palaces or having servants or wives or of going on hunts or the heat of battle. But—' She breaks off for a moment, a new thought occurring. 'I was always afraid of dogs.'

'You had no idea who you were until after the accident. After the Somnipradine?'

'It wasn't an accident.'

'But the report—'

'I reckon he did it on purpose.'

'Who? Do you mean your son? You think he caused the fire?'

'When I got home, he looked at me and I knew who he was.'

'But your son didn't know who he was. He was innocent.'

'He knew. Some people are here to burn down the world. They don't learn it. It's just inside them.'

'How could a little boy like that destroy the world? He had no power. He wasn't born a king.'

'Hitler and Mao and Putin weren't born kings either.'

'Even so you couldn't be certain it was him.'

'I was certain. I gave him a chance though. I put a cake and his favourite toy car and a box of matches in front of him and I waited. He lifted up the box and shook it at me and he laughed. It was a strange laugh for a child. Eerie-sounding.' She lifts the vape to her lips but doesn't inhale. 'It was the moment I knew he had to die.'

'Because he was your brother?'

'Because he would burn down the world if I let him live.' A whistle shrieks.

'Right, everyone out,' a warder is yelling. I get up slowly, making a production of putting on my jacket, trying to eke out the seconds. 'Thank you for talking to me.' Her eyes don't flicker. She reaches down and pushes her sleeve up to the elbow. The flesh is a sickening moraine of twisted scars. Unmistakable presentation. Prison napalm. Sugar in boiling water. Only my medical training stops me from flinching. 'Oh, Brigit.'

'They did this to me 'cos I stabbed my baby to death. Silly cunts. They should be down on their knees thanking me for saving them.' She pockets the vape and I think she's about to say goodbye when she adds, 'Tell you one thing, doc. If there was justice in the world, there'd be statues to me in Trafalgar Square.' She twists up her mouth and something very old looks out of her eyes. 'Made out of alabaster and gold.'

EIGHTEEN

Liv is driving too fast. I want to tell her to stop but she has the *kill crazy* face she adopts when she gets behind a wheel, and any sign of terror in her passenger only eggs her on. As we tear down a narrow street of brutalist housing improbably called Elm Avenue, she says, 'Let me get this straight. You visited a delusional child-killer serving life, on the hunch that she's a reincarnated Assyrian ruler from the seventh century BC, who killed a despotic madman calling himself the King of the World, and not her innocent toddler. I'm not clear. Which is the crazy part again?'

'Liv, I know how it sounds.'

'Are you sure about that?'

'I'm not insane.'

'Do you know who else says that?'

'Insane people. I get it. Can you humour me? Just for a bit?'

'Fine.'

'You don't have to believe anything supernatural or against the laws of physics, but something is happening in patients who are given Somnipradine. They're experiencing out-of-the-body memories.'

'And no-one but you has noticed.'

'Other people did notice, but the articles have all disappeared. Someone doesn't want us to find out.'

'So now it's a conspiracy?'

'I'm not saying that.' I think I'm not saying that. Liv slams down the accelerator and we skim through the junction as the lights turn red. She has a lot of repressed anger when it comes to traffic control. Over the blare of horns, she shouts, 'I just don't know what it is you think I'm going to see apart from psychosis!'

'It's hard to explain. You have to experience it to understand. The detail is incredible. The way their speech and body language changes.'

'I thought he was tetraplegic?'

'I meant Brigit. She grew up on a council estate. She was a drug addict, single mother with three kids before she was twenty-two,

116

yet she can recall in incredible detail how she was killed by an ancient king I had never even heard of.'

'You mean Ashurbanipal.'

I stare. 'How could you possible know that?'

'From what you've described, who else could it be?' Liv's grasp of general knowledge impresses me to the point of throwing up.

'The historical record backs up her story.'

'Which means she could have looked it up or seen a documentary that's she's forgotten.'

'But what about the detail that isn't in the record? The Elamite wives dancing naked for instance?'

'Unless there's something that directly contradicts it then it can't be proved or disproved. Frankly, it sounds like suppressed eroticism.'

'I don't—JESUS. Look out!' A lollipop man flies past the window, so close I see the whites of his eyes. For a split second I think we've hit him and invisible fists start pummelling my heart. 'God, Liv!'

'We were miles away.' In the side mirror I can see the small fluorescent figure brandishing his lollipop stick aloft. He looks like Charlton Heston calling down the wrath of the Lord.

'Do you have some sort of death wish?'

Liv is as cool as a scoop of our father's favourite *bingsoo*. 'Better that than a death phobia, baby sister.'

§

Liv is impressed by The Grange. We pull up in a swan's wing spray of gravel and Liv cuts the engine. 'Wow, remind me to come here if I ever part ways with my spinal column.'

'You couldn't afford here. This is a place for rich people to suffer.'

Liv continues to be impressed all the way to Darius's room. 'Hey, they have carpet on the floors.'

'Only down here. It's all laminate up in the medical suites.'

'This wood panelling is original, isn't it?'

'Yes, Actually I wanted—'

'Did you say Darius Colvin is single?'

§

'Your *sister*?' I know what that emphasis means. Liv is the ideal of Eurasian beauty. East meets West in glorious fusion. Unlike me, where East lost control and crashed into West at high speed. 'It's a pleasure to meet you.' Darius is trying hard not to notice the difference between us. I'm trying hard not to mind.

'As I explained, Doctor Song has taken time out of her busy schedule to facilitate the experiment in a medical capacity.'

Liv looks at me wondering why I'm talking like Jane Austen. 'Don't you think,' she says, 'it will be confusing if we're both Doctor Song. I'm sure a bit of informality won't queer the pitch. I'm Olivia. Call me Liv.'

'Lexie,' I add grudgingly, feeling weirdly exposed and naked as I do so.

Liv has drawn her seat up. 'You understand what we're trying to do today?'

'We're trying to trigger the memories.'

'And you are comfortable with this and give your consent?'

'Yes.'

'Do you believe that you are experiencing memories from a past life?'

'Yes. At least I think I do.' He glances at me, and I feel like a mother whose child is being tested.

'It doesn't matter,' I interject quickly. 'We just want to find out more about the mechanics of the experience. Whether it can be controlled in any way.' Liv frowns. She's trying to gauge his credulity.

'Did Doctor—Did Lexie explain what we will be doing?'

'Hypnotherapy?'

'Yes. Regression hypnotherapy to be specific. There are different techniques from Ericksonian to NLP. But we're primarily interested in the kind of memories you recall and whether you can manipulate them.'

'I'm afraid I will be wasting your time. I can't recall them at will. Believe me, I've tried.'

'You let us decide what's a waste. Even a negative result can yield some useful data.' Got to hand it to Liv, she's so smooth she could have been a silkworm in another life.

'Shall we get started?' They look up, surprised. Yup, I'm still here.

Liv recovers first. 'Shall we close the blinds a bit.'

'You want it dark?'

'Dim. Just to create a relaxing atmosphere with no distractions.' It's a grey day outside, and when I pull the blinds to slits, the light turns misty; all the hard edges disappear. Liv turns to me. 'Do you need to inject him?'

'No. It doesn't work that way. It seems to act as a trigger. To open a door that was locked inside the brain. There are patients here who've had larger doses and experienced nothing unusual.' I don't mention that I haven't found a single other case of recall in the hospital.

Liv shrugs. 'All right then. Let's get started.' We take our seats on either side of the bed. 'Darius, I want you to take a deep breath. Can you do that for me?' Easier said than done for a quadriplegic, but he draws in air through his nostrils then lets it out.

'Should I close my eyes?'

'That's up to you.' Liv starts talking in her silkworm voice. She's subtle, not using the usual cues about feeling limbs relax or walking along beaches of golden sand. Everything she says focuses inside his head. She tells him to concentrate on his breathing and gets him to listen only to the sound of her voice. She keeps talking. I keep watching his face. Every so often she asks a series of rehearsed questions. 'Where are you?'

'Here.'

'Where's here?'

'In hospital.'

'What are you wearing?'

'A tracksuit. A T-shirt. Grey socks.'

119

'Do you think rocks can fly?' He's startled. He stutters out a negative and a series of micro-expressions flicker across the muscles of his face. Liv looks at me. I shake my head.

'What day is it?'

'Tuesday.'

'What colour are your eyes?'

'Brown.'

'Have you ever invited a sheep to a dinner party?'

'No.' He isn't startled this time. Bemusement and curiosity flick by. I shake my head.

And on it goes. After an hour Liv looks at me. She pushes the chair away and stands up. 'Well, you're not trying to fake anything. That's something.'

'I'm sorry.'

'Please don't be. Your honesty was the most valuable control we had.'

'Perhaps we can try another time.'

'Perhaps. It was nice to meet you, Darius. I hope things get better for you.'

'Thank you.'

I walk her to the elevator hoping we might do it in silence, but Liv says, 'You must be disappointed.'

'It's a setback. That's all.'

'He seems like a decent man. A very sincere man. I can see why you want to help him.'

'I'm not in love if that's what you think. Something is happening to him. I want to know why.'

'He's been through a lot. Trauma can do strange things to the brain.'

'This is more than trauma.'

'Have you even considered the possibility that you're wrong?'

'I'm not wrong.'

'What if it's a narwhal.'

'What if it's—what?'

'Old story. A man goes looking for a unicorn. Many years later he appears with a narwhal horn and tells everyone that he's found the horn of a unicorn on a distant shore. They call him a liar. But the man is honest and he sincerely believes unicorns exist. To suggest they are impossible is such an anathema to him that he simply went on looking until he found one.'

'You're saying I see a connection because I want to believe there is one.'

'I think you need to believe that death is a comma, not a full stop.'

§

I feel my footsteps slowing as I approach Darius's room. I'm not looking forward to this conversation. Fingers on the door handle. Deep breath. Get it over with. 'Hi, I'm back.' An orderly has been in while I was walking Liv to her car. Darius is sitting in his wheelchair looking out of the window. He doesn't look round when he hears me open the door. Should I slip away? 'I'm sorry that didn't work out.'

'Please don't worry about it.'

'We can try again. Change the nuances. Maybe a different environment.'

'Yes, that would be nice.' He's still looking out of the window.

'Darius?'

'Yes?'

'Can you look at me?' He turns his face and gives me a pleasant smile. 'Liv says the experiment was a complete waste of time.'

'You must be disappointed.'

'Are you disappointed?'

'Yes. Terribly.' He turns back to the window. 'It was raining earlier. But I think they said we can expect sunshine by the late afternoon.'

Everything goes very still between my ears. 'Where are you?'

'I'm here, of course.'

'Where's here?'

'On the train.'

'You're on a train?'

'Yes.'

'Where are you going?' His chin juts up and he cuts me a look, not sure if he wants to share. I'm trying to formulate another question when he says reluctantly, 'Berlin.'

'Is that where you live? Berlin?'

'No-one lives in Berlin.'

'No?' His smile is teasing.

'People don't live in Berlin: they blaze.'

'What year is it?'

'Nineteen—Nineteen—' Something uneasy enters his eyes. Ask another question quickly. 'Can you tell me your name?' A gathered inbreath then a deep sigh.

'Jules. My name is Jules. But they don't call me that at home. That's why I'm leaving.'

'What do they call you at home?'

He flashes me a furious look then bites his lip. 'They call me Julia. Julia Elfriede Vogelsang. A girl's name.'

'Are you a girl?'

'No!' Emphatic. Angry. Replaced by a look of distress. 'I'm a man. I know I'm a man.'

'But your family doesn't agree?'

'That's why I have to leave.'

'That's why you're on the train.'

'Yes.'

'Can you tell me what's happening right now?'

His head tilts to one side and his eyes grow heavy. 'I think I'm sleeping. I took some M earlier. And it hasn't worn off.'

THIRD LIFE

Orlando at War

The memories of Jules Vogelsang

NINETEEN

'Berlin Anhalter Bahnhof!'

Jerk upright, eyes open but not totally awake. A sore patch where my forehead has been leaning on the carriage window. My trousers are bunched in accordion pleats at the knees. M hasn't worn off. Only seven left. Have to ration myself until I get a new supplier. Everything fuzzy and dreamlike. Am I really in Berlin?

Outside, put down my case and shelter under Romanesque arches trying to light up an *Ekstein*. Damn matches keep blowing out. Wind feels like it's all the way from the Russian Steppe. Need to find somewhere to stay, but now I'm here—finally—here in Berlin, can't seem to move. What if I'm wrong? What if there's no acceptance for a man like me?

§

'Can you describe what you're seeing?'

'Strange.'

'Strange?'

'Never set foot in the city, but already I can see how the place has changed. Nazi flags sticking out everywhere. Horrible. Makes me think of red apples ruined by blight. I've left it too late. Should have come here ten years ago. Would have if I'd had any sense.'

'But you're here now. And the Nazis party is in charge.'

'Hmmm?'

'Jules, is there a war on?'

§

A tug at my trouser cuff breaks my trance. Look down and find a legless creature clinging to a plywood board on wheels. A cardboard sign around his neck proclaims him as a veteran of the Ludendorff Offensive. Press ten marks into his hand. He holds the note up to the light and lifts his grubby, bandaged fingers in salute before wheeling himself off on his makeshift chariot. Dear Lord, if this is how Berlin treats its heroes, how will it treat a man like me?

Need to find a room. Newspaper would be the ticket. But none of the familiar old titles are there when I stop at a kiosk. New broadsheets have taken their place with names like *The Attack* or the *Racial Observer*. Walk on past the Reichstag. Its blackened corpse stands in the Platz der Republik while citizens hurry by, eyes averted. Makes me sad to see this Berlin. Not the one of my opiated dreams, but the one that eats through democracy like a disease.

A sullen-faced fraulein, with fat sausage plaits fastened to her crown, stands guard behind the counter. Her eyebrows are so pale they are very nearly not there. Gives her eyes a boiled-egg look. Shakes her head when I ask for a pack of Eksteins. 'We don't have any.'

'Karos? R6s? Lucky Strikes?'

'No. We don't stock foreign or degenerate brands.' Reaches under the counter then thrusts a pack of Trommlers at me. 'These are the approved label.'

The box is yellow with a picture of a brownshirt banging on a drum. Sort of image you would expect in a child's book: *The Little Prince* or *The Toy Soldier*. 'I thought Herr Hitler disapproved of smoking?'

'The Fuhrer knows that common men need relief from the stresses of the day. Besides, the militia receive a financial reward for every thousand we sell.'

So now I have the pleasure of paying for the blight corrupting the face of old Berlin. The fraulein is staring at my face as though something is puzzling her, a mystery she is determined to resolve. Suddenly the very-nearly-not-there eyebrows shoot upwards. She gives a little gasp. Was my voice a little too high? My jawline a little too soft? It doesn't matter. I take my cue to leave.

§

'*Where are you now?*'

'*I'm looking for somewhere to stay. Mother was in Berlin last spring. She stayed at the Adlon Kempinski and had a view of the Brandenburg gate. She said it was beautiful, with frescoed ceilings and a lovely old library where they served tea. Out of the question, of course.* "One month's allowance. It's all you can expect"—*Father's parting words to me. Didn't even let me say goodbye. I suppose I'm lucky he allowed me to fill my valise. I had never seen him so angry. His face very nearly showed emotion.'*

'*Can you tell me more about the falling out with your father?*'
Face falls. Eyes slide away. 'I don't want to talk about it.'
'*All right. Let's talk about something else. Did you find a place to stay?*'

§

My new landlady is a widow—stringy bun, dress at least twenty years out of fashion—her rough Berlin accent is polished with a thin veneer of gentility. Do I have a letter of introduction? Am tempted to claim that I left it behind last time I dined with the Queen of England, but instead take out my wallet make a show of opening it. She looks at the notes for a long moment then up into my face. Her bloodless lips compress. Something about me she doesn't like, but the hollows in her cheeks and the patches on her dress make an elegant case in my favour and, in the end, she doesn't ask too many questions.

Her sly-eyed son leads me to my room. Something of an exaggeration to call it that. It's a slope-roofed attic with barely space to stand up in. Junior is holding his hand out for a tip. The rogue didn't even carry my bag. Something about him makes me fearful, but the man inside me won't back down. 'Thank you. That will be all.' His eyes bug and I fear an outburst but then he shrugs and says in a saccharine voice, *Well, if there's anything I can do*, before slinking out the door. Not a full day here and already I have made an enemy.

Of course money is the real issue. My flamboyance before my landlady has cost me dear. Will have to pawn some of the contents of my valise soon. Mean to start looking at once, but take some grains of C to blot out Junior's menace. Soon the world is calling and won't take no for an answer.

Outside, everything is sleekly, clumsily, glamorously gauche. Nothing is truly old here. Berlin quivers like the legs of an epicene

teen who shouts out, *The past is dead. Long live the future.* I am
seduced. Entranced, hypnotized, I wander the galleries until hunger
drives me out. It's late and the sky is already a deep violet behind
the raw wound of the sun. It casts the city in a pall of dangerous
shadowy light. This is the Berlin I have been waiting for.

§

'Jules? Jules, can you hear me?'

'If course I can hear you.'

'What day is it?'

'Monday.'

'What if I told you it was Friday?'

'Friday, yes. How silly of me.'

'Who am I?'

'You're Doctor Song. Doctor Lexie Song.'

'How do you know me?'

A long pause. Chin down, brows together, thinking hard. 'How
do you know me, Jules?' *Brightening. A look of sudden clarity.* 'We're
old friends.'

'Jules, can you tell me if the war has started?'

'Not you too.'

'I don't understand. Are you speaking to me?'

'Who else? Everyone keeps saying there's going to be a war. I
won't give in to that kind of scaremongering. I came here to begin
life. War would end everything.'

'What are you going to do, now you're here in Berlin?'

'I'm going where all good Berliners go when times get tough.'

'Where's that?'

'To the cabaret.'

'Are there cabarets in Berlin? Now that the Nazis are in charge.'

'You're right, of course. Most of them are gone. Shut down by
Herr Goebbels because of their "Jewish tendencies". But—'

'But?'

Voice lowered. 'There are rumours. Whisper clubs. Places where
the old biting cabaret still takes place.'

'Have you found such a place?' A pause. Can almost see a nose being tapped.

'Perhaps.'

'How did you find out?'

'Scrap of paper. Blew up against my shoe when I was walking near the Reichstag. The burnings have stopped but you still see these charcoaled fragments around the city, caught in hedges or under benches. Usually, they are filled with words. Words that burn more fiercely than the conflagrations that tried to snuff them out. Words by Einstein or Kafka or Mann.'

'What did this one say?'

—Dream sweeter

with a taste of

Schokolade.

Entry free,—thaler P—

'What does it mean?'

'It's a whisper club.'

'Can you take me there?' A pause. Closes his eyes. 'Are you there?'

'I'm outside in…in Rosenthaler Place.'

'What do you see?'

'Little art gallery huddled between a tailor specialising in military attire and a typewriter repair store. Doesn't seem anything special about it.'

'This is the place in the flier?'

Doubtfully. 'Yes.'

'Go inside.'

§

Traces of scrubbed out graffiti on the door. Nonetheless, the interior is light and pleasant. White plaster walls and a scuffed wooden floor. Paintings hang from a picture rail or are displayed on free-standing easels. Don't see much that impresses me. All very modern and too many imitation *Groszs* or *Picabias*. Time and space exploding in fractured diamonds, that sort of thing.

Only one holds my attention. Standing alone on an easel. A rather bleak landscape—blasted heath, ash riven sky. Off-centre is a floating eye, incongruously placed, yet inescapable, as if something in the painting was shouting, *Wake up*!

'Through there.'

The proprietress— an impeccably dressed woman in her sixties with a wistful, pensive face—has obviously summed me up. Knows why I'm here. She points again to the curtain behind the painting with the omniscient eye. Not just a backdrop then. Saunter over with a display of casual confidence and—hand visibly trembling—reach out and pull it back. A door. The most ordinary thing in the world, but it reminds me of fairy tales where doors appear in the side of hills or in the middle of otherwise empty fields.

It opens on to nothing more than a wooden staircase leading down into dusty darkness. Throw a final glance at the proprietress, who gazes back at me like old Kharon on the shores of the Styx. Swear I can feel the press of a coin under my tongue. Still, nothing ventured. Descend like Orpheus or Gilgamesh wondering if I will find my way back to the light.

At the bottom is a door, heavily padded in red velvet quilting. Half expect a golden key in the lock, but there's only a very ordinary doorknob which twists without resistance and allows me to open the door a crack. The light inside is a dim glowing red. Takes me a moment to adjust, but a woman's voice—low husky tones with just a hint of sweetness; a spoonful of sugar in morning coffee—escapes through the gap.

'Ever been to a Nazi farm? The humans goose-step more than the geese.'

There's a titter of laughter. Not weak, but deliberately stifled. Even listening is a dangerous pastime nowadays. Press my face against the crack, needing to know more.

The interior opens itself up in an erotic fantasy of velvets and silks. Little tables illuminated by Japanese lanterns and a low stage where a single woman stands smoking a cigarette. It's clearly a rehearsal. A scattering of people—almost all women—sit at the tables drinking from champagne flutes. An obese *daddy* in a fedora is sitting at a table at the front with a waif in bias-cut satin, eyes consumptively ringed with kohl, straddling her knee. Her face is turned up in rapt attention, while her hand grazes the waif's nipples from time to time.

The woman on the stage blows out a plume of cigarette smoke. 'People say bad things about the Fuhrer. But remember how he kept us warm by burning all those books.' This produces hoots and catcalls, but she continues almost as though she hasn't heard. 'Don't be too hard on him. The Fuhrer loves the classics. They say he models himself on the Roman emperors. And just like this—'she mimes striking a match '—he goes from zero to Nero.' This time the laughter is unrestrained. I join in then stop abruptly, afraid of drawing attention to myself. Sitting down seems the wisest move. Creep towards a table at the centre, but the chair makes the most awful scrape as I take my seat, and when I look up, the woman on the stage is staring straight at me.

A heart-shaped face emerges from a pall of blue smoke, bobbed curls skimming the tips of her cheekbones. But it's her eyes that transfix. Ringed with sooty lashes like an Egyptian queen or some goddess of the midnight hour, they look straight at me. I know her.

§

'You know her? You've met before?'
    'Yes.'
    'Who is she?'
    Embarrassed laugh. 'She's you.'
    'Me? What do you mean?'
    'She's Lexie. Lexie Song.'
    'How can she be me?'

'I…I don't know. Her mouth. That gap between her teeth. I used to call her Crooked-Mouth…No, that's not right.' Nervously looking about. Clearly agitated. Move along.

'Does she recognise you?'

'No. Not by the way she looked at me.'

'How was that?'

'Disappointed.'

'Can you—'

'Doctor Song, you're needed in Ward C straight away…Doctor Song, I said—'

'I heard you, thank you. I'll be right there.'

§

'I'm sorry I was called away.'

'Please don't apologise.'

'Can you take me back to the cabaret?'

'Cabaret?'

'The whisper club. Where you saw the comedienne.' Distressed motions of the head. Looks away. 'The show's over.'

'Where are you now?'

'Back in the garret.'

§

Creep upstairs, relieved that everyone has gone to bed, and cautiously ease open the door to my room. Disaster awaits. Junior is inside going through my valise. His back is to me, but my gasp alerts him, and he turns, quite unperturbed, and holds up a shimmering sateen evening gown. My mother bought it for me at the Wertheim store on her last shopping trip. I remember how she raved about the biblical frescoes and the six-metre-tall statue by Ludwig Manzel in the atrium. 'You should have seen it, Klaus,' she said. 'Like a temple dedicated to some mysterious old god.' My father did not look up from his newspaper, 'Avarice,' he said coldly. 'The god of women.'

Junior's hands are back in the valise. He lifts another dress in cotton broadcloth and then another in rayon crepe. 'Amazing,' he says. 'Is this how young men are dressing in Munich these days?' Every cell in my body urges me to punch the rogue on the nose and evict him from my private property. Instead, open my wallet, begin pulling out notes.

Afterwards, sit on my bed letting the dawn find me through the open skylight and fill the garret with the metallic smell of the city. I feel trapped and hopeless. Rather as I did on the night Father threw me out for good.

§

'Tell me about that night.' Uneasy. Not sure whether to trust me. 'Please. I think it would help me to understand you.'
   'I would like that.'
   'To help me?'
   'To be understood.'

§

Halfway down the sweeping curve of our staircase before consciousness begins to resurface. Fuzzily. As if swimming up slowly through greenish murk. By the sound of it Father's VERY IMPORTANT dinner party is well under way. Clearly, I have lost time after I went up to dress. Must have taken M. C makes me jittery. Only M thickens the air so everything slows and moving feels like wading through water.

A wave of nausea throws me over the banister. Not a bad position from which to observe the guests while remaining, myself, unobserved. They look like actors in a play. Why do people lose their realness when you examine them at a distance? Father, granite giant, enthroned on a walnut *Biedermeier*, at the head of the table, a glass of muscatel in his hand. To his right is a bookish man—thick glasses attached to a rim of hair— and, opposite, a hawk-featured individual stirring his dessert with alchemic concentration. At the far end of the table, Mother remains invisible: her usual fate.

The bookish man is speaking. 'You are a sceptic, Herr Krauch?' Krauch continues to stir his dessert. 'Forgive me, Professor Boehm, but I am a man of science. To me the situation is simple. When our factories are overrun with rats, we exterminate them. There is no need to tell the people a fairy story about rats to achieve this end.'

Boehm adjusts his glasses, glances at my father then continues. 'You will forgive me, but I could not disagree more. Folklore is a catalyst of the instinct. It is a way to teach people who they truly are. Take for example my little nieces. They are at an age where folk tales are a delight. But now they see Little Red Riding Hood as an innocent German girl terrorized and tormented by the nefarious Jewish wolf. Cinderella does not merely marry a prince but ensures racial purity by expelling undesirable foreign elements, and—'

'But is it not too much for children?' Mother has forgotten that a refined *hausfrau* does not expect to join in the dinner conversation after the soup course. Father's face is stone, but Professor Boehm comes to the rescue, leaning towards my mother and taking her hand in his liverish paw. 'Frau Vogelsang, did you not teach your lovely daughter to be wary of strangers? To never go out alone after dark?'

'I suppose I—'

'And was she ever too young to be warned of these dangers?'

'No, of course—'

'There you have it. Children are never too young to be warned of danger. Should we not also make them wary of dangers that surround them? How easy it is to grow fond of a classmate or a servant without understanding that the loved one is nothing more than a façade disguising devious corruption. You would not want that for your daughter, now would you? We must be constantly vigilant—even children—constantly on the lookout for the Jew, the gypsy, the sexual deviant.' Father coughs and Professor Boehm hastily releases Mother's hand. 'Forgive me, Herr Vogelsang. It was indelicate of me to discuss this over dinner. If I may put it this way, the very essence of my argument is, that aliens belong neither physically nor spiritually to our race. Conversion is an impossibility.'

'An ape cannot transform into a man,' Krauch interjected.

'Precisely. I could not have put it better. And, as our worthy Krauch here says, if we are to stop the inevitable decline of the

West, we must eliminate rats. But first we must present a convincing story. A story not *to* but *of* the German folk, of their purity, of their fighting spirit. It is their very idea of folkdom that they must fight for. After all, the noble German peasant does not easily lay down his plough and lift up firearms. Science may fashion the rifle he holds, but it is folklore that motivates him to pull the trigger.'

Krauch lifts his glass. 'Science must, of course, bow to the arts.' Boehm begins a satisfied smile that somehow freezes on his lips half formed. The other heads turn to see what he was looking at, and suddenly the room shifts. The diners became frighteningly real, like characters from a dream who remain after your eyes open in terror. And no denying it, the curiosity in the room is me.

The M is wearing off. A church bell, which has been tolling deep inside me, now swings off balance and sends jangles down my nerves. Can't stop myself from letting a nervous laugh escape. It comes out silly and high-pitched. A muscle jumps in father's cheek. 'Is this some kind of jest?' For a moment I don't understand. Is he angry because I'm wearing his second-best dinner suit? Then mother cries, 'Julia, what have you done to your hair?' Reach up and pat the bare nape of my neck. I really did cut it off. Wasn't just a dream then. Sometimes with M I can't tell.

Father has lost the power of speech, chest heaving like a dying engine, and it's left to Boehm, once again, to come to the rescue. Applauds me with his fingertips. 'So charming. There is a tradition of it in the legends of the medieval period. A woman dressed as a man to champion female virtue. Saint Pelagia spent a lifetime hiding under a tonsure and a monk's robe until her death. And the knight's wife in *Der Borte* dressed in male garb on a similar principle.'

'Young people today will have their little ironies,' says Krauch, his lips pulled back less in a smile than a sneer. Mother, recovering herself, adds brightly, 'Shall I have Klara bring you up a dish of *Rote Grütze*?' Dear Mother. Thinks all situations can be fixed with a sweet taste in the mouth. I shake my head. 'I think I need a little air.'

Threw me out that night. Standing before me that proud face, impeccably Prussian. Men like Father are not born but carved from granite as if some inverted Medusa stalked their ancestry giving life to stone. Such a mix of contempt and disgust in that porphyry gaze, felt myself returning to petrification. He spits out that familiar/unfamiliar word. 'Julia, I do not know what you are. Your grandmother had Italian blood and possibly that has tainted you. Perhaps the fault is mine for allowing your mother so much say in your upbringing.' Make protesting noises, but I'm facing Goliath *sans* sling. Father addresses the ghost suspended between us. 'I do not know how long this has been going on beneath my roof, but I do know that you will leave this house forever and never come back.'

A high-pitched sound escapes. Am I laughing? 'Because I cut my hair? Really, Father, you're not serious. Tell me you're joking.'

'You'll find one month's allowance amongst your belongings. Expect not a penny more.' He makes as if to leave.

'Wait! What's mother going to say? Does she know what you're doing?'

'Your mother has had enough to deal with. She had to manage the scandal after you got yourself expelled.'

'That was years ago.' Father is unmoved. 'The gardener complained that you have been calling yourself Jules and acting unnaturally around his daughter.'

'It was nothing. A jape. That's all. Father—'

But he's already at the door. For a moment he pauses, considering, then glances over his shoulder one last time. 'You can keep the suit.'

§

'So you came to Berlin because you had no choice.'

'Exactly.'

'Did your father's Nazi sympathies worry you?'

'I don't know. I'm not a political type. I suppose it's selfish, not thinking of others, but I was young and afraid of him. I thought I would find a way to be at peace in Berlin.'

'Did you?'

Situation is becoming untenable. Junior is bleeding me dry and there's almost nothing left in my valise to pawn. Came home last week to find Junior strutting about in a brown shirt harassing a little Jewish girl half his size. Comment on the manliness of the act only for the witless wonder to square up to me. *So glad we crossed paths. Had heard the most fascinating talk on sexual deviants today.* He draws out the word 'deviants' savouring the thrill of saying it. *'It's true, Herr Vogelsang. Every word. They are destroying society alongside the Jews.'*

The little girl runs off and his sly eyes follow the path of her flight. 'Thing is, Herr Vogelsang, I can't seem to get it out of my head. Keep thinking and thinking about how it's the duty of a good citizen to report these things. What do you think? Should I do it?' Consider doing violence to the impudent upstart. Instead, mumble something about not being hasty, sleeping on it, he who leaps et cetera. He nods gravely. 'It's just so hard to think of anything else. If only I had a distraction. Money for the cinema say?' He takes the marks from my hand. 'And enough for a meal out afterwards?' More lucre crosses his palm. "Perhaps a drink or two…might I invite a friend?"

I should leave, of course, slip away in the night. But Junior's constant harassment has drained my faculties. The M I take to help me sleep leaves me tossing in my covers, while my morning dose of C makes me jittery and undecided by day. Sometimes I look in the mirror until my reflection blurs and shifts. The jawline too soft. The shoulders too skinny. The man I am is disappearing and I haven't the strength to fight.

During the night all hell breaks loose. Junior and his dun-coloured compatriots cause some kind of ruckus in the stairwell. Shrieks and howls. Entire building sounds as if it's in the grip of some fantastic night terror. Rumour has it that a man has been arrested. Apparently, he was caught holding hands with another man. Junior and his gang are quick to report him, and the criminal police—the ones they call the *Kripo*—waste no time in turning up, batons in hand. One of the men escapes but the other went on 'resisting' even after he was unconscious. Droplets of his blood stain the walls outside his door. 'Paragraph 175,' Junior says with his wolf's grin. 'Gets 'em every time.'

§

Head off at the earliest possible opportunity, walking aimlessly along the banks of the Spree. A belly cramp reminds me that I've eaten nothing since supper the night before, but I'm also out of cigarettes. Money won't stretch to both.

Purchase a pack of Trommlers at a kiosk and light up at once. A moment later a group of youths march past swinging their arms with military precision. They are singing what is becoming a familiar ditty. '*When Jewish blood runs off our swords, things are going to be better than great...*' Their high clear voices chill me more than the rain. Stand up and dizziness nearly cuts the legs from me. Can't sit back down though. Need to get away.

§

'*Where are you now?*' Mouth clams shut. Gives me a narrowed, suspicious look.

'*Who are you?*'

'*It's me. Lexie. We're old friends.*' Considering then relaxing. Slight nod to self.

'*Friends. Yes.*'

'*Tell me where you are?*'

'*Paradise.*'

TWENTY

JULES:

A waitress, sheathed in a cheongsam so short it barely grazes her stocking tops, places a glass of champagne before me, and too embarrassed to admit my penury, I let it sit untasted. The comedienne is finishing her act. 'Very religious people we Germans.

Known everywhere as people of the Book. Pity these days the book is Mein Kampf...'

I know her name now, Mopsa Hirsch, an ironic pixie who shakes us with laughter until we see the world more clearly. She takes a long drag of the cigarette then blows it out in my direction. 'If you're an informer, I can speak more slowly so you have time to write it all down.' Don't know what to do. Shake my head vigorously while laughter chimes around me. The dazzling gypsy holds my gaze a moment longer then shrugs and continues her set.

Other acts follow, a burlesque by a plump blonde, who half-heartedly throws handfuls of sequins at the audience while her sullen mouth telegraphs her displeasure at having to rehearse. The dark-eyed comedienne is talking to the barman—a middle aged daddy, whose rolled up sleeves are held in place by garters—but it's impossible to hear what they are saying.

Trying to decide whether the beautiful woman singing is actually a man in drag, when a smoky voice says in my ear, 'You don't like champagne?' Our soulful priestess of jest is suddenly at my side.

'No—Yes. I love champagne.' She lights a cigarette—which I can now see is a French brand—and takes a seat. She looks at me through fronds of curling smoke. 'You're new here?'

Try to speak but find throat is a dried-up stream. Wish I could quaff down some champagne. Voice comes out weak and full of hesitation. 'I was wondering if—that is to say if you might consider offering me a job.'

A frown. 'A job?' Her reaction is not encouraging.

'I would be willing to do anything. Wait tables, wash dishes.'

'I see,' she says, although it is not clear what she is seeing. The hope, which I carried bunched up inside me, is turning to stone. I feel hopeless. The waitresses are all tiny imps in alluring wisps of silk. My short blond cowlick and masculine features hardly fit the bill. Glance about looking for a solution to present itself. Piano catches my eye.

'I can play. I promise you, I'm good.'

She stares at me without speaking. 'You want to play piano?' The barman arrives—despite her female gender no-one would ever call her a barmaid! 'Everything all right, Mopsa?' Mopsa! That name from the nursery. A name for a fairy. She strokes her bottom lip with a fingernail. 'Wants to be our pianist.'

'We have Lotte.' Mopsa gives a tight nod and sucks in her lower lip. When she looks at me again it is through a gauze of regret. 'You see, it's not really practical.' Her eyes are unfocused and an apologetic smile plays about her lips. 'I'm sorry. You understand?'

'Of course. I'm sorry to have troubled you.'

She pulls a face. 'No trouble at all. Stay and enjoy the rest of the show if you like.' Can think of nothing I'd like better, but some violent urge propels me to my feet. 'I'm sorry,' I say again. 'A pressing business engagement—' Mean to go on but my chair falls over and the table lurches off to the side and the last thing I remember is the sound of the champagne glass shattering on the floor in a thousand crystalline notes.

§

When I open my eyes again, I am on my back, head cradled on Mopsa's lap. Close them again and hope to die in this one perfect moment. No such luck. The barman shakes my hand. 'Come on now. Wake up!' Mopsa is gentler. 'Easy now. Poor thing's half starved.' She strokes my cheek. 'Let's get you something to eat.' Helps me into a sitting position while the barman—whom I discover is known as Madam Flaubert for reasons never adequately explained—returns with bread and bratwurst.

Practically snatch it from her hands and bite off chunks like a greedy child. Have no inhibitions about accepting seconds and washing it all down with a couple of glasses of beer. Strength begins to return. Fingers tingle. Head clears.

Am reluctantly chewing the last mouthful of bratwurst when I realize Mopsa is gazing down at me, hands on hips. 'What's your name?'

'Jules. Jules Vogelsang.'

'Can you really play?'

Nod and offer a muffled, 'Mmm hmmm.'

'Show me.'

The piano is a rather battered old Bechstein but it's properly tuned and gives out sweet clear sound when I give the keys a tentative tap. What to play? Years of lessons from Frau Trinkenschuh make me bang out Brahms. Fingers are stiff and I play badly. Mopsa frowns and she and Madam Flaubert exchange glances. Fast as I can, segue into Jazz, Gypsy Wine followed by Musik Musik Musik. Lightness returns and infects the room. Madam Flaubert's expression becomes slightly less steely and two girls get up to dance.

Mopsa's touch on my shoulder brings it all to a stuttering end. Stare down at the keys afraid she is about to thank me for my time and ask me to leave. 'Lotte isn't always reliable,' she says slowly. 'She's never here on Mondays or Wednesdays.'

'And she's unpredictable on Tuesdays and Thursdays,' Madam Flaubert adds.

Mopsa sighs. 'She even called in sick last Saturday. I mean Saturday! Our holy day.' Madam Flaubert shakes her head in sorrowful agreement. Want to blurt out that I would never let them down, not if I had to give up my last crust, but am afraid to speak, to break the spell that I might be wanted.

Mopsa drums her fingers on the top of the Bechstein. 'We need a backup, a stand-in to cover Lotte's 'indisposed' days.' Before I can answer, she holds up a hand. It's white, slightly chubby, like a child's. Want to take the fingers in my mouth, one by one. What would they taste of? 'It won't pay much,' she is saying. 'But our wardrobe mistress, Ilse, can give you a clean collar and cuffs and you won't starve.' Holds out her hand and I take it in mine. There's a fluttering movement, like a bird's quick heartbeat then she pulls away. 'Deal?'

'Deal.'

§

'Darius—Jules? What day is it?'

'Saturday.'

'It's actually Wednesday.'

'Of course, Doctor Song. How silly of me.'

'You're smiling.'

'The world is just… Have you ever noticed how beautiful it is?'

'Even with the Nazis in charge?'

'Oh them. Tiny tin soldiers. They can have their guns and their boots and their great political speeches. There's only one thing I want.'

'What's that?'

'For you to love me.'

§

Life moves like water, limpid, glassy, suffused with light. Perhaps there is a moment like this for everyone, a moment when everything starts to make sense? In ancient days men left their homes to search the empty spaces of the earth; why risk life and limb except for the desperate need to find one's own tribe? I have found mine. Like some subterranean king, I descend into my realm each night and play and play—mixing blue notes and mellow loops and rich African rhythms—while suited satyrs whisk tiny nymphs from their barstools and whirl them around in what has become our very own *Jazzdämmerung*, our jazz twilight, because deep down we know this cannot last. Yet if we sense this is our final bite of the cake, we don't show it. *Live tonight; die tomorrow* is our frenzied toast and we willingly throw ourselves upon the bonfire of the illusive present and let it light us like martyrs to Beauty.

Isn't unusual for me to play all night, joined by a thickset daddy on the double bass and a tall skinny drainpipe of a girl on drums. Once a little mite of a thing, with hair like a dandelion clock, stood with us, a saxophone fixed to her lips. The haunting notes mixed with the wilder tempos of percussion and string, gave it a mournful soul-filled quality suggestive of sad *adieus* (the kind where there is no sense of *au revoir)*, of endings and points of no return. There wasn't a dry eye in the house.

My *doppelganger,* Lotte, rarely makes an appearance, but on those occasions when she graces the club with her languid presence, I loll at a table while flirtatious girls, dressed like French urchins, vie for my attention. They ply me with champagne and stolen kisses—sometimes a little C to be secretly shared in the bathroom—as the daddies look on with unmistakeable envy.

But Mopsa, lovely Mopsa, maintains her crystalline distance, a moth caught in amber, beautiful, untouchable. She treats me, as she treats everyone, with utter indifference. Eager greetings are met with nothing more than vague bobs of the head or cool polite smiles. On stage she is as sharp as ever—*People think Goebbels doesn't support comedy. It's not true. He said we could have all the comedy we want as long as we don't make it funny. But don't get me wrong, he's a great man. And behind every great man you'll find a woman. Now if only she would get up the courage to pull the trigger.*

'What about Paragraph 175?' a heckler yells. 'Our queer brothers are being arrested under our noses and you're making jokes.' Mopsa takes a drag on her cigarette and blows out loops of blue grey smoke. 'Be glad Goebbels can't count to 176 or we girls will be in trouble too.'

Night after night I watch her in awe and in grave danger of an accident of a urinary nature. Yet my clumsy overtures are unfailingly crushed. Sidle up to her as she sits sipping Scotch after a late-night show. There are signs of fatigue around her eyes and sweat has made a Celtic crown out of the curls on her forehead. Twins in bow ties and spats perform a tap dance while gazing down at the audience through improbably large monocles which they switch from eye to eye. In the club, no-one talks about personal lives. It's an unwritten rule. But you can pick things up if you listen closely. Swirl my glass until the ice cubes clink and screw up my courage to ask Mopsa a question. 'You're Jewish?'

'You didn't know?'

'No. I mean…you don't seem Jewish.'

'What does a Jew seem like?'

'I don't know. Religious?'

'Are all Christians religious?' I don't know what to say. The tomboys and the daddies laugh, and I'm dismissed, the stooge, the sidekick, there to contrast her brightness with my dullness. Is her cruelty intentional? Does she think the joke laughs at itself?

I hate her. I love her. Take to watching jealously for some rival to my unrequited affections. And in that, at least, I am happily disappointed. She treats everyone with the same superficial warmth that seems to armour her against all intimacy. No-one is special, with the exception of Madam Flaubert, with whom she is thick as thieves. Yet I cannot bring myself to believe she goes to sleep enfolded in those meat-crushing arms.

But it's not only her indifference which infuriates. There are times when she simply disappears.

TWENTY-ONE

'Mopsa vanishes?'

'Like a pantomime fairy disappearing in a puff of blue smoke. One minute here, the next gone. And the weirdest part is that no-one comments. Mme Flaubert wipes the bar and ignores the abandoned, half-filled glass. The daddies, who have crowded in so eagerly, float away suddenly released by the strange force of attraction. Where do you go, pretty Mopsa? Where do you go?'

'Do the others know?'

I ask, of course. My questions are rebuffed or disregarded, and it's clear that to inquire further would be deemed unforgivable gaucherie. No-one says a word. A thin mist of conspiracy hangs about the place, and only when it comes close to time for Mopsa to take the stage do Mme Flaubert's hands tighten around the glass she is polishing and her glance goes anxiously to the clock. But Mopsa never misses a turn, casting her coat and hat as she runs downstairs, cheeks cherry red.

"Of course I'm happy to say Heil Hitler? Who wants to say, "good day", in times like these...Does Goebbels love the theatre? Sure, he loves closing them down."

§

JULES:

Follow her once. Instead of rehearsing, I send a note saying I have a cold then stand in a doorway across the street—a shoulder against the jam, ankles crossed, smoking one gritty Trommler after the other—waiting. Time passes. Shadows lengthen. The next time I try to light up, the match stutters out between my numb fingers. I've been a fool. She isn't coming. Push the Trommler back into the pack ready to go. A woman is crossing the road, tight belt and hat pulled low on her brow. She is almost past me when something about her walk, that stiff, clumsy, almost childish, gait gives her away. Mopsa is on a mission.

I could close the gap in a few strides, but something holds me back. Mouth feels numb from C but the rest of me is crouched, a starving wolf with the lamb in its sights. Wherever she is going, it is not nearby. She takes a train and then another but gets off almost at once. I'm afraid I'll lose her in the crowd of men and women swarming up the stairs. It's hard to keep her in sight. Every so often she glances over her shoulder, forcing me to take evasive action. Practically knock over a woman, pushing a perambulator. Profuse apologies follow, raise my hat, admire the wrinkled tyrant ensconced in its chariot. Where is Mopsa?

The street is empty, and panic puts a noose about my neck. Tell myself over and over that it doesn't matter. She will appear again. I will follow. But the wolf inside me won't let go. Something dangerous scents the air. It makes me frantic. Run to the terminus of the street, where it bisects another, and search up and down. She isn't there. Turn back, retrace my steps more slowly until I am standing at the spot where earlier I collided with mother and infant. Nothing. She has vanished in the blink of an eye. Inside one of the buildings? There are no cafes or shops. A wilderness of windows looks back at me.

About to admit defeat when I notice a narrow seam running between two tenements. Too small even to be called an alley. Did Mopsa really squeeze herself through this narrow birth canal?

Where could it lead except to squalid back courts and open middens?

The smell hits me first, rotting cabbage and urine. Walls graze my shoulders and I'm forced to walk sideways, feet slipping on the damp cobbles. Bend my head to duck through a narrow archway but hesitate when I hear voices. Mopsa. Those unmistakable smoky tones. She's clearly straining against anger.

'Half before. Half after receipt of safe delivery. We agreed. You agreed.'

'Things changed.' A male voice, out of the gutter, but lazy, a rat king comfortable in his own territory.

'What things?'

'Don't matter. Things.'

Mopsa's voice grows a little louder. 'We're paying you a king's ransom.'

'You're paying me peanuts. It's worth a hundred times what I'm getting.' A little gasp from Mopsa and Rat King laughs nastily. 'Didn't think I knew that, did ya? Thought you'd pay peanuts and watch the monkey taking all the risk.'

Mopsa's voice falls like ash. 'Don't worry. You won't be taking any risk. I'll find someone else.'

'There isn't anyone else.'

'We'll see.' A cry from Mopsa, high and frightened. 'Let go!'

§

Mopsa's words seep down to where my consciousness is hiding. 'You fool. You poor, poor fool.' For a moment I slip through time so that I am back in Schokolade, my head resting on Mopsa's lap. Close my eyes, but she slaps my cheeks lightly. 'We can't stay here. He'll come back and he won't be alone.' Scramble up using my elbows then seize her by the shoulders.

'Did he hurt you? Are you okay?'

'I'm fine. He wanted to intimidate me, not kill me. I think.' Thin laughter fails to convince. Holding up a cardboard cylinder, the kind used to transport artwork, she strokes its edge tenderly. 'At least he didn't get this.'

'What is it?' But my words draw down a curtain between us. She frees herself and takes a step back. 'Better you don't know.'

'Tell me.' A mulish look, about to shake her head when a trickle of blood from my nose startles us both. Reaching up, I find it to be throbbing tenderly. Hold crimson-tipped fingers out to Mopsa. 'I've earned an explanation.' Bites her lip, looks away. She's not going to budge.

'Mopsa?'

Suddenly her eyes are all I see, possibilities shifting across them as she moves from suspicion to uncertainty to defiance. 'All right,' she announces. 'But not now. Not here.'

§

Her rooms are not far from Schokolade. We tiptoe up a tiled stairwell to the second floor, where she opens the door with a key. A spacious hall leads to a well-kept sitting room—a sleek *style moderne* sofa, two *Bergre* armchair, a *Bambrach* baby grand placed upon a French rug in the corner. 'You live here?'

'Sure. Why not?' The walls are covered in artwork, beautiful old pieces and several more of those strange landscapes containing the floating eyes.

'You like this artist?'

Mopsa is removing her coat. '*I am* the artist.' Astonishment makes me crass.

'You paint?'

'I used to.'

'Not now?'

'Not since they kicked me out of the Academy.'

'But why?'

'For the degenerate nature of my painting. Oh yeah, and for being Jewish.' Follow her mutely into the kitchen where she is running water over a towel.

'Don't you sell the paintings in the gallery?'

'Have you seen a customer?'

'I—' People go into the gallery all the time but, now I think on it, only as they might pass through the foyer of a theatre on their way to the main venue. With an elbow she closes the tap and wrings out the cloth. 'The Nazis are closing down Jewish firms and throwing people out of their jobs. The gentiles are too afraid to buy and the Jews are too poor.' She turns to me. 'We could really use a steak for that eye. You'll have a shiner by the morning.'

'It's nothing.'

She gives me a look. 'Don't be a hero.'

'I wasn't trying to be heroic.'

'No? As I recall, you came charging out of nowhere screaming threats. At least you got in one good punch before he knocked you out.'

'Hardly a hero then.' Take the towel from her and press it to my eye. It feels cool but her fingers would soothe more.

'It takes courage to fight a battle you don't think you can win.' She leaves something unsaid, and I feel her retreating again. Not this time. I've waited too long.

'I'll make some tea.' She makes as if to pass me then halts. Her eyes grow large and her gaze drops to her wrist, which she finds inexplicably imprisoned in my hand. For the thinnest splinter of time, we stay like this. On the very cusp. In the void between heartbeats. She might pull away or throw me out or melt, like a thawing rose, in my arms. Hope and possibility bloom in the silence between us. 'Show me.'

She pulls herself free but this time it is only to lead the way. On the large dining room table, with its cloth of Bruges lace, she opens the cylinder, and with a midwife's reverence, retrieves the canvas inside.

There are many beautiful pieces in the room, and Mopsa is no mean artist herself. But all fade to nothingness in comparison with the painting that now lies before us. My first thought is Giotto. Those deep sad blues that make the heart reply with its own dark timbres. But this is not a medieval Madonna stiffly presenting an infant with the scrunched-up face of a middle-aged man. The woman looking up at me, with eyes the colour of iridescent pea-cock feathers, is from a later age. An age that was beginning to turn its gaze from heavenly miracles to explore the infinite nuances

147

inside the human skull. Those flowers in her hair, edelweiss, star of Bethlehem? Jessamine perhaps? There's so much loneliness in her expression. A woman utterly alone, utterly unknown, and yet somehow, familiar?

'Beautiful.' It's Mopsa who speaks.

I appreciate art, of course. No-one of my class and education could be unaware of the great masters. But never before—in a hundred visits to museums—have I met its living embodiment and felt my pulse quicken. 'Who is she?

'We don't know. We believe she was painted by Giorgione of Castelfranco sometime in the early sixteenth century.'

'Bellini's student?' I can't think how I know that, but it doesn't matter because Mopsa is smiling at me.

'Yes. He's hard to pin down because he rarely signed his works. You can see here—' She points to a corner of the canvas. 'A 'G' and the date 1508 or possibly 1509.'

'What makes you think it belonged to him?'

'Because of a letter.'

'From whom?'

'Isabella D'Este, Marchesa of Mantua. Shortly after Giorgione died, she wrote to her agent saying that there was a rumour that the artist had painted a very original and beautiful *notte*, a night scene. But the agent was unable to locate it. There was some suggestion that it had been sold to the Contarini or Beccaro family, but the agent was doubtful about the quality of those paintings.'

'And you think you have it here?'

'It has been in the family for a long time. There were Jewish art dealers operating in Italy during the Renaissance, and my mother believed we were related to a known agent called David de' Cervi. Cervi means 'deer' the same as our surname 'Hirsch'. He had a connection to the d'Este family too. We know that he worked with Cesare d'Este, Isabella's great-nephew.'

'Then why didn't he sell the painting?'

'We don't know. Perhaps he couldn't get the right price. Or the deal fell through. Or maybe he just couldn't bear to part with it. I know I couldn't.'

'And it's been with your family all this time.'

'Yes. Sometimes locked away. Sometimes hidden in plain sight. The oddest part is that it has always been gifted from mother to daughter. We've held on to it for generations.'

Look back at those imploring, painted eyes. Wish I could fathom the message they are trying to communicate. A pricking thought makes me say, 'But weren't you trying to give it away to that man in the courtyard?'

A mistake. Mopsa's eyes widen as though I've slipped a knife beneath her ribs then she starts to reroll the canvas. Our intimacy is shattered. 'Mopsa?'

'It's different for you.'

'What do you mean?'

'I mean it's different.' Suddenly she is shouting. 'Out there. All you have to do is show the world your armpit and cry *Heil Hitler!* No-one is hunting you!'

'That's not fair.' Try to take her arm but she shakes me off. 'Mopsa? What did I say? Tell me.' Try to take her arm again. Again she shakes me off.

'My name is not MOPSA!'

'But—'

'Ziva. My name is Ziva.'

'I thought—'

'You thought I was named after a fairy?'

'I—Yes. I suppose I did.' Let my eyes drop unable to meet the appalled expression in her eyes. The carpet has a pattern of pale pink tea roses twined with a briar of thorns. A snort attracts my attention. Mopsa is laughing, a wild helpless sound that is as irresistible as it is repellent, pulls me in as a madman might pull a hapless passer-by into his frenzied dance. 'Why—why are we laughing?'

She is doubled over. 'What a world…what a world…'

'What do you mean?' Laughter is spurting out my nose. Mopsa grips the edge of the table.

'Everything—I mean everything— is upside down.'

'I don't understand.'

'Our heroes lie and steal. Hate is good. Tolerance is bad. Art and poetry go up in flames. Everyone cheers! Might as well join in the fun and burn the Giorgione myself.' She is crying now, the laughter simply the seismic shudder that precedes the flow of tears.

'Mopsa…Ziva, don't.' Grip her shoulders and hold her against me. Absorbing the hiccoughs and shakes. Gripping tighter when she tries to pull away. A gasp and her face lifts at the exact moment I lower mine. So close now our breaths intertwine like swans' necks and the moment of truth has arrived.

I have none of her clever words, but I speak with my lips against her cheek, her neck. My hands over her small hard breasts. Then down and further down until the hem of her skirt rises in my grasp as I sink to my knees: her thighs sweet; scent of almonds; a wisp of silk barring entrance; inviting; frightening; curtain drawn across the Pythia's lair. Brush with the tips of my fingers and she goes rigid then soft. With a groan, she lets go. She parts. Lets me in.

§

DARIUS:

'Hey, bro. Were you sleeping?'

'I—I'm not sure. I think I was dreaming.'

'Nice dream?'

'I don't remember.'

'Looked like it if that grin on your face is anything to go by.'

'Where have you been?'

'Sorry?'

'I haven't seen you in ages.' Seb blinks and glances to one side as though I might be talking to someone else.

'I was here yesterday.'

'Yes, of course. Yesterday.'

'Are you okay?' He peers into my face. 'You look tired.'

'It isn't easy living multiple lives.' I mean it to sound jokey, but Seb frowns. 'Is that really how it feels?' Mentally, I shrug. 'Ever woken up from a dream feeling more tired than when you went to bed?'

'Sure.'

150

'It's a bit like that, only—'

'Only?'

'More intense. I don't know how to explain. Dreams tend to hollow you out. The memories make me feel alive. But they can also be overwhelming. Think of having three…four times the number of memories a normal person has. Processing them is exhausting.'

'Is that why you're asleep so much of the time?'

'Am I?'

'Have you any idea how many times I've visited only to find you lost in slumberland. Yesterday, you were so deep you didn't twitch when Our-Lady-of-Sorrows Christian Women's Choir came and sang carols at you.'

'You're making that up.'

'If only. I begged the nurse for an injection of somni—whateveryacallit just to shut it out.' He pulls up a chair and straddles it backwards. 'So what's happening? Are you still a man born a woman dressing as a man?'

I pretend not to be annoyed by his tone. 'I'm still Jules Vogelsang if that's what you're asking.'

He looks at me in alarm. 'Now?'

'No. Not now. Now I'm just me.'

'How's the little comedienne? Still having the last laugh?'

'Playing hard to get.' I don't know why I lie. Why I don't tell him about the twilight Madonna or Mopsa's real name or how she turned into moonlight and melted into me. How, for one shining moment, I knew what it was to feel pleasure again. Perhaps I'm afraid of breaking the spell. Perhaps I'm afraid he's humouring me. Perhaps I'm an ungrateful shit. 'Seb, I—' The door swings wide and a lady from the WRVS pokes her head around. 'The choir is back and they want to sing you their version of *Funky, Funky, Xmas*.'

TWENTY-TWO

JULES:

The world is cracking around us. The audience at Schokolade dwindles night after night and even the acts begin to thin out. Lotte gives a final languid performance then disappears. Three days later her corpse floats in the Spree face-down. Suicide? Murder? Mopsa pleads with the authorities to investigate but they openly laugh in her face. When she insists, they grow sinister. 'Get out, Jew-woman. Go back and count your gold. We'll be coming for you soon enough.' Mopsa doesn't so much as flinch. 'Better come soon. It doesn't take that long to count to zero.'

Outside Mopsa grabs for her cigarettes. Drops the pack on the pavement, retrieves them but is trembling so much her matches go out one by one. Take it from her lips and light it myself, drawing deeply so that the tip glows before I hand it back. 'Was that wise? Baiting him like that?'

'Is it wise to roll over when your dog barks?'

That night atmosphere in Schokolade is febrile. Mopsa jitters through her jokes like an exploding Christmas cracker. 'Which race are Aryan athletes banned from? The human race. How many Nazi intellectuals does it take to defeat a Jewish one? I'll get back to you when we find one. What's the smartest thing to go through a Nazi's mind? A bullet.' The jokes come out so fast and hard the audience are bewildered. Their laughter is uneasy, strangled by the next quip. But Mopsa can't stop. It's as if she's swallowed every last grain of C I have hidden away. 'Hitler calls this a new age, but all he's really proved is two wrongs don't make a Reich. Two Nazis go into a bar. All the men jump on them and give them the hiding of their lives. As they lie dying, one says to the other, 'You idiot, that was a *bar mitzvah!*'

Mme Flaubert is glancing anxiously at the clock. Mopsa is overrunning her spot. She leans her meaty arms on the counter and whispers, 'Play the next act on. Play it loud.' Fortunately, the Kuckkuck sisters want a marching song for their skit. Start banging out *Alte Kameraden* for all it's worth and Mme Flaubert signals the curtain drop. Mopsa jumps back just in time. Doesn't stop her though. She's still yelling something about sauerkraut when Mme Flaubert finally drags her into the wings.

Am so jittery by the time we get home, I need some M. Mopsa isn't talking. Perches on the arm of a chair, head down, and stares at the floor. Dissolve some grains in whisky and pour it into two glasses. 'Take some.'

'I don't want it.'

'I'm not asking.' Expect argument but she takes it and downs it in one gulp, a sulky child swallowing hated medicine. But this is not medicine: it's magic.

Suddenly, we are in the eye of the storm, a strange silent place where life and death exist as equals. Bodies become worlds. Fingers are travellers. Mopsa runs her hand over the puckered well of my belly button. 'What are you?'

'A man.'

'What were you?'

'In agony.'

There are more words, but somehow their meaning disappears. Our eyes fill with fog and we are floating, half dreaming through pillowy clouds. Our fingertips are fireflies. Between Mopsa's thighs bloom butterflies. My tongue writhes, the serpent in our opiated paradise.

In the morning, light finds us through the chinks in the curtains. Our bodies glow. I have never been so happy. But Mopsa sits up suddenly, grasping the sheets around her. 'My love, what's wrong?'

'I dreamt we were at war.' Hold her tightly, feeling her breath in little puffs against my chest.

'It won't happen. The world will right itself. You'll see. The great civilizations can't go mad twice in one century.'

§

On our way to the club, we witness a group of brown shirts ransacking a family home. A family unit—mother, father, daughter, son—stand shivering against a wall. The mother has no shoes on. She is crying. But the others stare with shocked faces at a fire that is burning between them and the front door. It hasn't been going long and you can see the curling corpses of books as the flames consume them. Mopsa's feet slow to a halt. Hiss in her ear. 'We shouldn't stay.' But she is looking towards the doorway. Two brownshirts are heaving a large oil painting between them. It's too dark to see clearly. A landscape. Nineteenth century at a guess. They heft it towards the flames. Their leader appears in the doorway. He is clutching a silver menorah in one hand and has a ladies' fox fur around his neck. Visigoth tearing down Rome. 'Wait! What are you doing, you useless horses' arseholes?'

'We were following orders,' the smaller of the two brutes explains.

'Have you shit for brains? Kommandant Goering insists all artwork is to be taken to Central Headquarters.'

'Please,' the husband's voice squeaks out. 'That painting belonged to my grandfather.'

'And what good German did it belong to before he stole it from him?' the bigger brute snarls. The leader's approach is more direct. He smashes the candlestick into the husband's face and leaves him curled on the ground spitting out teeth.

§

On the edge of the stage, Mopsa sits, legs dangling, smoking cigarette after cigarette. The smoke is impenetrable. I can't reach her. 'Mopsa?'

'I'm thinking.' Stubs the butt out, reaches for another only to discover the packet empty.

'I'll get you another.'

'Don't bother.' The packet is a ball in her fist.

'We need to get out of here.'

'You want to go home?' Her eyes blaze through the smoke. 'There is no home. Germany is finished.' Feel my heart escape its moorings. For months now I have been wanting to hear these words. 'You're certain?' She throws the crushed packet on to the floor. 'Yes. But we need to take him with us.'

'Who?'

'Giorgione.'

'Are you mad? It's too dangerous.'

'I won't go without him.'

§

The argument rages for days. 'Mopsa, the Giorgione is wonderful. A masterpiece. But not worth risking your life for.'

'Art is all that is worth risking your life for.'

'You heard what he said, Goering wants to preserve art. He'll recognise its worth. He won't harm it. And after all this madness is ended, we can claim it back.' A stinging blow to the cheek makes my eyes water. Mopsa's face is red with rage. 'Do you think I would let that maniac put his filthy paws on it even for a second?'

And so it goes on. She slaps me. I slap her. By the end of the week her arms are dappled in bruises where I've dug my fingers in to shake her. But nothing changes. Mopsa's lips are still set in a sulky pout, her eyes barricaded against my pleas.

I try one last time. 'People are what matter. Beating hearts. Seeing eyes. No matter how beautiful the Giorgione is, it's nothing without you to see it.' See a flicker of doubt and push my point straight through her breast. 'Think, Mopsa, this isn't Einstein or some innocent child. It's pigment on canvas. Verdigris, lead, cinnabar. We don't even know what Giorgione 's motive was in painting it. Artists make their money from commissions. For all you know, it was just a meal ticket to him.' Another flicker, closes her eyes. Is she seeing things differently? Have I won?

Opens them again and her expression is so sad it tears my heart. 'My love, he might have been a monster, beat his wife, starved his children. You can't know he was a man worth saving.'

A little shake of her head. 'Is that what you think? That it's about saving the man? Men are flawed. Art transcends.'

On one thing we agree, we cannot just leave. A careful plan must be in place. But the noose is tightening. Mopsa writes to a distant cousin in America, but the response is not hopeful. They are already burdened with the pleas of closer relatives and have signed so many affidavits they doubt any more will be accepted. That same week Mopsa is followed home by an SS agent, who stands in the shadows opposite our apartment. He doesn't do anything, just smokes cigarette after cigarette flicking glow worm sparks into the night, but it spooks us and heightens our panic.

We apply for refuge in Britain only to find that the immigration standards have been tightened. Mopsa reads the letter in despair. 'They want fifty pounds deposited in an overseas bank. Don't they know it's illegal for us to have foreign currency?' We think of Palestine, but Mopsa worries for the Giorgione, and it doesn't matter in the end because the British restrict the immigration numbers. We hear that exceptions can be made to the fifty-pound rule, depending on an individual's training or education, and apply at once but the bureaucracy is painfully slow. Weeks go by and we've heard nothing. In desperation, I write to Mother begging for funds, but the letter comes back unopened.

We live in a nothing space, between one breath and the next, never knowing if we will be swallowed up or spat out.

TWENTY-THREE

'Jules, you must have been very scared.'

'We were. All our escape routes were cut off. No word from America, though Mopsa clung on to that hope for months. No route to Britain either.'

'You were trapped.'

'Not quite. We'd heard of a route that would take us to Shanghai.'

'Really?'

'No quotas, no need for affidavits or visas. It was our last chance. Only one thing holding us back.'

'Which was?'

'The Giorgione, of course. Mopsa had come to her senses. Knew we couldn't take it with us. Helga Zimmerman left last week, and a Nazi watched the whole proceeding to make sure she didn't take anything valuable with her.'

'Can you take me to the time when you hid the painting?'

§

JULES:

'That's your decision, is it?' Mme Flaubert's meaty fingers are polishing a glass while giving the impression she is hooking an eye from its socket.

Mopsa nods. 'We need to move the Giorgione.' For an instant she brightens. 'Have you heard any more about the rumours Peggy Guggenheim is sneaking out art in crates of bedlinen?' Mme Flaubert spreads her hands. She hasn't heard anything. Another dead end. Mopsa's shoulders sag. Want to put my arms around her but my hands are shaking so badly the only way to hide it is to sit on them.

'There is another way,' Mme Flaubert says. 'But you're not going to like it.'

Mopsa sits upright. 'Tell me.'

'Two words. Hildebrand Gurlitt.'

'Are you mad? He works for Goebbels' art commission.'

'Pah.' Mme Flaubert blows her cheeks out. 'He works for the devil, that one. And he has his protection, believe me. He's a second-degree *Mischling*. Jewish grandmother on the father's side. But he's clever and he has contacts, so they use him to buy and sell art.'

Head is pounding and I'm only half following what's being said. I want to go home and lay my head against Mopsa's welcoming breast, but Mme Flaubert has her attention.

'Rumour has it, he's buying Jewish art for his own collection.'

'They let him do that?'

'He's useful to them. For now.'

'And you think he would take the Giorgione?'

'Sure. They say he already has a Matisse and a Van Gogh. He's a shark. The night scene will attract him like blood in the water.'

Mopsa looks wildly about for a moment then shakes her head. 'It's too dangerous. 'A man like that will never return it.'

'Or his overlords will get wind of it and take it from him,' I suggest.

A silence. Mme Flaubert gouges the glasses clean. Mopsa chews the end of her thumb.' Unless—'

Heads whip round to face me. 'Unless what?'

'Unless Gurlitt doesn't know what he has.'

Mopsa pulls a face then frowns. 'You mean like telling him it's a fake.'

'No.' Mme Flaubert puts the glass down. 'He's too clever for that. Besides why would he protect a fake.'

'Because it won't be fake.'

'What do you mean?'

'I mean, it'll be an authentic Ziva Hirsch.' Hurry on quickly before she can dismiss me. 'We know he collects degenerate art. Why not something by you?' Light is beginning to dawn. Mme Flaubert and Mopsa exchange looks.

'You're talking about painting over a Renaissance masterpiece?'

'Can it be done?' Mme Flaubert asks.

'Of course.' My confidence startles them. But no more than it shocks me. Where has this idea come from? 'You can protect it with a glaze or use a water-based pigment.' I speak with authority. As though I've done it before.

'Ye-s.' Mopsa is thoughtful. 'I can use gouache. It's water-based. I can remove—' Breaks off, biting her lip.

'What is it? Don't you think it can be done?'

'It isn't that.' Her eyes go blank as though they've turned around and are examining something inside her head. 'I feel as though I've said those words to you before.' And now she says it, isn't there a prickling echo in the locked away chambers deep inside my mind? But there's no time to ponder the ghosts we conjure between ourselves.

'You're mistaken.' I don't say it, but M can make the mind play tricks. 'Have you used this technique before? Some time at the academy maybe? That could be what you're thinking.'

'No. Never. But it doesn't matter. It won't work. Why should he want to buy a painting by Ziva Hirsch. I was still a student. Hardly known.'

'You've won prizes,' Mme Flaubert reminds her.

'It's not enough.' A sense of deflation settles over us. Need a bump from C and, on queue, my nose starts to run. Am just about to sneak off when Mme Flaubert thumps the table. 'You had a successful exhibition last year.'

'What? No I didn't.' Mopsa looks at me, but I am as bewildered as she is. 'Who was that artist you used to talk about all the time? The one who lived near the Belgian border.'

'Karl Hoffman?'

'Yes.'

'Did you ever go to one of his exhibitions?'

'No, they were in Cologne. He emigrated to America after the galleries refused to exhibit him anymore.'

'But you know he was successful?'

'Yes.'

'How do you know?'

Mopsa looks baffled then irritated. 'I read about him. In the newspapers.'

'Then why can't Hildebrand Gurlitt read about you?'

'Because I've never been in the papers.'

'What if you were?' Conversation is making my head throb. One of us has lost their wits and I can't be certain it isn't me. Mopsa rubs her temples. 'This isn't getting us anywhere.'

Mme Flaubert lays her trump card before us. 'Freddy,' she says.

'Freddy?' Mopsa repeats the word without understanding.

'Frieda Kauffman.'

I know who Frieda Kauffman is. We all do. A club regular, a fat rich daddy who drinks champagne and smokes odoriferous

Nicaraguan cigars. She has a casual lazy air of wealth about her, and she never misses one of Mopsa's shows. Suddenly it's so obvious it hits me like a shot of M straight to the heart. 'Mopsa, don't you see? Her family owned a newspaper.'

'So what? They shut it down.'

'But if the presses are still there…'

Colour drains from Mopsa's face. She looks sick. 'Would she do it? Fake an article about me? What if Gurlitt checked?'

'He's not likely to trawl through the archives. Besides—' Mme Flaubert pats Mopsa's cheek with a clumsy hand. 'I hear he has a weakness for a pretty face. We'll make sure to include a picture of you.'

'But he could check with the gallery.'

'We'll choose one that has already shut down, the owners gone. Nothing too fancy. The idea is to make it so plausible he won't enquire too deeply.'

Mopsa gnaws at a knuckle. 'I don't like it. We're trying to con a conman. And there are all the other risks besides, Disguising the Giorgione. Fooling Gurlitt. And what's Freddy's motive in all this? Do you think she's going to risk her life for art?'

'She'll risk it for you.'

Mopsa shrinks in on herself. 'I need time. I need to think.'

§

'Jules, what day is it?'

Laughter. 'Hmmmm. What?'

'What day is it?'

'Saturday, our holy day of forgetfulness.'

'Where are you now?'

'At Schokolade…You are very naughty.'

'I'm naughty? Are you talking to me?'

'Hmmmm? No. This one. This one is a very naughty girl.'

More laughter. Expression suggests sexual arousal.

'Who are you with? Is it Mopsa?'

Guilty glance. Suppressed mirth. 'This is Inge…or Anke. She serves the drinks. And that's not all you serve now, is it my sweet?'

Staggered inhalation as though sniffing something up. Head falls forwards.

'Jules? Are you all right?' Lifts head to look at me. Pupils are noticeably dilated. Mouth mischievous.

'Do you know what they call me?'

'No.'

'Inge or Anke just told me. Young Orlando. You know after the novel by that Woolf woman. About the creature able to change his sex. Got it the wrong way round I think. But hey ho.'

Turns head. Listening to something. 'Uh oh. Got to go.'

'Where?'

'Time to play piano.'

§

Stumble over to the piano chortling to myself. I've taken the C too quickly. Feel it bursting inside my head in a glorious *pop!* And suddenly I see how right things are. Mopsa. Me. Our future a golden thread disappearing off into the darkness. Gurlitt will take the painting then Mopsa and I will fly away to Shanghai, where we'll sleep on silk cushions and blow opium fumes into each other's mouths.

Hammer out a crescendo so loudly that our fan dancer, Rosa, drops her appendages with a bang and treats the audience to more than they've paid for. Mme Flaubert stares daggers, but it strikes me as hilarious and I'm still laughing when Mopsa takes her place.

She stands for a minute blowing blue grey smoke and looking as cool as one of the neo classical statues along the Palace bridge. You'd never know she was boiling inside. Strikes me that Mopsa would make the perfect poker player. Perhaps we'll take it up in Shanghai and make our fortunes. Mopsa holds out a hand and Inge-or-Anke runs on to the stage with an ashtray. Mopsa crushes out her cigarette and waits until Inge-or-Anke has retreated. 'These are hard times,' she says into the microphone. A few catcalls and a *Too right* is thrown back by the audience. Mopsa ignores them. 'Hard times indeed. Especially for comedians. You've got to stay on the right side of history. Yesterday I tried telling a joke to a Nazi. "Three Germans walk into a bar—'

With perfect timing the big, padded door bursts open and young men in their National Socialist Storm Trooper colours come pouring in. The funny thing is that no-one screams, no-one moves. Mme Flaubert holds a half-polished glass in the air, while my fingers hover silently over keys. The audience is frozen. Not even the flutter of a mascaraed eyelash. We are shocked by how young they are. Hairless children quivering with sexual violence.

Without warning, they rush the stage, yelling and pointing. 'Jewish whore! Jewish traitoress!' Apparently every insult can be enhanced by the insertion of *Jewish* before it. One of them climbs up and pushes his shiny empty face in Mopsa's. 'Do you think you can mock the Fatherland?' Flecks of spit hit her face. She flinches but does not wipe them away. 'DO YOU?' Mopsa's eyes narrow. 'Why would I need to mock the Fatherland when jokes like you run around on two legs?'

Oh Mopsa, why can you never keep that clever mouth of yours shut? His hand is so fast we don't see it coming. My ears ring with Mopsa's cry of pain as she hits the floor, the after-image of his fist smashing into her chest burning in my retinas. Such casual violence. A civilised mind cannot process it. Mopsa doesn't get up. Just lies there, a curled-up autumn leaf awaiting the crunch of a boot.

But her pain is a gong summoning chaos. Chairs fly. Tables overturn. Flocks of screams rise into the air and mingle with shouts of rage and shattering glass. Somehow, in the midst of it all, find that I have mounted the stage and knelt at Mopsa's side. 'Mopsa? My love. Please, please—' Look up to find myself staring down the barrel of a luger. It looks enormous. Behind it a fat sausage finger rests on the trigger. 'You,' says Shiny-empty-face, 'Get up.'

Do so slowly, palms visible, submissive. He is staring closely at me, the blond cowlick on my forehead, the breadth of my shoulders. 'Do you know what we do to nice German boys who sleep with Jewish whores?' When I don't answer, he pushes the luger into my face and continues, 'We march them through the streets with placards around their necks so that everyone knows they are race defilers. Then we cut off this—' He rams a hand between my legs. A look of surprise then disgust crosses his face. The luger presses against my forehead. Close my eyes. Oh God, Mopsa, I'm sorry.

A second goes by then another. Tentatively open one eye. Shiny-empty-face has gone and his compatriots are heading for the stairs. A change of heart? New orders? No-one seems to know. Mme Flaubert is at my side and we help Mopsa to her feet. She mops the curls from her forehead and looks out at the devastation. 'Whoa, for a minute there I thought it might turn nasty.' Torn between hugging and shaking her. She is defiant. 'We need to get things cleared up. Show's off tonight. But we'll show them. We'll come back stronger.'

Mme Flaubert's voice is oddly gentle, a mother soothing a child. 'Yes. Yes. But not tonight. Leave it tonight.'

Mopsa looks mutinous but she staggers slightly and needs my steadying arm. 'Take her home,' Mme Flaubert insists. Under her breath she whispers, 'Freddy says, yes. She'll do it.'

TWENTY-FOUR

JULES:

We know as soon as we reach the landing. The apartment door is half off its hinges, and a triangle of chaos shows through the gap. Tell Mopsa to wait and push the door to one side. Worse than I feared. The furniture we planned to sell all splintered and cracked, rugs soiled, curtains torn, and Mopsa's clever landscapes with their wise eyes lie smashed and blinded on the floor. But these are in-cidentals, minutiae that can be mourned at leisure. What makes my mouth go dry and the hairs stand up on the back of my neck is the bedroom door, which lies open. We hid the Giorgione at the back of the wardrobe, but that now seems a stupidly obvious place. How could we have been so reckless, so hopelessly naïve?

Behind me, Mopsa has sunk down on the remains of a chair. She says nothing as I crunch across a mosaic of broken shards—all that's left of Mopsa's pretty Dresden dishes— towards the bedroom. A moment later I am back. 'It's gone. Oh Mopsa. The Giorgione's gone.' What reaction was I expecting? Disbelief? Fury? Instead, a slow blink, the world weariness of those in the know. Stare at her, the light slowly dawning. 'You know where it is.'

'At Schokolade. In the gallery above. You've been passing it for the last week. Only now it's a scene of a lovely Aryan family sitting around the kitchen table having a lovely Aryan supper in their lovely Aryan home.'

'You didn't tell me.'

'You didn't need to know.'

'You didn't trust me?'

'No.'

Feel as though it's my turn to be punched in the solar plexus. Mopsa's face is haggard. Staggers to her feet and comes over to where I'm standing. For a moment I think she's going to embrace me, but she reaches into my pocket and pulls out the pillbox I carry there. 'How long?'

Shake my head. 'I don't know what you mean.'

'Don't you? When's the last time you got through a day without jittering on cocaine? When's the last night you slept through without using morphine?'

' Lodovico! That simply isn't—'

'What? What did you call me?'

'I—I don't—'

'Is that what one of your little waitresses is calling herself now? Or did you think I didn't know?'

'It's not like that. They mean nothing.'

'Oh good. That makes it all better.'

'That's not fair.'

'Isn't it? All this time I've been trying to find a way out and you don't get out of bed until the sun goes down.'

'I'm a night owl.'

'Only because you're so high at night you don't know how to come back down.'

Take her by the hips. 'You love me at night. You love how I play.'

'Yes, yes. You're full of wild hedonism. Live for the moment. No thought for the future. Nothing practical.' Pulls away, biting at the knuckles of a hand. Her chest expands in a huge breath then she goes on in a calmer voice, 'You don't want to live life. You want to dream it.'

'That's not true. I tried. I contacted my mother.'

'One letter. I've been searching constantly. Begging anyone who might know someone who knows someone else who might help us.'

'I'm sorry,' I say stiffly. 'I had no idea I was letting you down.'

'Oh Jules,' She takes my hands and stares up at me. 'Think. Not just about not helping. Think of the danger you're putting us in. How long would you have held out if they'd taken the drugs away? You'd have led them straight to it for a grain of C.'

'You're wrong. I enjoy it. I don't need it. I could give it up tomorrow.'

Her smile is hopeful. But her eyes are sad.

§

'How are you today?'

'Fine. Fine. Thank you for asking.' Restless. Looking about.

'One of the nurses says you had a nosebleed last night.'

'It happens'

'I spoke to Seb. He says you have no history of nosebleeds.'

'I don't know him.' Sweat breaks out on his forehead. 'It's cold in here.'

'Let me get you a blanket…Is that better?'

'Hungry.'

'The nurse said you refused breakfast.'

'Makes me feel sick.'

Thought I could do it. Really did. Meant to get up bright and early, but terrible lethargy holds me down until noon when the cravings kick in. Then nausea and chills are my constant dreary companions. Make a few desultory attempts at cleaning up then try to read self into oblivion, but the gnawing wolf inside me won't let me forget. There's food in the kitchen but it turns my stomach to think of it. Sleep is a phantom that does not materialize.

Mopsa rushes in and out checking on me and offering snippets of news. Freddy is a peach. The article has been written and now appeared in a copy of the Berlin Post dated more than two years ago.

In bed, Mopsa holds me as I shake and sweat. I'm hungry but I can't hold anything down. I'm exhausted but sleep is only black wings fluttering at the edge of my vision. 'I can't—do—this.' Fingers stroke my hair. 'You can. My beautiful boy, you can.'

A stroke of luck. Gurlitt wants to see the painting. 'He'll be in Berlin on Saturday night,' Mopsa explains. Sit up and search her face. After all this waiting. It's happening. 'Do we cancel the show?'

'No. We go ahead. I don't want those Nazi bastards to think they scared me off. It'll be my finale. We'll slip out after my act. He'll be waiting at the Grand Hotel and he's bringing the money.'

'But what use is that? We can't take out more than ten *Reichsmarks*.'

'Oh Jules, haven't you been listening. We'll buy furs and jewels. They don't stop us removing those and we'll sell them when we get to Shanghai. They'll be our mobile bank accounts.'

'Yes. Yes. I remember now.'

Cool fingers stroke my forehead. 'Go to sleep. In a few days, we'll be safe.'

§

Am jittery when the great day arrives. Awake to harsh pure light that turns the world shades of platinum. Head's the clearest it's been in days. Mopsa rolls over into my arms and she smells as enticing as new bread. Draw her to me and she comes warm and sleepy, and our lovemaking is a thing of rapture.

§

Perhaps the withdrawal is not complete or it's the sheer enormity of what we are doing, but the jitters strike me again as soon as we set off for Schokolade. Night cleaves away day and somehow the pools of darkness between the lamp posts are filled with menace. Even Mopsa seems afraid, clinging on to my arm and glancing behind her as we make our way towards *Rosenthaler Platz*. Two policemen pass by on the other side and her legs give way. Only just manage to catch her then hurry on not looking back.

Mme Flaubert is cleaning glasses behind the bar. She gives a casual nod as we pass but her eyes are tense. Mopsa disappears behind the stage and I sit down at the piano. Start off with a little *Mein Berlin* and Mme Flaubert sits a Scotch—a double—on the lid. Down it quickly playing one-handed. Fingers are slick; the keys slide beneath them. Oh, for a single grain of M to take the edge off.

The night crawls by. Audience is thin and scattered. They perch on mismatched chairs around tables that no longer sit true. Freddy, flamboyant as ever, sits at the front, two waifs in tow, waiting for Mopsa. One by one the acts count down. The Kuckkuck sisters. The fan dancer. The tapdancing twins. I have a headache that sends jagged sparks across my vision. Rub them away with the back of a hand, and when my sight clears, Mme Flaubert is at the edge of the curtain beckoning urgently. It's the interval before Mopsa's act. Usually I play a few mellow musings while the waifs powder their noses and the daddies order more drinks. And tonight, of all nights, isn't it vital to keep up appearances? But Mme Flaubert's signals grow more urgent so down the dregs of my scotch and wander casually backstage.

Mopsa is there. She's white about the lips. 'Jules, they're coming for me.' I don't understand and it's left to Mme Flaubert to say, 'We've received word. The Gestapo are coming to arrest Schokolade's comedienne.' Everything beyond the curtain fades. It is only we three in a tiny pool of light.

'Are you sure?'

'Inge brought us the news. Her brother works as a plumber and overheard talk while he was on a job.'

'Then we've been betrayed.'

'Does it matter? You two have to go now.' Mme Flaubert shoves the Giorgione , carefully wrapped in its cylinder, into Mopsa's arms.

'Run!'

Grab Mopsa's hand and turn, but heavy footsteps are already coming down the stairs. Mopsa and I look at each other, our eyes saying what our voices cannot. Schokolade is a basement. There is only one way out. Mopsa squeezes my hand. 'I love you.'

And there it is, the grace notes that make this mawkish symphony of my life real. Bend close to whisper in her ear, and she closes her eyes, thinking she knows what I am about to say. 'I'm going out there.'

'What?' Her eyes fly open, wide, terrorised. 'No!'

'It's all right. What you said before about art transcending everything, I understand.'

'No! No! Whatever I said. You don't understand.' She's clinging to me, and I begin to unpick her fingers, talking quietly all the time. 'People aren't all that unique. We're good. We're bad. Brave, cowardly, loving, cold. The moulds were set a long time ago. And they don't matter.'

'What are you saying?'

'That I'm not special. I've lived before. Someone just like me. Hundreds of times. And I will again. Over and over until the celestial lights go out. But with the Giorgione, it's different. It brought something new into the world. You could copy it a million times yet never capture the uniqueness of its creation. It doesn't matter if I disappear out there. You'll find me again. I won't have lived the same life and my memories will be different. But it will still be me. We are all out there waiting to meet each other.' Bend down and kiss her forehead. Mme Flaubert has her gripped by the shoulders and we exchange a brief business-like nod then I'm out the other side of the curtain. The audience looks up, startled but don't give the game away.

'Yesterday I tried telling a joke to a Nazi.'

The Gestapo are at the bottom of the stairs. They freeze at the sound of my voice. Schokolade's comedienne is not what they expected.

'Three Germans walk into a bar.'

'Stop,' says my Nazi friend. 'Are these Germans pure Aryans?'

'Yes.'

'You can't use pure Aryans as the butt of a joke.'

'Okay. Three Jews go into a bar.'

The Gestapo creep closer, letting me finish my joke. It's fun to watch a criminal spool out enough rope to hang himself.

'That's better,' my friend says. 'But we don't just discriminate against Jews.'

'Okay, A Jew, a communist and a queer go into a bar—'

'Wait,' he says, 'What about gypsies?'

'All right, a Jew, a communist, a queer and a gypsy go into a bar—'

'You missed out negroes.'

'Sorry, my mistake.'

'And what about Slavs?'

'Slavs, of course.'

'And defectives.'

Mme Flaubert and Mopsa are at the back of the room. They shuffle into the shadows and towards the staircase.

'Right. A Jew, a communist, a queer, a gypsy, a negro, a Slav and a mental defective go into a bar—But my Nazi friend is frowning. '*Are you protecting Jehovah's Witnesses?*'

'No, I swear. A Jew, a communist, a queer, a gypsy, a negro, a Slav, a mental defective and a Jehovah's Witness go into a bar—'

Mme Flaubert stops halfway up the stairs, deliberately turning back as though listening to the joke. Behind her, Mopsa is a shadow that wavers, disappears. Is gone.

My heart implodes. Becomes a cold dead star, but my voice is still strong. '*Is the barman an Aryan?*'

'Sure.'

'Why is he serving them?'

'All right. He is serving them, but the beer tastes like piss. So the Jew goes up to the bar and orders another round. *Thank God for Herr Hitler,* he says. The barman's taken aback. *You mean it?* The Jew points to the others who are laughing and talking around the table. *Are you kidding? Before the Nazis arrived, those guys all hated each other.*'

TWENTY-FIVE

LEXIE:

Jules Vogelsang is dying. As a doctor I'm desperate to do something. But I'm helpless, listening to a death that happened decades before I was born.

'Can you hear me?'

Darius turns his head. 'Mopsa? Is that you? Are you here?'

'What happened? Where are you?'

'On the floor...the stage...the floor.'

'Did Mopsa get away?'

'It burns. It burns.'

'Jules, what's happening to you?'

Head twists from side to side. Desperate expression on face. 'Like...an...iron...fist...punched through me.'

'Did someone hit you?'

'Shot me.'

'Someone shot you? After Mopsa left?'

'Just a boy.'

'Who? The person who shot you?'

'Over there. Eyes as innocent as a Bermejo angel. After you left. Cold now.'

'Is someone with you?'

A long low moan. 'Hurts.' Sweat breaks out on forehead. Gasping sounds.

'Jules, what's happening?'

'I—I want—' Gurgling. He's choking.

'Get suction in here. Quickly. Jules? Darius? Can you hear me?' Eyes roll back. Neck arches.

'Where's that suction—Darius?' Eyes snap open. He looks at me for a terrified frozen moment. 'What is it? What do you see?'

'You need suction, Doctor Song?' The nurse rushes in. She aspirates sticky fluid from his lungs. There isn't much and she gives me a puzzled look.

I pretend not to be surprised. 'Thank you. I'll take it from here.' Darius is quiet now. Eyes closed, he looks exhausted. How much more can he take? I should let him sleep, but I need to know. 'Where are you now?'

'In a dark place.'

'Have you been here before?'

He ignores the question, sighs. 'I'm glad you got away.'

'Can you describe where you are?'

'Mmmmm?' A groan. Only half awake. 'Be happy.'

'No. Darius! Jules! I need to know.'

'I'm leaving now.'

'What do you see? Please...tell me!'

A long sigh. He starts to snore softly.

I want to make it to the staff lounge. I don't make it. Somewhere between Darius's room and the elevators the wall leaps out and hits my knuckles. Fuck!

'Doctor Song?' Seb's voice mixes with my meltdown. Did he see me punch the wall? Smooth my shirt. Try to sound professional.

'Can I help you?'

'I want to talk about my brother.'

'Of course.'

'I'm worried. His delusions seem to be getting stronger.'

'The intervals of his recall have certainly been increasing.'

He frowns. Don't sidestep a sidestepper. 'You seem to believe him.'

'I keep an open mind.' Can't tell him I've watched so much death that I can tell the delusion from the real deal.'

'Maybe this isn't the right place for him.'

Try to keep my face steady. 'He's still undergoing rehabilitation.'

'He needs psychiatric help.'

'He isn't a danger to himself or others.'

He makes an embarrassed gesture, sticks his hands in his pockets, looks halfway down the corridor. 'I think he's getting too close.'

'Close?'

'To you.'

'I'm not sure I—'

'You know he believes you are some sort of lost love he's been searching through time to find?'

'Of course, some attachment is natural—'

'This isn't natural. His obsession is growing. Every time I visit he seems further away. I'm not sure this is the right place for him.'

'What do you mean?' Panic chalk-squeals my voice across the air.

'He needs to get away.'

'Moving him isn't a good idea. We're still running tests. And—' And what? Jesus Lexie, think of something. 'Your brother's brain is dealing with complex issues. We don't know why these memories are being constructed, but it seems to be important to his recovery.'

'You think he'll remember what caused the accident?'

'It's impossible to say for sure, but there are huge holes in his recall and the new memories seem to be a way of filling in the blanks.'

His eyes look into mine. 'You don't actually believe he's mentally time travelling in and out of past lives?'

Keep it light-hearted Lexie. 'I keep an open mind.' He's still looking at me. Need to drive the point home. 'At the end of the day, he's better off here. Another facility may be reluctant to step in when we're still monitoring the effects of the drug trial.'

He blinks slowly, expels air out of his nostrils. 'Hmmm. I see. Thank you for your time.'

He's not convinced. Shit. Shit! SHIT!

§

The thing about death is, it has a sense of humour. You don't get one for weeks then all hell breaks through.

'Victoria, can you tell me how bad the headache is on a scale of one to ten?'

'Eleven.'

'And your neck feels very stiff?'

'Yes.'

'Morning, Doctor Song. I'm Kirsty. I'll be helping out today.'

'Where's Tiana?'

'Off with a stomach virus. Half the staff have it. I've come up from Cardiology.'

'I see. Nurse, can you—'

'She's seizing.'

'Oxygen. Hold her...Damn, can't get the Venflon in...'

'Temperature 105, BP 150/95.'

'Buccal midazolam. 10mg.'

'Heart rate 120.'

'Shit. Somnipradine. Let's get two ampoules on standby. And call her consultant. Who is it? Crossley? Virdee?'

'It's Miss de Sola.'

'Fine.'

'She called in sick. We're not to disturb her.'

'Jesus, get the Somnipradine and call Jimm—St James's. We need an ambulance transfer.'

'They're backed up. They say they'll have one as soon as they're free. But it could be hours.'

'Heart rate is down. Temperature 99.3. She's stabilising.'

'What do you want to do?'

'Shit. Phone. Another emergency. Fuck, am I the only doctor on call today?'

'Everyone's off.'

'Yeah, you said. Okay. Keep an eye on her until the ambulance gets here. I'll be right back.'

'Hi, I'm Doctor Song. What have we got here?'

'Male, sixty-two years. Liver transplant. Started complaining of short sharp chest pain, worsening cough, bloody sputum—'

'Nurse talking to him when he collapsed.'

'No carotid. Start compressions.'

'Ready to shock. Clear oxygen. Stand back.'

'Shock at five.'

'Rhythm?'

'Burts of VT. Still no pulse.'

'1mg of Magnesium, please.'

'PO$_2$ 78.'

'Adrenaline 1mg. We need a transfer to St James's.'

'They're backed up.'

'Call them anyway.'

'Let's try once more. Ready to shock. Clear oxygen. Stand back.'

'Sinus. We're back in VT.'

'Compressions. Infuse Somni—'

'No. Cancel that. Let's try Lidocaine.'

'Who the hell are you?'

'Doctor Sanchez. I'm covering Doctor Agrawal's shift. She's down with—'

'A stomach virus. I know. I'm Doctor Song. We'll get to know each other once the patient has a heartbeat. Where's the Somni—'

'You can't prescribe it.'

'Why not?'

'They've withdrawn it.'

'What did you say?'

'Withdrawn—Doctor Song?'

'When?'

'As of today. It's been taken off the market. Didn't you get the notification? There was a presentation last week.'

'Doctor Song…Doctor Song!'

'Charging again. Clear.'

'It's not working.'

'He needs Somnipradine.'

'Not possible.'

'We need the Somni.'

'I've got a pulse.'

'He's in sinus. Rhythm is holding.'

'Doctor Song, where are you going?'

'I've got a patient to check.'

'Who are you?

'Lexie Song. Victoria is my patient.'

'Was your patient. I called Time of Death at five past.'

'What happened?'

'She was asystole when I got here. I did what I could.'

'And you are?'

'The Locum. John Parry. Just arrived to cover someone sick—'

'Never mind.'

'My notes are here, but I've not written them up.'

'I'll do it.'

'You sure?'

The door clicks shut and the noises fade, more than is physically possible. Death brings its own hush. Victoria Ollerton is dead. She died four and a half minutes ago. I say it inside my head, trying to convince myself, as I stand here looking down at her body. Looking for what? A sign that something escaped. Some indefinable quintessence that's catapulting towards the stars seeking rebirth? I wait for something to happen. Nothing does. She looks like an empty shell. If I put my ear to her chest, would I hear the sea? In a minute the nurses will be back with the mortuary trolley. I save them some time by pulling the sheet over her face. It makes no difference: she's already anonymous.

The door bangs open. Finally a face I recognise. Prisha from Pharmacy. 'Doctor Song!'

'Yes.'

'There's been a mistake. It shouldn't have happened. I don't know how it happened.'

'I'm sorry?'

'It's never happened before. It shouldn't. We have procedures. There's no way—But with so many people off—'

'Prisha, just tell me what's wrong.'

'The Somnipradine trial. It's been suspended. They suspended it.'

'So I heard.'

'But one of the nurses says she brought two ampoules in here. I don't know how she was able to requisition it. It really isn't possible—I need to know. Was it used?'

Somewhere outside the door comes the long *beeeep* of an ECG monitor. Chrysanthemums. I didn't notice them before. Wilting in a vase. They're badly dyed, the colours of a child's drawing. A radio playing at the nurses' station. The audience laughs at an unheard joke.

'Didn't you know?' Prisha asks. 'Doctor Song, did you use the Somnipradine?'

Her eyes come back into focus. They're huge. Pupils swallowing up the irises. *'Did you use it—Doctor Song?'*

'Yes. Every last drop.'

§

Lead white. It's the only way to describe the colour Liv's face has gone. For a minute now, low gurgling noises have been coming from her mouth, but nothing that comes close to resembling human language so it's hard to know what she's thinking. I want to reassure her.

'It's okay. I know what I'm doing.'

She shakes her head while backing away then collapses on to an old beanbag, which collapses further until she is virtually sitting on the floor, head in hands.

'Liv?' She looks up. 'Tell me you didn't.'

'I can't do that.'

'When?'

'As soon as I heard your car draw up. I was watching at the window.'

She checks her watch. 'Seven minutes ago.'

'I guess.'

'You guess?'

'It's seven minutes.'

'They'll strike you off.'

'Maybe. But there's plenty of precedent. Isaac Newton, Marie Curé, Barry Marshall: scientists have been experimenting on themselves for generations.'

'That's great, Lexie. Because statistics are going to impress the GMC when they carpet you for faking hospital records and illegally administering a stolen drug to yourself.' She pushes her fingers up into her hair and looks like a beautiful mad woman. 'This is going to kill dad.'

'It might kill me.'

Her hands fall and she gazes at me as though hearing me for the first time. 'God, yes. Have you taken your pulse?'

'I haven't taken anything. It's only been seven—now eight minutes.'

Liv is on her feet. 'Sit down. No, not on the beanbag. Take the chair by the window.'

'*Your* chair. I must be dying.'

'Glib. That's great, Lexie. I'll write that on the death certificate. Now give me your wrist.'

'I had to do it, Liv. I have to know if…there's anything more.'

'Shut up. I'm counting.' After a minute she lets my wrist go. 'Pulse is a little high. Could be nerves. How do you feel?'

'Honestly? A little disappointed. There was an adrenalin spike at the start but it passed almost immediately. Then nothing.'

'Let's count that as a win. Maybe we can cover your tracks. No-one has to know.'

A prickling sensation. Not tears. Don't let it be tears. Turn my head until the light from the streetlamp fills my eyes. It wasn't there when we rented the apartment. The council installed it by stealth one day while we were at work, a stark metal stem with an ugly helmet protruding from the top, as though the architect had once heard a description of a flower but never actually seen one. It casts a harsh white interrogator's light straight into my naked pupils until I can pretend the hot tears are just a reaction to the glare.

I'm still sitting there hours later, when Liv staggers in clutching a tatty old dressing gown, with a ripped pocket, around her. Her hair is astray and there are pillow creases on her cheek, but somehow she still manages to look like a geisha. Unfocused, her eyes wander about the room then double-take and pivot back to me. 'Jesus, Lexie. You scared the life out of me. Have you been up all night?' The question being too stupid to merit an answer, I heave myself to my feet and put my head in the oven. Liv's words filter in from behind. 'Wow, you were Sylvia Plath in a past life.'

'No.' I try to flip her the bird and end up banging my head on the oven door. 'I was looking for a clean mug.'

'In the oven?'

'I found one in the bath yesterday.'

'Try here.' Liv starts going through a basket of washing. 'So who do you reckon you were? Nefertiti? Golda Meir?'

'I was nobody.'

'Statistically more likely, I guess. We can't all be King of the World.'

'No. I mean. I was nobody. I didn't remember anything.' Liv gives me a look that says she has no idea what is upsetting me but that she's sorry for my pain. It's why I love her and it gives me the courage to say, 'It's okay. It was a long shot anyway.' She starts a nod, which is interrupted as her eyes bug. 'Aha!' She pulls out a mostly clean mug from under a pair of jeans and holds it aloft. 'Now all we have to do is find the kettle.'

§

Darius is in the day room. He's working on a voice-activated laptop, and doesn't notice me come in. I've been avoiding him for three days, and my attempt to sound natural backfires into a parody of the robotic voice that insists that *your business is really important* before putting you on hold for an hour. 'I'm sorry I haven't made it for a while. Things have just been…' I let my spread hands finish the lie for me.

'I'm glad you're here now.' He smiles at me. That special smile he reserves for me, except until this moment I never noticed. In fact, he's so pleased to see me, I feel the immediate need to deflect.

'What are you working on?'

He gives me a guilty glance. 'Still trying to locate our missing Madonna. Jules Vogelsang was correct. Isabella d'Este did send an agent after Giorgione's death looking for a 'night scene'. Seb thinks I must have known the fact about the d'Este letter and forgotten it. I'm sure Seb thinks I'm insane. But it gives me something to focus on. Something real.'

Real. The word spikes through me sharp as an adrenaline shot straight to the heart. Mentally I give a big gasp and sit up clutching my chest. What the hell am I doing? I'm living proof that Somnipradine doesn't work. Liv's a hundred per cent right. I'm Dorothy back from a trippy trip to Oz and realising Glinda is a subconscious version of Auntie Em. Time for us all to wake up. The past can't help him. He needs to move forwards.

'Look, Darius, I—' My legs feel weak and I pull up a chair to sit down. Stupid move. It'll be harder to get away afterwards. My eyes are trying to roll away from meeting his, but I wrench them back. I owe him this much. I owe him the truth. 'I want to—' He interrupts me.

'.*real Something .on focus to something me gives it But*'

'Wh-what?'

'.*insane I'm thinks Seb .Madonna missing our locate to trying Still*' The big smile on his face winks off and he turns abruptly back to his laptop. 'Darius, are you okay?' The nape of my neck is prickling and there's a cold feeling deep in the pit of my stomach. I've felt this before, as a child lying alone on a hilltop when the sun went behind a cloud, and everything was thrown into shadow. A feeling of otherness, of not being alone, of shapes moving under the surface.

Out of nowhere a bell starts tolling.

FOURTH LIFE

The Twilight Madonna

The memories of Seteney, a free Adyghean woman
and
also of the artist Giorgione Castelfranco

TWENTY-SIX

SETENEY:

So, this is Venice? Shrouded in fog and smelling of fish. I can hear bells. Great coppery waves of sound shuddering in the air. If my wrists weren't fettered, I'd put my hands over my ears. No-one else pays the slightest attention. City folk.

'You first, milady.'

There is a man's hand on the small of my back. He shoves me forwards knowing my fettered ankles will throw me off balance. I almost fall from the gangplank, skirts up-billowing about me, but he catches my arm just in time and wrenches me upright. 'Wouldn't want milady to take her bath too soon.' He finds it comic to pretend he thinks me a lady. The first time he did it I looked up in wonder. Was one of our dark-eyed, black-bearded captors human after all? But he started making a rutting donkey's honking, which I took to be laughter, and hit me with his whip. It wasn't a hard blow. It was the kind you give to animals to keep them in line.

A smirk curls his lips to show a set of rotten teeth. 'Hurry up, milady. Your prince awaits.' I would like to tear his eyes out with my nails.

I have tried several times, which is what got me kicked out of Constantinople. They displayed me there, naked, standing on a small wooden crate. I don't know what they did with the male slaves; I could see only women. Most were young, like me. The older ones were using their hands to hide the marks of childbirth along with their modesty. There were even a couple of crones who wept openly because they knew they had no worth, and as soon as they were dead, their bones would be ground up as fertilizer and spread on the fields. Our captors didn't bother to fetter our wrists and ankles. Where were we going to go?

We stood there for hours. The sun grew hotter. The shadows shrank. Eventually they erected a canvas awning over us as it occurred to them that our pale skin was beginning to char and crack. It wasn't an act of kindness. They didn't want the meat to spoil.

Gradually the market began to fill up with buyers rat scuttling amongst us and gawping at our wilting flesh. I got used to being pinched and prodded, my jaws forced open, my buttocks parted, all in the name of a thorough inspection of goods.

As the sweat trickled between my breasts, I made myself think of home. Pale sunlight pushing through treetops. Cold wind in my face. So high. A world on top of the world.

'What about this one?' I blink. A billowing galleon is standing before the block pointing at me. Behind her, two Nubians stand guard, while to the side, a scrawny youth—her son presumably—stares sullenly at the ground. 'What do you think, dearest?' He shrugs a shoulder into a lopsided hunch. 'I don't like her.'

'Why ever not?'

'She has funny eyes.' The galleon attempts to meet my gaze then thinks better of it, feigning disgust by pulling her veils across her face. 'These Tatar girls make very good housekeepers. You need someone to keep house for you, don't you?' He gives another sullen shrug. Doesn't care either way.

Tatars! It's the only word they have for us. Russians, Poles, Galicians, Bulgarians, Mingrelians, Alans, we're all just Tatars to them. They care more about where their dogs come from. The galleon is haggling my price. 'Two hundred and fifty *Kuruş*? Are you trying to ruin me?'

'Oh, just pay the man,' the son says irritably. 'The heat's intolerable. Do you want us all to melt while you shave an *akcheh* from the price?' He throws an order at his slaves. 'Take the Tatar bitch and let's go.' As he speaks, he grabs my wrist and wrenches me from the crate. Then something happens. I don't recall exactly what. But there's screaming and blood and lumps of hair. None of it mine. A woman's voice is howling in rage, *Not Tatar. Adyghean! Adyghean!* An almighty bang! A star explodes behind my temples and everything goes dark.

I wake up in the bowels of a ship bound for Italy. Bare boards digging into my bones and water dripping on my head. The air smells of death. A slave woman, who—irony of ironies— it transpires actually is a Tatar bathes my bruises with a cloth dipped in seawater slops. I can't do it myself as I'm bound hand and foot. 'They were going to kill you,' she says matter-of-factly. 'They thought you were possessed by demons.'

'Why didn't they?'

'No-one knows. God must still be writing your story.'

§

The slave market is very small. There can't be more than ten of us, and three are children. It's conducted on the steps of a church, while other goods—bolts of silk, velvets, brocades, barrels of wine, fine jewellery, sacks of coal—are traded along with us. The Venetians are a strange lot: faces from all shores converge here. Hard to tell who belongs and who is just passing through. At least they let me keep my clothes on.

Their jabber sounds high-pitched yet lyrical, the music of children. But not meaningless. My Tatar friend was a woman of many talents, and she knew the language of our captors. While the ship rolled and I clutched my stomach, she stroked my hair and whispered, *Doman sia megio de ancuo*. Tomorrow will be better than today. We'll see.

A couple of nuns take nervous little rabbit steps in our direction, a tall skinny one and a little round one with rosy cheeks. No chance to call out with the slave broker watching, but I send silent pleas in their direction and cough and clear my throat a couple of times. It works. The rosy one tugs on the other's sleeve and they look over. I make the sign of the cross and point to myself. Do they understand? They exchange looks then tentatively move towards me. I smile. They smile. The scent of freedom tantalizes the air. The tall one looks me up and down as the rosy one turns to the broker. 'How much?'

They can't afford me. After haggling for a while and invoking God's law to rain down thunderbolts on the heads of thieves, the tall one shakes her head and draws the rosy one away. They go off to inspect the children.

Shoulders slumping, I watch as they pick out a small boy with blond hair. The sound of a pig vomiting attracts my attention. The broker is laughing his boots off. 'Did you think that was going to save you? Making out you were a Christian.'

'I am a Christian.'

'Oh yeah. What's the name of the pope?'

'I—'

'Thought so. Head full of that Eastern nonsense, have you? You won't fool anyone. You're among the real deal here in Venice.'

'I'm as real a Christian as you.'

'Not possible, dearie. The church doesn't allow Christians to be enslaved.'

'How much for this one?' An older man asks the question. He's well dressed, but the richness of his clothing doesn't disguise the coarseness of his face. He's sliced men to ribbons to get where he is, and he doesn't care who sees it. The broker gives a small bow. 'I can see you are a man of taste. A gentleman scholar perhaps?'

'I deal in cloth.' He lifts my arm and inspects it as if deciding where to make a cut. 'What are you asking?'

The broker picks his teeth. 'Not cheap this one. Tatar. Top stock.' He quotes a price higher than the one he gave the nuns and adds, 'Intact too. Thighs tighter than the Virgin Mary.' The merchant doesn't answer. Without warning he reaches out and pulls my shirt from my shoulders. Wilted yellow blooms of old bruises decorate my flesh. He turns to the broker. 'Do you take me for a fool?'

'No sir.'

'She's damaged goods. I'll give you forty.'

'Forty? You're taking the bread out my children's mouths.'

'The only children you have scuttle on four legs in the sewers. Forty and not a *solidus* more.'

'You insult me, sir. You wound me. Sixty ducats.'

'You're trying to sell a piece of tenderized beef. You won't get ten for her on the open market and you know it.' On and on it goes with the broker exaggerating my worth and the merchant undermining it. Things become quite heated, and I am wondering if I might slip into the crowd unnoticed, when the merchant yells, 'Forty-five. Final offer. Take it or leave it.' The broker grimaces and beckons over the scribe to draw up the contract. By the satisfied look on the merchant's face, I can tell I'm a bargain.

§

I try to kill him twice. After he raped me the first time, I hit him over the head with a vase and ran for the door. He caught me by the ankle and dragged me back to the bed where he tore at me with less care than he would have treated a cheap bolt of cloth. The next time I was more careful. I stole a breadknife from the kitchen then hid it under the covers. As soon as he climbed on top of me, I stabbed it into his neck. But he was too quick for me and rolled to the side so that it glanced off his cheek, opening nothing worse than an oozing seam.

He cut off my hair for that. Then he tied my wrists together and dragged me along the banks of the Grand Canal. All the time talking. 'Ever heard of Bona? No, of course you haven't. She was a Tatar slave who belonged to a nobleman of the house of Barbo. A very ordinary household slave. But every family in Venice knows the name. Because, despite the great good fortune that placed her heathen soul in a civilised and Christian country, she murdered her master.'

We are very near the edge of the water. I feel its closeness lapping away the edges of everything solid. Palaces disappear in the evening mist. Gondolas spectral-glide through the water. Venice is a city from a fairy tale. But I haven't forgotten fairy tales emerge from darkness. He drags me to the St Mark's Piazza. 'Do you see those pillars?' I don't answer. 'We call them the pillars of justice. They brought Bona here then they built a pyre and burnt her alive until she was nothing but ash.' An unexpected yank on my bound wrists drops me to my knees. Hand pincering my neck. Lips at my ear. 'That is the justice Venice metes out on slaves who murder their masters. Do you understand, Marta?'

'My name is Seteney.' A punch deafens my ear. 'I asked if you understood, Marta?'

'I understand.'

TWENTY-SEVEN

LEXIE:

'Doctor Song?'

'I'm sorry?' Couches. Coffee tables. Copies of *The Lancet*. In the staffroom. How long? How did I get here? A tea trolley is standing before me, and attached to it is one of the orderlies. She's looking at me with a slightly puzzled air. 'I asked if you wanted tea or coffee.'

'No. Thank you. I'm fine.' She gives a vague smile and turns to go. Clearly I haven't been acting too strangely. Ruin that by calling out, 'Wait!'

'Yes.'

'What day is it?'

'Day?' She looks alarmed. 'Friday.'

'And the time?'

'Half past two.' I do the calculation. That's more than twenty-four hours since I went in to talk to Darius. Somehow I ended up in here with no memory of what took place in between. I didn't go home. Liv must be frantic. The orderly beats a hasty retreat out the door and I make a grab for my phone. 'Liv, it's me.' I start talking before she has a chance to say hullo. 'I'm all right. I just got caught up with work.'

'Good to know.' There's no relief in her voice. Is she mad with me?

'I'm sorry about last night. I should have called, but—'

'Lexie, are you okay?'

'Yes, I'm just trying to apologise for not phoning you last night.'

'From the other side of the sofa?' Everything goes quiet inside my head. 'What did we do last night?' Liv sounds exasperated. 'Is this a joke?'

'Sure. Yes. You'll love the punchline. Just tell me, Liv. Please.'

'You came home at six-thirty. We had dinner. Then we watched some old episodes of *M*A*S*H* before you fell asleep and I had to put a blanket over you. I came in at seven this morning and you were gone.'

'That's it. I didn't say anything or do anything out of the ordinary?'

'You mean like phoning up and apologising for being at home all evening?'

'Thanks. You've been great.'

'Lexie, what is going—' I cut her off. I've already made an unnecessary apology so I guess we're even.

§

I find Darius outside on the terraces. He's more confident with the electric wheelchair now, and he's taken himself unnervingly close to the stone staircase for a better view of the lake. There's something in his stillness that makes all the excited words jostling in my throat go quiet. I stand beside him and look out over blue green waterlilies. On the water's edge, the tree branches are all downy with new leaves and a bud or two is poking through. Spring has happened, and I didn't even notice. Darius speaks first. 'Seb will be sorry. He loves cold crisp winter days.'

'Liv's the same. First snowflake falls and she's dragging me outside for a snowball fight.'

'You love your sister.'

'She's like me only better in every way. She pretends all this indifference and disinterest, but she's the most caring person I know.'

'It's different for me. I've always been there for Seb, protecting him. Now he has to take on being the carer.'

'He'll do it. Sometimes people just need the right circumstances to step up.' I take a big breath and let the cold air force the words I want to say to the surface. 'I need to tell you something.' At the same time he says, 'I know what you've done.' For a moment I'm not sure I've heard correctly. 'I don't—'

'You've taken Somnipradine.'

'How—how could you possibly know?'

'I saw the change come over you when we were last talking.'

'Changing, how?'

'I don't know exactly. You were just different.'

'I didn't make sense? I spoke about unusual things?'

'No, nothing like that. I just knew you weren't there anymore.' His certainty gets under my skin. I've lifted the lid on the genie and now I'm not sure I like what I'm seeing.

'You don't know me well enough to know. Not when my own sister didn't know.'

'I do know you. Lexie, I think—' His eyes say what neither of us can say out loud, that he's known me for hundreds of years. It's too much. I used to get lost in stories as a child and there was always that horrible jolt when I looked up and found myself in my Elastoplast pink bedroom and realised the dragons and the castles weren't real.

'So what happens now?'

'I guess we'll just have to wait and see.' Something shifts. The smile hovering on his lips doesn't reach his eyes.

'Darius?'

'Yes?' He might be making polite dinner party conversation with a stranger. 'Darius, where are you?' He blinks slowly as though mimicking surprise. 'I'm here.'

'Where's here?'

'Near…Near…' His eyes glue to the lake and seem unable to look away. 'I see water.'

'This water? At the Grange?'

'No. I think it's a canal. I'm walking beside it. With my friend, Marco.'

'Am I Marco?' He quirks an eyebrow at me to indicate how stupid the question is. So much for leading the patient. 'Where are you going?'

'Nowhere. Just walking. He wants to tell me something.'

'What does he want to tell you?'

'That he thinks I've lost my mind.'

TWENTY-EIGHT

GIORGIONE

'Ormesini? Are you mad?' Marco looks at me as though I need dragging to the Rialto to be cured of demonic possession.

'Ormesini needs his vanity stroked. I need money.'

'Won't the Maestro advance you a little?'

'Bellini won't spit on me. Not since I said DaVinci was a genius.'

'Sweet Jesus, Zorzi, why didn't you just tear out the Maestro's heart and piss on it? Didn't you see his painting of the Doge?'

'It's magnificent.'

'Then why side with DaVinci?'

We've come to a little humpbacked bridge spanning a minor canal and Marco skips up it. I am slow moving, a heavy carthorse not suited to Venice's narrow streets. Marco looks down at the green water, and together we watch a dead rat float into view, lazily rotate in an eddy, then disappear. I look down at Marco's curly head. 'Do you really not see something different in the way DaVinci paints?'

'There's a sort of softness in the colours, I suppose. Hey look, two rats. Let's take a bet on which one disappears first.' Marco's face is as clear as a new canvas. How can I make him understand?

'When Bellini paints, his figures are bathed in a constant celestial glow. But Leonardo's subjects are half in the shadows. Don't you see how he uses the dark to make us yearn for the light? Just as hunger makes us yearn for nourishment. I want to paint like that. I want to paint what is real.'

'Bellini's work is real! The technique used to create the fabric of the Doge's robe is incredible. I saw it. Shimmering like actual silk. I tell you Zorzi, there was a breeze when I viewed it, and I swear it moved.'

'Ormesini provided the fabric.'

'I didn't say he wasn't rich.' We pass the church of San Zaccaria, where eight of the city's doges drown in perpetuity inside their submerged crypt. Marco points with his thumb. 'I heard there was a fire there once and a hundred nuns died.'

'I heard it was ten.'

'Ten? A hundred? This is Venice. Tomorrow they will say a thousand.'

'Tomorrow the Turks may be victorious and we will all be sent off to be slaves of Bayezid II.'

'I'd take my chances over Ormesini. Have you heard what happened to Giuseppe the tailor who owed him for a yard of damask?'

'No.'

'Neither has anyone else. His widow still goes up and down the canals looking for him.'

'We don't know it was Ormesini. For all—'

'Look out!'

Pull my foot back just in time. A bundle of rags sprawled across the alley—half hidden amongst rotting leaves of cabbage and animal dung—is not a bundle of rags after all, but the corpse of a woman. My foot is hovering inches above her face and Marco's young voice rises from warning to laughter. 'You can thank me for stopping you wearing an old whore as a boot for the rest of the day.'

'She's not a whore. Look at her hands. They're rough and calloused. She's just a poor old woman who died in poverty. Probably a fishwife or a grave digger maybe.'

'Well, she should have had the wit to dig one for herself before leaving her corpse around for decent people to stand on.' Marco is looking back down the alley. 'Come on, before the militia arrive.' He's right. We should go. But something holds me back. 'See her skin. The patterns? All her experience is drawn upon it. It looks like old lace.'

'Lace chewed by rats and moths. Now hurry!'

For a while our flight occupies us, then Marco says, 'Why not paint Fiametta if it's money you want? She would pay handsomely. Or at least one of her clients would.'

'She doesn't interest me.'

'Doesn't interest you? Doesn't interest *you!* What's the matter? Did your mother drop you on your head? The coldest heart in

190

Venice would swell to see the looks she gives you.' He cups himself between the legs to emphasise that Fiametta's inflationary powers are not limited to a single organ.

'She throws the same looks at rich clients when she wants something.'

'She wants to be painted by you.'

'She wants immortality. To live on after death has eaten her flesh and crumbled her bones. That is not real.' Marco is shocked.

'You would rather paint old fishwives lying in the street?'

'I would rather paint life. Fiametta wants to be a Madonna or a nymph or a naiad. A Circe or Psyche. Anything but a real woman.'

Marco gives me a look that is shrewd beyond his years. 'People don't pay for real. Fiametta knows that. Why do you think she paints another face on top of her own? Because her clients want an angel to defile, not a woman who pulled herself out of the gutter.'

'And if she would let me paint Fiametta the whore, I would do it in an instant.'

'You're impossible. Next time she's in the studio send her to me if she wants a real man.'

'Why? Do you know where to find one?' Marco throws a punch and we play fight all the way to Baker's Bridge where I catch him in a headlock. 'Sorry, my young friend, but it's time for us to part ways.' Marco wriggles free. 'You're not still going, are you?'

'I am.'

'Zorzi, I'm begging you, leave Ormesini alone. He'll stab you in the heart then throw your remains into the Grand Canal. Send Lorenzo.'

'Why Lorenzo?'

'I still owe him five ducats after that last game of dice.'

§

I've made a mistake. I feel it as soon as I enter Ormesini's house. The servant who lets me in has a scar on his face and a look that clearly states, *step out of line and I'll tear your head off and piss in your neck.* He leads me through rooms which feel curiously cold—colder even than Venice's omnipresent antique dampness—and leaves me in a chamber clearly meant to impress: gilded ceiling, frescoes by Perugino, rows of antique books with names in Latin or Greek. I pick up a book of Roman poetry and try to peruse it. But still that strange chill. The way a chest is positioned in the centre of the room like an unoccupied catafalque. The sunlight that doesn't penetrate the shadows. The ashes of a doomed fire. Marco was right: you can taste the tomb in here. Fish scales lift on the back of my neck. Money or no money, I should go.

'You are the artist?' A woman dressed in green Damask silk is standing in the doorway. I make a clumsy bow. 'Signora. My great hon—'

'You don't bow to me.' She comes into the room crossing the Turkish rug so lightly she might be floating. Her eyes fall on the book in my hand. 'You like Catullus?' Her voice is strangely accented.

'Is it real?'

'Of course not. The original was lost centuries ago.'

I look down at the gilded cover. The workmanship is exquisite. 'It must be expensive.'

'Very. That is the earliest known copy.' She takes it from me and returns it to the shelf. 'He doesn't like his things touched.' She is the strangest creature I've ever seen. Her hair is boyishly short, barely to her shoulders. Has she been ill? A fever? But the eyes that look at me are clear and steady. 'You don't approve of such wealth?' Is she asking me personally or did Ormesini put these words in her mouth?

'How could I disapprove? As an artist, it's my job to increase the sum of a man's wealth.'

'Oh.' She lifts a bronze satyr and repositions it minutely. 'I thought it was your job to capture mystery.' I feel myself flushing darker than the bronze. I wish she would go but I'm also afraid that she might.

'May I ask you another question?' It seems unlikely my refusal would deter her so I nod weakly. 'Which do you consider to be the greater art, painting or poetry?' Is this what she wants to talk about, philosophy?

'Many minds greater than mine have debated it.'

'But what do you think? Is it painting or poetry?' With each word, she steps closer until I am forced to step back. As I do so, I'm reminded of a horse rearing up to escape a biting gnat, and the image amuses and shames me. What would Marco say? With great calmness I put my case.

'Which would you rather lose, your ears or your eyes?'

Her face is cold. 'Of course. You side with painting. But don't you think that to hear a poem is to have it in your heart?' She clasps her hands to her chest. 'It belongs to no-one. It belongs to everyone. Poetry can give courage to a child or comfort to the prisoner trapped in his lonely cell. What is painting compared to that but a commodity to be bought and sold and locked away in rich men's houses?' I am speechless. She burns with the fury of a new star. Her mouth opens to continue the onslaught but another voice speaks.

'Found each other, have you?' Ormesini is standing in the doorway. He's in his forties, well-dressed, not particularly tall. But, for all his refinement and the softness of his voice, I sense a beat of violence beneath his skin. I think if I put my ear to his chest, I would hear it as loud as a second heartbeat. Too late to do anything but bow smartly and say, 'At your service, sir.' He stares. 'You don't look like an artist.' A common response. My wide shoulders provoke images of sweat and ploughs and sturdy oxen driven across golden wheat fields. My grandfather's memory will never die as long as I stand six-foot-three in my stocking feet. I offer an apologetic smile. 'I was fortunate Maestro Bellini thought otherwise.'

Ormesini walks into the room, taking possession of it. He stops before the Moorish-style windows and peers towards the Church of San Giorgio Maggiore. 'What does your father do?'

'He has a farm. Olive trees mostly. Outside Castelfranco.'

'Rich?'

'Not especially.'

'Rich enough to let his son be an artist.' I concede the point. Battles between fathers and sons are dull to recount. He lifts a gold-hilted dagger from where it is displayed on a trapezophoron and holds it up, letting the light glitter on the inlay: a near naked figure hunting a lion. The blade is wickedly sharp. With one of those quick, unexpected movements, he is holding it out to me. 'What do you think?'

'It's beautiful.'

'Persian. Taken from the tomb of a nobleman. One of my collectors found it. Very rare to see one in this condition.' He's looking at me. Is it a question?

'Fortune has smiled on you.'

'Do you know how much it's worth?'

'No.'

'More than you'll earn in a lifetime.' I don't doubt it. 'Do you know why I bought it?' His questions stab like rapiers. Did he put Perugino through this before he let him paint the frescoes?

'No, sir.'

'Because I wanted it. Because I am the kind of man who can decide to buy a priceless object just because I fucking like it.' He laughs at the confusion on my face. 'The collector was a smart man. He knew what he had and exacted a high price.' He returns the dagger to the trapezophoron and stares at it contemplatively. 'Sometimes though you can get a bargain if you know how.' He turns to the girl. Is he expecting her to agree? But she stares ahead in silence, the petals of her face closed against him.

He looks back at me. Is this a test? The dagger is on the trapezophoron, the girl is so still she might be sculpted from Carrara marble. The antique, the girl and— The piece of the puzzle falls into place, a pattern in the clouds that can't be unseen no matter how many times you blink.

Ormesini's laughter is long and harsh. 'What appals you more, Castelfranco, that I rob graves or that I buy women? Only one is illegal in the eyes of the law.' He reaches out and pinches the girl's breast. It looks painful but she doesn't flinch. 'She's a block of ice this one,' he says almost affectionately. 'She was fire when I bought her, but a firm hand can douse a disobedient flame if you take my meaning.' I take it too well. All my life I've been slow to anger but something about this man makes an almost physical rage rise inside me.

'You brought me here to paint, sir.' Ormesini's eyes narrow. I've cut across his boasting and we both know it. No matter what happens next, I've made an enemy. 'Is it to be a portrait?' Rich men like to immortalize themselves in crushed ivory and powdered lapis.

Ormesini regards me through eyes narrow as arrow slits. 'A portrait, yes. Something majestic to hang in the entrance hall to remind people who I am.' I nod. This is a common request.

'And a second one. A full figure this time.'

'Of you?'

'Of her.' Not a muscle in her face twitches but something tells me she is shocked. 'Do you have something in mind?'

'A Magdalene.'

'You wish me to paint her as a penitent?'

'No. Paint the Magdalene as she is before her conversion. On her knees, yes, but for quite a different purpose.' He laughs wolfishly. 'Come now, Castelfranco. I've heard you know how to paint a whore.'

TWENTY-NINE

LEXIE:

Liv finds me staring into a mirror. 'My, my, who is the fairest of them all?' She pauses and looks back. It isn't exactly usual to see me glued, Alice-like, before the looking glass. 'Something wrong?' I don't know how to answer. I've spent my whole life not minding that I wasn't beautiful. Then to find myself suddenly wrapped up inside beauty. To see how men looked at me. To feel seen in that way and take it all for granted. Worst of all it felt right. As if some missing piece of me had fallen into place. Now it's the face looking back at me from the bathroom mirror that feels alien. Choppy bottle-dyed hair and Uncle Liam's chin. It isn't me. I can't explain this to Liv so I say, 'He's having the same incarnation as me.'

'What do you mean?'

'Darius. He's in my memory and I'm in his.'

'You're having unexplained memories?'

'Yes.' Shit, she doesn't know. My head has been so full of new memories I've forgotten to clue Liv in. I wait for her to laugh or say something sarcastic. Instead, she turns and walks into the living room. I follow in the manner of a naughty child. 'I should have told you.'

'You think?' She's pouring brandy into a glass like it's the apocalypse.

'I'm sorry. It's all been happening so fast. But it's worth it. The effects for Somnipradine are way beyond what anyone realised.' Liv drops into her chair and crosses her legs. Apart from the brandy swirling around in the glass, she looks like a therapist about to start a session.

'Okay. Deep breath. Slow down. Back up.'

I do two out the three. I breathe in. I back up. I don't slow down. Liv stops me several times to clarify. 'You're telling me you were having the memories while we were watching M*A*S*H?'

'Apparently.'

Then later: 'You call yourself what?'

'Adyghean. I think you call us Circassians nowadays.' She raises her eyebrow at the phrase, *you call us*, but says nothing. When I finally finish, there's a long silence. Liv stares down into her brandy and I consider making a joke about asking Bacchus to offer his pennyworth, but I'm afraid she'll take me seriously. 'Liv, I need you to say something. Please.'

'What do you need me to say?'

'Don't do that.'

'What?'

'Therapy speak. Just—just talk to me like we're two scientists discussing a theory. *Wo-mano a wo-mano*.' A number of emotions flit across Liv's face. None of them positive. I watch her wipe them away and turn a clean whiteboard expression to me.

'All right. Let me understand something. You were with Darius when the memories began. He noticed you change?'

'Yes.'

'And so he knew you believed you were in Venice?' I know where she's going with this and try to protest, but she holds up a hand. 'Bear with me. What are the chances that the person who gave him the wonder drug is also someone he knows from a previous incarnation? If you're approaching this scientifically, you have to agree that, far from some miracle of mental time travel, the likeliest explanation is that he absorbed your delusion into one of his own.' She quirks her lips. 'Occam's razor.'

'It isn't that simple.'

'Why not?'

Good question. 'It's hard to explain. You have to be there, to experience what it feels like.' Occam is probably thinking of slitting my throat. I feel a sly expression forming behind my eyes. 'You know, there's one way you could know for certain.'

'No fucking way!' She slams the glass down so hard it rings out a deep crystalline note, which comes as a surprise as we both thought Aunty Bong-cha too cheap to gift anything more expensive than glass. 'No fucking way,' Liv says again in case I missed it the first time.

'You don't know what I was going to say.'

'You were going to say I should inject your batshit crazy drug into my veins.'

'All right, that is what I was going to say. But more elegantly.'

'It's still no.'

'Will you at least come along and attempt to observe the memories one more time?' She doesn't answer. 'Your face says no, but that involuntary hemifacial spasm in your cheek says maybe.' She looks mulish. A sexy, beautiful pouting mule. Oh, Liv, I didn't understand what it was to be you when even your angry face looks a thousand times better than my best look. 'Please, Liv. Come just once more. If nothing happens, you can forget about it. I won't mention it again I promise.'

'And you'll do the dishes for a month.'

'The—what about the dishwasher?'

'It broke this morning, and we can't afford a new one till pay-day.'

§

This time, when Darius gives me the smile-that's-reserved-for-me, I return it full blast. Stupid move. Liv notices and starts drawing conclusions I can't openly contradict. A nasty little gremlin whispers in my ear, *what if she's right?* Darius is experiencing simple transference. He wakes up terrified and trapped, then along I come offering a shoulder to lean on. And me? I'm falling into my usual pattern of developing attachments for men I can't possibly have. Safe men. Unobtainable men. Men who can't possibly hurt me.

Liv and Darius have been exchanging pleasantries, but I can hear the nuances in her questions. *So Renaissance Italy is your area of expertise... You lived in Venice as a student?* She's trying to catch him out, breaking down the elements of his 'delusion' until he can see how it's all constructed from elements of everyday life. She calls it the Wizard of Oz conclusion. *Oh, Aunty Em, it's you!* It's her job and she's good at it. But it still makes me want to strangle her. Darius is polite, cooperative, not fooled in the least. I'd like to exchange a secret smile with him but Liv would spot it. She's moving in for the kill.

'I don't doubt the depth of your feeling, but what distinguishes these episodes from a powerful fantasy or a compelling dream?' Darius lifts his eyebrows, which is his version of a shrug. 'Why don't you ask your sister? She's there now.'

THIRTY

SETENEY:

Castelfranco stork-walks through the door the very next day, carrying a chest of pigments and squirrel-tipped brushes. A frame is ready in the middle of the reading chamber where the light is best, and he is absorbed in the business of preparing the canvas Assuming he hasn't heard me, I stand in the doorway, watching.

'Aren't you going to come in?' I would rather throw myself in the Grand Canal, but I obey and walk around the canvas to face him. He stops whatever he is doing and stares. 'What on earth are you wearing?'

I hate what I am wearing though it's probably the costliest item I have ever touched. An overdress of dark ruby brocade overlaid in gold. The sleeves are studded with pearls and caught in tightly at the wrists. 'I am dressed as the Magdalene.'

He raises a brow. 'Clearly her profession is more lucrative than art.' His mockery rankles.

'Artists may be rich. If they are any good.' I have touched a nerve. He snatches up a marble and begins crushing chalk.

'An artist may be rich if he sells his soul to the church.'

'You think it beneath you to paint angels?'

'I think it beneath all men to pretend to know Heaven when God has given us earthly wonders to explore. I don't like make-believe. Do you understand?'

'I understand why you are not rich.'

'My, my, you have her chirping like a little bird. She must like you.' Ormesini's shadow falls between us. 'Have you decided on the pose?'

'It's too soon.' Castelfranco points at the canvas. 'The surface has to be perfectly smooth. Layer upon layer of gesso, each sanded down before I can think of beginning. It's too early to talk of poses.' Ormesini drops into a chair and lolls back against the cushions. His head rolls lazily onto a shoulder. 'Indulge me.'

Castelfranco looks mutinous but I know it's a bad idea to openly cross swords with Ormesini, and I am the one who will pay the price of his impertinence. I raise my voice. 'What do you want me to do?' He blushes, clever enough to know he has made the situation worse. If I did not hate men as the lowest and filthiest of all God's creatures, I might come to like this one.

He comes to my side suddenly full of enthusiasm. 'I thought to have you in the moment before realisation dawns. You are at the height of your powers, your charm, your passions yet you sense something is wrong.' He searches my face for understanding. 'It's the unearthly intuition you feel before a crack of lightning. When all is darkness, yet deep inside you know it's about to happen.' I nod. I recognise that feeling. I felt it just after I saw the strangers in the forest. The moment before I lost consciousness.

§

I don't see him for several days then suddenly, when I least expect it, I am sent for. The ruby brocade is left out, and I have no choice but to wear it. When I arrive, there are more sheets on the floor and he has dragged a Savonarola chair and placed a small *scrittoio* before it. Several books are scattered on its surface. 'Sit, sit.' I obey, a little clumsily; the overdress is too long. He frowns and mutters something under his breath about tasteless ostentation.

'Open the book as though you were halfway through.'

'I do not read.'

'Yet you knew Catullus.'

'I knew the look of the spine. He has boasted of it often enough.'

'Place your hand upon a page as though about to turn it. And rest your hand on the others gently, almost caressingly.'

'Your Magdalene is a literary whore.'

'She is clever. We Venetians know the subtlety of courtesans. Her conversion is not a moment of blind faith but the culmination of pure reason.'

'The priests would not like to hear you say so.'

'They will not need to hear me say it. The art will speak for itself.'

'They will condemn you for it.'

'I have yet to meet a priest who gives two figs for what art has to say. Now turn towards the canvas. No, not like that. Twist from the waist. You are caught in the instant where your life changes. This is the divide. You are neither within the sanctity of Eden nor beyond its walls. A space so small not even angels would dare dance on it.' I do as he asks. He is like all men. He barks orders and expects women to obey.

When he is satisfied, he hesitates, biting at the end of his brush. In the long silence shadows form cameos on the walls. A gondolier shouts over the water to a courtesan crossing a bridge. A bell sounds in St Mark's Piazza. 'Remove your robe.' It is expected but my heart swings off course and drains the life from my limbs. 'I need to see you.'

What else can I do? Stiffly my fingers obey, while he turns his great head—an ox attempting courtesy—and stares fixedly out of the window. I might laugh if I didn't want to weep. Does he think it is only the act of removal that is a violation? I let the overdress fall to the floor. There's no need to undress further; I'm completely naked underneath.

God knows how long the idiot would stand there if I didn't discretely clear my throat. It comes out in a low growl and, startled, he turns then rubs his hands together business-like. He is with me in two strides, his expression interested yet distant. I know the look. It's the dispassionate expression of a physician or a butcher. Perhaps he will paint me as joints of meat. His lips part as though he is about to issue an instruction but no words come out only a low gasp as his gaze drops to my belly. Three letters are carved around my navel in armorial style. FMO—Francesco Mattia Ormesini. All pretence at objectivity is lost. Colour rushes into his cheeks then ebbs away.

'What's wrong? Don't you understand what it is to be someone's property?'

'This is—He can't do this.'

'He can.'

'You must appeal to the law.'

'The law allows him to do what he wants short of killing me. A few streets from here, they found a young Russian slave, by the name of Serafina, hanging from the rafters in her master's kitchen. The parts of her body which weren't covered in wounds were covered in burns. What punishment did her master receive? None. They couldn't prove that he intended to kill her.'

He looks raw, like a skinned rabbit. 'Marta, please—'

'My name is not Marta.'

'No?'

'No.'

'Tell me.'

I take a big gulp of air and spit it at him. 'Seteney.' *Seteney.* The word bursts out as the emptied chambers of my heart collapse. My hands lift from the books, as if by their own accord, but I don't know what to do with them: they don't belong to me. Uselessly they fall at my sides. I don't know who I am. Seteney would escape this place. Marta has nowhere to go.

'Seteney? Is that your Tatar name?'

'I am not Tatar. I am—' *What is their term for it?* 'Circassian.' He nods without understanding then reaches towards me. An unwelcome approach that has me cringing against the back of the chair. I close my eyes then force them open. I will not cower in the face of his depravity. But he merely lifts the robe and drapes it around me leaving only one breast exposed.

'Our Magdalene has hidden depths.'

THIRTY-ONE

GIORGIONE:

'Mother of God, what's got into you?' Someone is pulling at my sleeve. Marco—who for some unknown reason is upside down—wafts in and out of focus until I'm forced to turn my head and vomit into the surprisingly convenient gutter I seem to be lying in. A stray dog runs up to lick up the mess. 'Get up you ridiculous oaf.' Marco tries to pull me to my feet but I can barely sit upright before the world spins off its axis and I vomit again, unfortunately this time onto Marco's legs. 'Fuck you, Zorzi. You filthy cur.'

'You seem upset.'

'I've spent half the night looking for you.'

'Call yourself a friend? What were you doing for the other half?' He pushes his hands under my armpits and tries to lever me up. Alas, he is no Archimedes and we sink together back into the gutter. He attempts reason. 'Zorzi, we can't stay here.'

'You go. I long for death.'

'Death won't come near you. You smell too bad. Come on, the sweepers will be along shortly. Do you want to end up in the waste barges and sold to farmers for manure?'

'Why not? I am a pile of dung. Let me be useful.' He shakes my shoulders, a brave act considering the projectile nature of my stomach contents.

'What is wrong with you?'

'I am in love.'

'You dog. Fiametta has worked her charms.'

'No. No, it is another.'

'Who? Do I know her?'

'A princess.'

'A princess?'

'Locked in an ivory tower. Like Saint Barbara. Her pagan father shut her away for converting to Christianity, and also for being very beautiful.'

'The princess?'

'The saint.'

'But your princess is beautiful?'

'A face to make Venus cover herself in shame.'

'And does this goddess-shaming anchorite have a name?'

'Seteney.'

'Unusual.'

'Everything about her is unusual. Her eyes are the clearest lazuline, her skin is translucent pearl—'

'Her lips are rubies? Her hair is spun gold?'

'Exactly, except that her hair is dark, the colour of twilight.'

'Does she return your affections?'

'She has no idea of them.'

'That may make things more difficult. Have you spoken with her father?'

'I have no idea who he is.'

'I thought he locked her in a tower.'

'That was Saint Barbara. Seteney is locked away in the house of her master, Francesco Ormesini.'

'Holy Sainted Virgin Mother.' Marco crosses himself. 'You're in love with Ormesini's slave? What is she, a witch, an enchantress? Has she cast a spell over you?'

'She hates me.'

'Then at least she has wisdom. If Ormesini gets wind of this, he'll carve you so small your coffin will be the size of a snuffbox.'

'What am I to do? I love her and she spits in my wine before she offers it to me.'

'You must forget all about her. Do the painting, take Ormesini's silver then move to Milan.'

'You wouldn't forget her if you could see her.'

'I will never see her. Ormesini has her locked up with his precious art collection.'

'I must have her or die.'

'The two states are not incompatible.' Hands are under my armpits again. He's making a kind of grunting noise.

'Good old Marco. Always looking out for me. You're my friend, aren't you? You'll help me.'

'Sure. Sure. Just let me know what funeral arrangements you'd like.'

§

SETENEY:

Castelfranco is back and we are alone again in the reception hall. Except, of course, we are not alone. There are ears and eyes everywhere. Ormesini, however, keeps his distance. Does he want us to think he's lost interest? A game is being played here, but what? What?

Castelfranco is staring at me. He has done this for several days. I looked away at first but he corrected me. 'I need you exactly as I will paint you.'

'Can't you make sketches?'

'I don't work that way.'

There is silence for a long time. 'Would you like some wine?'

'Will you fetch it?'

'Yes.'

'No thank you.'

More silence. 'I cannot sit like this while you stare at me.'

He shrugs. 'We can talk as long as you don't move your head.'

'What can we talk about?'

'I would like to get to know you more.'

'You think every slave has a story?'

'Don't you?'

'I don't want to talk about that.'

'What do you want to talk about?'

'I don't know. Not that.'

He frowns. 'You moved.'

'No.'

'The fold in that sleeve is different.' He strides over and adjusts my cuff minutely then stands and studies it. His scrutiny makes me itch.

'She's not a whore.'

He looks up, startled. 'What?'

'Mary Magdalene. In the East, we call her first amongst the apostles. It's your tradition to debase her.'

He considers this. 'I think I would find your world a strange place to visit.'

'You wouldn't last a day.'

He smiles. 'Not if the men are as fierce as the women.'

'In ancient times the fiercest warrior of all was Queen Valdusa. She led an army of women fighters who fought the Circassian men led by Thulme. When they couldn't beat the Amazons, they had no choice but to marry them and from then on they fought as equals.'

'Who told you that?'

'My grandmother. She taught me many things.'

'You were close?'

'Before I was sent away. Yes.'

'Who sent you away?'

205

'My father. He sent my brother and I together when we reached the age of six.'

He is surprised. 'You have a twin?'

'Yes. I am the elder by nine minutes. I was also the larger one. My brother always claimed I pushed him aside in the womb in my hurry to get out, and that was the reason he came out lame.' He is nodding in the way people do when they have no understanding.

'Why did your father send you away?'

'It's our custom.' He lifts a bottle of linseed and begins adding it to a mound of pigment. The smell is oily, vaguely animal in nature. I don't know why, but it makes me want to cry. Don't let tears come. Force the tightness from my chest with words. 'We were *ataliqate*, children of the nobility. Our father was lord of our principality.' He says nothing but his fingers stiffen a little on his palette knife. I find myself saying. 'It was a very small domain. Really only a few hamlets. But my father was a stickler for tradition. It is the Circassian way to send a prince's children to live with the lesser nobility. That way loyalty between families is assured.' He is looking uncertain. 'It prevents the bonds of love between parents and children becoming too strong.'

Now he looks shocked. 'You consider that a bad thing?'

'Boys die in battle. Girls in childbirth. Is it better to see a mother tearing her hair out of grief with despair or a father beat his breast until it bleeds? You Italians are too sentimental. You would rather let the body rot than dare to cut off a limb.'

That night Ormesini takes me to his bed. He doesn't ask me anything and I don't bother to pretend to be surprised. We both know he was listening at the keyhole. Although my noble origins have done me few favours in this life, he is clearly offended to hear of them and perpetrates acts of violent *lese majeste* against my body to put me in my place.

I lie under him feeling his weight and his sweat. He is grunting, *Teach you...teach you,* over and over under his breath. When he is finished, he trails sticky beads of semen across me then forces me to thank him for these 'pearls of wisdom', and when my gratitude proves insufficient, he drags me to a chest, forcing me inside and locking the lid. Perhaps he will wait until I am half dead then pull me out for his amusement and watch me fish-gasp for air.

The darkness is thick as smoke. It stings my eyes and fills my throat. I can't breathe. No air. No-one can hear me. My spirit tries to ghost-soar, but it can't get out of the box. My heart is filled with snakes. I will die here. Alone. In the darkness. I will die!

§

'You're not alone. I'm here.'
  'Who's there?'
  'It's Liv.'
  'Liv?'
  'A friend.'
  'Show yourself then.'
  'You can see me.' I see her now. A woman. Elfin-looking. An enchantress? A fragment of a dream?'
  'Who are you?'
  'You've known me for a long time.' Yes, she's familiar. I know this woman. I do.
  'What do you want?'
  'I want you to leave this place.'
  'Leave. How can I leave?"
  'You can go back. To an earlier time. To when you were a child…'

§

Despite his limp, they place my brother on a horse. They have to hold him there as he wails and calls out to our mother in a shameful way until my uncle cuffs him about the ears. I, on the other hand, hold my father's eye without blinking then let them carry me off in a carriage without a backward glance.

We reach our new noble father's home after two days of hard riding and a short delay when Uncle Shumaf stopped to barter for some slaves. The lord's house is larger than the homes around it and set apart, but it has the same thatched roofing and plaited wood walls as the humblest dwelling. Easier to destroy when raiders come, leaving them kicking their heels in the ashes. The men go off to tend the horses leaving Beslan and me in the forecourt. Apparently we have arrived early and the lord is not at home. In silence we wait in the green air, our nostrils filling with the scent of pine needles. There is nothing to hear save for the sound of a cuckoo chiming down the seconds somewhere deep in the forest.

'Which sewer did you two rats escape from?' A tall dark skinny boy appears—the lord's son I presume—and offers us his greeting. Our men have gone to deal with the horses and we are alone. My brother pulls himself up. He's half a head shorter than me.

'I am Beslan and this is Seteney. We are the children of Prince Ezgbold.'

'Well, here you are dirt.' He pushes Beslan on to his back, causing him to burst into angry tears, which encourages the lord's son to aim a kick at his side.

'Don't.'

I am standing between them, the oblate sleeves of my gown hanging down from my skinny outthrust arms. A moment later, I find myself sitting on my even skinnier buttocks in the dirt, a sharp stone digging into my thigh. My nose feels odd and I find a smear of blood there. The lord's son has lost interest and is swaggering back indoors. He doesn't make it. A large stone hits him on the back of the head and knocks him down.

Beslan jumps up. 'You shouldn't have done that.'

'He isn't dead.' (I'm almost sure of this.)

'I didn't need you.'

'He was going to kick your ribs.'

'I fight my own battles.'

'Before or after you finish crying?'

'Take that back.'

'Shan't.' He takes a swing at me and I knock him down harder than the lord's son did. I brace, ready to hit him again, but he just sits there, a wounded fawn with huge diamond tears spilling over his lashes. He is pitiful and I should despise him for it. But what must it be like to be a small boy with a limping useless leg in a world that prizes only the strongest and bravest? It did not go unnoticed that my father offered him no words of encouragement in his farewell. I fall to my knees and put my arm around his shoulders. 'We're still friends. You and me. Forever.'

THIRTY-TWO

GIORGIONE:

Seteney's eyes are wide with horror. 'Are you mad?'

'Why does everyone keep asking me that? Very possibly. Will you let me in?'

'You were told to stay away.'

'I had to come. They said you were ill.'

'They said that to make you stay away.'

'Seteney, please. I have been standing outside in the cold for hours. I climbed this ladder unable to feel my hands. I may never paint again.'

Her expression is unrelenting. She folds her arms. 'Ormesini and his men will be back any minute. What do you think they will do if they find you here?'

'Seteney.' Frustration makes me slap the sill, which causes the ladder to wobble precariously. Far below, the solid cobble street rocks wildly and I emit a sound similar to a cat with its balls caught in a millstone. Seteney throws open the window and grabs my arm. 'Get in, you fool.'

'You do love me.'

'I want you out of sight before the whole neighbourhood comes running.'

As soon as my feet touch the floor, she retreats to the far end of the room. I want to say something comforting but I'm struck by the strangeness of the chamber. Bare boards and open rafters typical of an attic room but a bed luxuriously covered and, on every wall, an ornate mirror. They catch the light and play with it like water. 'Whose room is this?'

'His. All the rooms are his.'

'I meant—'

'I know what you meant. He keeps me here, his dog, chained up in my kennel.'

'An opulent kennel.'

'A cage is still a cage.' An angry step towards me and a dozen Seteneys bare their teeth. It's dizzying. Hard to think straight. Then she winces and holds her stomach. 'What's wrong?'

'Nothing. Leave me alone.' A wild look enters her eyes; her legs give way.

'Seteney!' A dozen Zorzis lift a dozen Seteneys from the floor and lay them on the bed. 'What's wrong? Did he hurt you?'

Her voice is faint. 'He always hurts me.'

'Worse this time?'

'He went too far. It's all right. He won't touch me until I heal.' There's some wine nearby and I pour a cup and hold it to her lips. She swallows a few sips. 'Thank you.' This passive woman frightens me. I want her to claw and scratch and spit in my goblet.

'What has he done to you?'

'Nothing he hasn't done before.' Her eyes are closed. The lids are blueish. I've seen daylight that colour just before it fades to black. 'What are you doing?'

Good question. What am I doing? My fingers have found the neck of her shift and I'm loosening it. 'I'm not going to hurt you.' Her eyes fly open. 'No.'

'I'm not going to do what he did. I'm not going to touch you that way.'

I soak a rag in a basin of water then help her to undress. Her flesh has been turned into a map belonging to an insane beast. Bruises form islands connected by rivers of livid scratch marks. She curls on her side. 'Don't look at me.'

'I'll kill him.'

'Don't be stupid. You'd be dead before you struck the first blow.'

'He can't do this.'

'He can.'

'Then—' It comes from nowhere. A solution is so simple it temporarily blinds me. 'I'll buy you.'

She whimpers several times then wipes her eyes. 'Thank you for making me laugh.'

'You think I can't do it?'

'He won't sell me.'

'Why not? Look at the way he treats you. He doesn't value you.'

'He loves me.' My gorge rises up and punches me in the lungs.

'Loves you?' I point to the palette of amethyst and carnelian shades covering her body. 'I can see that from the way he showers you with jewels.'

Her eyes close. 'It is how men love. By destroying.'

'Not all men.'

'No, not all men. But those men can't protect us from the beasts.'

I begin to bathe her arm. She's tense, a statue made of Carrara marble, no blood flowing under the skin. 'You should go.' Her lips are blue. It's costing her to speak.

'I want to stay with you.'

Her eyes open, stare at the ceiling for a moment then find me. 'No.'

'Then let me come back and see you.'

'It'd be suicide. For both of us.'

'Please.' I run the rag very gently over her breasts and feel something scaly and serpentine shudder through her. Her head turns towards me and I'm sure she'll say, no. Then she laughs, a short hollow expulsion of air more like a bark. 'Why not? What have I got to live for anyway?'

§

LEXIE:

Water puddles on the bathroom floor. I'd put a towel down earlier but it's already soaked. Liv will be livid. But I can't do it. Can't keep the shower door closed. Even the clear glass can't convince me I'm not inside Ormesini's chest. Ironic. Past life regression is supposed to free you of present trauma not provide you with new ones.

A bruise above my left breast. It wasn't there yesterday. Matches the ones that have mysteriously appeared on my thighs and back. Strange bruises that don't hurt to the touch. They ghost up during the night, subcutaneous nebulas of broken blood vessels tinted interstellar black shot through with weird traces of malachite and violet. Darius could tell me the exact shades. Not that he can know. Not him. Not Liv. Not anyone.

Is she angry? My altered alter ego. Raging up through the centuries from half a millennium ago. Wanting to remind me that a pretty face didn't save her from humiliation, from being less than human, from bites and kicks and punches, from violent rape, from being forced inside an airless coffin to smother for the pleasure an owner who dangles death, like the key to a door, then snatches it away as soon as she reaches.

She's so close. Last night, I woke up and felt her breathing under my skin. I've caught her in mirrors too, looking out of my eyes. She wants up. She wants out…She wants to tell me something.

§

SETENEY:

I don't know what he wants or what madness has possessed him, but he creeps back to my room whenever he can. He has lost his mind and now he comes to steal mine. All these questions he is asking me. Now I have one for him. 'How did you get here without the ladder?'

'I bribed the old woman who holds the keys when he's out.'

'With what?'

'I sketched her likeness. Possibly I allowed a little artistic licence to creep in.' He has charm, I'll give him that.

'How are the wounds of Christ?' He pulls down my shift to examine me.

'Have you no shame, talking like that?'

'Of course, I forgot. You say you're a Christian.'

'You don't believe me?'

'They say all Tat—' He corrects himself. 'Circassians are pagans under the surface.'

'Unlike you Italians, who invoke Zeus and Venus at the smallest provocation and hang little shrines at every crossroads. What do you call them? *Madonelle*?'

'It's not the same. Those carvings invoke the spirit of Our Lady.'

'And I see holy spirit in a tree or a stream. How is it different?'

'I don't know. It just is.'

'Do you deny that God is everywhere?'

'No. But—' The water on my back feels good. He never touches me directly, only with a soaked rag which is sweetened by herbs his grandmother would use when he hurt himself as a boy. He is still thinking about what I said.

'I heard you don't have churches.'

'There are churches. The Russian princes built them in the mountainous regions. Some choose to worship there. Some do not.'

'People choose not to attend church?' He looks so shocked I want to slap the silly expression off his face.

'Do you really believe you are closer to the Creator-of-All inside a house made of stone? You think I haven't seen your tortured god? Everything is dead inside your churches. But inside our sacred groves we stand amongst Her creation. The pulse of life is everywhere. God is everywhere.' *My grandmother's wrinkled hand covers mine. Her eyes are closed and she sways slightly in time with the shivering treetops. Listen carefully, little one. Holiness is all around us. In the rustle of leaves. In the high cold voice of the wind...*

'You said *Her!*'

'What?'

'You said, we stand amongst Her creation.'

'Him. Her. Do you think the Almighty is limited to a single form?' I'm glad my back is to him. I'm glad I can't see his stupid puzzled face. And I'm glad my bruises are healing so he won't be able to come here much longer. Why am I crying?

'Seteney. What's wrong? I'm sorry.' His hands are on my shoulders tugging at me, but I won't look at him. Before I know it, the great bear is kneeling in front of me, his clumsy form reflected over and over in the mirrors. How is this man an artist? 'Forgive me. The things you say. They're strange to hear. I'm a simple man

213

who knows nothing about the world except what washes up on Venice's shores. But I want to learn more.'

I cannot stop crying. In all this time I have not wept. Not when my father sent me away, or when the lord's son punched me on the nose. Not when I first bled and they forced me to wear the stiff leather corset day and night so my breasts would stay small and my movements be less wildly boyish. Not even when the slavers took me and Ormesini broke me into a million bits then ground me into dust.

'Seteney.' He doesn't ask me why I am crying or tell me to stop. He stands up and holds me by my shoulders, then kisses my forehead then my eyelids. His lips hesitate before mine. 'Do you want me to stop?'

Do I? 'No.'

§

That my heart should be so easily reached? I thought it was locked away in a box, neglected, shrivelled, eaten away by Ormesini's laughing demon face. He lifts me into the air in his arms. I am a child, an angel, a feather; I have wings. I didn't expect this. To come alive. Was I even aware of being dead? Nights and nights of dense grey pain. I was bones in the earth. But he draws me up. Fills out my flesh and paints in my colours. I am golden.

THIRTY-THREE

Lexie:

Another bruise has appeared on my arm. Just below the knobbly pisiform wrist bone. Pull my sleeve down and ask a question before Liv notices. 'Tell me what you're thinking.'

'Will you stop asking me that?'

'I need to know what you're thinking.'

'I don't know what I'm thinking.' Liv and I are walking around the park where we used to go as children. To be honest, it's little more than a gravel track surrounding a shallow duckpond and a couple of swings vandalised by the local wildlife. But it feels familiar and I think Liv needs that right now. She's walking too fast, arms hugging her waist, hands muffled in her coat sleeves. Her voice is so low I'm not sure if she's talking to me or mumbling to herself. 'You don't change accent.'

'No.'

'And there's no sign that you're speaking another language.'

'I think I am inside my head. But it comes out as English.'

'And you've only experienced one life.' I hesitate and Liv pounces. 'What?'

'I've had snatches of other things. But they're short, confused. I think I might have died as a very young child and sometimes I even get the impression that I'm wearing armour. But it's not clear. More dreamlike. Nothing like what I'm experiencing as Seteney.'

'The detail is astonishing. I'll admit that. I've never heard such an intricate delusion. And for the two of you to share the same narrative. I mean it isn't unprecedented. There are known cases of *folie à deux*, but they're rare.'

'You think the *deux* of us is about to engage in some *folie*?'

'I don't know. Not obviously. They're usually more specifically focused generally towards the murder of some specific target. You're not planning to murder anyone, are you?'

'It's not top of my to-do-list.'

'Then it's strange. My guess would be that he's drawn you into this delusion because he wants something from you.'

'What if it isn't a delusion?' Liv starts walking faster.

'I can't go there. If it's not a delusion, you've just rewritten the map on life after death. It's too much.'

'So what do we do?'

'I guess we see this out. Find out where you're going with it.'

§

Given an A4 notepad and an HB pencil, Liv could organise world peace. She takes one look at the haphazard notes I've been taking and disappears into her room with her laptop. At midnight, I tap the door tentatively and she makes a grunting noise which I take to mean, *come in*. I hold out a mostly clean mug. After all, boiling water kills off most things. 'Coffee?' Another grunting noise. She's sitting, cross-legged on the duvet, tapping furiously on her keyboard, so I sit down beside her and put the mug on the bedside table. 'Figured out whodunnit?'

The screen shows she's working on a spreadsheet. There are columns of data and charts with fat pie slices representing historical eras and jagged mountain ranges plotting things like history against duration. 'This took me to midnight.'

'Just the highlights then.'

'Okay. Let's take Darius. If we filter out the scary out-of-body experiences, which we can't separate from the endorphin effect on a dying brain, his first past life event is in prehistory, followed by Qing dynasty China then Nazi Germany.'

'And now back to the Renaissance.'

'Exactly. No progression. Though, if you look at this chart—' I glance at one of the spiking mountain ranges. 'It appears that the duration of the events is increasing. Dreams-the-People only takes a day, Refined Ink is more like a week and Jules Vogelsang takes place over a month. I wish you had recorded better data on the actual intervals. I would like to plot it out in terms of hours to be sure.'

'What about the lives themselves?'

'I think we can draw some conclusions. He is male in three out of the four incarnations. Only Jules Vogelsang is female and deep down she feels male. That reminds me, did you have any luck tracing her?'

'Nothing. After the war a lot of records were lost or deliberately amended. There's an Eva Hirsch who reached Ellis Island in 1947. Her occupation is listed as artist, but there's no sign of her afterwards. She might have changed her name.'

'Or she might never have existed at all.'

'Can't prove it. Can't disprove it. What else you got?'

'For Darius, the memories all centre around adulthood. There are themes. Dreams-the-People is an artist, Refined Ink falls in love with an artist, as does Jules Vogelsang, and Giorgione is one of the most famous, yet most mysterious, of the Renaissance painters.'

'I know where you're going with this. He's an art dealer so he remembers art-related past lives.'

'That's what I thought at first. But it's not the main theme.'

'No?'

'No. It's the loss of his true love. Think about it, Crook-ed-Mouth dies. Lodovico escapes as does Ziva Hirsch.'

'So logically, I—I mean Seteney—must be forced to escape.'

'Or die,' Liv says pragmatically. She can't see what the thought of dying as Seteney does to me so I deflect by asking, 'What about the painting? The Twilight Madonna.'

'I was coming to that. It features in two lives. Both Refined Ink and Jules Vogelsang see it. And, here's the clue, Eva Hirsch believes it was painted by none other than—'

'Giorgione.'

'Could it be the Magdalene that Giorgione is painting for Ormesini?'

'That's my theory. I think there's something significant about it. Something that Darius keeps returning to.'

'So what are you saying, these past lives are some sort of ra-tionalization? A coming to terms with the paralysis?'

'I don't know. I think…at least I have a feeling that something else is going on.' She sees my face and shakes her head. 'No, not in the way you're thinking. Not even a kind of coming-to-terms with his trauma. What if he's trying to work something out? Don't you remember that time I dreamt I was being robbed only to wake up and find I had left Nana's heirloom ring at the gym?'

'I remember your panicked screams.'

'Well, maybe it's something like that. He's using these past lives to remember something.'

'What?'

'I don't know.'

THIRTY-FOUR

'Can you hear me?'

'Yes.'

'Tell me more about the painting you did of Ormesini's slave.'

§

GIORGIONE:

'What is that terrible noise?' Marco has arrived at the studio. I didn't hear him come in.

'I'm singing.'

'I thought someone was skinning a dog.'

'Weren't you supposed to be carousing with Lorenzo tonight?'

'Claims he's sick. Shivering, headaches, can't keep anything down.'

'Sounds serious. Should we fetch a leech?'

'No. Sadly there is no cure for the common hangover. What's that smell?' He lifts a smoking stump of tallow and frowns at it. 'Have you been here all night?'

'Only since midnight.'

'You've been painting? At night?'

'We got it all wrong. Leonardo understands. Darkness doesn't obscure. It reveals. I realised it on my way to see Seteney. Twilight is more beautiful than dawn. The same way a face is more beautiful just before death. When the suffering fades and all that is left is serenity and the terrible splendour that comes with the passing of things.'

'Have you lost your mind?'

'I'm in love.'

'Same thing.' Dropping his cloak over a chair, he joins me in front of the canvas. 'Mother of God, who is she?'

'The princess.'

'You mean Ormesini's slave?'

'Yes. But she truly is a princess by birth. She told me that her father was prince of their region.'

Marco looks at me pityingly. 'You *are* in love.' He studies my work critically. 'All this from memory?'

'Yes.'

'Perhaps just a touch of artistic licence?'

'No.'

'Just a little?'

'No.'

'Just the teensiest, tiniest, itsy-bitsy bittiest little bit?'

'Not a stroke.' He looks again and the laughter leaks from his face. 'Zorzi, what are you doing? Ormesini will never let her go.'

A creak on the staircase. Marco glances over his shoulder. 'Are you expecting someone?'

'It's probably Signora Porzio after her rent. Ignore it. She'll leave if she doesn't get an answer.' But Marco is already at the door. He comes back a moment later, eyes filled with fear. 'It's *him!*' Ormesini. We stare at one other. Shadows grow bold. Colours corrode. The studio is bare, an attic space with only one exit. No escape. There is only one solution. 'Quick, behind the screen.' Marco throws himself at a shabby modesty screen, a gift to Fiametta by an enamoured count—admittedly a somewhat redundant gift in Fiametta's case. 'No, you idiot.' I make a grab for his retreating shirt tails. 'Hide the portrait there.' There's just time to secrete it behind the flimsy panels and to place a substitute on the easel before there is a knock on the door. Marco makes a move to answer it then pauses. 'Look busy,' he hisses and I grab a brush.

'Signor Ormesini.' Marco's bow is so low it borders on insolent. 'What a pleasure. Zorzi and I were just talking about you.' Ormesini gives him the look crows give before tearing out their victim's eyes and Marco falls silent. I feel naked, worse than naked, flayed. All the twisted roots of my muscle and sinew exposed. *He knows,* a voice in my head is screaming. *Knows about Seteney and me!* He can't know. Not for certain. I should greet him. Pretend nothing is amiss. But my heart is stoppering my throat.

Ormesini is impeccably dressed as always, from his velvet hat to his calfskin boots. He glances about, unimpressed by the bare floorboards with their fireworks display of paint splashes, then removes his hat. How many men has he brought with him? What are the chances that Marco will stand with me and fight? Unlikely. He's edging towards the door. He pauses to give me a look that says—*Sorry, but this isn't my battle*—but rushes back when Ormesini holds the hat out to him. He grips the velvet rim as though wringing the neck of a chicken then places it gingerly on the only chair.

Ormesini looks me in the eye. 'Forgive the intrusion. I wanted to see how my portrait is coming along.'

'Of course.' My lips tear as I force a smile. 'The very one I am working on.'

'It seems to be taking a long time.'

'I am sure you appreciate that art can't be rushed.'

'That's true,' Marco chimes in. 'Think of DaVinci. He can take years to finish.'

Ormesini is still holding my gaze. 'You are not DaVinci. May I?' He points to the canvas, and I stand back to allow him to inspect my progress.

He is silent for a long time—never a good sign—and it hits me that the paint is completely dry (I finished it weeks ago) making mockery of my claim to be 'working'. Marco's blanched face tells me he is thinking the same thing. *Do something*, his eyes plead. Lifting a nearly dry brush, I apply it to a corner of the canvas making no difference whatsoever then nod in a satisfied way. 'As you can see, sir. It is very near completion.' Ormesini still hasn't said anything. Marco attempts a rescue. 'Perhaps a cup to refresh you?' He lifts an earthenware jug, sloshing contents which are more vinegar than wine, and holds it out hopefully. Ormesini ignores him much in the way frogs ignore flies before spearing them on the ends of slimy tongues. 'It doesn't look the way I want it to.'

Now I am the one speared through. 'I can only paint what I see.'

'Then see something else. This isn't what I paid for.'

'This is exactly what you paid for.' I ignore Marco's agonized look. A man may threaten my life and get away with it, never my art. 'You asked for your portrait. I have painted it. What more can you possibly want?'

'You haven't given me a soul.'

'I'm an artist not a priest.'

'Are you trying to be funny, Castelfranco?'

'Not in the least.

'You think a man who buys and sells for a living has no nobility?' So that's it. He wants me to smooth out the rough edges and flatter his ego. Replace his jowls with chiselled cheekbones, the cunning glint in his eye with patrician hauteur. Perhaps he would like an arcadian landscape in the background or rays of celestial light. Well, think again, Signor Bigshot. I won't do it. A man must live or die by his principles. Compromise is the death of art.

Ormesini stands quietly radiating an aura of intense menace. 'You're going to fix this.' In the background, Marco's out-of-focus face has gone deathly white. He knows I will refuse. I wonder if he's going to faint with fright. I draw in a deep breath trying to find a diplomatic way to form my rejection, but all I can see is Seteney's face. Painting the portrait again will extend my relationship with the Ormesini household by several weeks. Can I compromise my art just for the chance of seeing her a little longer? Ormesini is tapping his foot. I give a small bow. 'Of course. If that is your wish, I will be happy to repaint it for you.'

There is a thud as Marco's unconscious body hits the floor.

Ormesini takes a fastidious step to the side as the contents of the wine jug spread a dark wound across the floorboards. 'You think you're being very clever, Castelfranco, don't you?'

'I don't know what you mean.'

'I mean I know what you're about. The jig's up on your little game.' Mother of God. He knows. Someone's told him. Stupid to think we could get away with it. If he's hurt her I swear—what? That I'll bleed to death on the floor, my heart pierced through by more blades than the Blessed Virgin. Words come stuttering out of my head. 'Whatever you may have heard, I assure you—' A groan rises from the floor. Marco is waking up, and I almost miss what Ormesini says next. 'You want to get paid twice.'

'What? No.'

'You think I'm stupid? Is that it?'

'No, sir. I—No.' Marco has pushed himself up onto his hands. His head hangs down and he shakes it slowly from side to side. A sudden gust makes the rafters creak and a pigeon lands on the tiles above our heads with a feathery thump. It begins cooing a musical heartbeat note over and over. Marco is still shaking his head. *Think of something. Fast.* 'The fault is mine. I accept that. Please believe me, I would not dream of asking for a second payment.' Ormesini smells a rat but can't figure it out. He stands, chewing his lower lip—*craving the taste of meat?*—while, behind him, Marco starts to mouth something but it's too low to hear. Is he praying? Ormesini clears his throat. 'Glad to see you're being sensible about things… Remarkably so. You'll start work immediately?'

'Of course.'

He lifts his hat from the chair. 'I'll take my leave then.'

'Allow me to see you out.' Together we head towards the door. 'Such a pleasure to see you. You must call again.' My hand has already clasped the doorknob when Ormesini turns his head. 'That screen,' he says as though noticing it for the first time. Blood drains from my head. 'Oh, that. A trinket from a satisfied customer.'

'Very satisfied indeed. That's come all the way from China if I'm not mistaken.'

'It really isn't anything special.' Ormesini tosses me a shockingly friendly glance. 'You're wrong. Look at the embroidery on those panels. You don't get work like that round here. *Suzhou* if I'm not mistaken.'

'Is it? Well, I mustn't keep you.' I throw the door wide.

'Let me take a look.'

'But—' The sands of time stop falling. Dust motes hang in the air. My mouth is ajar but no further sound emerges. Helplessly I watch as Ormesini starts across the room knowing nothing can save us, until Marco rears up and expels a perfect arc of vomit over his calfskin boots.

THIRTY-FIVE

'Seteney, it's Liv. Can you hear me?'

'Yes.' She's here. The enchantress. I hear her voice.'

'You're smiling.'

'That's because I'm happy.'

'I want you to tell me about the secret painting Zorzi did of you.'

'Painting?'

'Did he show it to you? Mopsa saw it. Lodovico saw it.'

'I don't know these names.'

'Can you take me to the time Zorzi first told you he had painted you as the Twilight Madonna?'

'No.' The enchantress is put out. Does she think she controls me?'

'Why not?'

'Because it would be rude to leave in the middle of a wedding.'

§

SETENEY:

I am laughing so hard my drink spurts from my nose and makes all the other women laugh even harder, except Aunt Ülkü who never fails to remind me how I constantly fail to live up to the high standards of an Adyghean woman. Even when I can't breathe for the tightness of my corset or I trip on my voluminous skirts. I ignore her. What has she got to complain about? The wedding has gone well.

Our Lord's eldest daughter has been safely dispatched to the matrimonial home, where the master of ceremonies lifted her veil with the tip of his dagger and proclaimed his satisfaction for all to hear. The air is sharp, a crystal sharp day where everyone is smiling, and I don't even mind when the crones poke me in the ribs and say it will be my turn soon. *You'll have something growing in that belly before you know it, dearie. Then you can kiss goodbye to that pretty waist.* I thank them for their good wishes and turn away, drawn by the juices of roasting lamb and calf hissing in the air.

I'm not the only one. A young man grabs the flayed skin of a calf before charging off with it on his horse, the others in hot pursuit. It is unseemly to watch men too closely, but their antics attract a crowd and who could blame us for applauding when the Lord's son jumps on the back of his horse or for laughing when Beslan falls from his and lands in the middle of a pile of discarded entrails. It makes me hold my sides and the corn beer I've been drinking misses my throat and gushes out my nostrils.

Beslan pulls himself up. He marches over, reeking of offal then pushes my shoulder roughly. 'Stop laughing. It makes you ugly. Like Aunt Elif.' This is harsh as Aunt Elif's nose and ears were cut off by her husband as a punishment for adultery, but it makes me consider how far the corn beer would have spurted if I had lacked a nose, which makes me positively howl. Through my tears, I see the hurt in his face. I am the one person who should never laugh at him. 'Beslan?' He ignores me, cloaking his ears with his shoulders and stalking off, his limp more visible than ever. Poor brother. If only he could learn to laugh a little at himself. It's hard to forgive a man his faults when he won't forgive himself.

I return to the revels, but I can't enjoy myself knowing Beslan is miserable, and eventually I make my excuses and go in search of him. It isn't easy. Everyone is soft with drink. They stagger in front of me, silly smiles dripping from their faces. 'Don't leave. Dance with me.' I'm twirled from hand to hand and have to duck under arms to get away.

Death stumbles out of the firelight into my path. He's an imposing figure, neither animal nor human. A goat's head on a man's body. Billy-Goat-Skin, the clown who appears at every wedding. My grandmother never laughed when she saw him. *The old gods are made to play the fool for now. But they won't forget the insult when the time comes.* He reaches for me. 'One kiss, pretty one, and I will make the flowers bloom and the wheat grow tall.' His skinny fingers skim my robe but I'm too quick for him, and, before he can catch me, I'm running towards the woods.

Beslan isn't hard to find. I hear him cursing before I get there. 'You think you can cheat me? Belly crawling sons of slaves. Get up, you dirty cocksuckers. I demand satisfaction.' His rages amuse rather than anger the other young men. Who would take up a cripple's challenge? No honour in that.

Creeping up behind Beslan, I touch his shoulder. 'Come home with me.' He jumps at my touch then spits on the ground. 'Go away. This place is for men.'

'Then what are a bunch of silly drunken boys doing here? Come.' I place a gentle hand on his shoulder. 'Let's go.' Beslan bites his lip, his pupils growing large and glassy while the others howl like wolves and stamp their feet to drown out the sting of my words.

'What's this? I was looking for my kin and instead I find a litter of squealing piglets.' A man, tall and bearded, is staring down at us. He faces us, hands on hips. 'Don't you recognise me?' No. Yes? I do know this man, but he's different somehow. I can't place him, not the way his face is blurred between the past and present. Beslan says it first, 'Uncle Shumaf?'

Of course. The name unlocks a box in my head. This is our father's youngest brother. I haven't seen him in over a decade and a half, but it's more than time that has changed him. That look in his eyes. What does it mean? But, even as I am still struggling to understand, something in my mind deer-leaps forwards and plucks the answer out of the air. I'm not the only one who met Billy-Goat-Skin roaming the night.

Beslan looks blank, but I know what Uncle Shumaf is going to say before he says it. Is this what Grandmother meant by the 'wisdom of women'? He opens his arms wide as if to hug us instead but stands motionless, crucified before the flames. 'My dears. I bring sad tidings. Your father is dead.'

§

GIORGIONE:

I'm halfway up the staircase when I hear movement coming from above. Faintly. A creak from a floorboard. The scrape of a chair. Enough to make me freeze, foot hovering above the next step, hand white-knuckling the banister. There's someone up there. In the studio. Ormesini? Back to take a closer look at the *Suzhou* lace? I should have moved the portrait. What was I thinking?

Another creak. The door is opening. I turn, too late to run, stopped in my tracks by Marco's voice wafting down. 'Zorzi, is that you?' He appears at the top of the stairs. 'What's wrong?'

'Nothing. I'm fine.'

'You're clutching your chest.'

'I thought you were *you know*.' Marco doesn't smile. He glances down the hall then points back at the studio. 'You'd better come up.' He stays silent until we're inside then blurts out, 'I've been with Fiametta.' Does he think I'm jealous?

'Did she make a man of you at last?'

'Not like that. She sent for me. She's heard rumours.'

'What sort of rumours?'

'Ormesini intends to kill you.' The colours drain out of me.

'He knows? About Seteney and me?'

'No. Of course not.'

'How can you be sure?'

'Because fish mamas aren't feeding your rotting corpse to fish babies at the bottom of the lagoon.' He makes a fair point, but the small flame of relief is quickly quenched by the realisation that Ormesini still wants to kill me. Marco is watching me anxiously. 'He wants the Magdalene to be the last portrait you ever do.'

'Why? I mean—for God's sake—I mean—why?'

Marco shrugs. 'Who knows? Ormesini is Ormesini. Fiametta says he's obsessed with his slave girl. He hides her from everyone, even loves her in his twisted way. And he can't stand any intimacy between her and another man. Not even that of an artist and his subject.'

'That makes no sense. He's left us alone, unescorted. Many times.'

'He's feeding you the rope and waiting for you to fashion the noose.'

'But he can't just kill me.'

'Can't he? He bursts in, a man betrayed. Crime of passion. A robbery gone wrong.'

'A robbery?'

'She's still his property. In this context, stealing her affections has the most literal interpretation.'

My legs are suddenly weak. I slump on to the chair and feel it creak under my too-large frame. 'What can I do?'

'Run. Far away. And then keep running.'

'What about Seteney?'

'Forget Seteney. If you want a slave girl, head for Constantinople. I hear the streets run every shade from ivory to snow with them.'

I'm not sure what happens next. One moment I'm sitting on the chair, the next I have Marco by the collar and I'm lifting him off the ground. I spit words in his face. 'I don't want a slave girl. I want SETENEY.' He makes a strangled squeaking noise in response, and it occurs to me that this is most likely because I am strangling him. My fingers loosen and he falls to the ground clutching his throat.

'Zorzi, you rancid excrescence on a whore's putrid tit.'

'It's possible I may have overreacted somewhat. I'm sorry. Let me fetch you some wine.'

'Is it the same stuff as yesterday?'

'Yes.'

'No thank you. My vomit tastes better. Where were we?'

'You were telling me I'm going to die.'

'I was telling you to get out.'

'I told you. I won't go without Seteney. Besides I have nowhere to go.'

'And that is why it is lucky that, for some unfathomable reason, I am your friend. I have a plan.'

'Does it involve courtesans and the exchange of large sums of gold?'

Marco looks hurt. 'It involves a relative of mine. Jean Perréal.'

'Jean Perréal. I know the name.'

'You should do. He is portraitist to King Louis at the French court.'

'A relative of yours?'

'We're not all peasants grubbing about in the dirt, you know.'

'I'm sorry. I've underestimated you. What is he, a cousin, an uncle?'

'As good as. My mother's sister's husband's aunt's second cousin is Perréal's wife.'

I squeeze my eyes tight shut then open them again. 'Marco, we are more closely related.'

'That is neither here nor there. The point is that Jean and I correspond. About you.'

'Me?'

'Yes. Don't go all blushing maiden on me. He admires your work.'

'He's seen my work?'

'Of course not. Where would he see it? Fortunately I have a flair for the picturesque and I left out your interest in painting the corpses of old women. He wrote back to me recently and he's particularly interested in your twilight portrait.' I can't help glancing at Fiametta's screen.

'But how can you possibly have discussed it so quickly?'

'Because, for some reason beyond the wit of mortal man to comprehend, the saints smile upon you. Jean is in Nice at the moment visiting relatives, and I happen to know a merchant who travels between the two on a regular basis. Half the journey. Half the time.' He flourishes his fingers in my face. 'Prepare to be amazed. I can get a response to my letters in less than a *fortnight*.' I have to admit it's impressive.

'Let me get this straight. You are saying that Perréal is willing to offer us protection.'

Marco's smile is a mile wide. 'Yes. For a price.'

THIRTY-SIX

SETENEY:

The sun is setting by the time we reach our father's home. It's taken a night and a day of hard riding to reach here, and my limbs are so stiff from perpetual jolting along narrow mountain tracks I have to be lifted down from the carriage. Horseback has been harder on Beslan. His face has a moony whiteness about it, and he fish-flops on to the ground and lies there cursing until helped up by one of Uncle Shumaf's men.

No-one comes out to greet us. The house is wrapped in silence. Where are the mourners? Where is my mother? An old slave opens the door a crack then wider when he sees who it is. 'They couldn't wait any longer. They've taken the body up the ridge track to the High Place,' he explains.

'Why aren't you with them?'

'There's been a sighting of raiders. I'm to stay behind and keep watch.'

'And what will you do if you spot them? Shake your arthritic bones to sound the alarm?' The slave shrugs. The jest is not new.

'We're weary,' Beslan says. 'We'll go in the morning.'

Uncle Shumaf evil eyes him and says, 'We will go now.'

The closer we get the louder it becomes. A deep thrum of human voices chanting the funeral dirges and the crackle of great pyres swirling constellations of sparks into the darkening sky. The sound enfolds us, draws us in and makes us part of it, so I can't remember the moment I first see my father. Only that he is there in my consciousness, sitting on a raised platform surrounded by costly gifts and tokens. So lifelike, I take a step towards him. 'He won't rot,' Uncle Shumaf whispers. 'They removed the viscera before I left.'

'Where is Mother?' Uncle Shumaf points through the mourners to a small figure sitting before the platform. So rigid. For a moment I wonder if she, too, is dead. But this is a wife's place, obedient before her lord. 'Mother?' I creep closer until I can see the scratch marks she has inflicted upon herself. How many hours drawing her long nails down her cheeks? Blood worms its way from the crevices and quivers in the night air, but otherwise she is perfectly still. The frenzy of her mourning is over and now she sits, dry-eyed, transfixed by the corpse.

Uncle Shumaf squeezes my shoulder. 'It's different for Beslan but no-one would mind if you wept a little.' I jerk step away from him. What does he mean? Who should I weep for? The great husk propped up on the platform or the woman who is little more than a memory of a memory? Beslan and I exchange looks. What a strange notion Uncle Shumaf must have of family.

§

'Zorzi, did you show the painting of the Twilight Madonna to Seteney?'

§

GIORGIONE:

My portrait of Ormesini hangs in the entrance hall, a magnificent frame haloing the canvas—scallop shells, Greek lyres and a dozen naked cherubim struggling to support huge cornucopias bursting at the seams with gilded fruits and flowers. Poor taste doesn't come cheaply. From the centre, Ormesini's painted eyes look down with kingly beneficence, a slightly disdainful smile playing about his lips as though his generosity comes at the price of his contempt. The perfect patrician in other words.

The old woman greets me with a toothless grin. If she knows of Ormesini's murderous intent, she hides it well. 'Hello you.'

'Hello gorgeous.' She blushes and flirtatiously pushes a thin straggle of grey hair behind an ear.

'Come for your money, have you?' A bag of coins is thrust into my hand. 'Here. The first instalment.' Ormesini's eyes look down at me. I imagine him stuffing the coins back in his pocket once they've been taken from my mutilated corpse. She catches me looking at the portrait. 'He's pleased, you know.'

'Is he?' The smirk on Ormesini's face twists a blade through my conscience. I've created a freak, a snarling street mongrel sewn up in a lionskin.

'Do you want to count it?'

'What?'

'The coins. Do you want to count them?'

'No. Your master's honour is enough for me.' If she recognises the sarcasm in this, she chooses to ignore it. A glance at the painter's bag under my arm. 'Here to finish the other one?'

'Yes.'

'You're almost done.' It isn't a question. As her rheumy eyes meet mine, I think, *she knows she's talking to a dead man.* Her scaly claw slips into my palm and squeezes it meaningfully. 'I will miss you.' Her flesh feels cracked and dusty—I'm caressing a cadaver—but I manage to curl my hand around her fingers and squeeze back. 'I will miss you too.'

§

Seteney is sitting by the window. Her hair is loose, and the red brocade gown has slipped a little, revealing the captivating curve of her shoulder. She starts at the sound of my footsteps, but when she looks round her lips part in a smile, a smile that makes my heart turn over knowing it's meant just for me. She slips down from the window seat and runs over to bury her head in my chest, surprising me with her recklessness. 'Are you sure? Is it safe?'

'Old Alessandra you mean? It's fine. She won't say a thing. She's in love with you.' I can't help glancing over my shoulder.

'What about—'

'Away on unexpected business. He rushed out of the house this morning. Didn't say when he's coming back.' Her fingers burrow deeper into my flesh. 'Our last days.'

'Don't say that. Never say that.' She pushes me away roughly.

'Italians! Our time is ending. We must accept it.'

'I won't.'

'Who is going to save us? Apollo? Neptune? Perhaps the Queen of Heaven is listening at one of your little shrines?'

'I have a plan.'

'A plan?'

'Listen to me.' I drag her over to the window and we sit, facing each other, on the cushioned bench. 'We're going to France.'

'I don't understand.'

'There's a painter there. By the name of Jean Perréal. He is known at the French court.'

'But why would he help us?'

'Because Marco has written to him.'

'Marco, your friend?'

'Yes. Perréal is a relation of his.'

'A close relation?'

'Close is a relative term. Does it matter?'

'Yes.'

'All right.' I try to remember. 'Perréal's wife is Marco's mother's sister's husband's aunt's second cousin. I think.'

She imprisons her face in her hands. 'Madness. Not even amongst we Circassians would the connection mean a thing.'

'Seteney, hear me out. He wants something from me.'

'What?'

'This.' She takes the canvas from my hand and unfurls it. Her reaction is not what I hoped. Eternity stretches between us as she sits in silence staring at it. 'Who is this?'

'It's you.'

'No.' She shrinks back.

'You don't believe me?'

'There are mirrors everywhere in that hateful room. I'm forced to look into them night and day, but I have never seen this woman.'

'That is because you have never seen her as I have.'

She looks into my face then back at the portrait. 'What are those flowers in my hair?'

'Jessamine. They only flower at night. I chose them because they remind me of you.'

'You've seen me during the day.'

'I've only seen you bloom at night.' I can't help myself. I touch the twilight strands of her hair very gently, very lovingly. 'This is the greatest work I have ever created. I will never better it.'

She's frowning. 'And this Perréal wants my portrait?'

'He wants its secrets.'

'Why?'

'I can't answer that. Not fully. But I can tell you that the Valois kings are not easy men to work for. To maintain his position as royal portraitist, Perréal must constantly be better than all his rivals. Constantly able to surprise. He needs new techniques: how to soften skin tones, how to diffuse them with light.'

'And you will do this for him?'

'In return for his protection, yes.'

'And when he's learned all you have to teach and sees you only as a rival, what then?'

'We'll move on. Go further.'

'Where?'

'Where? The ends of the earth. Scotland I suppose.'

'I don't know where that is.'

'It's very far away. A cold, hilly country constantly shrouded in mist. You'll like it.' She's biting her thumb, eyes darting from side to side. There is terror in her expression but there is also hope. At last she says, 'You would give up your secrets for this man?'

'I would give them up for you.'

She gets up, begins to pace. Mumbling to herself, 'It can't… it can't possibly…'

'What's that?'

'It can't possibly work. Do you think I can just walk out of the door?'

'Why not? We'll go now. You said yourself, he isn't here.' A curtain of anger drops over her face and she spits something at me in her native language, leaving me staring helplessly until she switches back to Italian. 'Have you ground your brains to dust along with the pigments? Ormesini's men would cut us to ribbons the moment we stepped over the threshold.'

'Didn't he take them with him?'

Eyes rolled. Fingertips pressed to temples. 'Of course not. He's not going to leave the security of his home to old Alessandra, is he?'

'I came through the front door. I didn't see anyone.'

'That's the point. You're not to supposed to see them. But he doubled the guard on the house before he left and made sure I was there to hear him give the order.'

A thought chimes against my skull and makes me sit up. 'The ladder. It worked before. We can do it again.' My words work no magic. Her face empties. I watch as she closes her eyes and breathes deeply, and when she opens them again her voice is resigned. 'He put bars at the windows. Didn't you notice?' I didn't notice. I've passed so easily in and out of Ormesini's lair that I've half forgotten that it's a prison. I should say something, but what? Half a plan. That's all I brought with me.

She shakes her head then slumps down on the window seat, close but not touching. 'Even if I could get away, his men are everywhere. They'd find us. Bring us back.'

Awkwardly I lay a hand on her shoulder and squeeze it gently. 'We'll find a way.'

'Don't say that.'

'Seteney?'

'Don't.' She shakes me off and jumps to her feet, casts about, a wild thing ready to dash itself against the walls. 'It's cruel.'

'I'm sorry. What did I—'

'You're trying to give me hope.'

'Is that bad?'

'You don't understand. Not since I awoke, bound in that cage, have I allowed myself to taste hope. Not a single drop. But the way you spoke, just for a moment, I…I believed you. I thought—' Her hands fly to her belly and press hard. 'I can't. It hurts too much. Too much.'

I'm on my feet, trying to reach her, but she is quicksilver and I am lead. My hands paw air but all that is left is the swish of the brocade on polished wood as she runs through the door. 'Seteney! SETENEY!' I don't care who hears. I have to reach her. But Alessandra steps into my path and holds up a scaly claw. 'Leave her be.'

'I can't. I need to make her listen.'

'She won't listen. Poor child. Every man she's ever known has betrayed her. Why should she trust you with your witless, half-baked abortion of a scheme so malformed it should have been drowned in a backstreet canal before it saw the light of day?' I have to hand it to Alessandra. She has a way with words. A dark cloud descends over me. 'Then it's hopeless.'

'Now, now dearie, I didn't say that. There might be a way to save her yet.'

'Tell me.'

She taps the side of her warty nose. 'Not here. Go back to your studio and I will slip away as soon as I can.'

THIRTY-SEVEN

GIORGIONE:

Smokey darkness fills the studio before Alessandra's knuckles finally rap against the door. Despite waiting in an agony of anticipation for what seems like hours, I give a scalded cat jump then fling it wide, all but dragging her into the room. 'Easy now.' She pulls back rubbing her shoulder. 'Is this the way to treat someone here to save your bacon?'

'Where are my manners? A seat? A cup of wine? Now tell me how to save the love of my life.' She accepts the chair and holds her hand out for the wine, which makes her pull a face and mutter, *cat's piss,* before spitting it luxuriously on to the floor.

'All in good time, dearie. We must settle the terms first.'

'Terms?'

'I have something you want, and you have something I want.'

'I don't understand. What is it you want?' A coquettish glance down at the floor then up between sparse lashes. 'Can't you tell?' Light is dawning from murky depths. No. No, not that. Please let it be money. Blessed Mother, I will pay her any amount, only let it be money. She bats her lashes once then twice then looks hard at me.

'But surely—I mean—after all—' Mumbled phrases about respect and 'deep regard' while Alessandra listens without expression. A drool of words like 'honour' and 'esteem' dribbles from my tongue until my voice gives out in a rasping wheedle. 'After all, it would be a violation. You wouldn't want that, would you?'

Her rheumy eye swivels towards my codpiece. 'Why do you think I'm here?' She stands up and starts loosening her corset. Oh no!

'Wait! Please! Look, I haven't even got a bed.'

'Slept on floors all my life. Don't reckon one more will kill me.' Her skirt is a puddle around her ankles. I can see the sagging outline of her breasts through her shift.

'What about your reputation? If it suffered damage because of me, how could I ever forgive myself?'

'Are you going to tell the master I was here?'

'No. Of course not.'

'Then I don't need to worry, do I?' Her claw reaches forwards and grabs my balls through the codpiece—an impressive act as they feel as though they have retracted close to my Adam's apple. 'Come now, dearie.' We progress, crab-like, towards a corner of the room. They used to say my father was led by his balls by my stepmother. I hope to God it was a more pleasant experience for him.

There's an arthritic creak as she gets down on her knees, and I can't help a pang of anxiety for her joints until she starts undoing the codpiece. A moment later her cracked lips are around my shaft. What's this? Sweet Infant Jesus, no. A familiar tingling stretches the skin. This can't be happening. 'Wait! How do I know you'll keep your word?' Her response is muffled but indisputable. 'Doesn't look like you've got much choice now does it?'

Her fingers are expertly massaging my balls. Truthfully, she could teach Fiametta a thing or two. Blood rushes from my limbs weakening my knees and turning my shaft stiffer than a surgeon's pole. Sweet Seteney I love you, but Alessandra's toothless gums are suckling me with the energy of a starving baby goat.

She pulls back suddenly and, breathless, we admire her hand-iwork. If Archimedes wanted a lever to move the world, he could do worse than my cock. Alessandra's wrinkled cheeks plait with pleasure. 'Just the way I like it, dearie.'

Before I know it, I'm on my back, the nightmare far from over, as she mounts me, fleshless buttocks thrust towards my face. Somewhere my mind is screaming, *Seteney*, over and over but the voice is growing fainter crushed beneath the mounting shudders brought on in response to Alessandra's gyrating hips. A red mist descends and I rear up to grab her hair. Some of it comes away in my hand. I could push her away in an instant, but I can't help myself. I want to do it. I am confounded…confused…I'm COMING!

Afterwards she dresses calmly while I lie, recovering, on the floor. A full moon pulses over the skylight and all that is left of our coupling is the faint smell that rises from the lagoon in summer. My chair is pulled up and she stares at me as though I were a fine hock of ham recently relished.

'Well?'

'Well?'

'Don't you want to know how to save your little Tatar? Or do you prefer homegrown to foreign muck?' Forgetting the blood is still pooled in my loins, I sit up and the room swims. Alessandra crackles with laughter. 'My, my. What a prince our Tatar princess has found.'

'Just tell me what to do.'

'What's wrong? Realised what it's like with a real woman?' I don't answer. Is punching an old woman a mortal sin? For a few years in purgatory, it would be worth it. Alessandra sighs and plays with her corset laces. 'There's plague in the city.'

The room starts to spin again though I haven't moved. 'How do you know?'

'Why do you think the master took off so fast?'

'But why hasn't there been an outcry? I haven't heard anything.' Alessandra doesn't answer, and I find myself saying, '*Carnevale.*' No. That's madness. Impossible. Might as well tell me the Holy

Mother was spotted selling herself to sailors at the *Arsenale*. 'The council of ten would never allow it.'

Alessandra straightens her skirts. 'More than one council in Venice, dearie. There are secret councils. Grey councils. Councils you might even call kingdoms. And we both know who the king is.'

'So why did he leave you behind?'

'Because it may come to nothing. Not the first time. A spark doesn't always catch. Besides I can look after myself. You think I reached this age by being Fate's fool?' It's true. She must be at least fifty.

'Okay, so Ormesini doesn't want to lose his profits. How does this help Seteney?'

'Supposing I told you she has plague?'

'What?' The room fills with crows. Black wings beat in my ears. Behind my eyes. Alessandra shakes her head wearily. 'I said, *suppose*. Not that she did have it.'

'All right.' I nod, but I can still hear the wings.

'Think about it. There are only two ways she can leave that house. Either in a box or because the men guarding her think she'll put them in a box.' I think about it, and it still makes no sense. Alessandra is unimpressed. 'And they call you a genius? Artists are all the same. As much depth as a layer of paint. All we have to do is give the appearance of pestilence. Dark circles under the eyes. A boil here a bubo there.'

The *Denari* drops. 'A disguise.'

'Bravo.' Alessandra's claws come together in a slow clap. 'Now all you have to do is persuade her.'

I'm on my feet, head full of putty and pigments when a thought occurs. 'Why are you doing this?'

'Perhaps I'm just a kindly old woman.'

'No, really.'

'I want something.'

'But I gave you what you wanted.'

'That was for information. Now you want my assistance.'

'You want me to pay you to help Seteney escape?'

'My, you're quick.'

My temper has always been slow but now I'm spluttering with anger. 'Of all the avaricious, blackmailing, greedy old—'

'The master always pays well for loyalty.' She examines her knuckles while I savour bile. Ormesini's purse is still in my doublet.

'How much do you want?'

'Not money.'

My throat is dry but I manage to gesture at the corner of the room. 'You want to—Again?'

'Men!' She's offended. 'You think a quick ride on your cock is worth risking my life for?'

'Then what?'

'The painting.'

'Which painting?' She doesn't answer. Doesn't need to. 'But you haven't even seen it.'

'Don't need to. *The best you've ever painted.* That's what you said.'

'You spied on us.' She gives me a look to say, if the Almighty didn't want us to spy, he wouldn't have made ears fit keyholes.

'It's a bargain, dearie. The real thing for a copy.'

'But Perréal?'

'It's your techniques he wants. You'll think of something.' She's serious. No way to persuade her.

'What will you do with it?'

'Ensure a comfortable old age. Told you, dearie. Old Alessandra's never been Fate's fool.' She holds out her twisted claw. 'Do we have a bargain?' I hope I crush her motheaten bones to powder as we shake hands.

THIRTY-EIGHT

LEXIE:

Liv is glued to her laptop when I finally get home. I toy with slinking past her and shutting myself away in my room. It's getting

239

harder to jump from life to life without a sense of living at twice the speed. Constantly weary and weirdly ravenous. I wonder if I'm sleeping or has Seteney taken over my dreams? But Liv has given up things to help me so I try a cheery, 'Hey, what's up?'

She drags her eyes from her laptop, tortured-genius-style. 'I found something.'

'I hope we can eat it because I didn't get lunch.'

'Sorry, cupboards are bare. It'll have to be takeout again.' I look for our dogeared menus while Liv talks to my back.

'I went somewhere new today.'

'Nice. I went back to the fifteenth century.' Pull out my phone and hand it to her. 'It's all here. My notes and the interviews with Darius.' Liv takes it from me.

'Anything significant?'

'I learned that my father had died.' The Freudian in Liv is immediately interested. 'Death of a father figure? How did that make you feel?'

'It was five hundred years ago. I'm over it.' I hold out the menu from Luciano's. 'I want pizza.'

'I want world peace, and at least we didn't already have it last night.'

'Fine. I'll have whatever you want as long as it has anchovies on it.'

'Don't you want to know where I was today?'

'If I ask, can we have pizza?' She angry-porcupines her shoulders at me.

'If you're not going to take this seriously—'

'I'm sorry. Really. Constantly switching between two worlds isn't easy. One minute I'm me, the next I'm still me but a different 'me'. I don't think like someone from the twenty-first century. I believe in God and demons and the magic of clouds. I hate being enslaved but I don't question slavery. It's a 'me' I didn't think I could be. Then suddenly I'm back and I'm just plain old, everyday 'me'. A 'me' who has to handle MRI machines and global networking and call menus that cut you off before you can speak to a human being. It leaves me confused and drained and also really hungry. So, I'm sorry, Liv. Tell me where you were today.'

'At a survivor's meeting.'

'Survivors of what?'

'People who have assholes as sisters.'

'Really?'

'It was for survivors of near-death experiences. Interested now?' The pizza menu congeals in my hand. 'Are you saying what I think you're saying?'

'Five members were on the Somnipradine trial.'

'How did you find out? They've signed non-disclosure. They're not allowed to tweet or post or talk to anyone.'

Liv taps the side of her beautiful nose. 'I have my ways.' This is not the goody-two-shoes, daddy's girl I grew up with. I can't keep the doubt out of my voice. 'You went there today?' She points at herself. 'Meet Soo Choi, survivor of a terrible skiing accident. I died three times on the operating table until the miracle of Somnipradine brought me back.'

'Wow, Liv. I didn't think you had it in you.'

'You're not the only one who can live other lives.'

'Tell me. I want to know everything. But first let me order pizza. You have no idea how little I've eaten in this life or my previous one.'

Over slices of a world pizza—a dozen slices, the classic taste of twelve international cities on a single dough base—Liv tells me what she's learned. 'There were about ten people at the meeting, but only four of the ones I was looking for.'

'And they talked about the trial?'

'No. They were clearly scared off. But I laid it on thick. Went on about how the memories haunt me. Even teared up a bit.'

'Impressive. Did you learn much?'

'Well, they clearly had no idea what I was talking about when I mentioned memories that might not belong to me.'

'Maybe they were afraid.'

'Not my impression. They looked completely blank. None of the shared glances that happened when I mentioned being on the trial.' Disappointment turns the cream cheese on my slice of New York sour. 'You're sure?'

'I'm sure. Reading reaction is pretty much what I do for a living.' I chow down Mexico City without thinking. The loaded jalapenos taste of sawdust. 'Of course,' Liv adds, taking a tiny fairy bite of her otherwise untouched, slice, 'I did meet the missing survivor just after I left, an elderly lady called June.'

'What did—ow!' The jalapenos kick in and my mouth turns to molten lava. She ignores my streaming eyes and carries on, 'She mislaid her bus pass and tried to walk. She'd missed the whole thing by the time she made it. Nice woman. Chatty. I walked her all the way to the train station.' She pauses to give me the chance to ask an excited question, but fire ants are perforating my tongue with pneumatic drills, and all I manage is a strangulated gurgle. Liv gives a weary shake of her head. She's seen it all before.

'She was the kind of woman who likes to tell anecdotes. Her cat sending an email, that sort of thing. And wait for it—' She drum rolls her fingers on the counter. 'She told me how she was still very confused after she got out of hospital following a stroke. So confused, in fact, she tapped a young man on the shoulder in a train station and said, *I think I'm your wife.*'

I'm sitting straight up. 'Then what?'

'Then nothing. He got on a train and she never saw him again.' Not knowing whether to laugh or cry, I stare dejectedly down at the pizza until Liv says. 'You ass!'

'What?'

'You don't get it, do you?'

'What? What don't I get?'

'It's you. You're the reason Darius is remembering.'

'I'm the reason?' Liv looks smug while managing to continue to look gorgeous while doing it. 'You're the trigger.'

'In English, please.'

'Okay. I'm not exactly being scientific here. I'm extrapolating from a dataset of eight subjects.'

'Piaget's theories of developmental psychology were based on observations of his own three children.'

'As we psychologists say, two Jungs don't make a right. But, if we're allowing wild conjecturing, here's my take. The four of you who claim past memories are you, Darius, June and—' She snaps her fingers. 'Prison girl.'

'Brigit Carlisle.'

'Whatever. Not one of you has a strange memory until you encounter someone you believe you had a bond with in a past life.' It makes sense. Does it make sense? I'm not sure. 'Are you sure?'

'No. It's a wild theory from a minuscule amount of data. Only think about it. Darius doesn't find himself back in prehistory until his first encounter with you in the MRI suite. Brigit Carlisle doesn't recall any royal connections until she sees her son. And June is the only survivor of the group to experience anything out of the ordinary when she meets her 'husband' in a random encounter at a train station.'

'So, continuing the theme of arbitrary speculation, what do you conclude, Doctor Song?'

'Well, if you give any credence to Eastern philosophy, it happens all the time. Why else do we encounter people every day and feel no connection then some random individual appears, and we feel like we've known them for years?'

'Hormones, subconscious patterns of behaviour, secret longings?'

'Could be. But whatever it is, some force is driving us towards them, as if they hold the answers to something we're looking for.'

'You said it before. He might be attempting to work something out.'

'I said a lot of things. All I'm certain of is that there is some connection between you two that goes beyond doctor/patient attachment.

After Liv goes to bed I lie in the clammy semi-dark. Did Darius choose me or did I choose him? Are we just pieces in some bigger game our subconsciouses are playing out? It feels real. When I'm there, I *am* Seteney. Liv doesn't know what it's like to stand inside someone else's soul. To look out through eyes that have never seen an aeroplane, who doesn't even have the concept of the

word. To feel that person's rage, her trauma. Ormesini's hands...
his breath, rotten meat and sour wine...spittle on my face...my
breasts...bile in my throat...his hate-filled cock...coming towards
me...no, no, NO!

'Lexie? You okay?' Liv's voice, sludgy with sleep, comes from
her room.

'I'm fine. Just a bad dream. Go back to sleep.' There's no reply.
I think she was asleep before I finished talking.

Try to calm myself with thoughts of Darius. That smile I feel
coming, even before it reaches his lips. The secret glances. Not
just, 'I know you'. But 'I have *known* you'. Ageless and untouchable.
Over and over. Loss and discovery. Discovery and loss. The thread
that can't be broken. The shattered man in the bed touching me
from another world, another life. Are they the same? How much
are we just the sum of our experiences? Our birthplaces? Or do
we carry an immutable core in the human BIOS, the firmware we
bring with us from incarnation to incarnation no matter what? At
what point do two people exist only as one?

Seteney is in love with Zorzi. Am I in love with Darius? The
circumstances are so different, so impossible to compare. We can
never make love, take a walk across a beach, cuddle up on a sofa,
float down the Amazon, trek up Machu Pichu. Yet I'm risking my
career, my relationship with Liv, everything that's worth anything
because I need to know that death isn't the end. Human life doesn't
end in a blank, and all those people I tried to save and failed weren't
wiped out by stupidity or ignorance or some pathetic random fuck
up just because shit happens. I need to know we all get another
chance.

THIRTY-NINE

SETENEY:

My stoicism is admired in the days that follow my father's funeral, the dutiful daughter swallowing her grief in silence. All around me, decisions are taken and arrangements made, but I am privy only to fragments which I gather together and sew into a patchwork of meaning. I learn that our father broke a leg while out hunting, and though his brothers did their best, keeping up a constant clamouring vigil—banging pots and playing rowdy games—to prevent him from falling asleep and succumbing to evil spirits, he fell unconscious on the third day never to awaken. I also learn that my mother is to join my eldest uncle's household. She will be cared for but never again enjoy the status of wife. My father's property is to be divided amongst his brothers. His children are forgotten as though we never existed.

Beslan finds me in the grove where Grandmother used to pick her herbs. I like it here, lying on my back, the trees encircling a bottomless well of sky, winds ghost whispering amongst the branches. Beslan walks through a fan of shafted light and sits down on a half-rotted log beside me. 'There you are.'

'Here I am.' We sit in silence for a while then he turns to look at me.

'Uncle Shumaf went to the tumulus, and asked Father's corpse three times if he would like to join us for dinner.'

'What answer did he receive?'

'Same as yesterday.'

'This is the sixth day. How long will they go on asking?'

'I don't know. A while I guess.' He pulls a flask from his tunic. 'Drink?

'I'm not thirsty.' He looks sad and I can't help thinking how rejected he must be feeling. 'Give me the flask.' I take it from him gently and drink deeply. It's stronger than I'm used to it, a little bitter. I follow its fire all the way to my belly where it glows softly, warming me. To my surprise, I find I like it and take another draught. Beslan looks pleased. He lifts his hand when I try to hand it back.

'First, a toast.'

'What are we toasting?'

'Your good fortune.'

'Mine?' He takes back the flask.

'Haven't you heard? Our loving father left you a dowry.'

'What?' I nearly spit out the contents of my stomach, and Beslan laughs so hard he falls off the log and drops the flask before righting himself and toasting me with a messy gulp that half runs down his chin. This isn't his first drink today.

'Not as clever as you thought with all that listening at doors. I heard Uncle Dizchin talking to Mother.' The laughter leaves his face and he digs a toe into the moss. 'Do you know what Father left me? His first and only son?' I can guess but shake my head. He makes a vicious movement with his foot opening a seam of red earth through the green. 'Nothing. Not a button from his coat.' I reach out to him, but he pulls away. 'I need to get away from here.'

'You want to go home?'

'No. Away. From everything. I need a fresh start. But how can I? You're set up. But what do I have?' He draws his knees up. Starts rocking. Poor Beslan. He's right. He wasn't born to be part of the fierce stark beauty of our world. I wish I could help him.

'Listen, I don't want the dowry. I'm never getting married. I'll tell Mother to give it to you.'

'She wouldn't listen.'

'I'll make her listen.'

He stops rocking and stares sadly into the distance. 'It's too late.'

'Too late? Too late for what?'

Several things happen all at once. I notice that something is wrong but I don't know what. I start to say something when a snapping twig alerts me that we aren't alone. Unfamiliar footsteps. Shadowy figures emerging from the dark spaces between the trees. They make no greeting and I can't make out who they are. Try to get up, but my head is spinning and my eyes won't focus.

Blinking only makes it worse. Where is Beslan? We're in terrible danger. Run! The world spins off its axis and I kiss the earth with my slack immobile lips. In the last moments of consciousness an insect thought buzzes at the edges of my mind: the flask Beslan used to toast me wasn't the same one I drank from. He switched them when he pretended to fall from the log.

My brother has betrayed me.

§

GIORGIONE:

'What if they don't believe me?'

'They will. They must.' There's something new in Seteney's voice. Something I've never heard before. I think it's fear. 'You must hold still, my love.' I'm trying to fix a 'bubo' to her thigh with wax, but she's shaking so much it won't adhere. She drops her face into her hands.

'What am I doing? Men have always deceived me.'

'I'm not like those men.'

'You say that now. But you won't be there.'

'I will. I promise, and the palanquin will be waiting for you.'

'What if you're not?'

'I will be.'

'But if you're not?'

'Then get inside and instruct them to move along. I will catch up as soon as I can. You have the money and the letter of intro- duction?'

'Yes.'

'Tell me the route.'

'I know the route.'

'Tell me anyway.'

'First to Verona then Bologna, Parma, Pavia to the Septimer Pass then Basil, Troyes, Paris. And freedom.'

The wax has melted. I dribble a little on to her thigh. 'This may hurt a bit.' She isn't listening.

'It won't work. The men know what plague is. They'll never believe me.'

'You're as pale as a ghost and your eyes are red from weeping. One look at you and they'll run.'

She gives a watery smile. 'I want to hear the plan.'

'You know the plan.'

'I want to hear it again.'

'All right. But hold still. I have some rouge from Fiametta and I want to mix it with a little azurite for a bruised effect.'

'The plan!'

'Alessandra will pretend to discover you fevered and delirious. She'll call for help. But as she examines you, she'll reveal this.' I tap the putty now attached to her thigh. I've painted it a glistening black. A work of art though I say so myself.

'Urgh, what's that smell?'

'Rancid lard and extract of fish entrails. I packed the pustule with them.'

'For the love of God, why?'

'It's not enough to look like you have the plague. You need to smell like you do. Don't worry. Alessandra will clean you up.'

'Then turn me into a dancing bear in Ormesini's wife's frills and flounces.'

'She'll turn you into a noblewoman of charm and mystery. You have the mask?'

'Yes. It's hidden in a blanket chest.'

'Good. The gondolier will be waiting at the bottom of the steps wearing a *melpo* mask. He has orders to take you to the mainland.'

'Where the palanquin will be waiting.'

'Where it will be waiting. Yes.'

'Why aren't you coming to fetch me?'

'I've explained before. We don't know how quickly Ormesini's men will become suspicious. If I'm seen with you the game will be up.'

'You'll be wearing a mask.'

'A mask won't hide my stature. It's better this way.'

'What will I do if you're not there?'

'I told you. Go on. I'll find you. But you must go. Ormesini won't be fooled for long. Promise me.'

'I—'

Fear squeezes my heart. 'Promise me.'

'I promise. I promise.'

Alessandra catches me on my way out. 'You have it?' Her claw comes reaching as her eyes search my face.

'Here.' I hand her the canvas, managing to release it only by an act of will.

I am cajoled in milky, midwifery tones. 'There now. That wasn't so hard.' Perhaps she understands, after all, that nature excluded men from the ultimate act of creation, and art is what we do to compensate ourselves. One eye on me, she unravels the canvas and lets out a low breath. 'Oh yes. Better than I remembered. Truly a wonder, I'll give you that.' There are tears in my eyes as she rolls it up again.

'You'll keep your side of the bargain?'

'Never fear, dearie. Old Alessandra is as good as her word.'

FORTY

GIORGIONE:

I must get the painting back. Perréal wants a masterpiece and I have none other to give. In desperation, I return to the studio and search through half-finished portraits and landscapes. There's much that's good, technically impressive even. But they all seem stiff and lifeless compared to Seteney's twilight beauty.

Sit back on my heels looking up at the skylight trying to think, but my head aches, a dull thrum behind my temples that grows worse the harder I try to ignore it. A cup of wine only makes the thrumming morph into a continual pounding until my skull becomes a cauldron seething with dark blood and red-hot pokers. Push myself to my feet. Need to get out. To think. To breathe.

Where to go? I need someone who will understand, someone with a flair for deceit and subterfuge. I know exactly where to go.

§

SETENEY:

There are no stars. Fog rolling in from the Adriatic snuffed them out and made the night turn secretive. These last hours I've floated like the moon over the blackness of the window, watching the canal slide away into oily darkness. Is the gondolier waiting down there? The lanterns along the *fondamente* are imprisoned in their own halos and illuminate almost nothing.

The window is hard to open through the bars and I manage only the smallest crack. I can't see anything, but the familiar salty scent of decay rises up. It's always there, that smell of rot. Despite all the pageantry, the gorgeous costumes, the gilded towers, the marble fountains, even the gondolas floating by like swanly ghosts, this is a city of death.

A shudder in the air. The big bronze *Marangona* peals over St Mark's Piazza. Cheers and laughter drifting down the water. Carnevale is under way.

'Holy Virgin's Sainted Tits, what are you doing here, dearie?' Old Alessandra is standing in the doorway, hands on bony hips. 'Have you lost your wits? You can't be seen whole and healthy. Hurry, get upstairs!'

Meekly I obey. 'Strip down to your shift.' No fire has been lit and, when I'm done, I stand shivering while Alessandra shakes her head. 'This won't do. You look as healthy as a heifer. Here.' She lifts a pitcher of water and throws it over me. My God! Why?

'Best you look as though you've been sweating. Now into bed.'

'How can I look as though I'm sweating when my teeth are chattering?' I slip under the covers gratefully, but, just as my head touches the pillow, I bolt upright again. 'My ear's burning.'

'A hot water bottle,' Alessandra explains, pushing me back. 'We want them to think you're flushed with fever.'

'With fever, yes. Not broiled!'

250

'That's good. Your cheeks are glowing. Lie back and I'll go fetch the men.'

§

GIORGIONE:

An elbow parries then thrusts into my side. As I try to regain my balance, a boot stamps down on my foot then moves off without apology. Carnevale! Something cracks against my shoulder and cheap lavender scent dribbles down my doublet. Luckily, it's not ink. Throwing scented eggs is prohibited of course, but it doesn't stop the revellers. There's no point in looking for my assailant either. No-one looks guilty behind a mask.

A firework explodes in front of the Doge's palace and the crowd gives a cheer and starts pushing towards Saint Mark's. They haul me along, ignoring how my kicking legs and flailing arms fight against the current until, without warning, a string of whirling *girandoles* goes off above our heads, spitting out tongues of blazing stars. The crowd screams in bibulous delight and surges forward again, almost dragging me down into the undertow of their stamping feet. But I'm quicker than that, and they don't know Venice the way I do. Especially at night.

Shouldering aside a hooded cat, who hisses beery breath at me, I slip down an alley and feel my way along the slippery walls, then it's up and over a load-bearing arch and in through an open window, where I startle a dozing dowager half asleep with her feet in the hearth. She gives a scream as though I am about to take her maidenhood, which considering her breathtaking lack of beauty, may indeed still be intact. A finger to my lips does nothing to quieten her howls, and encourages a sturdy Moor, brandishing a scimitar, into the room. What follows is straight from the ivory pen of Aristophanes: a chase round and around the dining table, jugs and vases flying, until the dowager lifts a set of fire tongs and throws them at my head. Fortunately her eyesight doesn't match the robustness of her lungs and she hits the Moor on the temple and knocks him out cold. With a bow, I thank her for her hospitality and, helping myself to a leg of chicken, I back out.

I'm still licking the grease from my fingers as I climb the stairs to Marco's lodgings. 'Marco, it's Zorzi. Let me in.' He's out. Of course he's out. As if he would give up an opportunity to join in all the drink-drowned debauch terrorising the streets. I'm about to turn away when a flicker catches my eye. There's light coming from under his door. 'Marco, can you hear me? Let me in. This is important.' Still no response. Does he have a woman in there? 'Marco!' Frustration makes me slap the door with the palm of my hand. I expect to feel my shoulder jar, at the very least splinters jabbing my palm. Neither. The door concedes defeat and creaks slowly open.

Marco is lying on his narrow bed, face turned to the wall. He doesn't seem to realise I'm there. Of all the times to prostrate himself before Bacchus. 'Come on. Get up. I need you.' He groans and rolls on to his back. The face that greets me is waxy; the eyelids shaded by midnight. They flutter open and his pupils fix on my face without recognition. 'What's wrong? Are you sick?' But even as I say it, I see them, a filigree of purple blood vessels, delicate as the veins on a fallen leaf. They draw my gaze inexorably towards a glossy black dome, so perfect it might be the roof of a cathedral in hell. My voice escapes in a squeak from the midnight terror rising inside me. 'Dear God. How?' He blinks and says something, repeating it several times before I understand. 'Wa—ter.'

A jug stands near the bed. Is he too weak to lift it? I pour some into a bowl then hold it to his cracked lips; it runs down his chin. Some must get in because he chokes and gasps and clutches my arm. 'He's coming.'

'Who's coming?'

'Ormesini…he—' He chokes some more, and a little worm of blood dribbles from the corner of his mouth. It looks more alive than he does.

'Easy now. Don't try to talk.'

He shakes his head, eyes burning fiercely. 'He's coming for you…tonight.'

Is he delirious? I search his pupils; they seem sane. 'Why to-night? Who told you?' A groan. Clearly he is in no state to be interrogated. 'I need to warn Seteney.' His fingers fumble at my doublet. It's costing him to speak.

'No… Just you…he wants…kill you himself. Safer for her if you stay away.' I stand, undecided. If he's right the very worst thing I could do is lead Ormesini to his house while Seteney is trying to escape. But, if he's wrong, I'll be leaving Seteney undefended. Marco's next words break into wild dog chase of my thoughts. 'Take me to the island.'

'What? No.'

'Doctors there…treat the lepers in the lazar-house…help me.' His words fill up my ears. I'm underwater. Have to shake my head to get rid of them.

'There isn't time.' The excuse is feeble. I know it. He knows it. His eyes are sculpted chips of glass.

'Take me…please.'

FORTY-ONE

SETENEY:

'Oh lamentations! Oh Lamb of God. Spare this innocent child. Take me. Take me!' The agony in Alessandra's voice suggests her thighs are being ripped apart as she gives birth to a litter of angry weasels. Heavy footsteps pound up the stairs, and she winks at me. 'Ready?' I can't speak for the fear blocking my throat but my silence proves sufficient. She rubs her hands together then commences wailing again. 'Blessed Mater Dolorossa, have pity on my ancient bones and spare this guiltless angel who—'

'What the fuck is going on?' The door slams open and two of Ormesini's meatier thugs come barrelling in. Through slitted eyes, I note one has a shaven head and the other a drooling lower lip. I don't recognise them. They're new, which means we have no history. Will this work for or against us? I have no idea. Drooler rubs his lip on a sleeve and looks at Alessandra, who is now rocking back and forth and calling on all the saints to come to her aid.

'They can hear you all the way to the Rialto.'

Stubble is more concise. 'Shut it or we'll cut your tits off.' Drooler shakes my foot. 'What the fuck is wrong with you?' I give the rehearsed response, groaning and thrashing my head from side to side.

According to the plan, he's supposed to draw back, anxiously enquiring after my health, but no-one has shown Drooler the script. He leans closer and flecks of spittle fall on my face. It's all I can do not to draw back while vigorously wiping myself clean. I attempt another groan but it sticks in my throat and only the barest thread of sound escapes. 'What's the matter with her?' Stubble enquires. Drooler is still scrutinizing my face. 'Reckon she's at it.' I should moan, roll my eyes, fake a seizure, but my limbs stay frozen disdainful of my pleading. Why doesn't Alessandra speak?

'Might be her womb,' Stubble says with an air of authority. 'When they start wandering, it causes all sorts of mayhem. Roberto the shoemaker's wife was suffocated by hers when she tried to birth twins.'

'You think she's with child?' The silence suggests a shrug. 'You, old woman. Has she had her yoke harnessed?'

'How should I know?' Alessandra's voice is watery with sniffles. 'Can't you—I don't know—check or something?'

'I don't know about that? What if it's catching?'

'The only way you'll catch what's up there is if you're in the way when she squirts the little bastard out her cunt.' Drooler laughs at his own joke and more spittle falls on me. A creak of floorboards. Alessandra is at my side. 'Let's see now, dearie.' Air rushes over my legs. No-one speaks. The only sound is my heart clanging louder than the *Marangona*.

'Holy hand-job of Antioch. It's the fucking plague.' Drooler gives a castrated cat yelp and jumps back. 'What'll we do?' Stubble cries. He's already backing towards the door, while Alessandra pleads on her knees. 'Don't leave me. Take me with you.' The slamming door answers her. A few moments later the front door gives an echoing slam.

'Good.' Alessandra springs to her feet. 'Let's get you cleaned up.'

§

GIORGIONE:

The gondolier takes one look at Marco slumped on my shoulder and refuses to take him. 'Please, I'll pay double.' He gives a *not-worth-the-hassle* shrug and glances past me to see if there's a better prospect. 'All right triple then.' I can't afford it. I have to think about the future, especially now that there is no artwork to offer Perréal. Should I haggle? Marco's nose is bleeding into my doublet. I can't think straight. Something is spooking me. A feeling of being watched. Reluctantly, I dig out my coins and watch dispiritedly as the gondolier helps himself. He counts them slowly, checking each one by crunching on it with his yellow teeth. The hairs on the back of my neck are rising. 'Can you be quick?' He glowers and begins the counting process from scratch. Am I imagining things or did a smudge of darkness detach itself from a wall and edge closer to us. 'Hurry, please.' He glowers again.

Temper, which has always been slow in me, rushes forwards at breakneck speed and grabs him by the curls of his beard. With the other hand, I push Marco aboard and join him under the *ferro*. 'Now row like the hounds of hell have your scent.'

Not until we are safely moving down the canal, do I breathe again. The fog blots the spread of my fury and the familiar sound of water slapping the edges of the gondola lulls me, at least until I realise that, after tonight, I'll never hear it again. So many things I'll miss about the city. Little things. Things I took for granted, things I didn't notice. All the importance of unimportance. When did I become a philosopher?

I think of sharing the thought with Marco, but his eyes are closed and his face is deathly pale. I'll miss sharing things with him too.

The mist grows so dense that time is suspended. We hang in nothingness, moving neither forwards nor backwards. Alone and unreal, the stuff dreams are made of. Perhaps I'll wake up in my bed. Perhaps Seteney is just a reverie conjured by a dying mind. Marco hasn't opened his eyes and I watch the gondolier, trying to avoid thinking of old Charon rowing the souls of the dead across the Styx.

The image is not helped by the welcome party awaiting us at the bottom of the landing steps. Two figures robed in black, both hooded and masked. The smaller one lifts his hand to prevent us disembarking. 'Woe,' he intones. 'Woe to those who enter the isle of Poveglia.' A lugubrious nod from his companion, who adds in falsetto accompaniment. 'Many enter. Few return.'

'My friend is sick.'

'Then he will find good company here.'

'Can you help him?'

'That depends.'

'On his condition?'

'On whether he can pay.'

The fund I have to start a new life with Seteney shrinks a little further. 'He can pay.'

They face each other then step apart. 'This way.'

My last words are for the gondolier. 'Wait for me. I'll be back.' Marco appears to be unconscious so I lift him in my arms and carry him up the narrow steps.

'Woe,' Falsetto says and his companion nudges him in the ribs. 'He knows.'

§

SETENEY:

I am wearing a gown that belonged to Ormesini's late wife. 'He'd kill you if he saw you in it,' Alessandra says cheerfully as she tweaks a ribbon. 'There you go. Grand as the Doge's missus.' The gilded mirrors don't agree. Beautifully attired women surround me, their worried faces all saying the same thing: a servant girl might pass unnoticed; why dress me up like a peacock pie? Even running away will be impossible. The skirts are several inches too long and I have to hold them bunched in my hands. This is bad. I've broken my rule. I've up-bellied myself before a man and let him take my quivering heart in his hands. More than my heart. My life.

'Time to go, dearie.' Alessandra leads the way as we slip downstairs. Something feels wrong. She's taking me away from the canal exit. 'I thought—'

'Change of plan. Aldo can't take you. He sent a message earlier to say he was sick.'

'Plague?'

'Bigger tips from foreign fares more like. Don't worry, he's sending one of his men.'

'Can we trust him?'

Alessandra makes a gesture only Italians make with their hands. 'It's fine. Aldo has a good reputation.'

'How will I know who he sends?'

'He'll be looking out for you, and, remember, he'll be wearing a mask called the *Melpo*. It's a very ancient mask. Been in Aldo's family for centuries. He makes a big deal about it apparently. Don't know why. Ugly thing. Looks to me like a bloke who's just come home to find his best mate porking his missus. Still, you can't miss it. Stands out it does.' She scans the hall. 'Not much time. They could be back any moment.' Lifting a chest, she pulls out a couple of items. 'Here. Wear this.' She hands me an oval of black velvet with two eyeholes. There are no ties. 'Hold it in your mouth. See?' She points to a button on the back. Is she mad? 'I won't be able to talk.'

'That's why they call it the *Muta*.'

So, I am to go hobbled and silenced. This is the shape my escape takes? Why not simply bind my hands and feet, and throw me in the canal? I should call it off. Go back before I'm discovered. But what will happen if I stay? No path is safe. Death lies behind every door. Alessandra wraps a cloak around me and tucks the hood about my face. She hands me a candle lantern. 'Follow the alley to the end then take the last passageway before the apothecary. Cross the bridge and Aldo's man will be waiting at the water's edge.' Her eyes glisten black and corvine. 'Oh to be young again. A few hours from now you'll be a free woman.'

I can't even bring myself to nod.

Outside, the mist ghost curls around the hems of my skirts. I must be quick. The moon's eye only pretends to be blind. I feel it following me as I slip across the cobbles searching for the entrance to the alley. Nothing is familiar. I've been locked up too long. My lantern only makes the night look blacker and I can't find my bearings. Should I ask for help? Drunken revellers stagger in front of me, their voices slurred beneath masks. Ghosts escaped from graveyards.

A hand grabs at my sleeve. *Come with me, pretty thing.* I shake it off only to be caught in the grasp of another featureless phantom. My lantern flies away, my hem rips. *Paradise awaits if you'll let my weapon prick you.* Muffled chortles give way to cries of pain when his weapon crumples under the force of my knee. And now I'm running. Stumbling down the alleys, blind as the moon. Why did Alessandra leave me on my own? No lady would be out at night without an escort. Why didn't Zorzi come? Am I the world's biggest dupe? What made me listen to him? What made me think his mad plan could work? What made me think love is real?

The world shudders to a halt beneath my breathless gasps. Years in a cage have weakened me. My legs have forgotten how to run. Doubled over, I clutch a building, feeling the render crumbling beneath my fingertips. I've left the revellers behind but I don't know what to do. Go on? Turn back? Mist tongues the air in breathy screams. A rat scuttles between buildings and is lost behind the pier of an arch. Above my head, a sign swings from a keystone: serpents entwining a winged staff. Something familiar about it. In the window, bottles, green, dusty, dangerous-looking. Is this it? The apothecary?

I retrace my steps. Five. Six. Seven, and a passageway opens up. Grimy, unpaved, narrow as a tomb. In all my nightmares, traps look like this. Who in the world would enter? Who but someone whose trap is already as large as the world.

Breath caged in my chest, I start down it. At the end is a little bridge, hump-backed, crooked, the balustrades rickety-looking. Before I can place a foot on the first step, a shadow falls over me.

The body belonging to the shadow steps out from under the bridge. Alessandra was right. His mask is unmistakable. The gilded curls, the down-turned mouth, this mask was made for the eyes of a different age. His hand imprisons my wrist. He indicates that we are to move with a jerk of his head but doesn't speak.

Where are we going? I thought we were taking the canals. I want to ask but I have no voice and he offers no explanation, simply drags me along behind him. Silently, we run through the slippery black alleys, he-rat and she-rat slithering through the shadows. I pray to the god of my grandmother to protect me, but She hasn't listened so far. Why would She start now?

FORTY-TWO

GIORGIONE:

Marco's face is pressed up against my shoulder, eyes closed fast like a sleeping child. If a sleeping child were the colour of paste and his lips stained the purple of crushed foxglove petals. He isn't dead. Please, Sweet Saviour, deliverer of men's sins, he isn't dead. I beg you. I swear I'll do nothing but good deeds for the rest of my life if you let him live.

The guardians move strangely along the winding path, the trailing length of their robes giving the I impression of floating rather than walking, while I stumble awkwardly behind. A quick glance over my shoulder shows that the mist has already swallowed the boatman. What if he leaves without me? I think of Seteney sitting alone in the palanquin, searching a blank wall of fog for my shadow. Has she even made it out of Ormesini's prison? I shouldn't have let her do it on her own. If Ormesini can't find me, he's bound to head home. I quicken my pace. The air pulses with death.

I hear the pest-house before we reach it. Its walls are made from groans and sighs. The guardians wait on either side of the door, solemn as stone atlantes holding up the temple of Zeus. As I approach, Falsetto bows and holds the door ajar. 'Woe,' he says. 'To all those who enter, woe.' He proffers his hand for a tip, which I ignore as I stagger past him and lose myself in the tenth circle of hell.

Moaning skeletons lie three or four to a bed. I can't tell who are men and who are women. Nothing human is left in their faces. It's hard to breathe. The air is soupy with faeces and blood and bloody faeces. In the midst, a stooped man with a monk's tonsure is holding a bowl of something to a hollow-eyed skull who takes listless sips.

'I need help.'

He turns, a younger man than I expected, but his face half eroded beneath leprous ulcers. One eye is a smoked glass disc. 'Are you the doctor?'

'I am Fra Benedetto. At least I was before this.' He gestures at the dead eye. 'Now I am just a man who tries to help.'

'Where are the other doctors?'

'There are no other doctors. Lay your friend on that bed there. The one with only one other occupant. He's lucky. We had a couple of deaths this morning.'

I lay Marco on the filthy bed, feeling hope draining out of me. He moans a little and mutters but does not open his eyes. Fra Benedetto examines him, taking his pulse and smelling his breath. He uses callipers to measure the bubo. 'How long has he had this?'

'I'm not sure. A few days.'

'Have any treatments been applied?'

'I don't know.'

Fra Benedetto leans down and sniffs along Marco's body. 'Possibly a concoction of vinegar, and he's definitely used onions. We'll start with bleeding. Then a poultice of eggshell and faeces mixed with chopped marigold leaves. Of course, a tincture of alicorn would be best.'

'Can you give it to him?'

'There isn't any.'

'I'll fetch it. Tell me where to go. I have money.'

'That won't work.'

'Why not?'

'It's not as simple as that. Unicorns are notoriously difficult to get hold of at this time of year.'

'Please, there must be something you can do.'

'There is one other treatment we could try. I warn you, it can be expensive.'

'Please. I'll try anything. What do you need?'

'A chicken.'

'A chicken?'

'The method is deceptively simple. As everyone knows, chickens are bottom breathers. Think about it, how else could they run about when deprived of their heads?' His logic is hard to fault. 'We simply pluck a few feathers from its arse then bind it, anus-down, on to the infected sore. Its breath draws the disease from the body of the patient. Of course, an advanced case like this may mean using two or three chickens, hence the expense.'

'And this works?'

'Not so far. But I am hopeful.' He's mad. And I'm mad for listening. But what choice is there? Marco will die without medicine, and time is running out for me to reach Seteney. I pull out some coins and spill them on to his palm. 'Is this enough?' Fra Benedetto inspects them. 'Perhaps just a little extra. I have to buy feed for the chickens after all.' I add a couple more and he beams at me. 'We will get started at once.' He reaches out to shake my hand then thinks better of it. 'Perhaps not so wise, eh. Let us get down to business. Name?'

'Giorgione Gasparini of Castelfranco.'

'Good. I will make the arrangements.' He bends down and pats Marco's arm. 'Don't worry, Giorgione. We will take good care of you.' I hope they will. With all my heart I hope— Wait! What did he say?

'No. You misunderstood. He's not—' A sharp tug on my breeches. Marco is awake and he's gripping my thigh.

'Marco, not now. I have to—' Another tug on my breeches, more insistent. He's trying to speak. 'What's wrong?'

'Don't…' I bend low. His voice is somewhere in the distance. 'Better if Ormesini thinks…you…' Life goes out of his fingers and they drop to the blanket. His eyes are fluttering. Consciousness is costing him.

'It's okay. Don't try to talk. The doctor's coming.' I grip his hand. It's cold. The tips are turning black. He swallows but can't get the saliva back down. Panic grips every nerve under my skin as I watch him struggle. 'Doctor—Benedetto, come quickly!' Marco's lips are moving and I press my ear close to hear. He gurgles out a single word. 'Understand?'

No. I don't. I don't want to. Because understanding confirms my worst nightmares: that Marco is dying and he is sacrificing his own memory to save me. If Giorgione Gasparini dies of plague on the island of Poveglia then Ormesini will stop looking. I will be free and perhaps Seteney and I can find peace after all. But how can I do that to my friend, my very best friend in the world? Marco doesn't try to argue with me. He's beyond speech. He looks at me with eyes that are wet and losing focus. I watch him struggle to remain conscious, struggle to send me a silent plea to take this last token of his love. I hear the squawk of a chicken. Fra Benedetto is coming back. There are tears in my eyes as I lower myself to my knees—I'm still too tall—and bow down to kiss him gently on the forehead.

'I understand.'

§

SETENEY:

Darting into one of wider, more populated alleys, Aldo's man slows down. Even behind the mask, I can see he's tense, eyes peeling the surfaces, looking for something. Groups of revellers surround us, carrying wineskins and squirting them liberally at each other, sometimes even managing to reach an open mouth. Some of it splashes on my skirts. Aldo's man pushes past them, but more are funnelling into the narrow spaces. We'll never get to the palanquin in time. I tug at his sleeve. Still no response. Who is behind that mask? Is it really a friend?

A door opens—or perhaps he shoulders it open—I'm not sure. As we flounder through, every eye turns in our direction. We're in a room occupied by men and women all wearing cat masks. The women are magnificently attired—oriental brocatelles, Genoese laces and Turkish Velluto trimmed with mysterious furs. They sit preening on the laps of men, who boldly fondle them inside their bodices and beneath their petticoats. At the centre, a man is doing handstands on top of a chair.

What is this place? A secret society? A den of vice? I know such places exist. Ormesini has threatened often enough to send me to one. Is that what has happened? Have I been sold? There is a pause then all the women point at me and start hissing and clawing the air. Why? What have I done?

Aldo's man is trying to clear a path, but they block the way and start pulling at my dress. One rushes forward to tear off my mask and we grapple until I accidentally rip her sleeve. An arm is revealed, muscular, hairy, belonging to a man. Word-lost, I let go and step back. The hisses have descended into growls, and now, as faces press up against mine, I see the bobbing laryngeal lumps in their throats and realise, with a jolt, I am the only Eve here without an apple.

The acrobat is screaming at Aldo's man. He speaks very fast with an accent I find hard to decipher. Something about favours and this being the last time, and just as I think we will be torn apart, a screen is pulled back at the far end of the room and a hidden door revealed. The acrobat produces a key and opens the portal, towards which we are manhandled like thieves, until we stand ejected on edge of a narrow waterway.

Aldo's man is unsure. He looks this way then that while greenish vapours rise from the canal smelling of rot. Is he waiting? Has something gone wrong? In the end, I see it before he does, the prow moving through the black water. It pulls up alongside us. 'You're late.' The gondolier is a short man with powerful shoulders. His mask stretches upwards in silent laughter, but his voice is iron-flat.

'Where's Domenico?' Aldo's man demands. He doesn't sound as I expected him to. The gondolier shrugs. 'Couldn't come. His wife's ill.'

'His wife?'

A shrug. 'Dunno. Maybe he said it was his mother. I don't know him that well.' Aldo's man looks back down the canal as if he's weighing things up then says on an outbreath, 'All right.' I feel a tug on my arm and the gondolier is reaching out towards me. Shaking my head, I shrink back, not wanting to go. This isn't part of the plan. No-one mentioned a second guide. But when did I ever get to choose my path? Aldo's man simply bends down and lifts me in.

I sit before my ferryman silent as the grave. Where is he taking me? 'Comfortable?' he asks. I nod. I'm sitting on velvet cushions next to a golden ornament of a stag whose body ends in a split fishtail. A strange motif. 'Off to the mainland?' I nod. I don't like the way his mask is grinning at me, gilt paint glinting in the light of the hanging lantern. He leans forwards. 'Late to be out on your own. Running away, are you?' Ice water rushes down my spine. How much does he know? I turn my head and look down at the canal. It's black beneath the mist glow. Other worlds float beneath us. Drowning seems a little thing.

We pass under a bridge and the world out-winks momentarily. Echoes and sighs. The water sounds alive. A soft warble joins in and accompanies us beyond the dripping stone. Looking up, I see the gondolier's teeth flash through the mouth-hole of his mask. He's laughing. 'Pretty price on your head, I'll bet.' I ignore him. The walls are sheer, nowhere to land. Windows glow above us like the stars of an overly regular god…

'Wake up.' My eyes split wide. Did I doze? Not asleep surely? Air fans my cheeks. The mask lies limply on my chest.

'Are we there?' What is this place? It's so dark. Am I still asleep? The lantern flickers near death. I can only make out shapes. A vaulted roof, like in a church, but water all around. We're floating in a canal: an underground canal.

The gondolier is laughing. 'Didn't expect this, did you now missy?' I'm dressed as a noblewoman; I try sounding like one. 'Take me to the mainland at once.'

'Oh, I intend to take you.' He cat jumps into the body of the boat and kneels before me. His mask grins insanely up, the head of an encephalitic child. 'How often?' I shake my head more to negate him than participate in the conversation. His hand skims my skirts, rustling the silk. 'How often did the greasy peasant boy dip his brush in your paint pot?'

The muta mask falls on to my lap. It takes my voice with it. Zorzi, where are you? 'Can't speak, is that it? What did you think, that it was all a big secret?' His wet dog breath comes through the false lips. 'Nobody hides anything from the master.' I have no need to ask the master's name. The ghost of Ormesini paralyses my heart. I can feel the last jumping beats trying desperately to restart it. His hand trails my cheek then he lunges. The boat rocks violently, and I only manage to stop myself tumbling out by clutching the golden ornament. Then he's pinning me down, slobbering in my ear. 'Master says I can have a little fun with you. All the boys are getting a turn. We drew lots.'

I squeeze out a name. 'Alessandra?'

'Who do you think ran the lottery?' He's pushing up my skirts when my hands turn to birds and start pecking at his face. 'None of that.' He slaps me lazily. 'I'm not going to hurt you. Master wants you there when he cuts Castelfranco's throat. He wants you to lick up the blood.'

§

GIORGIONE:

He's not there. The boatman's not there. Christ's weeping wounds, the bastard's gone. I've lost my cap, torn the knee of my breeches and flayed the skin from my palms falling on the stony path, and that cankered, dockside doxy's whelp has buggered off into the night in search of more fares.

I stare into the mist on the verge of weeping. My friend is dead. I've left Seteney to be hunted down by Ormesini. And I stand here abandoned on a tiny island like some banished Roman noblewoman. It's all my fault. What made me think any of this could work? If the moon was visible, I would get down on all fours and howl at it. Instead I stand, a Doric column of gloom marking the graves of the forgotten dead, and coming to the sad truth that the priests have been wrong all along. No loving Father created us. What could the storm-riven tide of sorrows that is our earthly existence be but an arse-fuck jest played on mankind by the egotistical inhabitants of Olympus? Every time they aim another kick straight into mankind's balls the celestial spheres must ring like the *maleficio* at an execution. *Woe*.

Such is my state of mind that it takes a moment to understand that it is Falsetto and not myself who has spoken. He joins me, looks to where the boat should have been, then adds, 'Many enter. Few return.'

'Is another boat due?'

He shrugs. 'Maybe Tuesday.'

'A week away?'

'That's if it comes.' I wonder if, in some far off, unimagined future, talking parchments will be invented to perpetually replay the unhelpful words of minor functionaries in an endless loop that offers no prospect of assistance. We stare blankly into the blankness until Falsetto tugs my sleeve. I wonder if he wants to hold hands. 'Of course, there's always the emergency vessel.' With every particle of my being, I swivel towards him. 'Emergency vessel?'

'We keep a small boat on the other side of the island for unforeseen circumstances.'

'It's available?'

'It's for hire.'

Naturally. I reach for my bag of coins. 'Lead the way.'

The boat is tied to a small jetty on the western side of the isle. It's small, rather weather-beaten, but most notably, it's half submerged in the lagoon. I look at Falsetto. I look at the boat. I look back at Falsetto. Have I missed something? 'It's a little worse for wear,' he concedes. 'A storm, you see.'

'It's sunk.'

'A temporary setback. The hole is quite small. Quite repairable.' He reached into his robe. 'I took the precaution of bringing a piece of cherrywood to plug it.'

'A hammer? Nails?'

'Alas, the workshop that contained our tools was blown away during the storm. Replacements should be coming on the next boat.'

'On Tuesday?'

'On Tuesday. Yes.' I'm standing inside an hourglass, the sands of time running out between my legs. Falsetto brightens. 'Here.'

'What is that?'

'Wadding. You can use it to pack the wood in place.' I take it, feeling the strange texture. 'Wool?'

'Feathers. Fra Benedetto provides them.'

It takes an hour of trial and error. Most of it error. But at last I have a seaworthy vessel. At least it doesn't sink too much. 'Will it last?'

Crinkling his eyes, Falsetto considers. 'Can you swim?'

'No.'

'Then yes.'

Now that I'm ready, I find myself hesitating. 'I must take my leave.'

'Yes.' He coughs discreetly and I press some coins into his hands.

'Thank you. Thank you for everything. I'm glad to be going but sorry you're stuck here.'

He looks at me in surprise. 'I'm not stuck here.

'You're not a leper or—or—'

'Fit as a fiddle.'

'Then why?'

He considers. 'I suppose I like cheering people up.'

There's a small gurgle from the boat. Stepping into it is proba-bly as foolish as letting Ormesini take my neck measurements. But

Seteney is out there, alone and at his mercy. Marco is gone and all my future lies beyond these shores. Gingerly, I place a foot inside then bring the other in to join it. The boat rocks sluggishly then steadies. The oars are light in my hands. 'Many enter—' Falsetto begins before making a ghastly contortion of his lower jaw, which I take to be a smile. 'And some return.'

He's growing smaller. I've begun to row without realising. Water seeps through the wadding and gathers at my feet. I try not to think about it. An onion moon reveals itself in layers and suffuses the world in shades of ivory and pearl. I've never seen anything so beautiful, a twilight world, neither heaven nor earth, but somewhere between in which all possibilities lie.

Hark at me. I was a painter before Seteney, a hack who knew how to hold a brush. She turned me into an artist, and here I am in the middle of the lagoon in a leaky boat, spouting poetry. If they're watching, Marco and the Reaper must be crying on each other's shoulders with laughter. Seteney will laugh too when I tell her. The water is slopping at my feet. Need to concentrate on rowing. 'I'm coming, my love. I'm coming.' The mist closes around me like a shining robe.

FORTY-THREE

SETENEY:

The world seesaws back into focus. I blink. What happened? The gondola. The vaulted ceiling, closer somehow. To my left, a splintered spike. The golden stag with the split tail has broken off. I recognise it now. The symbol from Ormesini's seal, the great silver stamp he uses to conclude his documents. Bloodless, my fingers are death-gripping its neck. At my feet is a shape, twitching slightly. I remember now; a while ago it was clutching its throat. Something wet drips off one of the antlers on to my skirts.

The ceiling is definitely closer. How long have I been sitting here with the waters rising about me? Has Zorzi left? Ridden off without me? Would he do that? I have a pain in my shoulder and my bodice is torn. I want to close my eyes and go to sleep. The thing at my feet makes a gruesome noise. But a swift stab with the antlers into its neck is all it takes to silence it. My words are the last things he hears as he up-vomits the contents of his veins. 'I am a freeborn Adyghean woman. Remember that when you boil with your master in the cauldrons of hell.'

Dropping the filthy carcass into the water isn't easy, but I succeed somehow without capsizing. The echoes snatch the sound of the splash and play a giggling children's game with it, passing it back and forth, while I listen frantic that someone will hear. But Venice is still revelling, and what's one more splash amidst a night of chaos? The body doesn't sink, of course. Floats away arse-up. A fitting end? I send his mask spinning after him. It gags, spewing and weeping from the mouth and eyeholes until it disappears below the surface. The sensible thing to do now would be to wait, to make certain that the tide doesn't wash the body out into open water, but there's no time. The waters are already so high I have to duck my head to prevent my skull cracking against the roof.

Keeping my eyes on the body, I reach for the oar and my fingers connect with—nothing? It's gone. It can't be. Yet the *forcola's* shallow claw is empty. Floating nearby, surely. I waste a full minute searching. But no. The night has claimed it. Breath turns to stone in my chest, and before I can gather my thoughts, some movement in the water sends the gondola bumping against the wall. The wooden hull makes a nasty crunching noise. Am I going to die? Green darkness and silence forever. I brace my hands against the wall's pitted surface. Another crunch then the hull steadies itself. The wall tears at my palms, but clinging to the stone blocks gives me the purchase I need to drag the gondola inch by inch towards the crescent gap at the end of the tunnel.

By the time the gondola noses out into the night air, my nails are torn off and my fingertips bloody, but at least I'm outside. Where am I? The world wobbles and light streaks the sky. The night has moved on without me. Am I too late? The thought of Zorzi standing, with his eyes trained upon the empty waters searching for me, burns worse than the pain in my shoulder. The grooms shaking their heads. *Time to go, sir.* Mustn't think like that. More pressing issues.

A wriggling serpent has appeared on the boat's bottom. It stretches and lengthens into a narrow stream. Sweet blood of the Saviour. Taking on water. How long before I sink? Will my skirts keep me afloat or drag me down? Think, Seteney. Think! The walls are slippery. Too sheer to climb. There are landing steps on the far side of the canal. I'll never make them. If only I could swim. Closer by, I can see one of those strange Venetian doors partially submerged, *porta d'acqua* they call them. Madness to think it might be open. Madness, the whole hare-brained scheme from start to finish. I should abandon all hope. Accept that I'm standing in my own coffin. Try the door. What is there to lose?

Up close, I can see that it's more a gate than a door, a lattice of iron filigreed with rust. I push. I pull. It doesn't budge. There's a lock on the far side. I feel for it with my outstretched fingers. No key. Hopeless. I'm going to die. I don't want to die. I thought I did. But I don't. I really don't. What can I do? The water pulses at my calves; the air tastes of blood. Will it take long to drown? Shouts and screams from St Mark's Piazza. A thousand voices rip open the sky. Yet no-one can see me; no-one can help me. I'm lost. Forget me, Zorzi. Forget me and live a long happy life. I wish I had told you about Beslan. Why that? Of all things, why regret keeping my brother's betrayal secret? My knees give way and I sink, as though praying, into the slippery chill.

Heneguash is an underwater goddess. My grandmother knew her name. She drags the unwary by their hair down, down to her breathless palaces and makes their bloated bodies dance the *kabardinka* for her entertainment. Sometimes, it is said, she comes to the aid of a helpless traveller.

My eyes fall on the hinge. It's nearly rusted through. Just below the water level and wholly invisible until I knelt down. Will it be enough? Hitting it with my hands proves useless. Struggling to my feet, I brace myself with one arm, and lifting my drenched skirts with the other, I aim a kick at the most corroded part. The force sends pain exploding through my foot and I nearly lose my grip. Wiping the tears from my eyes, I clench my jaw and kick again. And again. And again. Something gives. The hinge is loose. Heaving my whole weight against it, I feel the metal dissolve into powder. The gate tips drunkenly, opening up a cat's-width gap. It isn't enough. It's all I have.

By the time I'm through, my skirts are torn and my shoulders covered in a trellis of rust-trimmed welts which weep a thin mixture of blood and canal water. I take a few steps until I'm fully on terra firma then stop to wring out my skirts. Where am I? All I can smell is a tomb-like chill. I feel my way along a sloping passage that leads to a flight of stairs. A lantern near the top throws down patches of feeble undefined light, and I steppingstone-hop up them only to find myself in a short corridor. At the top it splits in two, both directions disappearing into gloom. Which way? I have no idea. I take a left. Perhaps I can find my way out through an unlocked door. I approach the first one I see and press my ear to it. It seems quiet, and my fingers have just closed around the handle, when raucous billowing laughter burst through.

Flinging myself into the shadows, I cower there, a bedraggled fish creature, waiting to be discovered. The door remains shut. The voices behind it are drink drowsy and slurred. They're singing about a maiden who lost her virtue to a lustful swan.

"There was a young girl called Leda
Who allowed a swan to invade her
She pulled out a feather
Shouted, 'Aren't I clever?'
Then everyone knew Zeus had laid her."

Gathering my sodden skirts, I run full tilt in the opposite direction. Night air pillows my face before I know I am outside. The sky is blue grey—barely night at all—and I stand, breathless for a moment, watching the last stars wink out. *Wait, Zorzi. Please. Please wait. I'm coming.* I'm on a balcony. Too high to jump. It straddles the canal, an umbilicus between two buildings. At the end is a worm-eaten door. No lock. I tug at it, like a rotten tooth, and it gives way in a gasp of splinters. Behind it, is a long black gullet which might lead anywhere.

It's eerily quiet inside. My breathing is louder than my foot-steps as the spiral of the staircase winds me down, down until it thrusts me out into a soaring sacred space. I am in a church. A roof like the inverted hull of a ship. Not one apse but three. I choose the middle and run, feet slapping on the chequered marble floor. I don't care who hears. I must get out. I must find Zorzi.

The door is bolted from the inside—no-one is expected to break out of God's holy sanctuary—and escape is easy. I throw myself through on to the piazza and stand there panting. I don't know where I am. Limping, I set out in one direction only to find myself turned around. Determined, I try again and find myself back where I started. Despite its Christian piety, there is something unholy about this city. Venice is a maze not even besotted Ariadne could unwind.

I try again, braving the larger alleys in the hope of orienting myself. Sleepy-eyed revellers are still wandering the streets but my transformation into bedraggled madwoman is amulet enough against their advances. I feel safe for now. Then a hand claps itself over my mouth and drags me into a doorway.

I try to scream.

I have no voice.

I try to kick and claw.

I have no strength.

'Calm yourself, woman. It's me.' The vice-like grip loosens. I turn my head and am greeted by the mournful lips of the mask belonging to Aldo's man.

'He—he—' I point wildly in the direction of the attack. 'He tried to…Did you know?'

'He wasn't the man I thought he was. I swear.' Aldo's man pats me down like a child. 'Did he hurt you?'

'No.' When a man asks that he is not asking if you are bruised. He's relieved. His shoulders relax.

'I found our man with a slit throat in an alley near where we tie up the boats. I've been looking for you ever since.' I want to thank him. I want to tell him he is an honourable man. All I manage to squeeze out is, *Zorzi*.

He half leads, half carries me to the rendezvous, while my heart hurls itself against my ribs and my lungs breathe fire. *Please be there. Please. Please. Just be there.* Aldo's man rows me to the landing point, and before we reach it, I hear the wicker of horses. He waited. Thank God, he waited.

Aldo's man ties up the gondola before helping me up the steps. I feel I should say something to him. To thank him for his bravery and constancy. 'May I see your face?'

'That's not a good idea.'

No. Probably not. I must say something though. 'I will never forget you.' He hesitates then lifts the lower half of his mask to show that he is smiling.

'Goodbye.' He bows and quotes a Venetian proverb about luck being like trying to hold an eel dipped in olive oil. Or maybe not. It's hard to tell. His accent is thick. Then he is gone, and I hurry towards the figures by the horses. There are two men. Both tall. But neither the size of my love. Lead weights attach themselves to my ankles. My steps slow. 'Where is Zorzi?' Their stares tell me that my efforts in the boat to make myself more presentable have been in vain.

One of them lifts something down from the saddle. 'Change into these. You'll look less conspicuous dressed as a man.' He hands me a burlap sack. 'There was a problem with the palanquin. Can you ride?' Can I ride? I, who felt the power of a horse between my thighs before I was five years of age. I, who have ridden stallions that breathed fire along mountain paths so narrow goats trembled to walk them. 'Yes. I can ride.' He makes as if to turn away. 'Zorzi?' He shrugs. 'No sign of him. Can't wait any longer. Need to get out of here. Word is that one of Ormesini's men's been found dead in a canal.' I want to ask questions but his companion is preparing the horses. 'Hurry it up. We leave in five minutes, with or without you.'

Pretending modesty, I squeeze behind a pillar and strip off my damp skirts. I'm a bedraggled rat. Blood and slime ooze from my cuts and scratches, and God knows what my face must look like. Would Zorzi recognise me now as the woman in the painting? Not that I ever was. No matter what he says. There isn't a woman, alive or dead, who ever looked like that. Not even Signora Giocondo made famous by Maestro Da Vinci's otherworldly touch. She was no flesh and bone woman because Zorzi, my Zorzi, didn't paint a woman. He didn't paint me. He poured all his technique—his eggshell, his glaze, his squirrel-tipped brush hovering over a dish of crushed azurite—into painting something more than the simple facts his eyes recorded. You see he didn't paint me at all. He painted something he found inside himself. He painted love.

'Are you dressed yet?' I jump.

'Almost.' Clumsily, I pull the breaches and doublet on and don a ridiculously large cap. 'Ready.'

'Right.' He pulls up a chestnut rouncey. It's happening. We're leaving.

'Can't we wait a little longer?'

He looks at his companion who shakes his head. 'We're dead men if we stay. Are you coming or not?'

I'll find you, Zorzi said. *But you must go. Ormesini won't be fooled for long. Promise me.*

I look over my shoulder, straining my eyes in the sad grey light. Surely, in this night of miracles, there will be one more. The curtain does not lift. Zorzi doesn't appear. The men are looking at me.

Promise me.

Find me, Zorzi. Don't give up. Keep looking even if it takes all time. I dig my heels into the horse's flanks and fly towards the future.

FORTY-FOUR

As I pull up to The Grange, a flurry of wind detonates an explosion of mineral-coloured leaves overhead. The season is changing. How long has it been, seven months, eight? They say a busy life passes more quickly. Try living at twice the speed. Down by the lake, Darius is sitting looking over the mirror reflection of the water. An inverse world looks back up from the depths.

'They said you were here.' The only place to sit is a low wall and I drop on to it beside him, almost knocking over a pot of Japanese anemones. Was I ever graceful without thinking about it? Darius is still staring at the water.

'Thought I'd take a last look.' He glances up, and I feel his smile coming before it reaches his lips. 'I'm going home in a few days. Seb's been getting the finishing touches to the house done.'

'How do you feel about it?'

'A little daunted. It'll be strange at first, I suppose. We've had to make a lot of changes.'

'I'll be there as often as I can. I'm looking into changing my hours.' There's a bit of a silence then I say, 'I don't suppose you've…?'

'No. Not a flicker. You?'

'Nothing.' Seteney rode off into the dawn, and I haven't been able to find her since. I'm all alone at night again with the voices of the dead creeping out of the gangrenous shadows. *Why didn't you save me? Why did you let me die?* My phone pings and I ignore it. Darius sighs. 'All the records say Giorgione Castelfranco died of plague on Poveglia.'

'But we know otherwise.'

'Do we? What if I died on the water?'

'You would know. You felt Refined Ink's heart attack. You suffered Jules Vogelsang's last moments.'

'But not Dreams-the-People. He disappeared without trace.'

275

'There were other memories afterwards. Not just this… nothing!' My phone pings again and I flick it to silent. I'm not on duty for another ten minutes. Whatever it is can wait.

'Perhaps we've remembered all there is.'

'I don't believe that. You don't believe it. Did you try the techniques Liv recommended?'

'Yes.'

'And?'

'I told you. Nothing. Face it, Lexie. The effect wears off. Whatever doors Somnipradine opened are closed now. To both of us.' His words fill me with grey pain.

'It can't end like this. It just can't.'

'I'm sorry.' Darius looks helpless. I can see that he wants to reach out, hold me, comfort me. Instead, we sit in our separate worlds inches apart and all time flowing between us. A flock of ducks lands on the lake's glittering surface then takes off almost immediately, honking their way into the distance. I glance at my watch. In four minutes I have to be on duty.

'There is one thing we can try.'

He looks at me curiously. I'm finding it harder to admit than I thought, and he has to say, 'What is it, Lexie?'

Big breath. Push the adrenaline down. 'I kept a dose.'

For a second he's confused then understanding jolts across his eyes. 'How?'

'I recorded two doses when one of my patients died.'

'And you kept it all this time?'

'In my fridge. In a jar marked, Double Chocolate Chip Peanut Butter Cookie Spread.'

'In your—I mean, is that safe?'

'Not for your arteries. But, if you mean from Liv—it's safe. She won't even read the label in case her fat cells absorb calories telepathically.'

He stares over the water, sucking in his lower lip then twangs it back out. 'Only one dose?'

'Yes.'

'You or me?'

ME! We say it over the top of each other.

'I said it first.'

'Did not.'

'It should be me.'

'On what basis?'

'I've shown the most—' He searches for a word. 'Aptitude. Four lives versus your one.'

'But I only had one dose. Besides I'm younger and fitter.'

'I have less to lose.'

'I need to know.'

'You will know.'

'I need to experience it.'

'You think I don't? I need to know what it feels like to reach out and touch someone. To climb a set of stairs. To walk until my feet hurt.'

'Well, I need to know death isn't the end.'

We go on like this. Children squabbling until he says, 'There are a million good reasons for you to do it.' I glance at him sharply, knowing he isn't finished. 'And there are a million good reasons for me to do it.'

'So what are you suggesting?'

'We let fate decide.'

'What? Flip a coin, you mean?'

'Why not?' There must be a million reasons why not. But, right now, I can't think of a single one, except— 'Do you have a coin?' He looks at me in surprise. 'No, do you?' I feel in my pocket and pull out my bank card and car keys. 'Who carries cash nowadays?'

'Are you sure?'

'As sure as I can be.' For good measure I empty out my bag. Crumple tissues. A box of tampons, mostly empty. An unfinished novel. Leaflets for a play whose season is over. A pen with no ink. And, right at the bottom, a half-melted caramel, furry with fluff and stuck to a tarnished ten pence piece. I hold it aloft. 'Jackpot.'

'It's fate.'

'It's disgusting, but it'll do.'

A quick surgical procedure separates the coin from its sticky mass and I wedge it between my thumb and middle finger. 'Heads or tails?' He swallows visibly. 'Heads.'

'You sure?'

'You're the lioness.' I'm so tense I almost can't do it. Darius has thrust his neck forward, using the only force left in his body to reach me. 'Please, Lexie. For Zorzi.' The coin flies in a high arc, briefly catching the light, and lands several feet away in a mossy bank. I scramble after it flinging curses into the wind. 'Do you see it?' The slabbed path stops six feet or more from the bank. Darius can't reach it, can't see what I can see. My eyes scan the ground. There are a million good reasons it should be me. A million reasons I should tell him that I've spotted the stiff tails of the lions passant. That I've won. That I should be the one to take the final dose. 'Lexie?' I can't speak because I'm looking down at the face of a dead queen.

§

My stuff is gone. I'm standing in the doorway of our living/kitchen/dining room, looking at a ghost ship. A faint metallic breeze wafts in from the open window. Is that how the thieves got in? Which makes no sense as we're five storeys up and the front door is made of cardboard. Liv appears from behind the kitchen counter. She has a box of mould in her hand which may once have been raspberries. 'You're back.'

'What happened?'

'I'm cleaning.'

'Why?'

'Because I sent you a million texts and you didn't answer. It made me nervous.' Automatically, I reach for my phone and turn it on. All those pings. They were from Liv. She sent me ten. Anything over eight suggests a crisis. 'What's wrong? Is it Dad?'

'Yes…no, not really.'

'Liv, you're scaring me.'

'I went out to dinner with him last night.'

'Nice to have gotten an invite but okay.'

'Not this time, Lexie. This is serious.'

'I can tell by your *this is serious* voice.'

'It's about Somnipradine.' My entire musculoskeletal system goes hypertonic. Shit. She's found my stash. I try not to look at the fridge. How much has she thrown out? 'What about it?'

'Dad told me the reason they withdrew it.'

'Oh, is that all?' My spine softens. 'I think I already know the answer to that one.'

'No. No you don't. The withdrawal has nothing to do with past lives or out of body memories. Somnipradine is killing people.'

'*What?*'

Liv looks sick. 'It's true. He showed me the research. People are dying.' An invisible drummer sits up inside my amygdala and starts performing a Heavy Metal solo. I can barely hear myself say, 'But the trials were in the last stages.'

'It happens. Something to do with the temporal lobe and unforeseen differences in human brain structure. Perfectly healthy people have just keeled over. There's some talk about lesions in the brain being discovered, but I don't think anything has been confirmed.'

'How did we not know?'

'Because they've been covering up the death rate. There's going to be a massive stink. Lawsuits. Everything.'

I can barely bring myself to ask the next question. 'Liv, did Dad say what dosage is lethal?'

'That's it. We just don't know. There have been cases of someone having ten doses and showing no side effects and, in others, as little as two have been deadly. The inconsistency in dose made the correlation harder to spot. And most of these patients were near death which muddied the waters even more.'

A horrible thought strikes me. 'Dad, does he know about me?'

'No. It would kill him if he knew. Thank God they withdrew it when they did.'

'Thank God.' I walk casually towards the fridge. Liv is blocking the door. 'Why all the panic?'

'What?'

'I mean, you could have told me this tonight. There wasn't any need for all those texts.' Liv looks sheepish, the way she does when she has to break her deeply felt scientific beliefs or when she comes home at seven a.m. with her heels in her hand and her lipstick smeared.

'I don't know.' She twings a nail against the raspberry mould. 'I just got the feeling you were going to do something stupid.'

'Wow, supportive.' I make a gesture to suggest I'm starving and need in the fridge, and she steps to the side.

'Come on, Lexie.' Her voice is wheedling. 'You can't exactly blame me.'

'Where is it?'

'Where is what?'

'My Double Chocolate Chip Peanut Butter Cookie Spread.'

'Oh that. I threw it out.'

'Threw it OUT? Threw it out where?' Liv is staring at me like I've lost my mind. She points at a pile of binbags. 'In there somewhere…What are you doing?' Pretty obviously I'm tearing them open and emptying the contents onto the floor. 'Have you gone mad? That stuff is more toxic than Somnipradine and the jar is so old it was last in date somewhere in the Middle Ages.'

'I just—really want some.' My fingers curl around the edges of a squat glass jar just as Liv says, 'I know what's going on.' I freeze. 'You do?' An accusing, though perfectly manicured, finger points at my abdomen. 'You're pregnant.'

'I'm what?'

'Aren't you?'

'In what fucked up, upside down, lunatic world would I be pregnant?'

'I don't know, the world where you think you're some sort of Renaissance damsel about to be saved by your knight in shining armour?'

'He's an artist and he didn't save me.' Oh Zorzi, why didn't you come? The *stapes* is the smallest bone in the human body; my heart feels smaller, harder. 'What did you think, he sent his reincarnated sperm through time for me to harvest from of a man lying in a hospital bed with a *broken neck!*'

Liv looks like she's about to cry. 'You've been so weird lately, and I just felt—something.' She's right, and I might as well be the contents of a bedpan on the colorectal ward right now. Liv has looked out for me and taken care of my screwups my whole life, and now, on some deep, inexplicable level, she knows I'm about to do the most dangerous thing I've ever done—risking my medical license, risking jail—and I'm shutting her out. I want to tell her so badly, the words stick to the roof of my mouth. Suddenly, her hand is on my shoulder making me rabbit-in-the-headlights freeze. We don't do this. We dual with words, our sarcasm sharpened to the finest points, but *touch?* Never. It nearly undoes me.

'I'm sorry things didn't work out the way you wanted.'

'Me too, Liv. Me too.'

DARIUS:

We're under a canopy of trees. Gusty winds. Something indefinable in the air. The day is disappearing, and the night knows what we're up to. It isn't easy going. We've left the thoughtfully paved paths, the paths designated for the broken and the helpless, and now the wheelchair is bumping over roots and ploughing up mud. I lift my voice in a rusty whisper. 'I want to get down beside the lake.' Lexie gives a grunt. 'I don't think I can get any closer. The wheels have started to spin.'

'Are you sure?'

'I'm spattered in mud up to my crotch. Yes, I'm sure.'

'Sorry.'

'Don't be.' She parks the chair and slumps down on an artfully placed boulder to catch her breath. 'This is fine. Nobody is going to interrupt us here.'

We're silent for a minute. Nothing is quite real. Our forest is a fringe of trees. Our lake only a sizable pond. This is my life, a window-dressed reality that looks like freedom but doesn't quite live up to the hype. She leans in and her soul salmon-leaps in her eyes. 'You don't have to do this.' Strange to view her from this perspective, face tilted up to look up at mine. How it was meant to be. I've been thinking of her as a giant, but she's small, smaller than Seteney or Lodovico. Only little Crooked-Mouth stood closer to the earth.

'Please. I don't want you to do this.' Her eyes glint; she's holding back tears. What wouldn't I give to be able to brush them away.

'I have to find her.'

'You have found her. I'm right here.'

'It's not enough.'

'Why? Why isn't it enough?'

'Because there's a pattern. Every life, I find you. I lose you. I need to know what it means, if there's a chance for us.'

'And what if Zorzi never finds Seteney. It doesn't mean we're doomed. Maybe Liv is right. None of this is real. Maybe it's all just a kind of mental modelling, your brain trying to fix broken memories.'

'Except I haven't remembered anything that belonged to me. Besides, there's another reason I have to do it.'

'What reason?'

'If I don't, you will.'

She feigns outrage, considers lying, admits defeat. 'So this is it.'

'I guess so. She stares at me an instant longer then gets to her feet and reaches for her bag. The vial comes out, half-filled with its innocuous clear liquid and she cleans the stopper with an alcohol wipe.

'I want you to know I gave Seb a recording confirming that I did this of my own free will.'

'You told Seb?'

'I had to. You'll need proof if…if things go south.'

'It won't save me.'

'It might mitigate things a bit.'

She plunges the needle in and draws out the liquid. 'They'll crucify me.'

'I'm sorry.'

She shrugs. The vial is dropped back in the bag and she holds up the syringe. 'Ready?'

'Ready.' My sleeve is pushed back and she injects me in the vein that slithers down my forearm from the crook of my elbow. We lock eyes, astronauts on countdown. 'I love you.'

'I love you too.' She struggles to say something else then clamps her jaw and falls silent. I've no watch but an invisible clock starts counting down the seconds in my head. At ninety-six she frowns at me. 'Anything?'

'No.' We wait.

'Now?'

'No.' Nothing happens. The night stretches into mediocrity. An orange haze dulls the stars. At fifteen minutes a horrible thought occurs. 'What if I've become immune to the drug's effect?'

'It's possible.'

'I mean, what if access to the past is a onetime offer. Once closed, the door is locked forever. What if I've wasted the world's last chance to get at the truth?'

'It's possible.'

'Of course, it might just be taking a while. After all, neither of us had an immediate reaction before. What do you think?'

'It's possible.'

'Lexie?'

'Yes?'

'Look at me.'

'I am looking at you.'

'Come closer.' She leans in, eyes restless, barely able to hold my gaze. Absence is staring back at me. Abandoned fortress. Empty fishbowl. Her soul has disappeared. 'Where are you?'

'Leaves drip, dripping. Like drops of rain…'

'You're not Seteney.' She starts to answer but, before I can make sense of the words, something goes *pop* between the hemispheres of my brain. A kind of sheet lightning that burns away the world. and fills my eyes with flame. When my vision clears the trees have vanished and Lexie isn't crouched in front of me anymore. A phone is ringing.

CROOKED-MOUTH:

Leaves drip, dripping. Like drops of rain. Fall to earth. Wrinkled. Dead. Not like rain. There were birds. Where are the birds? Dig with stick. Earth hard, like stone. Before there were tiger nuts and crickets and cowpeas and lablab and bambara. In the before, Honey Bird came. Call out now. High then deep-down low. She does not come. Call again. Then again. She does not come. Follow path to water hole. Feet have memory. Belly has memory. Hungry, tight. Know this place. That tree. I am there, climbing that tree. Leaves. Many as raindrops. In my mouth. Around my head. Like shivering hair.

I laugh. Dreams-the-People laughs. Carries-Short-Spear hits him on head side. I don't laugh any more.

Tree is not like in the Before. Leaves all gone. Bald. Like First-Father's head. Branches are bone dead. Turn away. But belly speaks. Growls. Voice is an angry leopard. Chases me to tree. Climb. Climb. The branches are bone. I reach. Snap! Snap!

I, a leaf falling—

There is no telling, but not the ground. Not wrinkled flat. Blow away. Pain sparkle dazzles. Breath pant panting. Branch touches me all over. Like First-Mother's caress. I don't eat the Black. Not today. Laughing. I am Honey Bird. Bones feel hollow. Climb. Pull. Clamber. Reach. There!

Crusty dry. No bees. Sticks to roof of mouth. Chew. Swallow. Hard to get down. Not so sweet. But good. Good to eat. Save some. Share with others.

Dreams-the-People sits on rock. He looks at the watering hole. He says, 'The water was deep. Now it is not deep.' He knows I am there.

'I have honey. Bees are gone but here.' I hold out precious comb. He takes from my hand. Gives small lick. Gives back.

'I do not need more. Aurochs feeds me. Gazelle feeds me.'

I am amazed. 'In the Black?'

'Yes. In the Black. Aurochs speaks to me.'

'What does He say?'

'He says Crooked-Mouth's voice is a lapwing at night.'

How to tell this? His words make things. When First-Father points, he says, 'This is the river.' And the river is there. Only the river. Dreams-the-People makes the river a song. He makes it a shining path through dreams. He makes my eyes see new things. Makes new thoughts in my head. He makes me a lapwing at night. He makes *me*.

He stands up. Carries-Short-Spear is big. Killed-a-Leopard is big. Dreams-the-People and I stand eye to eye. Fingers reaching, touching shapes of his marks. One for the river and one for Aurochs. One is for the zigzag sky when clouds roll overhead. They make me feel things. I want to tell but I have no telling. I say, 'If I found an egg, I would give it to you.' He makes his mouth big and curving. It makes my heart a new day.

Pad pad of feet. This way coming. Freeze still. Voices. Killed-the-leopard speaks. 'I hunt. I bring back kudu and hare and zebra and ox. What does Dreams-the-People bring?' I look at Dreams-the-People. He does not make his mouth big and curving. He turns and walks away. His leg is pain of him. He does not look back.

'You killed a leopard,' Carries-Short-Spear says. 'The leopard came and you killed it. Who has Dreams-the-People killed?' I am behind the rock. Freeze still. Listen. Killed-the-Leopard speaks. 'First Father says Dreams-the-People sees things in the Black.'

'No-one can eat what lives in the Black. You bring back kudu and hare and zebra and ox.'

'But kudu is not here. Hare is not here. Zebra and ox have all gone.'

'First-Father is hungry.'

'We will find them. We will go far then further.'

'Dreams-the-People will eat. Who has he killed?'

'Dreams-the-People has knowing. He sees things in the Black.'

'First-Mother and Second-Mother and Crooked-Mouth and New-One are hungry. But Dreams-the-People will eat.' Kills-the-Leopard is silent. I think him pushing out his bottom lip. Carries-Short-Spear says, 'First-Mother and Second-Mother and Crooked-Mouth bring bambara and tiger nuts and honey and eggs. Dreams-the-People eats. What does he bring?

285

'What can we do? Dreams-the-People must eat.'

'Let him eat the Black.' Silence. I think-see Kills-the-Leopard looking at Carries-Short-Spear. I think-see Carries-the-Spear looking away.

'Where?' asks Kills-the-Leopard.

'The river is high. The river is fast. Dreams-the-People is a lame kudu.'

'No,' says Kills-the-Leopard. 'You can eat a kudu.'

My heart is a wild animal. My heart is birds bursting out a tree. It is zigzag sky and belly rolls from clouds. Dreams-the-People is not a kudu. He is words and thoughts and seeing. Where has he gone? I can't find him. He is not at the honey tree. Is he hiding in the bush? My heart is crawling ants. My breath is spiky tree thorns. Dreams-the-People, where are you? Your brother is going to BETRAY YOU!

FORTY-FIVE

DARIUS:

The phone is ringing. A glance at the old station wall clock tells me the working day finished an hour ago and, if I go right now, I might still get a jump on the traffic. Surely it can't be so important that it won't wait until tomorrow. I pick the phone up. 'Yes?' Dottie's voice is on the end.

'It's Mrs Dolby. She wants to speak to Sebastian.'

'He's not here. Take a message.' Dottie gives the kind of snort that suggests she is suffering at the hands of the patriarchy rather than simply being asked to do her job. 'He's not answering her messages.'

'I really don't know anything about it.'

'She's going to the police if she doesn't get to speak to someone.'

My heart sinks. What has Seb got himself into this time?

'Shall I put her through to Mr Carnegie?'

'No, no. I'll handle it.'

A moment later Mrs Kathleen Dolby's cobwebby voice speaks. 'I'm sorry to trouble you.'

'No trouble at all. Darius Colvin here. How can I help?'

'I'm trying to get hold of…of…Oh, what was his name? Very blond…charming manners.'

'Sebastian Colvin?'

'Yes. That's right. He came to see me in…in that month—the one where things grow?'

'July?'

'No. The one with buds.'

'May? June?'

'No. Like snow?'

'December?'

'Johnny Mathis sang it.'

'April?'

'Yes.'

'Mrs Dolby, if you could just tell me what the problem is.'

'I'm trying to. It was—oh what was his name again?'

'Sebastian.'

'Yes. He came to see me. I'm sorry. You see it's hard for me. I lose words.'

'That's okay. I have your record here. It looks like he visited you on the nineteenth of April so that you could discuss selling your husband's collection.'

'I was going into a…a—one of those places with old people sitting about.'

'A nursing home?'

'Yes. That's right. I can't live by myself anymore.'

'Your husband had a valuable collection. I remember it now. Mostly German artists. There was a particularly fine Max Ernst and a Francis Picabia amongst it.'

'Yes. His mother left it to him. There was some hoo-ha because it was supposed to go to the eldest living female member of the family, and Robert was an only child. Some second or third or fourth cousin came crawling out of the woodwork claiming the collection was hers. Jennifer, that was her name. Now why do I remember that?' I must make some noise that hints at irritation as she adds hastily. 'You're a busy man, Mr Colvin and I'm holding you back.'

'Darius, please.'

'I am not comfortable calling people I don't know by their first names, Mr Colvin.'

'Of course, Mrs Dolby.'

'Good. Then let me come straight to the point. I want my painting back.'

'I see. Which painting is it?'

There's a pause. 'It's—it's—'

'Take your time, Mrs Dolby.'

'It's the one I never liked.'

It's my turn to pause. 'I'm afraid several pieces have already been sold. The Ernst and the Picabia went very quickly.'

'I don't think this one will be sold. It wasn't valuable. But it was Robert's favourite.' My eye flicks through the record. The collection was eclectic. Plenty of dross amongst the diamonds.

'Can you tell me more about it?'

'That's the thing. I can't remember what it looked like.'

I turn my annoyance into a cough. 'That will make it more difficult. Do you know the artist?'

'No-one famous. His name might have begun with an 'M'.'

I look back at the record. 'Marowitz? Minz?'

'No. No. I would know if I heard it.'

'Perhaps if you slept on it?'

'Are you trying to give me the runaround, like your brother?'

'No. Mrs Dolby. Certainly not.'

'Because the other Mr Colvin is being very shifty with me.'

'I assure you I would never do anything to damage our relationship.'

'What did you say?' Is she a little deaf. I raise my voice. 'Our relationship. I wouldn't damage it.'

'There is no need to shout, Mr Colvin. I'm old. Not stupid.'

'I sorry, I—'

'No need for that. I remember now. The painting was damaged. We had a leak you see. All Robert's fault, of course. The last words I ever said to him were, *Will you get that bloody roof fixed?* Fell off the ladder the next day. Stupid man.'

I look back at the record. 'Yes, three paintings were listed as spoiled, one with a recommendation for restoration and the other two were deemed essentially worthless. But I don't have images here so I'll have to check them out.' I don't say that the records are sloppy and that Seb hasn't included all the detail he should have. Mrs Dolby sighs. 'Ugly thing. Should have gone in the bin. It probably would have except Robert had made a clause in the will that it was to be sold collection intacto.'

'But you'd like it back?'

'I want something to remember him by. And they wouldn't let me keep the ladder.'

§

At the top of the stairs, I try calling Seb, but he doesn't pick up. After three goes I give up and leave a text telling him what I'm going to do. I won't be able to call again once I'm in the cellar as the signal doesn't penetrate that far. There is no reason for this I can fathom, except that it's a cellar and meant to creep people out. Nothing else for it then. Down the uneven steps I go, ducking my head to avoid the bulges in the ceiling.

The wormy smell hits me as soon as I enter, and the damp blanket atmosphere settles against my skin. The Dolby crate is stacked against a wall only half full, the best already gone to auction. Inside, there's a passable neo-Dadaist portrait in monochrome and a decent looking sketch that might be a Jorg Immendorf. Trust Seb to miss it. Near the back are two still-lifes in oils. They've both had water penetration, though one looks salvageable. Not important enough to be worth it. I'd need daylight to be sure. Three were listed as damaged. Where's the third? I check again and find it trapped against the frame of a larger painting. It's smaller than the rest and has suffered more than the others, with colours so badly run I might as well be looking at abstract expressionism.

I lay them on a convenient trestle table and take my phone out. It isn't ideal but I only want a record for Mrs Dolby. Surely a photograph will jog her memory. I only hope she isn't too disappointed though I'm pretty sure she's forgotten the extent of the damage. The fluorescent tube throws a harsh clinical light across the canvases. Details leap out, colours recede. The least damaged one has a tear in the corner. It looks like an early Joan Miro but it isn't signed and the cost of authentication probably isn't worth it.

Something is niggling me about the little one. I place it between the other two. Perhaps it was closer to the leak so suffered the most. Yet the outer canvases are disfigured by several long runnels, raindrops sliding down glass, while the middle one radiates a sunburst of damage from the centre, as though it was lying flat when the water hit it. And the more I look, the more I think I know this painting, that I've seen it somewhere before. Gaudy transavantgarde palette, that faint detail in the corner which could be the innocent outline of a vase or the sensual curve of a woman's hip.

It used to hang above Seb's bed.

§

The *Lost Lass* bobs a little against its anchorage. It looks sadder than I envisaged, green paint peeling off in places, rust intruding in fungal colonies along the hull. I'm glad the new owner hasn't changed the name. It leaves something of my mother still living on in this tired old hulk—not new when she bought it—and the scene of childhood innocence where the loss of a favourite ball could be the cue for tragedy and dissolve as quickly as a sugar lump melting on the tongue.

Seb is sitting at the fold-down table in the kitchen area. There's a high flush along his cheekbones and he's rolling an empty whisky glass between his palms. He doesn't look up when I descend the ladder. 'How did you know I was here?'

'Elimination. I went to your house and your passport was still in the kitchen drawer. After that, I called every friend and searched every haunt I could think of. This was the only place left. You had to be here.'

'No shit Sherlock.'

'Piece of piss, Poirot.' There's an empty bottle of Jack Daniels next to him and several empty beer cans roll freely on the floor. He swirls the last drops around the bottom of the glass. 'You want to see it?' I nod dumbly and he gestures towards the tiny bedroom at the rear. Instinct holds me back. Hairs prickling the back of my neck. Is it a trick? He glances up, puzzled, then mutters, 'Oh, for fuck's sake,' places his hands down heavily on the table and lurches up. A moment later he's back clutching a stretched canvas on a tabletop easel. It's protected from the light with tissue paper. He pushes it across the table. 'Knock yourself out.'

I don't move. Time turns to aspic. I can hear a clock ticking and it doesn't strike me as weird. It's as if I've moved out of my body and am looking down from the dizzy perspective of Dali's *Christ of Saint John of the Cross*, that strange painting of the Messiah as a nuclear warhead hovering over the world's rim. I see myself blink at Seb then look down at the easel. In slow motion my trembling hand reaches across and lifts the tissue. I hear my gasp, a low rumble at the back of my throat. But the odd thing is, I can't see the painting. Only my reactions to it. I hear myself say, 'The water damage—that's how you knew.'

'I'm right. You know I'm right.'

'Yes.' Seb, little brother Seb, who couldn't tell Van Gogh from Van Helsing has hit the jackpot. 'This is—' It can't be. It's impossible. A billion to one. A meteor strike. Divine intervention. Yet my lips shape themselves around sound, breathe meaning into it, exhale, 'Giorgione.'

Seb looks a little taken aback. 'You're very certain.'

'Am I wrong?'

He turns the canvas over and points to an inscription, faint but still legible. *Per mano da maestro Giorgio da Castelfranco 1510.* It can't be real. After all, Big George was careless of posterity, and there are only two other inscriptions attached to his work. The discovery of a third should be enough to make the work suspect. But it doesn't. Some instinct is telling me that this is the real deal, some logic-defying intuitive spark that knows more about the way the universe works than human reason can explain. Giorgione painted this image. I can feel it in the tingling of my fingers.

Seb turns the canvas around and places it gently on the easel. He gives me a lopsided grin—the kind that makes me feel I'm part of a children's mystery entitled, *The Colvin Boys and the Hidden Treasure*—and, despite myself, I can't help grinning back. I look back at the portrait. It's far from complete. A fuzzy nimbus of smeared pigment surrounds the face. 'You've been restoring it yourself?'

'You've forgotten I've had training.' There's a note of pride in his voice. 'Once the frame was off, the tacking edge revealed the palette. Look, you can see there's an oil glaze over the original. Not unlike DaVinci's technique.'

I nod. 'It's what gives the skin tones that soft enamel look.'

'But it's thicker, more widely applied. Almost as if the artist knew his work would be in danger.'

'Even so, to try to do this yourself—'

'I'm very careful.' The Jack Daniels has formed its own glaze across Seb's eyes and his pupils are large and unfocused. He waves a hand dangerously close to the surface of the paint. 'Cotton buds. A little water and hours and hours of patience.' His laugh comes out in a snarl. 'Didn't think I had it in me, did you big bro?' I should answer him, offer reassurances, but I'm looking at myself looking at a painting I can't see.

Not knowing what to say, I retreat behind closed eyelids. The *Lost Lass* rocks gently under my feet. Something plops into the water nearby, probably a water vole. *My mother reading Wind in the Willows. I was always Ratty. Seb was Mole.* When I open them, Seb is placing the tissue paper back over the portrait. He does it very lovingly, a sense of ownership evident in the hunch of his shoulders. 'Seb?' He doesn't look round. 'You know you can't keep it.'

His shoulders freeze. 'Don't intend to.'

'All right.' I'm talking very gently as if to a child clutching a sick kitten. 'We'll put it back. No-one has to know it was ever gone. We can claim that we didn't realise the importance of the under-painting at first. You can take credit for the discovery and think of the Old Man's face. The commission alone will be incredible.' His back is still to me, fingertips on the edge of the canvas. He inhales and exhales deeply several times. I watch his shoulders relax and he gives a small nod then throws his answer in my face like a glass of iced water. 'Sorry, big bro. No can do.'

'What? Why not?'

His look is pitying. 'Because I've already sold it.'

'What are you talking about?' He doesn't answer at first. Rummages under a bench and pulls out another bottle of Jack Daniels. 'I owe some people money.' He holds out the bottle. 'Drink?'

'No. What people? How much money?'

'Bad people. A lot.' He pours three fingers into a glass and swallows it back, shuddering slightly as it hits his stomach.

'Seb, we can fix this.'

His empty glass comes towards me as if he is the toastmaster at a wedding. 'That's my big bro. Always fixing his messy little brother's scrapes. Not this time. A quiet word, a few quid to the right people ain't going to cut it. They get the portrait or they kill me. Simple as that.'

'The police—' Seb starts laughing. 'I don't think Plod is quite up for these guys. They're not messing around. They took me into a dark room and showed me a cow they'd butchered hanging from the ceiling. Except, when I got up close, the cow opened its eyes and started mouthing something. And I realised I was looking at a man.'

'Jesus.'

''Fraid not. Crucifixion looked like the easy option compared to what they'd done to him.'

I feel sick. 'What are you going to do?'

He laughs louder, the earsplittingly note of hysteria in his voice vibrating so sharply I expect his glass to shatter. 'What happened to 'we', big bro? Not so easy to step outside your safe little life now, is it?' I blink several times. I'm looking into the eyes of a stranger, glassy and unreachable. Seb is hiding behind him, badly frightened and desperate, needing me to take control.

The shock shivers out of me and I become practical. 'Look, this is ridiculous. You're just digging yourself into a deeper hole. Gangsters? Stolen masterpieces? These are scenes from a bad movie trailer. I'm putting a stop to this now.' I take a step towards the painting and he responds exactly the way the film script would dictate. He reaches under the bench and pulls out a knife. I recognise the serrated steel blade, the worn wooden handle.

For an instant I'm transported back to childhood. My mother cutting bread for picnic sandwiches stuffed with ridiculous fillings—strawberry jam and salted potato crisps, tuna and cornflakes, chocolate spread with cheese. Seb and I vying to steal bites before we even set off. And Seb is so like her in this time-capsule of watery light, except he's taller, of course, and a man and the knife is now an old rusty artefact from a forgotten age. Can it even cut bread? Irritation is beginning getting the better of me, and when Seb makes an unsteady attempt to thrust it menacingly, I push past him 'Don't be an idiot. We have to go. *Now!*'

Consciousness doesn't register at first but my fingers go searching, groping the broken filaments of tweed at my shoulder, exploring the mushy wetness at the centre 'You cut me?' I ask it like a question even as I examine the redness spreading across my fingertips. It isn't a deep cut but the sense of betrayal stuns me, as though I'd offered Mother Theresa a donation and she'd punched me in the face. I recover almost immediately but it's enough. Seb has the painting and he's already scrambled up the ladder. I hear his footsteps thudding above me.

'Seb! Don't do this!' I lurch after him, stemming the blood flow with one hand. It slows me down and his taillights are disappearing by the time I'm on dry land. Where is he going? No time to think. There are lights at the junction. With a bit of luck I can catch him there.

But the lights turn green as I approach and he's already moving away. Fleetingly, I catch his wild expression reflected in the rear-view mirror and plead with him even though he can't hear me. 'You don't have to do this. Seb! Please.' He cuts his eyes away and speeds off.

Rain starts to come down like a curse. Where is he going? The chase veers off down narrow country roads, cutting between farmers' fields and disappearing between avenues of trees. He's driving an XR—why did I never question where he got the money to buy it? It handles like a hot blade through butter compared to my old carthorse. Keeping up is impossible.

Something skitters out in front of me and I'm sure I've hit it. Instinct stamps my foot down on the brake pedal and the car lurches dangerously. Stopping is the only sensible action but Seb's lights are up ahead—the only blessing of the early-fallen winter night; no streetlights to confuse the eye. If I give up now, I could lose him forever.

The headlights catch the harrowed outlines of trees, hag-fingered branches chittering at the sides of the car. I try not to think about what it's doing to the paintwork. By some miracle I'm closing the gap between us. Is there something wrong with his car? The rain is so heavy now I can't see the separate drops, only a flexing lens of water covering the windscreen. Seb has stopped. Has he changed his mind?

I ease my foot on the accelerator, offering a silent prayer to some unknown god of happy outcomes. Then I'm looking at something that makes no sense at all. An owl. Filling the windscreen, the blank prophecy in its eyes reflected in the headlights. My hands swerve away and the car follows. The last sound I hear is not any sound at all, but the impossible, illusory beat of wings as it rises ghostlike into the darkness while I soar after it through constellations of shattering glass. Until my head hits the ground and I have the strangest feeling—a spring recoiling followed by a bright white heat flooding my body.

It's the moment my spine snaps.

§

I'm back. It's still dark. Time hasn't moved much. 'Lexie?' I shout her name but there's no answer. A figure sits in front of me, so still, I momentarily lump him in with the scenery. 'Seb?' Between his fingers, Tinkerbell glows on the end of a roll-up which is burnt down almost to his knuckles. 'So, you've remembered.' Darkness floats in his eyes and they have that opaque unreachable look they had on the houseboat last November. I look about. We're in a small clearing further along the lake's edge than I've ever been. Night hangs in blank canvases between the trees. The ground is arthritic with roots. How in God's name did I get here? 'Where's Lexie?'

'I have no idea. I found you on your own.' I nod though I recall nothing. There's something disturbing about the emotionless way he's looking at me, as if he isn't Seb at all, as if my little brother vacated the premises in a rush and handed the keys over to a cold-eyed stranger.

'I'd like to go back now.'

He sighs and throws the roll-up into the bushes. 'I'm sorry.' Without another word his hands take hold of the back of the wheelchair and we start moving towards the lake. The water has an evil sheen. 'Seb stop. It's not safe.' No answer. Not even a grunt. The full horror of my helplessness comes home to me. Is he trying to scare me? He isn't going to hurt me. Not Seb. Little Seb who couldn't get through a reading of *The Three Bears* without bursting into tears.

I can smell the water. Does water have a smell? Clingy dampness. Mud sucking at our toes. Seb and I searching for minnows and toads in the garden pond. Acid-yellow fishing net clutched in his chubby fist. 'Please. We can talk about this.' I spout cliches as the black water comes closer—*I won't tell. Who would believe me? I love you.* The water isn't deep. I read somewhere it was originally a skating pond, barely three feet at the centre. But none of that matters to a man who can barely raise his head. Left on my own, I could drown in a facecloth. What will they say afterwards? An accident. A mishap. *Why was he left so near the water?* Will they blame Lexie?

The front wheel sticks on a branch and he struggles to free it. 'You'll never get away with this. You'll be caught.' More clichés. Change tone. Appeal to reason. 'Seb, think about what you're doing. You don't want to kill me.' He barks out a laugh, low and harsh. It doesn't belong to him. It doesn't sound human.

'Why worry. You'll be in your next life soon enough, won't you?'

Will I? Suddenly I don't know any more and I'm terribly afraid. 'Seb?' My voice is much quieter. 'If—if you do this, promise me you'll tell Lexie I'm sorry and I'll find her again.' I don't know how he meant to answer or, if indeed, he would have answered at all, because at that moment the undergrowth explodes and Crooked-Mouth hurtles from the trees like a madwoman.

She throws herself on top of him, a screaming ball of prehistoric rage, and they roll beyond the arc of my vision in a spitting zoomorph of arms and legs. 'Lexie. Run!' Crank my head around till I think it will detach. Seb is on top raining down blows. She's fighting back but she's losing. He's too big, too powerful. 'Seb, for God's sake. You'll kill her. Seb! I don't care about the painting. I swear! Just let her go.' No answer. I can't see them anymore.

Sound paints vicious strokes across the blurred air. Scalpel screams. Graffiti cries. Thick gouache of pulpy thuds spatters pigment across flesh. The moon fills with Crimson Lake.

It goes on and on. Then? Silence. Darkness hums in my ears. 'Lexie?' I scream it out. 'LEXIE!'

My cry is a beacon. Wands of light shoot out of the black spaces between the trees, crisscrossing my location and catching me in a web of beams.

—*We've found him.*

   —*Down there.*

   —*Fuck, right at the water.*

I blink and blink, unable to shield my eyes. A broad cherubic face, in a uniform that confers the full authority of the law upon him, is hovering before me. *Darius? Darius Colvin?* I think I nod. Nothing makes sense. Sirens. Doppler screams in the distance. Clouds shred themselves on pointy stars. Did my brother try to kill me? Another face, jolly Cockney barkeep in a paramedic's hi-vis jacket. *Bit chilly for a swim, sir. What say we get you back? Careful now—* this is not to me—*Keep it smooth as possible. That's it. You're wasted as a plod, big strong lad like you. Put him down gently.*

The world turns on its axis. The police are leading Seb away in handcuffs. His shoulders tense as he passes me but he doesn't meet my eyes. Doctor Song is crouched by a tree—the other Doctor Song, Liv. She's wiping blood from her sister's nose. 'It's all right, Lexie. Look, he's okay.' Crooked-Mouth lifts her head. One of her eyes is shut but the look in the other is proto human. She sniffs the air then gets unsteadily to her feet and staggers towards me. Her hands reach out to touch my face and a tear escapes her good eye, and all I can say is, 'I remember. I remember.'

FORTY-SIX

LEXIE:

Darius looks up at me from his bed, exhausted, pale but otherwise unharmed. He has a question in his eyes. He doesn't need to ask it as it's there in my eyes too. *Do we live forever?* Sink down in the chair beside his bed. The seat is padded but shooting stars of pain explode along my tender spine. My arm is in a splint—humeral fracture, probably caused by Seb's foot stamping down on me—and hurts all colours of the rainbow despite the painkillers. Bruises are ghosts under the skin for now. By tomorrow I'll look like Satan's dalmatian. Darius' eyes trace the gauze covering the left side of my face then focus on the bloodshot organ I'm squinting through. 'I'm so sorry.'

He looks forlorn. What must it have been like to find yourself rooted to the spot in the middle of a poison garden? I should say something comforting—the modern equivalent of *a mere scratch, think nothing of it, dear boy*—but I'm not quite there yet. Instead, I whisper, 'Was it all a dream?'

'Not from where I was standing.' Liv is in the doorway clutching fresh nightwear to save me from the humiliation of wearing what she terms 'hospital *hate couture*'. 'Wow, you look like shit.'

'It's not as bad as you think. Mostly soft tissue swelling.'

'I meant the hospital gown.' She hands me the pyjamas and I notice for the first time that they're her silk *Fleur du Mal's,* her favourites. It's Liv's way of saying she loves me. While I'm pushing down the lump in my throat, she turns to Darius and says in a guarded way, 'I think you should know your brother has confessed.'

His eyes telegraph pain but his voice is steady. 'To trying to kill us?'

'Yes. And to other things. Gambling debts. Drug addiction. He was in way over his head. The people he was dealing with are part of the Albanian mafia.'

'And—' I break in but can hardly bear to ask it. 'The Twilight Madonna?'

'They're doing their best, but Dad isn't hopeful.' Dad. Of course Dad. Who else would Liv go to with the Freudian hairs in her nose twitching? *Lexie's acting so strangely. Something's wrong.* And Dad, the man I thought didn't care dropped everything to pull strings and make enquiries. But it wasn't Darius who threw up red flags. It was his brother, Sebastian.

I don't remember the fight, only waking up afterwards with Liv's beautiful face hovering over me and wanting to reach out and stroke her cheek but being in too much pain so whispering her Korean name instead, *Wolha,* moonflower, and thinking it had never sounded so perfect. Later I asked, *How did you know?* A shrug. She avoids my eyes. *I just had a feeling. I kept trying to ignore it but then I found myself dialling 999.* Liv. Beautiful Liv. Amazing Liv. She went against everything that defined her neat clinical life to listen to the secret logic of her heart.

After she's gone, Darius and I sit in silence. The questions in our heads are so big, small talk seems ridiculous. 'Lexie?' I look up, searching for his smile but can't find it. 'I understand.'

'Understand? Understand what?'

'That you can't be with me. Not after all this. Not when—' He swallows hard, glances down the length of himself. 'I'm like this.' I want to say he's wrong, that he's the love of my life and nothing else matters. I really do. But fire ants are eating my brain and I feel so confused. I'd like to lie down and close my eyes and sleep for a

299

very long time. Instead, I stand up sharply and it feels like ripping off a full body plaster in one go. My eyes well up and I mutter, 'I think I need to be alone for a bit.' I head for the door without saying goodbye and Darius stays in bed unable to follow me with anything but his sad eyes.

The corridor has that vacuum-packed, dead space feel about it that spaces which are interconnections between other spaces usually have. I wander down, having to stop and catch my breath at every third or fourth pace. The thought of going outside and breathing lungfuls of cool autumn air appeals but is impossible in my current state. Can't face going back to my room either; the too cheery faces and upbeat comments, the constant reminders to stay in bed for my own good. Maybe it's true. Doctors make the worst patients.

Voices are heading my way and I duck through a door, not considering where I'll end up. At least not until a mop smacks me in the face. Push it out the way and sink down on between the buckets and brooms. I'm so tired. Not the *I could do with a nap* tired. The tired that buries your consciousness so deep not even dreams can reach you…not even screams. Sleep teases the outer edges of my brain, while thoughts, memories—thoughts of memories; memories of thoughts—pneumatic drill their way through my head. Times. Places. None of them mine.

There's Mopsa, outside *Schokolade*, a shadow between great blocks of shadow, frozen as gunfire shatters the moon. Or Lodovico, on his knees at prayer, opening his eyes wide with the sense that something has vanished from the other side of the world. And little Crooked-Mouth, head thrown back, watching strange birds whirl in an endless vortex of twilight sky.

All of them me. None of them me. Versions of versions of versions. What-ifs and could-have-beens. Angled mirrors. Infinite regression. *Mise-en-abîme*. Did I have a say in any of them?

Freight train, carrying all the baggage of my pasts, thunders through the tunnel of my ribs, making me gasp. Can I commit myself to Darius only to lose him again? Huge crushing pain inside my chest. Maybe that's why we forget, why we shed our skins in the black corridors connecting one life to another. Because we can't know the pointlessness of replaying our inescapable patterns and go on living.

It's so hot in here. Sweat sprouts, swampy palms slip slide. That pounding sound? My heart? Open my mouth to gasp at the air. Too fast. Snapping it down in starving bites. The world is sliding away. I'm going to fall off. What's wrong with me?

What would Liv say? *You're the physician, baby sister. Heal thyself.* All right. Fine. Patient history: Female. Thirty-two years of age presenting with shortness of breath, centralised, diffuse chest pain radiating to neck and jawline. Non-smoker. Some substance abuse, mainly alcohol and sleeping pills. Recently administered a single bolus of the experimental drug, Somnipradine—*Two doses, Liv. You said as little as two have been deadly. Not one single lousy shot*—Best guess, Doctor Song? You're experiencing an acute myocardial infarction.

What else is on the menu? How about, ventricular tachycardia with a side of oxygen deprivation. We recommend you follow it with a generous helping of plunging blood pressure. And why not finish off with the house special: thrombal occlusion of epicardial coronary arteries leading to cell death of the underlying subendocardium. We can, of course, arrange for a hearse to pick you up afterwards.— Oh, Darius. I'm sorry.—Fluttering arrhythmias. Hurricanes and thunderbolts. The wires are cut and Pierrette falls to the ground. Systolic function slowing. Little bird. Little bird. Wings beating frantically against the moon.

Slide onto the floor. Dead weight. I'm drowning on dry land. Fire scouring my nostrils, my eardrums. Around and around and around we go. Discovery. Loss. Revelation. Regret. The colours come, the colours go. Eternal carousel. Our lives. All lives. Over and over for all eternity. Blackness bulging into my fading pupils. Soggy beats of my heart further apart. Frogspawn of spittle trailing from my lower lip. An organ playing. Underwater tones, Claribels and Voix Célestes. That sound? A lapwing calling at night. I'm not breathing.

Aberdeen. The smell hits me first. Fish guts. Then blood. Then the urine the tanners use to cure the skins. I've forgotten what it's like to be back in a city. Zorzi's lip is curled and I can tell he doesn't like what he sees. Not that he sees much beyond the length of his arm these days. A great sigh escapes between the grey curls of his beard. 'Not exactly Venice.'

'Not exactly.' Did Venice ever really exist? It was never a real place. Not even when I was trapped inside it.

A cart trundles past filled with night waste followed by a staggering woman in a ripped shift. She reeks of cheap spirits and yells out in an unintelligible patois, but I get the gist. She wants the world to know that she feels like the contents of the cart. I don't judge. There's little of the buying and selling of human cargo here, but life has taught me that there is more than one way to enslave a human soul. 'Is it far?' A shrug from the Chief's man. He's more used to our island life, where he struts around with his oversized brotherhood singing of bloody victories over the Macdonalds. At least until the women put their hands on their hips and call them home whereupon they go running off like lost lambs.

The Chief's man looks up towards Castlegate then back the way we've come. We're standing in Shiprow where we disembarked at what they call the 'herborie'. Clearly he is lost. 'Ask him.' I spot a man with a confident air giving orders to the barrel-chested dockers.

'Ah canna dae that, mistress.'

'Why not?'

'He's a Macdonald.'

'You recognise him?'

'Naw, but ah kin tell.'

'How can you possibly tell?'

'By the way he's staunin.'

'The way he's standing?'

'He stauns like a Macdonald.' The resemblance is lost on me but I've lived long enough among the island Scots to understand that the Macleods and the Macdonalds hate each other with a passion akin to great sexual attraction. The true tragedy would be if they ever made peace. What would they sing about?

'You need to do something. We can't stand here all day.'

'Wait here. Ah'll mak enquiries.'

Big sullen drops of rain fall from the slate sky. If we stay where we are we'll be soaked through. Zorzi tugs my arm. 'There's shelter over there.' The shallow entrance to a wool merchant's home provides an inadequate roof, and we huddle under it watching a curtain of water slough animal dung and bits of straw and ribbons of vegetable matter down the hill. The damp starts to up-creep into my joints. By nightfall, my fingers will be useless knots. 'Why am I here?' Zorzi grunts. 'We think the Jew will be better persuaded if he sees you.'

'If he sees a woman as old as the hills?'

'You're not old.'

'Only lined and wrinkled and covered in age spots.'

'You're beautiful.'

'I sag in more places than a wet tent in winter.'

'That's not what I see.'

'You can't see your hand in front of your face these days.' He looks away. End of conversation. My anger won't be contained. It out-belches, hot, sulphurous. 'All this on the word of the Chief?'

'We can trust the Chief.'

'Trust him? He thinks his clan flag was a gift from a *fairy!*'

'You have seen the flag. They set great store by it.'

'I have seen *a flag*. The needlework is Ottoman. Ormesini had embroideries, hundreds of years old, and I recognise the style.'

'It came from the other side of the world.'

'No doubt. Recovered from the bloody hands of some poor Mohammedan who fell foul of their crusades.'

'I trust the Chief.' He sets his face. I know that look. I've watched it harden over the years. He wasn't the same man who found me. He'd lost his friend. His home, his reputation. Perhaps if we'd had children.

'And how did the Chief find out?'

'His own man saw it.'

'He saw it.'

'He saw a description of it.'

'And who gave the description?'

'A French sailor. He was recovering from ague in Deer Abbey and had it on good authority from the monk, who attended him, that he had seen the most astounding Madonna.'

'Where?'

'In the lodgings of a Jewish merchant in Aberdeen.'

'So the chief's cousin—'

'I didn't say it was his cousin.'

'They're all his cousins. The Chief's cousin read a description by a delirious French sailor from a monk who knew a Jew in Aberdeen.'

'It's more than we've had to go on in years.'

'Oh Zorzi, more of nothing is still nothing.' He doesn't answer. His eyes are panes of glass into a room filled with darkness, and I wish I had said, Yes, yes, it's a good omen. Perhaps we have found her after all this time, all this searching. But I've watched hope die too often. The ashes are cold. I can't rake over them again.

The Chief's man reappears. 'Ah wis spikin wi a wee wifie feedin her bairn. Wa're tae gang up tae Netherkirkgate where oor man is waitin for us in his lodgings.' Zorzi thanks him, although I can tell he has no idea what he just said. It's good of the Chief's man not to speak in Gaelic but, even after all this time, the Scots tongue is still harder to swallow than a mouthful of knotted eels. 'What did he say?' Zorzi asks from the corner of his mouth. 'Just follow him. He knows where the Jew is staying.'

The lodgings are respectable, and we're shown into a small clean parlour by a maid. Despite the comfort of the chairs, the Chief's man prowls about, hunching his shoulders around his ears and peering into the shadows. 'What's wrong?' He starts, his hand reaching for his sword hilt before he recovers himself.

'Ah huv niver seen a Jew.'

Zorzi and I exchange glances. 'He's a man. Like any other.'

'Aye. But no a Christian man.'

Before I can reply, the door swings wide and there he is, Don Benjamin Rodriguez. His smile is warm, and he offers a bow in the Spanish style. 'Welcome. I am sorry I cannot offer you the comforts of my home in Castille. It was my wish to invite you to dine with me. But, alas, my cook is afflicted with the inability to prepare anything without boiling or mincing it to death. The Scots, I have discovered, are a sober race, who look askance at the sensual pleasures of flavour.'

He offers his hand to the Chief's man, who recoils as though the devil has tried to pinch his pimply arse. There is a pause. A fishtail flick of hurt flashes in Rodriguez' eyes then dives deep below the calm of his expression. Zorzi moves forwards and takes his hand warmly. The sight of a Jew is no more surprising to a citizen of Venice than a Mohammedan or Moor or Saracen would be. 'Thank you for agreeing to meet with us. I am Marco Ghirlandaio and this is my wife, Catterina.' In his excitement, he's switched to Italian, but Rodriguez appears to have no difficulty.

'You are the miniaturist who is so popular with the Scottish nobles.'

'They find it amusing that such a large man paints such small pictures.'

'Your story must be quite intriguing.'

Zorzi shrugs. 'A man must eat, and he must go where he can earn his crust.' There is an expectant pause. Rodriguez says nothing, and it's left to Zorzi to blurt, 'You know why we are here?'

'The message I received was somewhat puzzling. You believe I have something that belongs to you?'

'I know it sounds strange.' Zorzi's voice is pleading. 'I don't expect you to believe me without proof.' With that, he pulls me out from behind him and Rodriguez gets his first clear view. The pause is longer than before. Rodriguez glances at Zorzi then back to me in confusion.

'Look closely,' Zorzi urges. It's clearly uncomfortable for Rodriguez to study the face of another man's wife, but he makes a show of it, while I stand there, gritting my teeth, and letting the room grow stiff around me. On another floor, the maid is clattering pots. A candlemaker goes by in the street shouting about the quality of his tallow, and I find myself wondering if we are enacting some version of the old legend of a king who brings a statue to life. Only in this case I begin as a living woman and end up sheathed in marble.

Eventually, Rodriguez lifts his gaze to Zorzi and starts shaking his head. 'Forgive me. I really don't—' The sentence dies, severed by some internal jolt. He whips around and his gaze is fire. It strips away my crinkled flesh and reads the bone. 'Dear lady, come to the window, please. The light in here is not all it might be.'

I follow him to the diamond panes and he close-searches my face. 'Remarkable…the resemblance…those peacock feather eyes… remarkable.'

Zorzi can't contain himself. 'You see now. You see.'

Rodriguez is still looking at me; he nods. 'It could be no other.'

'I must have the painting back. I can pay. The chief of the Macleods sets great store by art. He is willing to be generous.' Rodriguez makes an apologetic gesture. 'I am afraid it is impossible.' Something happens, too quick to follow. One moment Rodriguez is sadly shaking his head. The next Zorzi is shaking it for him. He has Rodriguez by the neck of his doublet and has lifted him from the ground. 'Give it back, you cocksucker…you lover of little boys…you—'

'Zorzi!' I have never seen him like this. He's possessed. I grab his arm and try to pull him away, but he's turned to iron and won't budge.

'You baby-eating, Christ killing whore's—'

'Help me. Before he kills him!' The Chief's man rabbit blinks then hurries to my side. Together we manage to pull Zorzi back a few steps and Rodriguez falls back. I expect him to run from the room, but he gets up slowly and silently straightens his clothing. His hands are shaking. Zorzi is a raging bear straining against captivity. 'Don Rodriguez, forgive my husband, please.' He ignores me and addresses Zorzi directly. 'Senjor Castelfranco, I have long wished to make your acquaintance.' A hand shields him from protest. 'Do not deny it. That would insult both our intelligences.'

Zorzi's anger goes from fire to smoke. He slumps, and suddenly the Chief's man and I are struggling to hold him up. Rodriguez walks over to a dresser and pours a goblet of wine. 'They mourn you on the streets of Venice.'

'Still?' I can't help the frisson of fear in my voice.

'Still. All they talk about is tragic Giorgione of Castelfranco who died of plague on Poveglia.'

'That isn't all they talk about.'

'No. They also speak of the mysterious twilight painting. His greatest work. The Marchioness of Mantua, Isabella D'Este, offered a prince's ransom if it could be discovered.'

'Ormesini—' I didn't mean to out-blurt the name, but its taste is poison and I need to spit it on the ground.

Rodriguez nods. 'Who does trade in Venice without coming across the house of Ormesini?'

'He is alive then?'

'Barely. An old man walking the rim of life. But his sons carry on the business, and they are an unscrupulous pair. I, myself, do not trade with them. But one hears rumours.'

'Do they believe we are alive? Do they seek vengeance?' Rodriguez stares across a millennium and a half of persecution. He knows what it is never to be safe. 'You would be wise to stay hidden. They believe you have the painting.'

Zorzi stirs. 'You have it.'

A shadow passes over Rodriguez' face. He takes a small step back. 'Please believe that I was unaware of your claim to ownership.'

'Where is it? Tell me!' His face is red and puckered. How can this be the man I love? Rodriguez looks at him sadly. Did he have ideas about the great painter from Venice? How cultured and civilised he would be? Did he think they would discuss the School of Athens and Leonardo's astronomy over a jug of wine?

'Please, Don Rodriguez. Not knowing is killing my husband.'

He heaves a sigh, puts the goblet down. 'Dear lady, it would be my greatest pleasure to please you. But, alas, I sold it two days ago.'

§

The world is ending. Apocalypse-lit stars hurtle in fiery cataclysms towards the Earth. Seas burn. Mountains crouch down and pots and kettles rise up into the air, as though the Almighty has taken it into His head to follow the next ascension with a tray of refreshments. A fist of air lifts me and shakes me violently. Death's foetid breath drools in my ear yet, beneath the fear, I find myself thinking, *I've done this before.* My eyes—which are open—open again.

Blankets are caught in a sweaty tangle around my ankles and I haven't the faintest idea where I am. My shoulder is being shaken. 'Zorzi?' The clouds of sleep part and I see it's the Chief's man crouching over me. 'What is it? Where is my husband?' He downsquirms his brows and bites back his lower lip. 'Gone.'

'Gone? What do you mean, gone?' A new apocalypse is dawning inside my head. The Chief's man's eyes roll to the side.

'Ah shouldna hae telt him.'

'Told him what?'

'Ah foond oot whar yer man hae'd gang tae.'

'My man? What man?'

'Thon agent who the Jew gied the painting tae. He didna leave Aiberdeen straight aff, an he wisna oan the road afore this evenin.'

'Are you sure?'

'Ah hud it on guid authority.' He means he heard it in a tavern.

'And my husband has gone after him?'

'Ah telt him it wis a richt gipe idea tae ging fleein intae tha nicht like the de'il wis efter him. But he wouldna listen.'

'How does he mean to purchase the painting when a prince's ransom was paid?'

'Ah dinna think he means tae pay, mistress.'

'He's going to *steal* it?'

'He said it couldna be theft because Rodriguez was no a Christian gentleman and must have stolen it hisel.'

'Stop!' My hands fly to my ears. I can't listen to this. The candlelight doesn't illuminate much but I can sense a blush in the Chief's man's voice.

'Whit would ye huv me dae?'

'Find me a horse.'

§

A full moon follows us down the coast road, throwing stardust in our eyes, so that I see Zorzi everywhere and nowhere. In a tree. In a rock. In the hunch of a ruin. There are swarms of insects buzzing in my ears and crows death-throwing in my stomach. We'll never find him. Beneath my thighs the horse's hooves chant, *Too late. Too late. Too late.* As dawn breaks, we stop a sleepy farmer heading to his cowshed, and the Chief's man asks what he has seen. Not much by the blank look. The Chief's man gets back on his horse. Nothing is said. We ride on.

By Stonehaven our steeds are sweating and so are we. Mine has developed a limp. 'We'll need tae stop an change the horses.'

'No, keep going.'

'Mistress, that shauchly nag'll no mak it another ten steps nivir mind a mile.'

'Let me be the judge of that.' But the decision is taken out of my hands when the equine monstrosity limps forwards, stumbles and throws me from the saddle. The shock of the ground knocks the wind from my lungs and the world spins. The Chief's man is off his horse and dragging me to my feet before I know what's happening. 'What—what did you say?'

'Say, mistress? No a word.'

'You yelled something as I fell.'

'Mah lips nivir pairted. Ah swear it.'

'You did. I heard—' It comes again, loud as a woman's ecstasy, from a thicket of oaks less than a stone's throw from the road. The Chief's man and I stare into each other's eyes then we're running as though Auld Nick and all his demons were after us, except we're running towards hell instead of away.

Despite the fall and the joint pain that sometimes makes it hard to get out of bed in the mornings, I'm first to reach the trees. The scene is tranquil. Scotland's strange pale sun halos the leaves. An untethered horse licks moss from the roots of an oak. In the middle, a man lies on his back on the ground. He might be sleeping except for the red stain pillowing his head.

Zorzi is there. He's been there the whole time only I wasn't ready to see him. He's sitting a few feet away, head in his hands, a roll of canvas at his feet. I don't know what to say, but the Chief's man arrives at my side and says it for me. 'Fuuuuuuuck.' I lift a surprisingly calm finger and point to the man on the ground. 'Tend to him.' Whether this means staunch his wound or bury the body, I don't know but I'll think of that later. Right now, I have Zorzi to deal with.

He doesn't lift his head as I sit down beside him. Relief, exhaustion and anger jostle each other inside my head. He's alive. I should be grateful. But who is he, this man sitting next to me hiding his face? Would my Zorzi attack a man unprovoked or justify theft because he worships differently. I watch the Chief's man tear a strip from his shirt and wrap around the figure on the ground. That is something. At least Zorzi is not a murderer.

It's left to me to break the silence. 'All the time I was in Venice, the Church never saw me as a Christian woman. Yet you never treated me less for it.' He drops his hands but fixes his gaze at the ground. My toe prods the canvas. 'Was it worth it, my love?' Why won't he answer? I might as well be talking to the horse. I lift the roll and shake it at him. 'Is this all you care about? Smears of pigment on cloth? Would the world end if I tore it in two?' Anger leaches into his silence but he does nothing to prevent me. I look at him closely and then my hands are unrolling the canvas until it's spread across my lap.

There it is. I remembered it exactly. I didn't remember it at all. The ways the eyes looked through their veil of sadness. The night blooming jessamine. The twilight background with its crown of stars. We have travelled the noble houses of Italy, France and Scotland, and never was there a painting such as this.

'It's a copy.'

'I know.' It's a good one. But the differences are there. The chin a little too sharp, the blossoms not quite translucent enough. The signature that reads, *Got ye! Ranald Gallda, son of Allan, 4th of the Macdonalds of Clanranald.*

The Chief's man is standing before us. 'Is that it? A gey braw thing, nae doot aboot it.'

'It's a copy.'

'Ye're sure?'

'Yes.'

'Nae chance that—'

'No.'

He shrugs a shoulder. 'Aw well. The Chief'll no be oot o pocket efter aw.' He offers his hand. 'Come oan. Ye'll need tae get going.'

'Going? Go where? Our lives are in ruins, and I'm too old to go on the run again. I'm too tired. Let them come. What does it matter? It's all over.' Zorzi stares at the ground. The Chief's man's hands are on his hips.

'Weel, ah dinna ken if that's hoo they tak in Italy. But ah'll gie ye some Scottish advice. Stop yer greetin and pull yersels togither. We're no beat yet.'

'We're not?'

'Naw. Thon laddie on the ground is injured but he's no ready tae meet his Maker. No today onywise. Tak yer man an get him oan the horse.'

'What happens when he wakes up?'

'Ah'll tell him ah saved him frae a robbery. Looks like the blow wis frae behind. He'll no know whit's hit him, and ah'll say ah chased the robbers aff an retrieved his wee paintin. He'll be nain the wiser.'

'You'd do this for us? Fugitives? Imposters? Thieves?'

'Aye weel.' He hikes his plaid and back-thrusts his shoulders. 'Yer no Macdonalds noo, ur ye?'

§

It's a blue grey day on the island. North winds push oceans of clouds across big skies. Galleons of shadow navigate moors and slopes, on doomed voyages, as they pass beneath my stumbling feet. Zorzi is missing.

I thought we would go back to our old routine when we returned, but he disappeared inside himself, barely eating or speaking. Something inside him is broken and I don't know how to fix it.

The Chief came to see me this morning. 'Ah hear yer husband is no weel.' I was feeding chickens and didn't look up.

'Nothing to worry about. A head cold picked up in Aberdeen. City life doesn't suit him, that's all.'

'The portraits urna finished.'

'Such delicate work.'

'Is that richt? Ah'd hae thocht sic wee paintings wid be quicker.'

'The process is complex. Miniatures require a greater degree of care. The smallest error can be ruinous.'

'And tell me this. Does he paint better when he's richt up against the canvas or when he moves further away?'

'Closer, naturally.'

'So ah wid be richt in thinking that he'd manage better if he was inside his studio than awa frae it, as he's been the last twa days?' I gape. After nights and nights of silence, I was relieved when Zorzi didn't come to bed. So he was working late? A little absence to make the heart remember. I didn't object. I didn't think to check.

As soon as the Chief has gone, I shake the feed from my hands and run through a cloudburst of chickens straight through the gates of the Keep and across the fields and goat tracks and peatbogs that roll more like seas than land.

I find Zorzi on a beach staring at the stretch of water they call the Hebridean Sea. 'Zorzi!' I want to say more but I'm out of breath. He stiffens at the sound of my voice but doesn't turn around.

'I can't see anymore.'

'Is that what's wrong? We'll get you glasses. If the ones the tinker brought are no good then there must be someone in Aberdeen who can help.'

'It isn't these!' He stabs a fist into his eyes so hard I wince. 'My inner vision's gone. I can parrot the faces, who come to sit for me, well enough. But that's all. The portraits are flat. Lifeless. They don't *breathe*.' I should tell him that he's wrong. That his painting is as good as ever. I say nothing.

'I thought finding my painting of you was the answer. Night after night, I lay there thinking if I could see my Madonna again she would tell me where I was going wrong. I thought she would explain how to rekindle the spark. But all she told me is what I've lost.'

'Did she mention what a churlish old fool you've become?'

'Among other things.'

'I knew I liked her.' My joints feel as though they're about to give way so I sit myself down at his side. We watch the sea slurp the shore. Our knees touch.

'I'm finished as a painter.'

'I know.'

'How will we live?'

'I'm good with chickens.'

'Is that enough?'

'No, but we'll get by.' He isn't persuaded. I need another way to reach him. 'Have you heard the story of the king who was lost and found?' He barely reacts but I plough ahead. 'There once was a king whose kingdom had suffered many hardships. The people were poor and unhappiness was widespread.

'One night the king has a dream in which he hears a prophecy telling him that a greater king will come and bring peace to the land. The king is a good man and he wants his people to be happy so he says he will step aside and let the greater man take the throne. "Ah", says the prophecy. "There's just one snag. We don't know where he is."

"No problem," says the king. "I will send my best men out to scour the kingdom from east to west, from south to north."

"Ah," says the prophecy. "There's another snag. Only you can do it. And you have to dress as a beggar."

"A beggar?"

"Rags. Sandals. Begging bowl. A little dirt smeared on your face and in your hair wouldn't hurt." The king is taken aback, but he is a good man, who hates that he has not been a better ruler, so he agrees to the prophecy's terms.

'Out he goes into the kingdom in search of the greater king. He comes across a woman, who is weeping by a well. She tells him that her husband is dead and the well is blocked and her children will die of thirst. The king looks down into the dark pit and is very much afraid, but he can't let the children die of thirst, and so he climbs down and unblocks the well. When he returns the woman is overjoyed and asks how she can reward him. He tells her that the only thing he wants is to find the greater king, but she has never heard of him and so he moves on.

'He travels the length and breadth of his land asking if anyone has word of the greater king, but no-one ever has. The days turn into weeks. The weeks turn into months and the months gather together and become years.

'One day, in despair, he is walking through the forest when he comes across a stag with its leg caught in a trap. The animal is very big and its antlers are sharp and fierce. As the king approaches, it rears up and paws the ground yet the king is unafraid. Very much impressed by the king's demeanour, the stag calms down and waits patiently while he frees him. Once loose, the stag asks if there is any favour he might do in return and the king asks the question he always asks. The stag considers it thoughtfully.

"Here, in the forest, I am the king," he says. "But I am not the one you seek. However, there is a rumour amongst us that a great king is approaching the throne." The king is very excited and blurts out, "Where did you hear this rumour?"

"From the squirrels. They are terrible gossips."

'And thus the king hurries back to his palace eager to greet the greater king. Such is his enthusiasm that the animals all start following him. And when the villagers see a beggar being followed by stags and hares and crows, they start following him too. And when the townsfolk see the forest creatures and the villagers following a beggar, they join in as well.

'By the time they reach the palace, everyone is afroth at the idea of meeting the greater king. Into the throne room they spill, the children whooping for joy and the squirrels besides themselves with excitement. At last they will meet the great ruler who will save them. Yet the throne is empty and covered in cobwebs. No-one has sat in it in many years.

'The laughter dies and the king falls to his knees. In that moment he might have died of a broken heart but just then the prophecy reappears in the garb of a beautiful woman. In a voice loud enough for all to hear, she says, "Hail to the greatest king of all."

'The king is astounded. He mutters something about a mistake having been made. But the prophecy shakes her head. "Let me ask you something. Were you ever hungry?" The king nods earnestly. "And did you learn to share a crust when you were given one?" The king nods again. "And when you were cold, did you learn what it is to be allowed to share a fire?"

"Yes, indeed."

"As a beggar you were often despised and driven away with harsh words and sharp stones. What did you learn from that?"

"Never to despise others." The prophecy smiles, a little smugly truth be told, and announces to the assembly, "As a fire will spread from a little spark, here is a man who walked amongst you doing nothing but deeds of kindness. His virtue has spread across the kingdom. Brother no longer fights brother. Peace prevails. Crops flourish and no child goes to bed with an empty stomach."

'And so saying, she raises him up and leads him to his throne. "Hail to the king, who lost himself and found a greater king in his place. Hail to the greatest king of all."'

My story finished, I bait my breath and wait. Zorzi says nothing. I nudge him with my knee. 'What do you think the story tells us about the king?'

'That he was an idiot?'

'Well, yes. He spent years and years looking for something he already had.' Silence falls with the dusk. Zorzi is looking out over the waves, and I look with him, watching the Hebridean sea turning from blue to slate. There's nothing more to be said. We sit there, locked in our separate disappointments, the western isles sinking, like our spirits, into shadow. I've lost him. Somewhere along the road, Zorzi went down a different path and I didn't notice, just

315

kept on going, practical Seteney, muse and chicken breeder. So this is how our last years will be spent, side by side and oceans apart.

'He knew.' Zorzi's voice is almost inaudible over the crash of the waves.

'What?'

'The king. Deep down he knew what he had.'

'Then why did he take so long to realise? Was it the Prophecy? The journey?'

'I don't know. If the idiot could explain himself he wouldn't be an idiot, now would he?'

There's truth in this, but it's hard to see where it leaves us. 'Was it because I grew old?'

'No. Never.' He touches my face. It pierces me. 'I suppose I had a dream of the kind of man I would be. Of the things I would give you.'

'I didn't want things.'

'I wanted you to live like a queen.'

'You left me living like a pauper.' A thousand responses flicker over his lips then fade into the dusk. He hangs his head. 'I know.'

After a bit he asks, 'Do you think we'll meet again in Heaven?' He's thinking that we haven't much time left, and the Church doesn't see me as a Christian woman. I want to say that a loving God would not be unkind enough to separate us, but the world has taught me never to rely on the kindness of strangeness.

'The way I see it, Fate did everything she could to keep us from one another. We were separated by birth. By rank. Even when we were in the same city, Ormesini prevented us from being together. You nearly died in that storm crossing the English Channel. And I had the sweating sickness. Twice! I think it's going to take more than a little thing like Death to keep us apart.'

'You really think so?'

'We lose each other. We find each other. Maybe that's enough.'

We go on sitting. Our knees still touch.

AFTERWORD

DARIUS:

'The castle! Can you see, Daddy? Can you see?'

'Daddy can see fine. There's nothing wrong with his eyes.' Lexie bends down and starts trying to clean strawberry juice from a squirming Mopsa's face. Her lips are stained Marylin Munroe cherry red, whereas the rest of her looks like an extra from *Cannibal Ecstasy*. She wails like the apocalypse and wriggles free.

Before she can run off, Glinda of Oz appears in the guise of Liv, who hurries towards us carrying two ice cream cones topped with chocolate flakes and spirals of raspberry sauce. They're melting already. Mopsa immediately stops wailing.

'Want me to calm the savage beast?'

'With more mess?'

'I thought she could smear it on her dress. Looks like there's some clean spots.'

They go off hand in hand and Lexie watches them, shaking her head. 'Our little IVF miracle.'

'A woman who was found dead in a cupboard shouldn't be too picky.'

Lexie's lips quirk but she doesn't answer. She's been quieter since the heart attack. Less spiky. She's seen death and believes it's a doorway now, not a blank wall. She points towards the slope that leads down to the formal gardens. 'You want help or are you going to run down on your own?' She's quieter now, but not entirely lacking sass.

Down in the garden the air is warm and dewy. This morning, curtains of cloud parted and let the sun through as we made our way here, hurtling stupidly fast along the narrow road to Mallaig—*what possessed us to let Liv drive*—to catch the ferry in time. Under the stillness you can sense movement. A buzz in the air. Tiny clods of earth sifting and sorting. Near my chair, a battalion of metallic ants marches up the stem of a sunflower. It's everywhere. The endless Möbius loop of life.

Lexie is looking up at the fairy tower where the precious flag of the Macleods is displayed. 'I can't believe it's taken us so long to visit.'

'Me neither.'

'Did we ever really live here?'

'It's feels familiar but strange at the same time.'

'A lot has probably changed in five hundred years.'

'I don't know. I thought I would feel more.' She nods absently at a caterpillar breakfasting on a Begonia leaf then says almost to herself, 'The memories…they aren't as strong as used to be.'

'I know.' A sharp glance. Is she surprised, relieved?

'You don't doubt them though?'

'No. Do you?' She shakes her head emphatically while trying to persuade the caterpillar to climb on to her finger. It sniffs her —*do caterpillars have noses*—then sine-waves its way back up the leaf. She wants more and so I have a stab at explaining what I don't really understand myself. 'For a while the memories were all I had. They kept me alive. Gave me something to live for. But now I have you. I have Mopsa. The way is forward not back. I don't *need* the memories anymore.'

'I guess.' She's not convinced. Biting her lip, she adds, 'It's just I miss them.'

'Me too.'

Mopsa comes running up and flings herself on to my lap. 'Beach, Daddy.'

Beach it is.

§

The waves have painted charcoal pictures on the black volcanic sand. It looks like a story written in a forgotten language. Lexie is setting out a picnic while our miracle splashes in the water with Liv. She is a miracle. Not many children can claim that their parents were brought back from the dead…can they? She's not our only miracle. Some feeling has come back into my right hand. I can

319

move my fore and middle fingers just a little. I'll never be whole, of course. Broken spines don't fix themselves but perhaps I'm whole in another way. A way I might never have found without the car crash. There are nights I even come close to forgiving Seb.

Lexie worms her toes into the sand. 'Peace. Perfect peace. How long do you reckon we've got before she savages Aunty Liv?' She studies my face and frowns. 'Whatya thinkin'?'

'Do you think we'll see her again next time?' I mean the Twilight Madonna. I mean in the next life. She uproots a baubled piece of bladderwrack and starts bursting the pods. 'I don't think we have a choice.'

'So this is what we do for eternity? Lose each other. Find each other. Reach for the Madonna and watch her slip away?'

'I guess.'

'But why is this our pattern? What makes us special?'

'Maybe nothing.'

'Meaning?'

'Maybe we aren't any different. The pattern of discovery and loss is the template of every love story. Who gets forever? We all go round thinking we're a novel. Perhaps we're just a series of short stories.'

'Who do you think we'll be next time?'

'Best not to know. There's a reason we forget.' With a pang, I wish with all my heart that I might reach out and tweak a lock of her hair. I content myself with asking, 'What made you so wise?'

'Easy. All the women who came before me.'

'Ah.'

Together we turn to watch Mopsa. Liv makes *save me* motions behind her back. Lexie waves. I wish we could get a glimpse of the northern lights, but it's probably too early in the year. The ocean breathes in, breathes out. Waves are swallowed up, smash themselves to smithereens on the shore then reappear.